SEX HELL

A LOVE STORY

JOE CANZANO

😊 Happy Joe Control

www.happyjoe.net

Library of Congress Control Number: 2015917431
ISBN: 978-0-9906365-3-3

DEDICATION

To everyone who's searching for that special someone.

SMART WORDS

"Imagination is more important than knowledge."

— Albert Einstein

1: Bad Sex

Debbie liked sex. She just didn't like it with other people.

She dug her fingernails into Mike's naked back and closed her eyes. She figured this would hide any signs of anxiety, or at least make it easier to imagine she was banging someone else. She couldn't see much without her glasses, anyway, and they were on the nightstand, right next to a flickering electric candle. Meanwhile, her bra and panties were somewhere on the floor, and her skirt was bunched up around her waist, and her body was bouncing against the mattress, and the mattress was squeaking like a hundred rusty hinges.

Stay positive! she thought. *I can always masturbate when he leaves.* She made herself moan and then gripped Mike tighter. He was on top of her, grunting like an ape on an exercise bike. His burly body was slapping against her, and she let out a screech, hoping it sounded sexy—but how sexy could it sound when she felt like she was bonking a crash test dummy? Her bed kept squeaking and went *badump.* Her mind zipped through snippets of her favorite fantasies, but tonight every vignette fizzled and died. Her fiery imagination was missing in action, and it looked like she was stuck with the guy on top of her.

She needed to forget about it. How ridiculous that she'd wanted to have an orgasm tonight. Orgasms rarely happened with a guy—and never with *this* guy—and it was almost time to start faking it as usual.

"Oooooh, yeah, baby," he said. "Oh, yeah!"

"Oooh," she said. "Uh, yeah."

She heard the sound of Mike's Chihuahua in the other room, barking and scratching at the closed door. She opened her eyes just to give them a roll of frustration.

"*Yip! Yip! Yip! Grrrr!*"

Why had he brought that dog over here, anyway? Supposedly, it needed to take a walk. And supposedly, it didn't hate her—but she had her doubts. The dog didn't even look like a dog. It was a rat with peg legs. It was a snarling sausage from the planet Sausagero. It was another distraction.

"*Yip! Yip! Grrr!*"

Debbie took another deep breath and imagined that moment when Mike would be back in his car and heading for home. Funny, a few of her nerve endings started to tingle, and now she felt a hot spark of hope between her thighs. Yeah, soon she'd be alone, reading a book, eating popcorn—and suddenly she was feeling it! Meanwhile, Mike reached down and cupped her jiggling bottom in both hands and kept pumping away. Hey, that wasn't bad! He was finally hitting a sweet spot; he was actually doing something that felt good. She whipped her hair around and stared into his face. The light from the trashy candle showed Mike's chiseled features. He was straining in the shadows and heading for the goal line, and maybe she was, too. It was building, like a ripple growing into a wave—and now she was close, so close, and maybe this was going to work after all.

Oh, yeah! Oh, yeah! Oh, yeah!

Maybe this was the night!

Then he shifted a bit and started sucking on her left nipple. He also reached up with a big, ignorant hand and twisted it.

What? *Now why the hell was he doing that?* She'd told him not to do that. Licking a nipple was fine, but no twisting. They were nipples, not control knobs on an old radio.

"Mmm!" he said. "Mmmm!"

"Hey, stop that," she said with a wince. "Don't do that."

Mike stopped just as the dog finally ceased barking. He looked at her through the flickering orange light with a steely blue stare.

"Do what?" he said.

"I've told you before," she said, squirming a bit. "Licking is great, but twisting is no good—because it hurts."

Mike frowned, but he also stopped twisting. He grinned and pushed into her harder than ever. "I'm sorry, honey," he said. "Don't worry, I'll take care of you." He grunted a few times. "Who's your daddy, huh? Who's your daddy?"

Inside her head, Debbie screamed a silent wail of defeat as every orgasmic spark fizzled and died—gone, gone, gone. She banged her fists down on the bed sheets. *Dammit!*

"Mike, I don't want to have sex with my daddy."

He stiffened for a second, and then he scowled and rolled off of her. His fat erection pointed at the ceiling, fading fast like a wilting banana.

Debbie froze and tried not to panic.

"What?" she said. "Why did you stop?"

Somewhere in the shadows, Mike crossed his bulging arms across his chest. She heard him swear in the prickly summer heat, and then he was quiet. The only sound in the room was the whoosh of a ceiling fan as it sent an ominous sigh across the zebra-striped bed sheets. And then the dog started barking again.

"Why did I stop?" he said. "How the hell can you ask me that?" He snorted and ran a few fingers through his tennis ball haircut. "Your body is like a minefield, Debbie—and so is your head. I should wear a freakin' demolition suit before touching you."

"That's not true!" she blurted. "I just have things I like and things I don't like. You're the same way."

She groped around for her thick glasses. She put them on and leaped into "damage control mode." It was where she seemed to live. Another relationship down the drain.

Okay, maybe not yet. She just had to stay calm. She tried to smile and look cute in an owlish kind of way, with her dark hair flowing straight down past her shoulders, and her roundish face, and her lips so small and quivering, and her eyes so big and brown.

"I'm not like you," Mike said, narrowing his stare. "I've done it underwater. I've done it in a cemetery. *I've done it on a freakin' horse!* You're so picky."

Debbie paused and imagined Mike and some copulating skank rolling off the back of a prized thoroughbred.

"I'm not picky," she said. "There are just certain things I don't want to do."

He gave an indignant snort. "Yeah, but by 'certain things' you mean a lot of things. Most girls like all that stuff I was doing—not to mention *other* stuff I've tried to do."

"You're not doing it with 'most girls.' You're doing it with me. And for the record, the average girl does not want to have sex with her father—and not every girl likes it *every* way."

Mike reached over and pulled the chain on a lamp. He sat up on the edge of the bed and stared at a crooked picture of Wile E. Coyote hanging on the wall while Debbie glanced at his naked body.

He was sexy in a muscle-covered, Greek statue kind of way. So what was he doing here in her little apartment? And what was he doing with her? There had been a hundred other girls in that gym with better bodies, and most girls past the age of fourteen wore a bigger bra. But for some reason he'd started talking to her, and for some reason he'd kept doing it even after she'd acted uninterested and then dropped a dumbbell on her toe. She'd tried to look unfazed while limping off in the direction of the Juice Bar, only to have him hit on her again the next day. It was probably a good move on his part, since she'd quit the gym a week later.

That had been about three months ago.

Mike got up and looked for his boxer shorts. They were on the hardwood floor where he'd tossed them, right near a beat-up night table that held an old-fashioned alarm clock resembling a soup can with two bells on top. Next to the clock was an e-reader and a pile of paperbacks—mostly sci-fi. He pulled on his underwear and gave her a grim look.

"I'm sorry," she said with a sigh. "I guess I have a few issues."

For some reason, she envisioned a bowl of popcorn. One of her issues was that she'd rather be eating popcorn than having sex with

Mike. Or maybe reading a book. Books and popcorn were so much simpler, but then she might end up alone forever, ugh.

Mike shrugged. Outside the door, the dog started barking again.

"Debbie, I'm sorry, too. I didn't know about the 'daddy thing'—but now I know." He gave a long sigh. "I'll just put that on the list of things you don't like, okay?" Then he shook his head and looked at her with his "what am I gonna do with you, Debbie?" kind of smile that she found so annoying.

Still, she didn't want him to leave. Then again, she wasn't going to ask him to stay. She watched him pull on his jeans and a black T-shirt and then strap on his shoulder holster, making sure his .45 Glock was secure. Then he added a light sport coat and a NY Yankees baseball cap. He walked toward her and gave her a kiss on the cheek.

"I gotta go," he said. Then he opened the bedroom door and the Chihuahua came racing into the room.

"Yip! Yip! Yip! Yip! Yip!"

It bounced around like a puppet on a string, leaping and panting and barking. It ran to where Debbie sat on the bed, staring at her and snarling with a frothy kind of fury.

Debbie slid fast across the sheets and tried not to look too aggravated. But every frantic yip was like a stressful little sword stabbing into her brain. Mike ran over and yanked the leash dangling from the dog's tiny neck.

"Cut it out, Sugar! Debbie hates that stuff."

"No, no, it's okay," Debbie said—because she needed to compensate for the evening's sexual train wreck. "You don't have to go," she added in a lukewarm voice.

"I have to get up early tomorrow."

"Okay. I understand."

"Debbie, don't worry about the whole sex thing. We can do it again tomorrow."

"Yeah, sure." She gave a weak smile and then started chewing on one of her fingernails.

"I can't wait," she said.

As he dragged the dog toward the front door, she mumbled to herself. She could certainly wait. Yes, she could.

2: The Diner

"I like Mike," Debbie said. "But I'd like him better if the sex didn't make me suicidal."

Debbie de La Fontaine was sitting in a booth by a window inside the Sunshine Diner, across from her best friend, Cynthia Crush. Of course, that wasn't Cynthia's real name—that was her punk rock name. Cynthia was a songwriter/bass player searching for a band. She also worked at the diner as a waitress, along with Debbie. Tonight their shift was over, and they were eating some food. They'd ditched their ketchup-perfumed waitress uniforms, and Debbie now wore a loose, knee-length black dress and white sneakers.

Debbie shivered in the sprawling air-conditioned dining room, a place constantly ringing with loud conversation and clinking silverware. She picked at her feta cheese omelet and shuffled around a few French fries. As usual, her face was scrunched up in an expression of worry.

"Why should I have to apologize for my preferences?" she said. "And why do my preferences always cause problems? Am I the only girl who hates having her nipples tortured? Am I the only girl who doesn't want 'doggy style' or 'crocodile style' or whatever? There have to be other girls who hate the animal kingdom. And why is it so hard for me to have an orgasm with a guy?"

Cynthia tossed back her uneven strands of pinkish blond hair and dipped another French fry into the glob of ketchup on the plate in front of her. She looked concerned, and she looked like she was plotting to eat the rest of Debbie's fried potatoes—but she was a good friend. She was also busty and curvy in a mid-sized way, and Debbie knew guys liked her, especially when she wore stretch pants. Tonight her stretch pants were a happy-looking shade of aqua, while her top was pink and loose fitting.

"Everyone's different," Cynthia said in her laid-back voice. "Lots of girls have the orgasm issue. And I agree, it's not cool for Mike to try and make you feel guilty about stuff you don't like; you shouldn't have apologized. But do you really hate 'doggy style'? Man, I love that."

"I feel too self-conscious. Maybe if I had a better butt."

Cynthia rolled her eyes. "Debbie, be serious. You have a great ass. I mean it's half the size of mine. I've got two of your asses in my pants."

"Not two."

"Okay, one-and-a-half. But I don't want to quibble over half an ass."

"Guys like your butt, Cynthia, and you know it."

"Some guys do. The ones who like big butts. But where are they lately? Nowhere."

Debbie shook her head and considered taking another bite of her omelet, but didn't. It would probably upset her stomach. Most food did. She said, "It's not fair. I'm good at lots of things, or at least a few things. Why am I not good at this one thing that every dumb animal on the planet seems to figure out? I hate sex. I really do."

"You can't say that," Cynthia said. "Because you love to masturbate, right? If you hated sex, you wouldn't be doing that all the time."

Debbie's eyes popped open. "Shhh! Don't say that in here!" she hissed. "I don't do it all the time. Just when I'm in the mood."

Cynthia shoved a fry into her mouth and nodded her head. "And how often were you in the mood today?"

"Three times."

"A slow day, huh?"

Debbie frowned and wiped the lenses of her thick glasses with a napkin. "Yeah. Maybe I need to go back to therapy."

"You're going to need an operation on your fingers first. And you keep saying you hate sex, but if you keep doing it with yourself then you don't hate it. Maybe you just hate it with Mike."

"Yeah, maybe," Debbie said. "Maybe I hate it with Mike because he doesn't know me the way my fingers do. But how can anyone? I've had these fingers my whole life."

"Well, most people don't fantasize about their partner, anyway."

"I don't have a *partner*, Cynthia. A partner is what you have when you own a law firm. I have a *boyfriend*—at least if I don't blow it again." She reached down into her small purse and pulled out a crumpled piece of paper. "And that's why I made these notes," she said while trying to decipher her scribbles. She'd jotted it all down this morning while eating a bowl of Captain Crunch cereal. "I created a plan."

"A plan? Wow, there's something different. Since when do you have a plan, Deb?"

"It's my new thing. It's supposed to keep me from getting stressed. If I know what I'm going to do, I'll feel better about it."

She smiled and chewed one of her fingernails.

"Okay, so what are you going to do?"

"I'm not sure. I spilled milk on that part."

"I see." Cynthia nodded and ate her last French fry. Then she eyed Debbie's pile of unfinished food. "The way I see it, love with anyone is a million-to-one shot. Maybe he's just not the right guy for you."

"But he is the right guy!" Debbie wailed. "We have so much in common."

"Oh, yeah? Like what? You don't even know what he does for a job."

Debbie shook her head. "Why is that so important? I don't identify people by what they do for money. If I did, we'd both be waitresses— but in reality, I'm a writer and you're a musician."

"Yeah, but we just carry dishes. Your guy is walking around with a gun, right? So he's not doing something harmless."

"He works for the government, Cynthia, and he's definitely not a crook. Or at least he's a legal crook."

"So what do you have in common? Being a 'legal crook' isn't anything."

"But it is! We're both rebels. We're both, you know, pirates."

"They used to hang pirates, Debbie."

"Good. I wish someone would hang me."

"No, you don't."

"I'm going to die alone."

"No, you're not."

"I'm going to die alone!"

"No, you won't."

"I will die alone, Cynthia! I will!"

"Uh-huh. Are you going to eat your fries?"

"Of course not! They're going to hang me, remember? I don't want my last meal to be so greasy."

Debbie pushed her plate a bit in Cynthia's direction, and Cynthia started picking away at the food. She seemed fairly nonchalant, like she expected Debbie to change her tune pretty quick.

"You know what?" Debbie said. "I'm not going to die alone."

Cynthia nodded again and kept eating. "Mmmm—good. You're making progress. Why the big change in plans?"

Debbie banged her fist on the table. "Because there's more writing on the back of my note! I rewrote the part that got ruined by the milk—see?" She shoved the crinkled piece of paper into Cynthia's face. "I'm going to make things work," Debbie said. "I'm going to have good sex! I'm going to do whatever it takes, and maybe I'll get a plant."

Cynthia hesitated, and then said, "You know, you were doing okay until the horticulture thing came along. A plant?"

"Yeah, I read that plants help relieve stress, so I included one in my plan. I'm sure Suzy Spitfire would do it differently."

Cynthia laughed and shook her head. "Suzy isn't real, Deb. She's a character in your novel."

"She's real to me. I keep telling you, Cynthia, there's a higher plane of existence. *I know it!* This world isn't real in the sense we believe— and imagination doesn't only happen in our heads. Imagination happens on a higher plane."

Cynthia sighed and lowered her voice. "Okay, fine, but let's talk about the 'lower plane' for a second. That creepy old woman is staring at us."

"What creepy old woman?"

"The one over there wearing a garbage bag."

Debbie turned her head and gave a quick glance across the bustling dining room, where she saw a white-haired woman sitting alone at one of the round tables in the corner. This was unusual, since those tables were usually kept open for bigger groups. Also, most women in New Jersey discovered hair dye by the age of thirty.

The woman was not actually wearing a garbage bag. She was wearing a dress with the dark green color and sheen of an outdoor trash collection sack, but it was not a garbage bag. So Cynthia had been exaggerating.

Debbie started to turn her glance away, but then the woman waved at her. She gestured with her fingers, displaying a movement that said, "come here."

Debbie winced. Oh, no! Now what?

Debbie whispered, "Cynthia, that woman wants me to come over there."

"Yeah, I see that. Hey, better you than me."

"What do you think she wants? Money? Do you think she wants money?"

"Hard to say. She looks like she could use a couple of bucks, but I have a feeling it's something else. Maybe she heard you screaming about masturbation."

"I wasn't screaming about masturbation!" Debbie screamed. Then she dropped her voice back to a whisper. "That was *you* talking about masturbation. Maybe you should go over there."

"I'm not going over there—you go over there. She's looking at you. She's still waving her hand. You better go see what she wants."

Debbie looked at the old woman again and forced herself to smile, but she had a feeling in her stomach, and it wasn't good. It was like the feeling she'd had as a kid at the end of summer, when school was about to start again and everything felt tight like a stretched rubber band, and she was going to have to return and see all those laughing kids who thought she was so weird.

Yes, she'd eaten her chap stick in fourth grade, big deal. And she'd made her own clothes out of old curtains, so what? And then later she'd thought astronomy was more interesting than pep rallies and cheerleaders and people moving a dirty little ball across a field—really, what part of that was so strange?

"Okay, I'll go see what she wants," Debbie said.

"Cool! And don't worry, I've got your back."

"Gee, thanks. Thanks a lot. Try not to choke on my omelet."

Debbie got up and walked through the clanging dining room. She tried to keep a smile on her face as her white sneakers plodded across the spongy red carpeting. She tried to ignore the typical New Jersey crowd as they gorged themselves on onion rings, ice cream, and double-deluxe bacon burgers. They were loud like foghorns and big like walruses, and they owned screaming kids and giant Sport Utility Vehicles filled with soccer balls.

Debbie frowned. There was no reason to be so nervous. This was a meaningless moment in her life that would be forgotten ten minutes from now. This woman probably had nothing interesting to say, but Debbie soon found herself standing in front of her.

"Hi," Debbie said.

"Hello," the old woman replied. "So I understand you're having problems screwing your boyfriend."

Debbie blinked. "Do I know you?"

The woman seemed even older up close. Her hair was wispy and white and tumbled from the sides of her skull like heaps of dead grass, while her face was crisscrossed with bottomless wrinkles that looked like canyons on the moon.

"No," the woman said in a gravelly voice. "You don't know me, honey, but I can help you. Why don't you sit down?"

Debbie narrowed her eyes. Then she glanced back over at Cynthia, who smiled and waved her hand. The bitch.

Debbie found herself sitting down across from the woman. She also noticed that the woman had a tiny plate in front of her that held a taco. Hm, Debbie loved tacos, but they definitely upset her stomach.

"My name is Velva," the woman said. "And we've been destined to meet ever since you kissed your first boy."

Debbie raised an eyebrow. "Billy Baldwin? That was gross. I was wearing a ton of lipstick. He probably thought he was kissing a jar of putty."

"Maybe. But he still told his friends he banged you good."

"What? Are you kidding me?"

"No. It's a thing guys do. They lie about how much sex they've had."

"But he didn't have any! All he got was a lot of goop on his face, and then I told him to leave because I had to study astronomy."

"Astronomy? Do they teach that stuff in school?"

"Not really, but I was studying it on my own in my parents' backyard. I was going through an awkward phase." She sighed and bit one of her fingernails. "By the way, tonight offers a stunning view of Coronas Borealis."

Velva reached for a cigarette. There were rules against smoking it inside, but apparently she wanted to feel the nicotine against her gnarled yellow fingers. She looked Debbie in the eye and said, "Honey, you need more help than I thought. And you need to be more serious."

Debbie shrugged. "I'm not good at being serious. Being serious involves talking about stuff I don't want to discuss. Anyway, how do you know about me? Are you some kind of witch or something?"

Velva grinned through her crooked yellow teeth.

"Yep," she said. "I'm a witch."

Debbie cocked her head. That was not the answer she'd been hoping for.

Velva laughed. "I know you don't believe me and I don't blame you. I look too classy, right? Let me give you a little taste of my power, so you know I'm not just blowin' smoke."

Velva stared at the taco on her plate, and it started to pulsate like a beating heart. It had rockin' rhythm, too, and for a second Debbie swore she heard a mariachi band and a few maracas. Then she heard a distant voice chanting poetry in an ancient Mayan dialect—and she somehow *knew* it was Mayan, and that it was a complaint about the "fucking Toltecs," and then the taco lifted a bit off the table and spun around a few times. Finally, it stopped spinning and just hung there, suspended in the air. A few strands of shredded lettuce smoldered a bit.

Debbie eyed the wayward Mexican entrée with mixed feelings. On the one hand, it was probably a dumb trick. On the other hand, her stomach felt like it was turning upside down because it often felt that way. And then there was the fact that the diner didn't even serve tacos.

Velva cleared her throat with a grating sound and gave Debbie a crooked smile. "Think of something that turns you on, honey. Go ahead, anything."

Debbie narrowed her eyes. She was about to make a wise-ass remark, but then—*poof!*—there was a puff of smoke and the taco was gone. In its place was a wise-ass bowl of popcorn. It hovered for an instant and then settled down on the surface of the table with a subtle click.

Debbie just stared. This was white corn with fat, puffy kernels— her favorite kind. And there was no butter! She could tell it had olive oil sprinkled on top along with some salt, just the way she liked it. She reached out and touched the popcorn and discovered the kernels were definitely real.

She felt her heart pounding. At this point, it would probably be best to go home, but for some reason she didn't move.

Velva cackled. "Go ahead, try it. It's pretty damn good. Now do you want to hear the deal, or what?"

Debbie shrugged and forced herself to look indifferent. "I'm not hungry," she said. "I'm listening."

Velva smiled again, and she once again showed her teeth like jagged yellow pebbles. Then she leaned close to Debbie and lowered her voice.

"I've got a desire to be younger, okay? And you've got a desire to have better sex. And for a small price, I can fix your problem. All I want is a little bit of your youth. Gimme about ten or twenty years; let's call it fifteen. In exchange for that, I'll fix your sex life. No more awkward fumbling around. No more faking orgasms—*oh! oh! oh!* And no more having to do anything you don't want to do. Hell, you can just eat snack food all night and read a book, and he'll be happy as a pig in a pie store. And you won't have to die alone."

Debbie hesitated and then screwed up her face like someone who'd just swallowed a shot of paint thinner. "Are you kidding me? You want me to give up fifteen years of my life just to avoid ten minutes of humiliation a couple of times a week? That's ridiculous. No way."

Velva rolled the cigarette a bit between her crooked fingers and smiled. "Look, honey, I can tell you want this deal, so I'll cut you a break."

"No," Debbie replied. "I don't want anything."

"And I like you, babe, so I'll make it easy."

"You don't have to bother, no kidding."

"I mean since you're a good kid, I'll sweeten the pot."

"I'm going back to my table."

"Ten years," Velva said with a grimace. "Just give me ten."

"So long," Debbie said.

"Five years! Only five!"

"Velva, I'm not interested."

"Three years! What's three years? Hey, the last three are usually awful, right? You're drooling, you're in a diaper, your kids don't give a shit—it sucks."

Debbie shook her head. This was getting ludicrous. First, she didn't want to give up any of her life over something as stupid as bad sex—and second, three years wouldn't do Velva much good. She'd need about three decades just to get her pulse back.

"Velva... I mean, uh, have you considered dying your hair?" Debbie said. "It's just a thought."

Velva tossed her unlit cigarette onto the table. "Okay, it doesn't have to be your youth. You can sacrifice your cat's youth, but then we go back up to ten years. Those little bastards usually live at least that long."

Debbie paused. For some reason she found herself not getting up.

"I don't have a cat," she said.

"That's okay, you can get one."

"Why don't you get one?"

"It doesn't work that way. It needs to be someone's sacrifice because that's the way these black magic spells work. Somebody's gotta get the shaft. What about a dog? Do you have a dog?"

"A dog? No—no dog." Now Debbie jumped up from her seat. "I'm really not interested, Velva."

Velva started to speak again and then stopped. She looked at Debbie and cackled, and then she handed her a business card. It was bigger than the standard size. It was also styled to look like a movie marquee, and it featured a glamour shot of a young woman's face. Her teeth gleamed like new shower tiles, and her hair shined like a glossy haystack, and the word "Velva" was written at the bottom in embossed silver along with a phone number.

Debbie was conscious of Velva staring at her as she studied the card.

"Yeah, that used to be me," Velva said, referring to the photo.

Debbie wasn't sure what to say. She found herself contemplating the horror and havoc that can be caused by time. "You were beautiful," she murmured.

Velva gave a laugh. "Yeah, I was—a couple of months ago. Take the card, honey. For just a little effort, I can get you a big payoff. Trust me, you'll be interested soon."

3: Mike's Place

Mike eyed his cell phone and scratched his head. Should he call her, or what?

He looked around the room and clenched a fist.

His house in South River was neat. It was a brick ranch on a wide, quiet street of brick homes with bursting green lawns. There was a sturdy oak tree in the backyard, overlooking a dense wooden deck, and in the center of the deck was a built-in barbecue grill that shined like an armored vehicle. Everything was solid and strong—or was it?

He frowned and shook his head. Everything was so right and yet somehow it was freakin' wrong. He reached over to a folding TV-tray and grabbed the remote control that operated the table-sized television screen hanging on the wall; he instantly felt better. It was so perfect—a digital escape into a world of football, baseball, and basketball. But then, he wasn't such a typical guy. No, he also watched mixed martial arts.

Okay, maybe that was typical, but then there were the cooking shows. Yeah, he did have a feminine side, despite the snotty words of a few ex-girlfriends. In fact, he loved to watch the Lucy Lolliboo show on the cooking channel, and he smirked at the coolness of his cosmopolitan nature. No one sucked a flaming banana pop like Lucy.

His eyes wandered across the official "NY Jets throw rug" sitting on the floor. His dog, Sugar, was sleeping on it. He looked at the official "NY Jets clock" on the wall and saw it was almost midnight. He was going to call her. After all, she was just getting home from the diner, and there were no sports on TV. Plus, enough time had gone by since last night's disaster. The poor girl. Sure, some of her hang-ups were crazy when they happened—but really, they were no big deal. He'd had plenty of great sex with other girls, and they'd been the wrong girls. They'd been girls in love with his ripped abs and his flashy Corvette and his presumed membership in the McNormal mainstream—but Debbie wasn't like those girls, and neither was he. Not really. He needed to talk to her.

He gripped his cell phone tight and felt his heart leap as she answered. But she sounded tentative, even wary.

"Uh, hi, Mike," she said. "What's happening?"

"I was gonna ask you that, Deb. How was the diner?"

"Oh, it was okay. I mean except for the witch."

He laughed. "Did some old lady spill ice cream on you again?"

"Yeah—exactly. But at least it was chocolate."

"Deb, I want to tell you something."

"What?"

She sounded nervous. He had a good ear, and her voice always got higher when she was up on her anxiety cliff. Damn, she probably thinks I want to break up with her.

"I like you, Debbie. I like you a lot."

No response.

"Debbie? Debbie, are you there?"

"I'm here. That's good... I like you, too."

"Don't worry about the sex thing, Deb. The sex is fine and everything will work out."

"Okay."

"No, really. It's gonna be fine. It's not that important, anyway. You're more important to me than sex."

She hesitated. "That's a nice thing to say."

"Is it? I've got a lot more nice stuff for you."

"Where?" she said with a laugh. "In your pants?"

"No—that's not what I meant. Debbie, you sound stressed out."

"Me? I'm fine."

"Are you sure?"

"Absolutely! In fact, I'm going to get a plant."

"A plant? You mean in a pot or something?"

"Yeah, for my apartment."

"Oh. Is that what you're stressed about?"

"I'm not stressed!" she shouted. Then she sighed and lowered her voice. "I'm fine."

"Okay... So how's the new book going?"

He instantly heard her voice change. "I've just started it," she said. "I'm only ten thousand words into it. I'm thinking it will be about ninety thousand when it's done."

Mike smiled. She suddenly sounded more confident, like a seasick person stepping off an ocean liner.

"Ninety thousand sounds like a lot of words."

"It's a lot if they're terrible, but it's really not a lot."

"You'll have to let me read it when it's done. What's it about?"

"It's a noir-flavored sci-fi comedy about a female space pirate—but underneath the action and absurd humor, it's basically a love story."

"Cool. What's it called?"

"Suzy Spitfire Kills Everybody. And right now, Suzy is thinking about how she wants to rob a casino located in the ancient spaceport city of Choccabon—but it's a million-to-one shot, and she needs help to do it. She's tired of going at it alone. *She's fed up with only getting things to work right when she's alone!"*

Mike paused. "Right," he finally said with a shake of his head. It was time to talk about the real world. "Debbie, I gotta go down to Washington for a couple of days, and I was wondering if you could watch my dog. My sister can't do it this time."

He held his breath, waiting for her reaction.

"What?" she said. "Are you talking to me? Are you talking about the Chihuahua?"

"That's the only dog I've got."

"Oh. Do you think that's a good idea? Because I think he hates me."

"What are you talking about?"

"He keeps snarling and trying to bite my face off. Do you want a girl with no face?"

"Sugar likes you fine, Debbie, and besides, he can't reach much higher than your kneecaps. Plus, I can bring over a plastic barricade and you can lock him in the kitchen. So what do you say? I'm leaving around four. How about I come over a little early, like one o'clock? We could have some fun. You know, maybe even a romantic moment, right?"

"Romantic?" Now she sounded nervous again. "What do you mean?"

Mike laughed. "Deb, you worry too much. I'll be over at one o'clock with the dog. We can take him for a walk and it'll be great."

There was a long hesitation now.

"Sure," she said. "Bring him over."

"Great. See you then."

Mike hung up the phone and walked into the kitchen, where he grabbed a carton of milk from the refrigerator. As he chugged it down, he thought about the situation with Debbie.

When the sex was bad, Debbie's insecurities caused her to blame herself, but is that what he wanted? No, it wasn't—but it was better than blaming him. If it was his fault, it was a much bigger disaster, and Debbie didn't understand this. A guy has to perform.

He swore and crumpled up the milk carton. Dammit! He should've kept pumping, but he hadn't. He sighed and washed his empty glass, scrubbing it too hard. Then he glanced at the kitchen counter, at the pair of heavy drumsticks he'd placed there about an hour ago.

He felt his mood improve, and he smirked. Everyone has secrets, and his would jolt a few jocks right out of their sweat socks. Even his parents had no idea, and his two older brothers, who he admired, had no clue. They all thought he was just like them, but they were wrong.

He grabbed the wooden sticks in his rough hands and grinned. Sure, the wizard he'd bought them from had once been a heavy metal drummer—but he'd demonstrated the power of the sticks, and Mike had been impressed. Certainly, it was the first time he'd ever seen a pair of drumsticks that could magically make a country singer disappear. Hopefully, the old guy would give him a few more lessons.

He looked at the clock above the sink. It was time to stop worrying about his job and his love life. He had to go move some iron.

He grabbed a couple of death metal CDs and headed down into the basement.

4: Juan Carlos

Juan Carlos played a few slippery licks on his Epiphone Casino and grinned. He sounded good tonight and he knew it. He scanned the crowd in *Ronnie's Martini Bar* to see if anyone cared—no such luck.

Still, he liked the room. It was his kind of place, a dark and sparkling mix of brick and oak and glass bathed in soft golden light. The gentle lighting made everyone look more attractive, if not less ridiculous. The patrons were young and stylish, with shiny gelled hair, slinky dresses, five-inch pumps, and flashes of tribal tattoos on milky white shoulder blades.

Juan was perched on a stool in a shadowy corner far from the front door, with a nice view of the bar as it stretched down the length of the room to the city street outside. He liked his position; he could see whatever was coming. He had no specific threat in mind, but there was certainly no harm in being careful. He bent a couple of strings in a special way, held the notes for a few seconds, and then slid his fingers down the neck. He heard a nice airy sound that no one else seemed to notice, but he only shrugged. The lack of interest was expected.

He'd played at *Ronnie's* enough times to know his job. He was here to create a cool, jazzy vibe that made it easier for pretentious hipsters to spend money on overpriced drinks. One thing he'd learned from hundreds of gigs was that all kinds of people liked their liquor.

Income, education, and fashion varied from place to place, but the quest for a good buzz was universal, and so was the management's desire to sell a maximum amount of booze.

The room was crowded tonight. He stroked the lower notes of a ninth chord with his big thumb and then slid it up two frets. It echoed with a sweet late-night sound through the Fender Twin on the floor—wow, he sounded great. He glanced in a mirror on the wall and shot himself a sly smile. He had a long brown ponytail, a mustache and goatee, and a face that went well with the room. Of course, his face went well with every room, and that's what made him such a hit with the women. They thought he was irresistibly handsome, and they loved his accent due to a childhood spent in Argentina. But all this love from the ladies sometimes caused trouble—like the trouble he spotted now.

Manda huevos! What was she doing here? He felt his head spin. Certainly, this crazy girl was not here to buy a martini.

She was wearing a blood red dress pulled tight over her curvy, full-figured frame. Her hair was a trashy shade of artificial auburn, and her eyes were the color of smoking avocados.

Juan felt himself start to sweat, and he looked away. Maybe if he pretended not to see her she'd disappear, but how to ignore a charging bull? She was barreling through the room. He switched gears and feigned a look of surprise, lifting his eyebrows. Then he flashed a blinding smile. Surely, her heart would melt—again. Surely, she would forgive him for a few unreturned phone calls. And of course, she couldn't yell at him while he was in the middle of a song.

"You bastard!" she yelled.

He kept smiling but stopped playing.

"Valentina," he said, trying his best to sound cordial. "How very nice to see you. I've been meaning to give you a call."

Valentina sneered. "You lying piece of shit! I never should've gotten involved with a guy like you."

A few people near the bar glanced at the scene and laughed.

"Don't be so upset. I was going to call you," Juan said. "I've just been so busy."

"Busy, doing what?" she spat. "Jumping on top of every girl in New Jersey?"

Once again, Juan feigned a look of shock. "How can you say this? Is this what you think? Let me buy you a drink, and we'll talk like rational people."

"I'm not rational!" she shouted. "And you're not a person—you're an asshole. An asshole I'm going to clobber with this pocketbook!"

It wasn't a big pocketbook, although it could have easily held a brick. Most likely it only held makeup and some credit cards. Still, Valentina wore a lot of makeup and really loved her retail, and it hurt when she hit him with it—over and over and over.

Poom! Poom! Poom!

"You asshole! I hope you die, you fucking asshole!"

Juan grimaced and held up his right arm to shield himself from the blows, while his left hand stayed wrapped around the neck of the guitar. People at the bar were definitely watching now, and most of them were laughing.

The bouncer walked toward the situation, but he took his time—probably because the woman seemed crazy and probably because it was just too funny. Luckily, Valentina stopped the assault before he reached her.

Her chest heaved like a pair of quivering cantaloupes as she scowled at Juan. He tried to recover a little dignity, but of course he still noticed those monstrous bobbing flesh-boulders. Yes, despite her outburst, he would've happily taken her home with him—because he was a man, and that's the way he was built. But she obviously wasn't in the spirit of forgiveness.

"Don't you ever talk to me again!" she screamed. Then she turned and charged back toward the front door, easily parting the crowd.

The bouncer gave Juan a glance and laughed. In fact, everyone in the room was laughing. Juan knew the guys were laughing because he was a dog, and Valentina had found out the hard way, and that was life. But the girls were laughing, too, and he guessed it was for a different reason, and for an instant he felt a pang of regret, and he sighed. He was a dog who'd gotten what he'd deserved.

Juan gave a sheepish grin and went back to playing his instrument. For the remainder of his set, guys would come up and talk to him about the brawl, and he'd joke about it, and they would think he was a cool dude. Hey, a girl is mad you didn't call her? That's the way to do it. A real king has to conquer and move on—or so they say.

Juan finished the rest of his set without any more beatings. Normally, he'd hang around a bit and have a few drinks and maybe talk to some of the ladies—but would any of these women be interested in a smirking scoundrel? He smiled, because they would be. Everyone wants what other people want, and he was obviously wanted by someone, even if it was "dead or alive." But tonight he decided to leave early. He had some big things on his mind—bigger things than Valentina. He had a meeting with a witch.

Juan tossed his gear into the back of his Toyota Corolla and pulled the car out onto George Street, a bustling road lined with shops, cafes, and ethnic restaurants. He punched the radio preset to 88.7 WRSU, the local radio station for Rutgers University, and heard a Spanish song about love. He sighed once again. How many songs were there about the topic? Too many.

He was tired of the games. What had he promised Valentina? *Nada!* He'd met her in a bar, and he'd gone home with her after she'd had a few glasses of wine, and it had been her idea! She'd asked him to come back to her apartment, and it had been a great time. She was fabulous in bed—most big girls are, because they like sex the same way they like food. They'd done it several times, and then in the morning she'd given him a good-bye blowjob that had been even better than the pancakes and sausages she'd cooked, and those had been tasty pancakes, oozing with butter and sweet sticky syrup.

But so what? Was he supposed to marry the girl? If he'd returned her calls, how would it have gone? Yes, he could've ended up back in that hungry hole between her thighs—and if she'd played her cards right, he would have. But he wasn't looking to fall in love, and he'd done her a favor by not calling. All she needed to do was get over it.

He was tired of being such a love god—but of course, he couldn't help himself. He loved women, but only for a few hours at a time, and definitely not the next morning.

Maybe the witch could help.

5: Debbie's Plan

Debbie put down her phone and stared at the wall with a blank expression.

She pondered which was worse: the thought of babysitting Mike's horrendous dog, or the thought of having horrendous sex with Mike. Her head was whirling, and she just wanted it to stop.

What would her blazing protagonist Suzy Spitfire do? Probably shoot someone. But unfortunately, Debbie was the only one here and she didn't feel like going out. She pressed her fingers to her aching temples and scanned the room, trying to focus on other things.

She lived in a sparsely furnished one-bedroom apartment in Highland Park, in an old brick apartment building. Her place had little furniture because furniture usually involved shopping and shopping usually involved money. Her collection currently included a dinged up wooden futon and a badly abused desk, both hauled from the curb on "garbage night," but on top of the desk was a shiny MacBook Pro where she spent her time typing. There was no sign of a television, but she gave the internet a good workout.

Debbie walked into the cramped kitchen. She glanced out the dark window at the fire escape, which always made her nervous, and then grabbed a box of animal crackers from a cabinet above the refrigerator. For some reason, animal crackers never upset her stomach. There was no chance she'd become a vegetarian; camels, gorillas, and sheep just tasted too wonderful.

She fidgeted with her glasses and then bit a fingernail. She had to call Cynthia. She just had to. She was tired, and Cynthia probably was, too—but Cynthia was a night person who rarely went to bed before 4 a.m. So she called and felt a wave of relief when Cynthia answered.

"Hey, Debbie, didn't I just see you talking to a witch? Let me guess, you're calling to tell me that you're gonna take her offer, right? The one with the big payoff?"

Of course, Debbie had told Cynthia about Velva. Then Cynthia said, "You know, I'd like to see if she's got any spells that can get me a boyfriend. I'll let the sex part take care of itself."

"Forget about the witch," Debbie said. "Mike called me. He said he liked me, and he said the sex didn't matter."

"Okay, that sounds great. So why do you sound so stressed?"

"He wants to come over here tomorrow!" Debbie wailed. "He wants me to watch his dog while he's in Washington, and I think he wants to have sex before he leaves."

Cynthia laughed. "Debbie, most girls would be *happy* about that. I wish I had a hot guy who wanted to come charging into my bed. Anyway, didn't he just tell you the sex didn't matter?"

"Yeah, but it's not true. I know it matters."

"How do you know?"

Debbie sighed. "Because even when it doesn't matter, it causes problems that matter. It causes arguments and tension. It's an area that requires compatibility but I never seem to be compatible. That's how it's always been and now I'm freaking out! I need a little more time before we do it again."

"Hm, so what are you going to do?"

"I don't know. I was thinking maybe you could come over first. Then he'll come and you'll already be here and I'll say, "Sorry, Mike, she just came by and I can't get rid of her.""

Cynthia gave a short laugh. "What? So you want me to be an annoying 'third wheel' who just popped in and won't go home. But aren't you just postponing the inevitable? I mean he's gonna be back, and I'm not moving in with you."

"I'll be okay by then. I'll go back to therapy."

"You've been saying that for six months, and you never go. How long is he going to be gone?"

"A couple of days."

"I think you're gonna need more than forty-eight hours of therapy, Debbie... Why don't you tell him you're on your period?"

"I had my period last week."

"Well, maybe he won't remember how long it's been."

"Cynthia, I've already had it twice this month, okay? Three times would be pushing it."

"Debbie, I think you need to talk to Mike."

"No! I need to stall him off. That's the way I do things."

"You mean push them out of your mind until they turn into a disaster?"

"Exactly! So are you coming over here or not? I need you here at one o'clock. Please."

Cynthia sighed. "All right, I'll be there. I guess I'll witness the grand fiasco—or maybe get a little whiff of romance."

"Great. Thanks, Cynthia. You're the best!"

"Don't mention it. And get me a six-pack."

Debbie hung up the phone. She took off her glasses and rubbed her eyes. She really had a headache, and she needed to sleep, but she was too nervous to sleep.

She walked into the kitchen and picked up a bottle of aspirin. She gulped down two of them and hoped they wouldn't give her an ulcer, because hadn't she just read that aspirins could cause ulcers? Crap! She should have taken something else! Hopefully the internal bleeding would be minimal.

For an instant she considered going back on anti-anxiety drugs, but the thought of relying on those meds forever freaked her out. She was determined to go natural even if her heart exploded. Besides, a lot of those drugs interfered with her ability to have an orgasm—not a very good side effect, doc. What good is a happiness pill that takes away one of the best kinds of happiness?

She finally headed to the bedroom where she was hoping to get some sleep. But it was unlikely. Her stomach was in knots, and she felt like she was standing on a high diving board, looking down at the water and wondering why everyone wanted her to jump.

She stared at herself in the mirror. What did Mike see in her, anyway? Her nose was too small. Her eyes were too big. Her hair was too straight and her lips were too thin! Velva was right—she needed help.

She took a few deep breaths and tried to relax. Maybe she'd read a book. She plopped down onto her bed and opened *Cat's Cradle*, a Kurt Vonnegut novel she'd read a hundred times. It didn't matter. If it kept her from thinking about sex with Mike, it was just perfect.

6: Suzy Speaks

"What are you doing, Debbie?"

Debbie was drifting off to sleep when she heard the husky voice of Suzy Spitfire inside her head.

"Hey, Suzy," she said. "What's going on?"

Suzy laughed. "Just my usual hatred of the boring world around me. You know, people painting their white picket fences and all that kind of bullshit. But you should understand."

"Yeah, I understand. So what color are you painting your picket fence?"

"I used my picket fence for target practice long ago. Then again, I suppose it was my parents' fence, but whatever. Anyway, I met this mystical guru named Shelba, and she says she's got a deal for me—an easy way to get a big payoff. I'm thinking I can use the payoff to outfit my ship better and then rob that casino in Choccoban."

"I think you should watch your step."

"I'm very careful, Deb."

"You're *not* very careful, Suzy."

"True, but that's why you love me. Besides, I'm heavily armed."

"Goodnight, Suzy."

"Goodnight."

7: Velva

Velva needed a cigarette. She needed a bunch of them, but the little fuckers were nowhere to be found.

She was rifling through the wreckage of her kitchen, tossing stuff from the top of a cluttered counter—a greasy raincoat, a frayed pocketbook, a pile of moldy old magazines, and a cat. The cat screeched as it landed in a cardboard box filled with rumpled clothes. The box was next to other cardboard boxes overloaded with books, newspapers, shoes, and assorted trash. The cat said *rrrrrrow!* and darted like a black streak through a nearby doorway.

Velva cursed and scanned the rest of the room. In the corner, she saw a smudge-covered door with three cracked windowpanes, and a pockmarked wooden table covered with dishes, and piles of paper, gloves and hats, and an old lamp. The lamp had a rusty wire handle on top, and it looked like something that had once been hanging from the back of a horse-and-buggy. Next to the lamp was the upturned lid of a mayonnaise jar, overflowing with the remains of a thousand dead cigarettes, and an empty tin that had once held anchovies.

On the walls were movie posters. The posters spanned a fat chunk of Hollywood history, and featured the official marquee images of movies like *Gone With The Wind, Pretty Woman,* and *Body Heat.*

Velva cursed again and coughed a few times. Then she shoved her hand into the pocket of the black terrycloth robe she was wearing and found her cigarettes. Hey, this was great news! She grinned just as another cat poked its headlight eyes out from under the table.

"Lookie here, Bart," she said. "I found my smokes. This could be the beginning of a good night."

She picked up a pack of matches from the table and lit up a Virginia Slim. She took a long drag and then blew a choking cloud of smoke into the room.

The cat leaped up on the table and sniffed at the empty anchovy tin. Then it sat down in a pile of stained napkins and started licking itself behind its rear thigh in the style of a feline contortionist.

Velva coughed a few more times and sat down. She took another drag on her cigarette and coughed again.

"So, Bart, what's on the agenda for tonight?"

The cat didn't even look at her, but a voice from somewhere near her feet said, "He's going to find himself a sexy little feline down the street, while you'll be at home finding yourself a nice case of lung cancer."

Velva frowned as a tiny red monkey came swaggering out from under the table.

"What do you want, Carl?" she said. "Did you come here to make trouble? I don't see your social life rocking the planet."

The monkey sat by her feet and laughed. It was only about eight inches high, but he spoke in a voice that sounded big for such a small creature. "In this world, I'm just a monkey—and I'll admit, that's not as great as most people might think. But in my world, I'm a king, and don't you forget it."

Velva sneered. "Okay, Your Majesty, I'll try not to step on your crown. What kind of color is red for a monkey, anyway?"

The monkey gave a snort. "It's the perfect color for a monkey that doesn't give a rat's ass about what he's *supposed* to look like."

"Great, why don't you take your rosy red ass back to your world and leave me alone? I'll call you when I'm ready."

The monkey laughed again. "And when will that be? You've been saying you'll be ready for a while. Just remember, you're getting older every minute. People are going to think you saw all these movies when they came out, ha-ha."

Velva took a drag on her cigarette and considered killing the mini monkey with a nearby butcher's knife, but it was a silly thought. The demon inside would just flee and she'd be left to clean up the slaughtered carcass of a dead primate. Besides, she needed that demon.

"Not all the movies are old, you evil piece of shit. And yeah, I'm getting old right now—but pretty soon I'll have a nice little pipeline to eternal youth and beauty, you'll see."

"Oh, really?" the monkey said. "So you've finally got somebody?"

"What do you mean, 'finally'? I was only kicked out of the fucking International Union of Witches two months ago. Christ, you act like I've been this old forever. But yeah, I've got a couple of idiots who will be perfect."

"That's great. But wouldn't it be easier to just try and get back into the group?"

Velva grimaced, and her black eyes smoked. "No chance! Those bitches can rot in hell!" Then she cackled and said, "Sorry, it's just an expression. I didn't mean it as an insult."

"I'm not insulted," the monkey said with a white-toothed grin. "But the word 'hell' isn't really correct, and nobody rots. We're very busy in my dimension, so send your people through. When are they coming?"

"I'll probably be hearing from the girl pretty soon. Any minute now."

The monkey whipped its pinkish tale around, obviously enthused. He looked sly and said, "Do you feel any guilt for what you're about to do, you miserable old hag?"

Velva eyed the butcher's knife again and then glanced at Kathleen Turner hanging on the wall. Kathleen was all wrapped up in William Hurt, but of course she was really thinking about murder and Velva could relate. She blew some more smoke and said, "Of course not. I have to think about myself first, right? That's what I do—the same as you."

"That might be true some of the time, but not all of the time."

"Are you saying you're better than me?"

"You bet your floppy old ass I am. You're just a worn out slut in the gutter of nowhere."

Velva seized the knife and threw it. Carl leaped to one side and watched it bounce off the grimy floor and then clang against a rusty radiator.

The monkey shook his head. "Just send me the people, honey. I'll take care of the rest."

Velva smiled like a crooked razor blade. "Fuck you."

The monkey just laughed and disappeared.

8: Too Big For Me

The doorbell rang like a gong of doom. Was it one o'clock already?

"Oh, no," Debbie said with a moan. "That's him! Okay, remember the plan, Cynthia."

Cynthia was slouched on Debbie's worn out couch, swigging a bottle of Corona. She was wearing a pair of baby blue stretch pants and a loose cotton T-shirt.

She raised her eyebrows like she'd just been asked to solve an algebra equation.

"Plan?" she said. "We had a plan?"

"Yes! Sort of! But first I need to change this stupid outfit."

"Debbie, you just changed your outfit. You look fine."

"No, I hate these jeans. I look terrible! I look like a stick."

"Debbie, most girls would kill to be as thin as you. You don't need new pants; you need a tray of cupcakes."

"I'm too nervous to eat!" Debbie said as she ran into the bedroom. "Get the door and tell Mike I'll be right there."

Cynthia sighed and slowly rose from the couch. She sashayed across the hardwood floor with the beer in her hand, taking another slug before opening the door.

Mike stood there in a gray sleeveless T-shirt and a NY Yankees baseball cap. His chest looked wide like a boxcar but twice as strong. He stared at Cynthia, and he blinked. She thought his expression was funny—obviously, he was surprised to see her, and obviously, she had a serious chest herself, even in a loose cotton T-shirt. Then the little dog at his feet started to bark.

"*Yip! Yip! Yip!*"

The dog bounced against Cynthia's leg while Mike yanked its leash, trying to jerk it away.

"Get down, Sugar!" he said. "Cut it out... I'm sorry, Cynthia. I guess he wasn't expecting you."

"No problem," Cynthia said with a smile. "From what I hear, I'm just a third wheel who won't go home... So, what's up, Mike?"

He gave her a quizzical look, but she just turned and walked back into the room, vaguely wondering if his eyes were watching her curvy hips. Ah, well, it was unlikely—after all, his girlfriend looked like a stick. She sat back down.

"Where's Deb?" Mike said.

"Oh, she's contemplating her eating disorder. She's also changing her clothes."

From the other room, Debbie screamed, "I'm not hungry! I'll be right in!"

Cynthia took another swig of Corona. "She's not hungry. She'll be right in."

Mike nodded. "How's the band?"

"Pretty much the same, which means it doesn't exist. So, do you want to play some drums?"

"I wish I had the time," he said with a grin. "I'm more of a fan now, but I like all that stuff you do—no prisoners and no apologies. Who needs all that fancy playing and singing, right?"

"Sure, right—I think," she said. "I'll let you know when I'm making noise somewhere. By the way, did you ever get a tattoo?"

"Nope. How about you?"

"Yeah, I did it, and I can't believe it took me so long."

"Oh, yeah? Where is it?"

"Do you wanna see?"

"That depends. Is it gonna get me in trouble?"

"No," she said with a laugh. "Better luck next time. But here's what I've got."

She stood up, turned around, and lifted her T-shirt a bit. She knew he was now staring at the image of the Warner Bros. Tasmanian Devil playing a bass guitar on her lower back.

"Do you like it?"

"Yeah. Part of the devil is cut off, but it's great."

She pulled her pants and panties down a few more inches, exposing the rounded top of her bottom. She felt her heart beat a little faster, but what the hell, it was all in good fun.

"Okay, now I see it all," he said. "I like it. Yeah, very nice."

She dropped her shirt and turned back around. "You didn't see it all," she said with a quick smile. "But I'm glad you like it."

She found herself staring at him for a long second, while he was staring back at her. Then he glanced away.

"Hey, what do you know?" he said. "Debbie got a plant. She told me she would. It's got leaves and flowers and everything." He pointed to a small pot that held an African violet, sitting on the dining room table.

"Yeah, they're supposed to de-stress her. From what I've seen, she needs to get a few more. I'm wondering if she can fit a greenhouse in here."

Mike went over and examined the wilted leaves. "This plant seems to be dying."

Cynthia shrugged. "She should've picked a different one—but that's how it goes, right? I don't think she's given it a thought since she brought it in here. Death is imminent."

Mike looked ready to comment on the plant's desperate condition, but then the dog started jumping around like he had springs on his feet.

"*Yip! Yip! Yip!*"

Mike said, "Sugar, shut up! I mean it. You need to behave."

Cynthia watched as he bent down to chastise the dog. His massive biceps moved like writhing pythons. She felt her nipples getting hard just as Debbie walked into the room.

Debbie glanced at Mike and Cynthia. Well, well, someone brought the big guns today, and that was fine. It was nice to have a boyfriend other girls noticed, and Cynthia was a real sucker for guys who spent too much time moving around big pieces of iron. She'd probably even showed him her new tattoo. Hopefully, she wouldn't accidentally stab anyone with those iron-tipped boobs.

Mike said, "Hi, honey," and gave Debbie a quick kiss on the lips.

"Hi," Debbie said as she moved back and adjusted her glasses. She pointed at a bulging arm.

"You look very sharp, Mike. Are those permanently attached?"

"No one's yanked them off yet. You look good, too, Deb."

Debbie ran a few fingers through her tangled dark hair and tried to believe it. She was wearing another casual black dress and her favorite white sneakers. As always, the dress was loose and hugged nothing—but there wasn't much to hug, at least the way she saw it. Then again, was this the best she could do? Why the hell didn't she have better clothes? Oh, wait, she hated to shop. She didn't like buying clothes over the internet, and going to the mall meant dealing with the crowds and a possible panic attack.

"Thanks," she said. "I see your dog hasn't gotten any bigger."

"No, not today. But he will, as soon as I feed him somebody's German Shepherd... I thought we could take him for a walk. By the way, are you allowed to keep a dog in this building?"

Now that was a good question. Debbie realized the answer was probably 'no,' but she'd never actually bothered to check.

"Sure," she said. What the hell, it was only for a day or two. Maybe Sugar would grow to love her. Or maybe she could duct tape his mouth shut.

Sugar growled and gave her a vicious look. Apparently, the little demon dog could read minds. Calm down, doggy, it was just a joke.

Cynthia noticed her beer was empty. She got up and walked into the kitchen. Mike instantly grabbed Debbie's arm and lowered his voice.

"Is Cynthia gonna be here all afternoon?" he said. "I'm just saying, because I thought we could—you know." And he raised his eyebrows up and down a few times, like a lascivious yo-yo.

Debbie fidgeted with her hair and tried to stay calm. "I know, but I can't just ask her to leave."

"But why is she here?"

"She was having a boyfriend crisis, so I asked her to come over."

"She doesn't have a boyfriend."

"She met some guy and he's...jerking her around."

Debbie looked away as her cheeks got hot. She didn't like lying, and she especially didn't like lying so badly. Why hadn't she bothered to come up with a better untruth? Ugh!

She started to bite a fingernail just as Cynthia returned. Debbie watched Mike's face grow dark as Cynthia sipped a freshly opened Corona, signaling she was sticking around.

Cynthia seemed amused. "Are you two talking about me?"

"No," Debbie said.

"Yes," Mike replied.

"Oh," Cynthia said. "I should probably be going."

"Okay," Mike said.

"No!" Debbie shouted, and she felt her face turning red—she hadn't meant to yell with such desperation. "I want you to stay, Cynthia. I want you to feel better about your...problem."

"Right," Cynthia said, "my problem." She took a long swig of beer. "I drink too much, and my problem keeps getting worse."

Mike said, "Debbie says you met a guy, and he's causing trouble."

Debbie shot Cynthia a sharp look, and Cynthia shrugged.

"Oh, yeah," Cynthia said. "This guy just won't communicate with me, you know? He thinks he can just stall things off, and that isn't going to work. Do you think communication is important, Mike?"

Mike's face got serious as a chunk of granite. "Yeah, it is. I take communication very seriously. It's one of the things I like so much about Debbie. She tells me everything."

"Right," Cynthia said.

"Right," Debbie said. Then she forced herself to smile. It was easier to do if she imagined she were pummeling Cynthia with a heavy object.

In one smooth motion, Cynthia chugged the entire bottle of beer and didn't spill a drop. She grabbed her sack-sized pocketbook from the couch. "I'm gonna go," she said, giving Debbie a warm glance. "It's all for the best. Call me later."

Debbie's mouth dropped open and she started to say something, but then Cynthia gave Mike a sunny smile and headed out the door, swinging her lively hips as she went.

Mike stared at her big rocking butt, watching her go. Then he turned toward Debbie and said, "Sure, you can call her later."

"Call her what?" Debbie snapped. "A traitorous bitch?"

"What?"

"Did I say something?"

"You seem mad at Cynthia."

"Mike, I'm always mad at Cynthia."

"I thought you liked Cynthia."

"I *love* Cynthia. I'm just mad because I don't want to have sex."

There, she'd said it, and she immediately regretted it.

She felt a wave of guilt and shame washing over her. But she gave him a sideways glance—would he understand what she was talking about?

"What are you talking about?" he said. "Debbie, why are you so worried about sex?"

She sighed. "I don't know. I just don't think I'm very good at it, and I guess you expect me to be better."

The dog started barking again. *"Yip! Yip! Yip!"*

Debbie wished she could be somewhere far away. But then she might end up alone, ugh! She suppressed the urge to bite another fingernail. Then she saw Mike looking at her with a spark in his eye. He was grinning and waving his arms in the air.

"Debbie, you're so crazy," he said. "You just need to think of sex more like a game. The best guy in the world still strikes out sometimes—even Babe Ruth used to go oh-for-four. Even Joe Montana threw a few picks. Even Michael Jordan missed a few layups. Do you understand?"

Debbie screwed up her face, trying to decipher his analogies. She guessed they involved sports, but she hated sports. She'd never been good at any of them. Sports involved coordination and red-faced kids in physical education class screaming at her because she couldn't catch some dopey object—like the world was going to end if a rubber ball bounced past her, big deal.

"I don't know what you're talking about," Debbie said. "I think sex should be romantic. I'm not interested in scoring a goal in the World Series."

Mike gave a little snort. "We've done it lots of times, and I thought it *was* romantic. I thought it was pretty freakin' good. So now you're telling me it was bad?"

"No!" Debbie blurted. Better not go down that road. "It was great. It's just that lately, well, I've been having a little pain."

Mike's eyebrows shot upward. "Really? What kind of pain?"

"Oh, it's nothing—probably nothing. It just hurts when we do it, and I'm…going to get it checked out. I think maybe you're…too big for me."

"What? Are you kidding me?"

His face broke into a huge grin.

Debbie shrugged. "Well, maybe—yeah, that might be it. Yeah, exactly. You're too damn big for me!"

For a second, he was silent.

"That's incredible," he finally said, shaking his head. Then he quickly added, "Of course, I mean in a bad way."

He reached out and grabbed her shoulders. "Debbie, don't worry about it. You'll get used to it—girls always do! We've got so much in common… We can't let my giant dick come between us."

She stared into his eyes. Was this conversation actually happening?

"Right. But I'm a little sore right now, so I think we need to take a break."

"Of course!" he said, puffing out his chest. "We don't have to do it now. You should've told me about this problem. But there are other things we can do."

"No!" Debbie said, rushing in to stop a spurting onslaught of inconvenient images. "I can't do those things…without thinking about how much I need to do everything. So we should wait."

"Oh," Mike said with a grin. "That makes sense. We'll have to wait… So, do you want to walk my dog? Or maybe lock him in your bedroom and make some popcorn?"

"Now that's a great idea," Debbie said, suddenly feeling like a giant dark cloud had evaporated.

"Great! And you can tell me about this book you're writing. I'd like to read some of it."

"Oh. I don't think you'd like it."

"Of course I'll like it. I like everything about you, Debbie. In fact, you're the most interesting person I know."

"Really?"

"Yes."

He stepped forward and hugged her hard. She found herself wrapping her arms around his body. She felt the bulging muscles of his arms and chest enveloping her, and she had to admit it felt pretty good.

"Debbie, I love you. I really do."

The good feeling vanished as a stab of alarm shot through her head. Love? Crap!

"That's nice," she said.

"Do you love me, too?"

She hesitated, trying to get her mouth to move. "Maybe," she said.

Now why had she said that? Maybe because it wasn't impossible—at some point in the future.

Mike seemed unconcerned. He just grinned again and said, "Don't worry. It'll all work out. I know it."

Debbie kept smiling. Her face seemed to hurt.

9: The Deal

The rain was pouring down, pounding the grimy blacktop. There was almost enough water and wind to loosen the layers of dirt glued to Debbie's battered Honda Civic—almost, but not quite.

Debbie gripped the steering wheel hard. She scrunched up her face and peered through the deluge as the wipers sloshed across the windshield. It didn't help that one of the wiper blades was ripped and hanging by a few desperate strands of rubber. Inside the car, empty paper coffee cups and depleted bags of snack food were scattered around.

Over in the passenger side, she noticed Cynthia using her Chuck Taylors to rustle through the mostly empty bags of Doritos on the floor. Cynthia said, "I can't believe we're going to see a witch. But weren't you supposed to bring the dog?"

"No!" Debbie said. "Do you really think I'd sacrifice Mike's dog? I have a plan."

Cynthia picked up an open bag of corn chips from the dashboard. She noticed there were a few chips left and smiled.

"I didn't really think you'd hurt the doggie, Deb. But another plan? That's three in one week. Besides, the witch wants a dog, so what's the point?"

"Cynthia, I didn't tell you this, but here's the problem: Mike said he loves me."

Cynthia stared at Debbie for a second and then bit down hard on a stale Dorito. "Okay, let me get this straight. There's a big, hunky guy out there who wants to live with you for all eternity. Gee, that *is* a crisis. You better hope some skuzzy loser comes along and saves you from all that happiness."

Debbie grimaced as a Mercedes SUV blew past the car, splattering the Honda with a filthy wave of water. Then she sighed. "It's a problem because I'm not sure if I love him, but what if I do? Or what if I will—eventually? Or what if I don't and I should? Anyway, I have to make this work, at least for now."

"Why do you have to make it work? If it's right it should work by itself."

"I have to make it work just in case Mike is the right guy. I have to make sure I don't blow it because of the sex! And then if it's still wrong I can break up with him later."

"Debbie, that is *so ridiculous*."

"I just want to talk to the witch, okay? Maybe I can negotiate."

"Ha, what are you going to do, offer her a hamster instead of a Chihuahua? What's the life span of a hamster? All the ones I had died in a few weeks."

"I'm not going to offer her a hamster. What kind of person do you think I am? I'm going to offer her a family heirloom."

"Excuse me? You have an heirloom? And why would she want that?"

"I don't know!" Debbie snapped. "Maybe because she's a witch, and she might want something nice. So I'll give her something nice that I totally don't care about, like my grandmother's wristwatch."

"So you want to give up your granny's wristwatch in exchange for lots of great sex. You know, my grandmother would totally get that. I don't think Granny's seen any action in thirty years."

"Exactly! My grandmother would want me to be happy. It's not like I really care what time it is."

Cynthia laughed. "All I can say is, this witch better not turn me into a frog. I mean if we're both running for the door and I get 'frogged' and you don't, I'm gonna be pissed."

Debbie shrugged. "I hope that doesn't happen, but if it does I'll get you a nice bowl to live in. I'll change your water every day."

Cynthia tossed the empty bag of corn chips onto the floor where it settled into the snack food graveyard. "Okay, but I don't want any little plastic castles or anything like that. I want to look sad and lonely every second so you'll feel maximum guilt."

Debbie grimaced again and then plowed the car through some deep puddles. She was entering the Washington Heights section of East Brunswick, located right off the main artery of Route 18, near a collection of strip malls and a sprawling car dealership. Debbie had never visited anyone here. It was a tight little grid of streets and stop signs, and a hodgepodge of houses, with beat-up bungalows standing next to overdone mini-mansions.

"Just look for number twenty-six," Debbie said. "Hey, this is it."

Cynthia peered through the rain and then shook her head.

"Beautiful. Oh, wait, I meant to say 'terrible.' I'm surprised there aren't any bats flying out of the attic."

It was a small cape cod in dilapidated condition. The outside of the house was covered with ratty green shingles, while the yard was buried under weeds and bushes and groping vines. There was a chimney that leaned to the left, and a tree that leaned toward the ground. There was also a driveway, but it was covered with jagged gravel. Debbie decided to park a bit past the house, in an inky black puddle just beyond a couple of potholes. She took a deep breath and turned off the car's headlights.

She glanced at Cynthia. "Don't be so negative. She's an old lady, and she probably has a hard time taking care of the place."

"I suppose. But couldn't she use a magic spell or something to mow the lawn?"

"Cynthia, do you really think a witch wants to waste her hard-earned magic on landscaping? Come on, let's go."

They ran through the rain, up a walkway of broken slate that led to the front door. Debbie rang the bell while Cynthia looked around with nervous eyes, like she was searching for goblins hiding in the high grass.

The door swung open, and there was Velva.

She looked about the same as she had in the diner, although

tonight she wore a murkier green dress the color of pond scum, along with a bunch of necklaces that formed a deep layer of fake pearls. There was weedy white hair around her head, and a smile that looked like a garden of crooked, yellow tombstones. She pulled a cigarette from her mouth and blew some smoke.

She coughed and said, "Come on in, Debbie. Oh, you brought your friend? Great, you can come in, too. Maybe I can help you both."

Debbie forced herself to smile as they walked into the house. Wow! The place was even worse on the inside than it was on the outside. The living room was filled with stained stuffed chairs, two smelly sofas, some baby-poop colored carpeting, and piles of junk—old lamps, empty fishbowls, heaps of clothing, piles of newspapers, and a collection of hubcaps.

On the walls were movie posters. *Romancing The Stone* caught Debbie's eye, where Kathleen Turner was happily swinging on a vine with Michael Douglas.

"I know what you're thinking," Velva said. "You're wondering where I got all this great stuff, right?"

Debbie and Cynthia looked at each other and said nothing.

Velva laughed. "I know the place is a disaster, but it didn't look like this a couple of months ago. This used to be a nice little house. I had Kentucky Bluegrass on the front lawn, and a kid pissing into a fountain. And in here I had some gorgeous leopard print rugs and a top-of-the-line entertainment center from Sears. All the shit you see now is because of a little disagreement with the International Union of Witches. But don't worry, I'm gonna beat those bitches at their own game and get my youth back—and my vinyl siding, too, you hear me? So, do you want anything to drink?"

Debbie said, "No, thanks."

"I'll take a beer," Cynthia said. "I mean if you've got it in a bottle."

They followed Velva into the kitchen, where she cleared a space on top of the cluttered old table. Then she opened the grungy refrigerator and pulled out a bottle of Budweiser. She handed it to Cynthia, along with a bottle opener shaped like a seashell, and they all sat down.

Debbie kept looking around with quick eyes. This place made her feel itchy. She bit a fingernail and considered how she was probably going to get fleas. She glanced over at Cynthia, who was examining the bottle of beer. And now she was drinking it. Well, Cynthia probably figured if Velva wanted to do something horrible, she could do it easily enough without the aid of a poisoned beer. Or maybe Cynthia just liked to drink.

Cynthia looked at Debbie and smiled. Debbie told herself to relax. Up on the wall, Kathleen Turner was lying in bed with some guy. She looked ecstatic, but it was only a movie. Besides, with a body like that, why shouldn't Kathleen be thrilled?

Velva crushed out her cigarette in the upturned lid of a mayonnaise jar and said, "Here's the deal: I cast a spell tonight, and you'll have great sex from now on—no more problems, no more hassles. Then you bring me the dog, and we'll be all set."

Debbie fidgeted with a burnt match she found on the table and then looked at Cynthia, who shrugged.

"How do I know you're telling the truth?" Debbie said.

"What have you got to lose, honey? You'll see the results right away, so you'll know it works, and if it doesn't work, you don't have to give me the dog. But if it does, you pay up."

"Will it hurt?"

"He won't feel a thing."

"I'm talking about me. Will it hurt me?"

"Nope. It's real simple. You'll be fine."

Debbie felt a nudge in her ribs as Cynthia spoke from the side of her mouth. "Tell her about your granny's watch. Negotiate!"

"Oh, yeah," Debbie said, squirming a bit. "Velva, I can't give you my boyfriend's dog. I just can't do that. So how about if I give you my grandmother's watch? It's…very important to me."

Velva laughed. "Oh, really? Do I look like a collector of old junk? Wait—don't answer that. No, the sacrifice has to be something alive that you actually care about." She leaned forward and narrowed her eyes. "Look, honey, I think the dog only marginally fits that description, right? So I'm already cutting you a break. Besides, I'll tell you what—I'll try not to kill the dog. I'll just take about ten years of its life. So that's ten less years of torture for you. The way I see it, this is a total win for both of us."

Debbie took a deep breath and considered the witch's indisputable logic. Plus, it wasn't really Mike's dog, anyway; it was his mother's dog. His mother had moved into a development in Florida that didn't allow pets, so he'd agreed to take it. And wouldn't Mike's mom want Mike to have a girlfriend who made him happy? Wouldn't that be more important to her than a dog she'd ditched the second a space opened up in the adult community of her dreams?

Debbie sighed. "I can't do it. I'm sorry I wasted your time. Let's go, Cynthia."

She got up to leave, slumping her shoulders a bit. This had been a crazy idea, but 'hopeful' and 'crazy' were often related. Cynthia smiled and also stood up, and they both started walking toward the door—but then Velva shouted after them.

"Wait! Honey, I'll tell you what, do you have a plant?"

Debbie turned around.

"A plant?"

"Sure, why not. You're a good kid, and I'm feeling generous. A plant could hold me over for a bit."

Debbie cocked her head. "Hm, I do have a plant."

"Okay, but is it a plant you *care* about?"

From the corner of her eye, Debbie saw Cynthia glancing at her sideways. "Deb, I don't think it's a good idea—"

Debbie's eyes lit up. "I love, love, love that African violet!" she said. "But I guess I'll just have to make this monumental sacrifice."

Velva grinned. "Great! So an African violet it is." Then her expression grew dark, and she pointed a crooked tree-branch-of-a-finger in Debbie's face. "But don't try to stiff me, honey. If I fulfill my part of the bargain, you need to keep yours."

"Hey, Debbie…" Cynthia said.

"Sure, I'll keep it," Debbie said. What was the big deal? She'd even throw in an extra pot of petunias. "Now turn me into a sex goddess."

Another smile slithered across Velva's crinkled lips as she looked at Cynthia. "You need to leave the room."

"Oh? Why?"

"Because the spell has to be directed at only one person. And besides, you're already a sex goddess."

Debbie stared at her friend, and Cynthia blushed—something Debbie had never seen before.

"Sure, yeah," Cynthia said. "I guess I'll just wait in the next room. I'll, um, try not to have sex with anyone in there."

As Cynthia exited the kitchen, she turned back toward Debbie and raised her fist. "Good luck, Deb. Death or glory! Or maybe a great orgasm—with someone else!"

Meanwhile, Velva lit up another cigarette and cast her gaze on Debbie. "Honey, I need your panties."

"What?"

"I need something appropriate to stick in the 'circle of sex.' "

"You have a circle for my panties?"

"Not yet. I'm gonna make one."

"Really? Where? There's so much junk in here."

"It's a small circle, okay? Who's the witch here, me or you? I need something that's close to your sexuality. I'm thinking a pair of panties is pretty close, right? Unless you brought a vibrator."

Debbie hesitated. Then she reached into her purse, where she found her Pocket Rocket clitoral stimulator. She handed it to Velva.

Velva's eyebrows went up a bit as she turned it over in her hands. "Well, well... I've never owned one of these things. I never needed one, but until I fix my situation, maybe I should join the modern world. Does it work?"

"Sure," Debbie said.

"How often do you use it?"

"I've killed a few batteries. Or maybe a few thousand."

"Interesting... So why is it in your purse?"

Debbie shrugged. Was this is a trick question? "Because sometimes I want it when I'm not at home."

"Oh. Well, that's perfect," Velva said with a laugh. In fact, she seemed downright gleeful as she reached into her own nearby pocketbook and pulled out a pack of Ernie Ball "Skinny Top Heavy Bottom" electric guitar strings. She put them on top of Debbie's vibrator.

Now it was Debbie who found herself with raised eyebrows. "Guitar strings? Why?"

Velva looked away quick. "It has to do with the universe. The strings represent the natural rhythm you're gonna have—right. Now gimme a few of your hairs."

"From my head?"

"Yeah, of course. What kind of joint do you think I'm running here?"

Debbie winced and yanked out a few hairs. The witch grabbed them and wrapped them around the pack of strings. Then she reached under a few old newspapers and found a mostly melted candle. She lit it and smiled. She also reached under the collar of her dress, through the wreath of plastic pearls, and pulled out a chain with a seashell on the end.

Debbie leaned forward to examine the piece of jewelry. The shell had a stone embedded in its center. Was this a talisman?

"Yeah, it's a talisman," Velva said. "I've spent my whole life charging it with power, and now I'm gonna put it to good use. What's the matter?"

"Oh, nothing," Debbie said. "I just didn't think a seashell would be your style."

"You were expecting something more glamorous, right?"

"Right—exactly." *Like maybe a rusty can opener.*

Velva flashed a cracked yellowy smile. "I told you, honey, I'm having problems with the Union. Pretty soon it will all make sense. Now, are you ready?"

"Sure," Debbie said, and she felt her stomach dropping toward the floor.

"Gimme your hand."

With some hesitation, Debbie reached her hand across the table. Velva seized it.

The witch closed her eyes, rocked her head a bit, and started muttering and moaning—low and slow at first but then faster and louder. *"Oh, oh! Yeah! Right there! Mmmmmmmm! Harder! Do it harder!*

Shove it in! Shove it in there, motherfucker! Shove that hunk of man meat right through me! Ahhhhhhh!"

For the next few minutes, Debbie listened to the witch slobber, swear, and scream through an unseen sex romp. On the one hand, it was totally gross, but on the other hand, certain moments actually turned her on—and it was funny how this contrast applied to so many sexual experiences. At the very least, the old lady definitely needed to invest in a sex toy, or maybe one of those industrial strength robots Debbie had seen on the internet.

"Oh, yeah! Oh, yeah! Oh yeeeeeeees! Grrrrrrrr! Arrrg! Oh! Oh! Sluuuurp! Blah! Bleck!"

For some reason, Debbie recalled a visit to the zoo in third grade. She didn't remember seeing any sex there, just a bunch of kids comparing her to an owl. Of course, owls were smart and fierce, and after all these years she wondered if they'd known that. Mainly, they'd only cared about the bird's big eyes.

With one final wail, Velva threw back her head and gasped. There was a moment of silence as she paused to catch her breath, and then she opened her eyes and smiled.

"It's done," she said.

"Oh," Debbie said. "You mean just like that?"

"Yep, just like that."

"That didn't seem to affect me at all. When is it my turn?"

Velva cackled a bit. "It'll be your turn real soon, honey. Real soon."

Debbie cocked her head. Somehow she wasn't feeling all warm and fuzzy. Somehow, getting a sex spell from a witch she'd met in a diner wasn't giving her the sense of euphoria she'd expected.

Debbie fidgeted a bit in her seat. "So what happens now?"

Velva took a puff on her cigarette. "Now you go home and have amazing sex, just like I promised."

"Okay... But my boyfriend is in Washington, so I guess I'll have to wait."

Velva cackled again. "Yeah, sure, sure. I'll be calling you, okay?"

Debbie felt a tightness in her chest. The witch seemed awfully pleased with herself, but not in a good way. Then again, she'd just spent ten minutes having sex with an imaginary stranger—and that always worked for Debbie, too. So there was no need to worry. There was no need to panic. There was no need to throw up in Velva's kitchen.

She was hunting for an inconspicuous spot to vomit when Cynthia's head poked into the room.

"Is the big shebang over? Because I have to get home."

"It's over for Debbie," Velva said. "But I wonder what I can do for you."

"Me? I don't need anything. I'm a sex goddess, remember? Although I could use someone to do it with. This goddess is a little rusty."

Velva blew a stream of smoke. "I might be able to help with that. Of course, you'll have to give me something in return, how about—"

"No!" Debbie said. "Cynthia wants to wait and see how things go with my spell first, right, Cynthia? And we really have to be going." She jumped out of her chair and grabbed Cynthia's arm. "Let's go."

Cynthia glanced at Velva and smiled. "Maybe some other time. And while you're at it, can you get me a drummer for my band? Anyone who'll actually show up will be great."

Velva smiled. "Okay, but take my card and have a few Magic Mints."

She reached into a drawer and pulled out a business card for Cynthia. Then she handed each girl a tiny white box with a silver label across its lid that said "Magic Mints."

"Wow," Cynthia said. "Will these grow a beanstalk?"

"No," Velva said. "But they'll make you grow hair on your chest."

"Gee, thanks. And why would I want to do that?"

"You wouldn't. But I'm all out of lollipops, so take what you can get."

Outside, the rain had turned into a misty spray. Debbie hurried Cynthia through the twisted undergrowth on Velva's front lawn and then shoved her into the car and gunned it toward Route 18.

Debbie gripped the steering wheel hard and tried to take deep breaths.

Cynthia looked over at her and sighed.

"Don't worry about it, Debbie. I know how you are—worry, worry, worry. Just relax and everything will be fine."

"I just made a deal with the devil, Cynthia."

"Ha! I don't think it was quite so dramatic. Besides, the deal doesn't sound that bad. Even if Velva does know what she's doing—and that's a big if—it's not like you gave away your soul or anything. Hey, you negotiated. You got her down to a plant!"

Debbie just shook her head.

10: Crash

Debbie maintained a white-knuckle grip on the steering wheel, even after dropping Cynthia off at her place. Cynthia lived across town from Debbie, in a studio apartment she rented from her aunt. Debbie had declined an invitation to come in and have a drink because her stomach felt jumpy, and she just wanted to get home.

She drove past the Stop and Shop supermarket on Raritan Avenue, a main artery that headed into the city of New Brunswick. The parking lot was empty, and the blacktop was shiny and wet from the storm. She jumped in her seat as a strong gust of wind bounced an empty Dunkin' Donuts coffee cup against the windshield of her car. Out on the street, everything looked ominous. Somebody was walking a pair of smirking poodles past Szechuan Wok. The mechanical monsters inside Lenny's Laundromat were churning. There was a teenager eating a slice of pizza in front of Stacy's Salon of Beauty, where many a face had been brutalized.

Debbie ground her teeth as her car idled at a traffic light. The light changed, and she revved the motor. She just knew something catastrophic was going to happen. Her mother had always told her not to talk to witches. Wait—her mother had never told her that. Her mother had told her not to talk to men and to maybe consider getting contact lenses, but she'd said nothing about witches. Thanks a lot, Mom, for screwing that one up big time.

Debbie looked around with jittery eyes. What would the witch's deal do to her? Was she going to be turned into a newt? Hopefully, she would be turned into something bigger, or maybe something that could fly. Then again, flying was a bad thing. She had enough stomach problems here on the ground. The thought of soaring above the earth was nauseating. It was probably more stressful than driving. Damn—she better hit the brakes!

Screech! Badump!

Holy crap. She'd just rear-ended somebody.

Debbie hung her head and then considered bashing it against the steering wheel. Here was one more problem she didn't need. Why hadn't her mother given her any advice on how to drive a car? Mom was having a bad night.

Her mind started racing. Was the other driver hurt? Had she just paralyzed someone? She saw a shadowy figure inside the other car, and it seemed to be moving. Her chest heaved with panic. She struggled to keep calm as she exited the vehicle.

The other driver was also getting out. Debbie braced herself; he was probably a lunatic. He was probably going to chop her up with a machete—every lunatic carries a machete—or at the very least, he'd start screaming. But wait! He was smiling. He didn't look injured, and his eyes looked more friendly than insane. She felt a wave of relief. As a matter of fact, he was cute. Maybe he was just a cute guy who was only going to sue.

Actually, he was more handsome than cute. His hair was tied back in a sexy ponytail, so dark like dirty mud, while his eyes were soft and deep as gourmet coffee grounds. When he spoke, his voice had an exotic, Hispanic accent.

"Hello," the guy said, and he held out his hand. "I am Juan Carlos. It's nice to meet you."

Debbie was still for a second, but then gave him a soft handshake. "I'm Debbie," she said, while trying to remember the basic rules of a car accident—things like never admit fault or apologize.

"Oh, my god, I'm so sorry!" she blurted. "I just wasn't thinking. It's all my fault. I'm such an idiot. I'm really, really sorry! Do you want my insurance information?"

He smiled again. "I don't know if it will help me. I have no insurance."

"Oh," she said. And then she shrugged. Insurance and taxes and anything that involved filling out forms had never interested her, although she did have car insurance—her mom had told her to get it. So Mom was finally on the scoreboard tonight.

"So, how does this work?" she said.

"I don't know," he replied with a wave of his hand. "You're the first person to hit me since I stopped paying the premium. I guess you can sue me for all I'm worth, ha-ha! Just don't take my guitar."

She cocked her head. "I hit *you,* Juan. I think that means *you* would be suing *me.*"

"Ah," he said, and his eyebrows shot upward. "Do you have a guitar? I suppose I could use another one." He looked at his rear bumper. "It doesn't look like you did any harm, so why not forget it?" Then he opened his eyes wide and raised a finger. "Or how about you buy me a cup of coffee? At any rate, we need to move these cars."

Debbie felt her stomach churn a bit. "Okay, sure," she said, and then stopped herself from biting a fingernail. What the hell, she loved coffee, and maybe it would take her mind away from thoughts about that damned witch.

They pulled the cars off the road and parked them along the curb. By coincidence, there was a glowing coffee shop right in front of them, and it was still open.

He flashed another warm smile, and she thought he resembled a bullfighter. She could easily picture him in a toreador outfit, but did she find the image of a man strutting around in gaudy tight pants while driving bloody swords into a bull to be exhilarating? No, of course not, because she didn't believe in the execution of defenseless animals. Then she snuck a glance sideways and saw that he had a great butt, and she considered how a bull had horns, and was therefore not truly defenseless.

"So, Debbie, why were you out in this horrible rain storm? What could you have been doing? Were you going to see your boyfriend?"

Debbie hesitated. This would probably be a good time to lie about the whole 'witch thing.'

"I don't have a boyfriend," she said.

Okay, that wasn't quite the lie she'd intended.

"Ah, well, I'm surprised. You seem so beautiful and intelligent."

She felt herself blush. "Oh, yeah, I'm intelligent," she sputtered. "Once upon a time I even passed a driving test."

He laughed. "It's true you crashed your car, but you looked fabulous doing it. And that is what's most important."

Was this guy kidding? Here she was, once again wearing a plain black dress and her white sneakers, and with her hair looking like a pile of wet squid. This guy had low standards, but was that a bad thing? Not really.

They entered the coffee shop. There was a pink neon sign in the window, and the sweet smell of South America drifting through the room. Inside, they found a combination of soft bluish lighting and cherry red tables, and a few people sitting around staring at digital devices. Debbie and Juan went up to the counter and ordered some coffee—and they both wanted cappuccino! Juan insisted on paying.

"Hey, I thought I was buying," Debbie said. "You know, in exchange for you ignoring some whiplash."

"I wouldn't think of it," Juan replied. "My neck hasn't felt this wonderful since I climbed Mount Everest."

"You climbed Mount Everest?"

His eyes got big. "Did I say that? No, that was an exaggeration, but I saw a television program about climbing a mountain while I was lying on the sofa, and my neck felt wonderful. Let's sit by the window."

They took a table that overlooked the street. It was a nice little nook that offered a stunning view of the traffic outside as well as a UPS store.

"I was born in Argentina," Juan said while sipping his coffee. "My family came to this country when I was twelve."

"I was born in New Jersey," Debbie said. "When I was twelve, I broke my arm roller skating."

He laughed. "You're a funny girl. You make lots of jokes."

She smiled. "Yeah, isn't it annoying?"

"No, not at all."

"Give it time."

"Are you a comedian?"

"No, I'm a writer, at least when I'm not waiting tables. I'm writing a novel."

He raised his eyebrows with obvious interest. "That's wonderful. Is it about a beautiful girl with dark hair and glasses, who meets a handsome stranger in a car crash? And she takes him home with her, and they have a night of tremendous passion, and then they live happily ever after?"

"Uh, no," she said, stirring her coffee rapidly with a straw. "Maybe I'll write that book tomorrow."

"Maybe you're writing it now."

Debbie fidgeted a bit in her seat. Was it warm in here? She definitely felt like a steamy wave was washing over her. This guy was interesting. This guy was sexy. This guy was—holy crap, she wanted to have sex with this guy. She totally wanted to fuck him. She wanted to fuck him right here in this coffee shop.

Juan smiled once again. "Too bad they only serve coffee here. I could do with a glass of wine. Are there any bars nearby?"

"I've got wine at my place," Debbie said with a rush. "It's right down the street."

"Oh, that would be wonderful. What are we waiting for? Let's go."

Debbie leaped from her chair so fast it fell over. And then she was driving her Honda fast down Raritan Avenue, toward her apartment on South 1st. Juan was in his own car, following close behind. She felt like she was in a dream. She'd never done anything like this before. Usually, it took at least a few hours before she'd consider ripping off her undergarments, depending on how much she'd had to drink. And she always had reservations. She took a deep breath as chaotic thoughts whirled through her head. *Okay, stay calm. You haven't done anything stupid just yet. No, that won't happen for at least another ten minutes.*

They crashed through the door of Debbie's apartment. The Chihuahua started barking, but he couldn't interfere much because Debbie had locked him in the kitchen.

At any rate, she hardly heard the yipping beast. Within seconds, she was in Juan's arms. She was kissing him, and his tongue was in her mouth, and their tongues were greedy and groping—and she liked it. He pushed her against the wall and a framed picture of Wile E. Coyote tumbled to the floor and shattered. What the hell, that was fine, she could repair it with some tape from the ACME.

She was panting a bit. "Juan, I don't usually do this sort of thing with strange men."

He squeezed her bottom in his big hands. "I would only be a strange man if I didn't want you in my arms."

She laughed at his cornball line. Then she grabbed his hand and pulled him into the bedroom. Damn, she'd forgotten to make the bed—for the three hundredth day in a row. But he was on top of her in a flash, kissing her. His lips tasted like coffee, but she loved coffee. He was kissing her neck, and then unbuttoning the top of her dress.

He said, "You are so sexy, Debbie."

She said, "Juan, I lied. I have a boyfriend."

He looked into her eyes. "He's the wrong man for you." Then he reached down and stroked her a bit, so lightly she hardly felt it. But it was good.

"You know," she said, "you might be right."

He kept kissing her, and he kept touching her. Was his finger inside her panties now? He wasn't jamming it in there, either, like a plumber working on a drainpipe—no, he slid that digit in nice and slow. She was excited, no doubt. But then he got up! Where the hell was he going? Get back here! Oh, he was taking off her sneakers.

He smiled, and she grimaced. She probably shouldn't have used double knots, but how was she supposed to know she'd end up naked with a sexy toreador tonight? And he was getting it done, holding her ankle and yanking them off—good. Then he pulled off her socks. Damn, she'd meant to paint her toenails. Still, her toes were okay, but she suppressed a frown—if he started sucking on a toe it was all over because she hated that foot fetish crap.

He wasn't going for her toes. Whew! He was sliding off her panties. Ha, she'd meant to shave a bit, but it wasn't like she had a jungle down there. She was always neat, but without the glassy porn star pubes of a ten-year-old. She was a woman, dammit! And she had some hair.

Now his tongue was going to work. Good! Nice thing for a guy to do. Plus, this was different from what she'd experienced before. This guy knew a few things. For one thing, he wasn't trying to crush her most sensitive parts into pulp. He had a light touch—just enough—but most of all he had *rhythm*.

And that's what had been missing. Of course! All those morons who'd come before him, flicking their tongues like epileptic monkeys, slurping away like little boys attacking ice cream cones. What she'd needed was a guy who could keep time. *A guy who could count to fucking four!* That's the way. Oh! Oh! Oh!

She ran her fingers through his hair. "You're so pretty, Debbie," he whispered. "The second I saw you, I wanted to be right here."

She gave a short laugh and then moaned a bit, and she wasn't even faking.

This went on for a while. Was she taking too long? She knew that she was—she always took too long. Damn! This was not going to happen. Why did it take her so long? Why could she never do this with a guy? He must be getting exhausted. His jaw would lock up, and his tongue would die a valiant death. But then he said, "Relax, Debbie… This is so perfect."

Then he glanced to his right where she had some books on her nightstand.

"You're a fan of Douglas Adams? And Kurt Vonnegut?"

"Yeah," she replied, breathing hard. "Oh, yeah."

"Mmmm, I like them, too," he said between licks. "I especially loved *The Hitchhiker's Guide to the Galaxy.*"

Debbie pushed hard against his mouth. "Yeah," she said. "Me, too!"

"You are one cool frood Debbie! You certainly know where your towel is!"

"Oh, yeah! Oh, yeah!"

"And I loved *Slaughterhouse Five*. What's that phrase he keeps repeating? *So it goes. So it goes. So it goes!*"

"*Ahhhhh!*" she said, and so she came, with a violent orgasm—wave after wave after wave.

And then he stood up. At some point he'd taken his clothes off. He was lean and muscular, with the body of a dance instructor or maybe a lightweight fighter. He had an erection that was long and fat like a plantain.

Debbie wasn't obsessed with size, but she liked it. On the one hand, all the talk about size was overrated—but on the other hand, all the talk about how "it didn't matter" was ridiculous. Of course it mattered. There had to be enough, and if there was more? Yeah, that was better. Juan was definitely better.

Debbie didn't mind using her mouth. Of course, it could get tiring after a while, especially if there was no end in sight, on and on until her jaw was cramping and falling off her face—but hey! Juan didn't seem to care, because he was busy shoving that slab of squash between her thighs where it belonged. He kissed her hard and started pumping.

"Oh! Oh! Yeah!"

The bed went *badump, badump, badump!*

He was pounding her pretty good. She was moaning in his ear.

So many times, Debbie had just wanted to get sex over with so she could go eat snack food—but not this time. Sure, she'd still make popcorn, but this time it could wait.

He looked into her eyes. "Does that feel good, Debbie? I want you to feel good."

"Mission accomplished," she murmured.

"I want to do this again, Debbie. I want to be here with you again."

She groaned. "I'll give you a key to my apartment. Feel free to let the dog out."

"I want you naked every night, Debbie. I want you naked, and, uh…" His voice trailed off for a second, until he glanced back at her nightstand and saw a dog-eared copy of *Dune*. "I want you naked on a pile of Frank Herbert novels. I want you naked on the sands of Arrakis!"

Debbie's orgasm crashed through her head, splintering her brain like a giant bell. It was ringing like a celebration. It was ringing like she'd won an Olympic medal, and a war had just ended, and she'd been given a lifetime supply of animal crackers.

And then Juan had an orgasm. She anticipated it, and she saw he was about to pull out—but she told him no, she took the pill, the best money she'd ever spent, and he gripped her tight and held onto her hard—oh, yeah.

Then Debbie had another orgasm. This time it happened while she was furiously stroking herself, beating the hell out of that thing in a way that only an owner can do. Juan gave her a hug as the spasms jolted through her. They reminded her of an earthquake, but not one of those wimpy tremors that rattles cups and dishes across California every few weeks—no, it was more like an epic disaster that levels cities and obliterates entire cultures. So it goes.

And then it was over. Debbie put her forearm over her eyes as she gasped for breath. Did she believe in god? She had some doubts. *But oh god, oh god, oh god, please let me get fucked like this again just once before I die.*

Juan gave her a soft kiss on the neck. "You're so beautiful, Debbie. We'll have to do this again sometime."

"Oh, yeah," she said. "Sometime soon."

"But right now, I could go for a snack. Would you like to go to a diner?"

"No. But I could make popcorn."

His eyes got wide. "I do love to eat popcorn," he said.

Debbie felt her heart skip a beat.

11: Washington, D.C.

Mike grimaced and banged his fist down on the steering wheel of his cherry red Corvette Stingray.

The car was idling at a stop light on a honking stretch of Pennsylvania Avenue in Washington, D.C. As the light changed, he gunned the engine and watched the cream puff dome of the capitol vanish in his rear view mirror.

He shook his head. He'd just left a meeting in one of the digni-fied-looking office buildings nearby, yet he couldn't seem to remember much about it. Why the hell couldn't he concentrate? He knew why. He was thinking about Debbie. He was thinking about the magic of love when he should be thinking about the magic of the universe—and that was bad, because he had a job to do, and it was something important.

He smiled. What would Debbie say if she knew? What would his father think? Unknown to these people he cared about, Mike was a member of The Confidential Ultra Force—a super secret government agency dedicated to the most ludicrous possibilities. The C.U.F. dealt with space aliens, time travelers, evil spirits, and better ways to predict economic disaster. Mike was currently hard at work on a highly clas-sified project called "Magic Patriot Freedom Flag."

His mission was to find people capable of harnessing the power of magic and enlist their aid. Certain government bigwigs believed magic could do a better job of protecting the country than a missile defense program, and maybe even predict the future unemployment rate with more accuracy than the average Ivy League egghead. At the very least, they would get the same bad results for less money.

Mike knew he had a freakin' great thing going. He knew guys in the CIA, and they definitely had the shallow end of the shark tank. They were mostly stuck in Third World countries, swatting at blood-stuffed mosquitoes or dodging the spit of angry, reeking camels. Meanwhile, he was living in the U.S.A. and doing super cool stuff, and he was learning quite a bit, too. Why just the other day he'd levitated three bananas and a dozen eggs for almost a minute, and then turned the whole mess into a protein-packed omelet.

He swung the car into the Marriott Hotel parking lot and walked through the bustling lobby, looking low-key with his luggage, Levis, and NY Yankees baseball cap. He didn't wear the kind of clothes his brothers wore, business suits and shiny shoes as stiff as cement. He didn't spend his days counting other people's money. They could keep all that soul-sucking bullshit. All he needed was some adventure, and maybe someone to talk to—someone to really care about. Someone like Debbie.

He snapped on the lights and swept his eyes across the room. It seemed safe enough in a no-frills kind of way. He saw a basic double bed, a television, a small bathroom, and a balcony that overlooked a swimming pool a hundred feet below.

He removed his jacket and threw it onto the bed, right next to a briefcase and a canvas bag. He also took off his shoulder holster and gun and tossed them down near the jacket. Finally, he took a breath and unzipped the bag.

He hesitated. Debbie had said she was in pain, and of course every guy likes to think he's huge enough to cause a little struggle and discomfort, but how many times had she had her period this month? He was pretty sure a girl only has that stuff going on once a month, right after the full moon or whatever. "Besides," he thought with a grim smile, "I'm not that huge."

He reached into the bag and pulled out a small pair of bongo drums. They were two different sizes, joined together. He grinned and recalled how he'd traded a salami sandwich for them from the same wizard/drummer who'd sold him the magic drumsticks; luckily, the average musician was usually pretty hungry. He put the bongos on the bed and banged them a bit. They had a decent sound, but it didn't matter. What mattered is that he'd been lugging them around for two weeks and he finally felt ready to test them out.

He reached into his pocket and pulled out a folded plastic baggie. From inside the baggie, he retrieved a few strands of dark hair. He rolled the hairs around in his rough fingers, and then he stopped. Should he really do this?

He trusted Debbie. He wasn't really checking up on her—no. He was just trying to see if this crazy spell he'd learned from that old wizard actually worked. In fact, this was a perfect way to test the spell because he was confident of the outcome. After all, Debbie was the girl he wanted to marry and maybe have kids with, even though she wasn't doing too well with the dog or the plant and kids were a lot more trouble. But he'd worry about that stuff later. Right now he wrapped the strands of hair around the piece of wood that connected the two drums.

He once again recalled his last sexual encounter with Deb, and he was once again disgusted with himself for getting so easily distracted. Then he pulled out a notebook and read from a page, reciting a short verse above the piece of percussion:

> *"The universe speaks, see how it grins*
> *Hear how it talks through a couple of skins*
> *Bang me a beat, a pattern so fit*
> *Is my girl true, or does she waver a bit?"*

The bongos immediately started to play. It was a little eerie, since no one was actually tapping them. Mike stared with wide eyes and listened as the drums banged out a slow, pounding beat, like they were warming up. Next they broke into a fast roll, like they were getting ready to rumble, or maybe just rumba—and then they were playing a variety of patterns in a messy conglomeration.

He broke into a grin. He'd done it! This was amazing. This was incredible. This was—hang on, wait a second. His grin drained away. Why were the drums settling into a tango pattern?

They should be settling into a virtuous 3-beat, something peppy yet pure. They should be banging out something a couple of senior citizens at a church social could waltz to while they were waiting around to die. But instead, the pattern sounded hot, steamy, and lascivious, like two people in tight outfits tugging every which way as they glided and grinded across a dance floor. How had he screwed things up? Something was definitely incorrect.

His mind started racing, trying to remember the details of the spell. If the drums played a bossa nova beat or some slow jazzy thing, it would just indicate a little flirting, or maybe a quick kiss, or a few fast seconds of perverted groping. But a tango! The tango was sultry and smooth, with suggestions of slippery undulation and grunting gratification. A tango beat meant Debbie was doing it with some other guy.

In a flash, he imagined it. Who was the bastard? He envisioned skull-splitting violence, and broken bones, and his fierce form of retribution—and then he pictured Debbie, so cute and sweet, and the angry images in his head disappeared.

There was just no way. It simply could not be. Debbie believed in honorable things, like loyalty and truth—and of course, his previous attempts at magic had not been stellar. He'd turned a few cats into cockroaches, and he'd turned a few cockroaches into snakes, and he'd turned the pest control guy into a cantaloupe. Luckily, he'd been able to reverse that last one before the melon got soft.

He paused and reached for his phone. With a pounding heart, he pressed it hard against his ear as it rang. He swore at the sound of a voicemail message. She usually answered his calls. Where the hell was she? What the hell was going on over there? He paused again and forced himself to speak in a sure, steady voice.

"Hey, Deb, this is Mike. I'm thinking about you. I hope you're okay."

He disconnected the call, and then realized the drums were still going at it like a couple of people doing the same. He mumbled a few words and they stopped.

He shook his head and stared at the wall. Maybe he'd try again later.

12: The Morning After

Debbie rarely had happy dreams. For some reason, she was usually under stress. She was a little girl being chased by a rabid dog, or she was locked in a spidery basement, or maybe she just had to dodge a falling piano.

Tonight was no exception. She dreamed she was naked in bed with a handsome stranger, and she'd had sex with him, and it had been amazing. They'd eaten popcorn together and fallen asleep in each other's arms—and now he was gone, and the only thing that remained was the yip, yip, yipping of her boyfriend's dog in the other room as the sun shone through the blinds onto the barren sheets of her bed.

Oh, crap!

Debbie sat up straight. Where was Juan? He wasn't here, and Sugar was barking in the kitchen because she hadn't fed him. Also, he was probably mad that she'd just cheated on Mike. Ugh!

She called out, "Juan? Juan?"

Debbie collapsed back down on the bed and stared at the ceiling. What the hell? What the hell had she done?

She groaned and groped around for her glasses, squinting through the thick lenses at the grinning clock on her nightstand. It was Saturday, and she was supposed to work tonight. Well, maybe she would and maybe she wouldn't—it all depended upon whether or not she committed suicide.

She leaped to her feet and ran into the living room. As she expected, there was no sign of a slinky toreador-shaped love machine. She ran into the bathroom but he wasn't there, either. She stared at her naked body in the full length mirror. She was too skinny, her breasts were too small, and her face was sort of cute but still kind of average—of course he was gone! Why would he stick around to be with her?

She went back into the living room and noticed her African violet was dead. Funny, she didn't recall it being so close to death yesterday. And it wasn't just dead; it was withered and black like an incinerated spider. She shook her head—whatever. Then the Chihuahua starting barking extra loud and she threw up her hands.

She took a deep breath. If she was going to kill herself, she should probably feed the dog first. There was no telling how long it might take for someone to discover her rotting corpse. Then again, Mike would be back from Washington in a few days, and he'd hear the dog barking, and he'd break down the door. He was a "break down the door" kind of guy, though she'd never seen him do it. But she just knew. Maybe she should leave the door unlocked and save the landlord a little trouble.

She bit one of her jagged fingernails and tried to prevent a panic attack. *Stay calm!* Maybe Mike wouldn't find out. But then again, she didn't like being a liar and a cheater. How would she feel if Mike had spent his night in DC with some other girl? And hey, how come he hadn't called her? What a bastard! He'd run off to Washington and hadn't even given her a call on a lonely Friday night. Maybe she wouldn't have cheated if he'd called! Maybe she wouldn't be sitting here right now rationalizing her wanton lust and infidelity.

She went back into the bedroom, searching for a robe to cover herself. While she was putting it on, she noticed her cell phone sitting on the nightstand. Damn, someone had left a message. Could it be from Juan? Her heart leaped at the thought. Oh, wait—it was from Mike! Oh, crap! So he had called last night. In fact, he'd called a couple of times while her phone had been in silent mode. He'd called when she was meeting with the witch, and then again about an hour later. But those had been bad times to call, because she'd been busy buying some black magic and then fucking some other guy. She smacked herself on the forehead. Could this get any worse?

The phone rang. It was Mike, and things were now worse.

She caught her breath. *He knows! He must know! He must know and he's going to hate me!*

She rubbed her pounding head and then with a shaky finger hit the button.

"Hello?"

"Debbie? Hey, what's happening?"

His voice sounded fairly neutral.

"Hi, Mike! I'm great. How are you?"

"I'm okay... Are you okay? You sound stressed."

She told herself to get a grip—after all, he couldn't know. There was no way.

"Why do you say that?" she said. "I'm fine."

"I can tell when you're stressed. Your voice changes. It gets higher."

She cringed. *Stay calm. Stay calm. Do not commit suicide!*

"No! I'm all right," she said, trying to summon a bullfrog-like baritone. "I'm...not stressed at all."

"I called you last night a couple of times. I sent you a text."

Oh, crap. She looked at her phone again and saw he'd sent a text message right before she'd gotten naked with Juan. Her heart was pounding, and she was in deep trouble. She was sinking into a tar pit of deceit, and her nose was about to start blowing bubbles into the hot goo, and maybe it was time to stop the lies. Maybe it was time to come clean.

"I was reading a book. I fell asleep with my phone in silent mode. I'm sorry I missed your call."

He hesitated. "That's fine. Maybe you were bored without me."

He paused again, like he was waiting for her to agree.

"Oh, yeah!" she blurted. "That's why I fell asleep—because I was thinking about you." She winced and shook her head. "Wait, that's not what I meant. I meant, uh, when are you coming back?"

Now there was a long pause. "Pretty soon. Are you sure you're okay?"

"Yes! I'm fine. And your dog is still alive."

He laughed, but it sounded forced. "Are you plotting against my dog, Deb?"

"No! Why would you say that? What would I do, sacrifice it to a witch?"

"What?"

"Did I say something?"

"I don't know. I'll call you later."

"All right. That sounds great. I'll just sit here and work on my novel."

"Good idea. See if you can keep that Suzy character out of trouble. Then try and get some rest. You sound tired."

Debbie hung up the phone and hung her head. She slapped her hands to the sides of her face.

She wanted to scream! She wanted to crawl out of her skin. She wanted to run and hide and explode and then be transformed into somebody else—somebody with another chance, or at least somebody with a prescription for Xanex. Again.

"I blew it," she said with a moan. "I totally blew it."

She sat in silence for what seemed like a long time. And then she heard a voice.

It was a voice flavored by whiskey and bar fights and high adventure in outer space. It was a voice that lived inside her head. It was the voice of Suzy Spitfire.

"Hi, Debbie," Suzy said. "I see you've got a problem."

"Yeah, I do, Suzy. And it's all my fault. I hate when that happens."

Suzy laughed. "It's not so bad. Stop taking things so seriously. There's nothing wrong with ditching a dude who can't rock the hell out of your roller coaster. Besides, it's not like you were married... Look, it's nothing I haven't done myself a few times; face it, he's the wrong guy for you. In fact, my mystical guru, Shelba, introduced me to a guy last night, and what's left of that bed will never forget us—and neither will the bar or the pool table or the washing machine. Just pick up the pieces and move on. Or better yet, leave the pieces on the fucking floor and walk out."

Debbie tried to laugh but just sighed. "That's easy for you to say, Suzy. You exist on a higher plane. I only exist in New Jersey."

13: Velva and Peach

It was a dark and smoky kitchen, and Velva glanced around. She took a long drag on her Virginia Slim and then grabbed a cantaloupe sitting on the countertop, right near a rusty old toaster and a pile of gooey black bananas. She dropped the melon on the cluttered kitchen table.

She grinned and reached into the pocket of her robe to grab a butcher's knife. With one violent move, she cleaved the melon in two. She cackled a bit, because it felt good to do a little cleaving. Then she blew a stream of burnt tobacco from her hairy nostrils and fingered the seashell hanging from a chain around her neck.

She said, *"Fruit, sister, speak and stitch—talk to me, you cutesy bitch."*

Poom! The surface of the cantaloupe shimmered with the image of a young woman's face. The woman had pineapple-gold hair decorated with a fresh-looking pink flower, as well as cherry red lips and blueberry colored eyes. All things considered, her face looked comfy on the surface of a melon.

She smiled. "I heard that, Velva. And yes, I am pretty cute."

Velva gave a sarcastic laugh. "Hello, Peach. I see you're looking rather smug today."

"And I see you're looking like a hag. So what can I do for you? I've already said everything I'm going to say."

"No, you haven't," Velva spat. "You left out the part where you help me get back into the International Union of Witches."

Peach rolled her eyes. "If you're going to ask me so nicely, how can I refuse?"

"Cut the crap, Peach. You know I can only be so nice." Then Velva sighed, trying to look more sad than angry. "Look, can you give me a hand here? I'm really at rock bottom."

Peach laughed. "The bottom might be deeper than you think. Anyway, I thought you didn't want to get back in. In fact, I seem to recall a few words like, 'those damned bitches can rot in hell because I don't need them and furthermore blah bah blah so there.' "

"I never said 'blah blah blah.' You're putting 'blahs' into my mouth."

"Who's quoting me? You didn't want any help, blah, blah, blah—and that's good, because no one's going to help you."

"It's not fair!" Velva wailed. "I didn't do anything!"

Peach stared from her cantaloupe with two stern eyes. "You know the rules, Velva—no using magic on civilians for frivolous gain. But that's what you did, and now you're paying the price."

"It wasn't frivolous! I just wanted a part in a stupid TV commercial, and the producer was being a real prick."

"You mean because he thought you had no talent?"

"Exactly!"

Peach laughed again. "Velva, why don't you just forget the whole 'actress thing.' Witches are not actresses. We don't pretend to be things—we *are* things."

"I can't believe you're my sister."

"That makes two of us. Anyway, you can apply for reinstatement in a hundred years, so what's the big deal?"

"But I don't want to be old for a hundred years! I need my looks back now."

"One hundred years, Velva," Peach said. "And don't try to get around the situation by doing something sneaky. Remember, that's how you got yourself into this mess."

"Ha! If no one's going to help me I've got every right to help myself."

"You never learn, do you? Mom always said that."

"What did she say?"

"She said, 'Velva never learns—she's such an asshole.' "

"She called me an asshole?"

"No, I added that. But she was thinking it."

"You were her favorite."

"Of course. I was competing with an asshole."

"I don't know why I called you. You're not even a witch anymore."

"That's true; I'm something better. Go take a vitamin pill. You look like hell."

Velva started to respond, but the image of Peach vanished.

Velva swore at the piece of fruit. Then she picked it up and threw it across the kitchen, watching it sail into the wreckage of the living room where it crashed into an old lamp—*splish!*

"Motherfucker!" she said. "That bitch. That god damned bitch!"

A voice from the floor snickered, and a little red monkey appeared.

"Are you having issues with your sibling, Velva? Are you still mad that she wouldn't share her tricycle with you?"

Velva crushed out her cigarette and then reached into a pocket of her robe for another one.

"What do you want, Carl?" she said with a sneer. "Have you come to rub things in my face?"

The monkey's nose twitched. "I won't deny your face could use a good rubbing—with a piece of sandpaper, ha-ha."

"Thanks. Remind me to leave a few poisoned bananas lying around, okay?"

"The Union might let you back in if you stopped acting like a jackass. Speaking of which, where are my two visitors?"

"They'll be coming soon."

"Oh, good. So you've decided to go ahead with your plan to make everything worse."

"It won't be worse! I need to look good, and I can't wait a hundred years to do it. I could be auditioning right now for some great part, but I'm stuck in this withered old sack of skin."

Carl gave a snort. "You could still do auditions. Maybe you could be in a commercial that helps people quit smoking. You could say, 'Before I started smoking, I looked fabulous. But now I look like this.' "

"One of these days, Carl, I'm going to kill you."

"If I don't kill you first."

"You're a bastard of a demon who gets off on watching others."

"And you're a bitter old bimbo who blames everyone else for her self-centered stupidity."

"I'll call you when I'm ready, Carl."

"I'll be waiting."

The monkey swaggered under the table and disappeared.

Velva frowned and blew a stream of smoke.

14: Girl Talk

Debbie turned away from Cynthia's stare and rubbed her teary eyes. She was sitting at the small desk in her apartment while Cynthia lounged on the nearby couch. Despite Debbie's hysterics, Cynthia looked calm, with her pinkish blond hair not overly combed, and her right foot crossed over her left ankle, showing her frazzled pair of Chuck Taylors. Debbie appreciated Cynthia's sense of eternal calm and thought it was so sweet of her to stop by on her way to work the lunch shift. Cynthia was the best friend a girl could have.

Meanwhile, Mike's Chihuahua, Sugar, was running in circles like a buzz saw, making yipping noises and trying to prove he wasn't so small. Debbie considered barricading the raging beast in the kitchen again but changed her mind. After all, she deserved to suffer.

Cynthia waved her hand, which was holding a bottle of Corona, and said, "It's not the end of the world, Deb. You cheated on Mike because he was the *wrong guy* and it's that simple. Besides, how serious were you? It's not like you were engaged or anything. It's not like he left you sitting here with a diamond. He left you here with his dog, and I think that deserves a little leeway."

Debbie glanced at Sugar, who yipped in agreement and then sniffed at her purse that was hanging on a chair near the front door.

Debbie wiped a tear from her eye. "We *were* serious, or we could have been, maybe, I think… I mean I've never cheated on anyone before! And now I did it with a stranger—a guy I met in a car accident. How could I have been so stupid? I'm a slut like my mother. And my father."

"No, you're not," Cynthia said in a soothing voice. "Your parents cheated with everyone. You just did it with one guy."

"But that's how it starts! My mom started out with one guy from Dad's garage, and then it was another guy from the garage, and then it was every guy with a wrench in his pocket. And my dad was furious, even though he was already banging every bimbo on wheels."

Debbie shook her head and wiped away another tear. It had all been so disappointing. Would she disappoint her own kids one day? She looked at Cynthia through red-rimmed eyes. "Have you ever cheated on anyone?"

"How do you define 'cheat'? I've flirted a bit."

"I know you flirt," Debbie snapped, but then stopped. She hadn't meant to use that tone, and she cursed herself for being so silly. She softened her voice. "Flirting is different. I'm talking about cheating."

"Okay. So you mean full-blown infidelity?"

"I mean mind-obliterating sex that shakes the walls and causes the destruction of a Wile E. Coyote picture."

"Whoah, now that is intense. On a positive note, Wile E. is great at putting himself back together."

"Yeah, but this time Wile E. is dead. He's got an anvil of guilt crushing his skull. Seriously, have you ever cheated?"

She was hoping the answer was yes. *Please, please, please say "yes."* She didn't want to be the only cheater in the room.

Cynthia sighed. "I've cheated on diets, and once in sixth grade I cheated on a test about ancient Egypt. I peeked at Jeanne Silverstein's answers. Did you know the great pyramids were not actually hotels for space aliens? I think we both failed that one." She flashed a warm look at Debbie. "Okay, I've never cheated on a guy I was involved with, but so what? I'm still young. Besides, I haven't had a boyfriend in so long I've forgotten what it's like. It's kind of hard to cheat on a stuffed animal. You made a mistake, Debbie, and you can't change it, so stop beating yourself up."

Debbie once again noticed Sugar sniffing at her purse. She considered stopping him but decided she didn't care.

"I think I need to be alone," Debbie said.

"What? Why? I thought you loved me."

"I do, Cynthia. You know I'd swim rivers of blood for you, and I swim like a cinder block... And I also really appreciate you coming over here, but now I want to be by myself. Besides, you have to work pretty soon." She forced herself to smile. "There are people out there in danger of losing weight. Go put a stop to it."

Cynthia smiled back. "Yeah, I guess I'm kind of like a superhero, or maybe a super server. But really, you should think about why you cheated with this other guy because you're not a cheater, Debbie. You're just someone who's looking for something."

"Oh, yeah? Like what? A sexually transmitted disease?"

"Like real love."

"Does 'real love' exist?"

"I don't know—ask the internet."

Debbie felt a jolt go through her head.

"Hey, Juan's a musician," she said. "Maybe he has a website. Or a listing of where he's playing."

"What? Now you want to find him?"

"No, of course not. Okay—maybe."

"Deb, you've got to stop looking for trouble."

"I wasn't looking for trouble. I was just driving home."

"Right. I think if Mike was the right guy for you, you wouldn't have done it. And I think if Juan doesn't want to see you again, he's not the right guy, either."

Debbie massaged her temples and then removed her glasses. She started wiping them with a napkin. "You know something crazy?" she said. "The sex was amazing, and I keep thinking about it. I keep thinking about *him*."

"Yeah, that's normal," Cynthia said with a shrug. "But it's also over, and the dirt-bag has left the building. Maybe you should just leave it alone."

"Maybe you're right. Yeah, maybe I should. I'm sure Juan meets lots of girls more attractive than me."

"Debbie, that's ridiculous. You're plenty attractive. If I were a lesbian, I would totally go for you."

"Well, thanks. If I ever break free from this heterosexual nightmare, I'll call you... Cynthia, do you ever worry about turning into your parents?"

"No, I don't," Cynthia said as she drained her bottle of beer. "But they spend a lot of time worrying about what I'll turn into. They can't seem to figure out that I've turned into this, and I'm done. I'm not gonna be a lawyer, or a doctor, or a stock broker. I'm just Cynthia Crush—a bass player forever in search of a band. And maybe a real man."

She gave a hollow-sounding laugh, and Debbie laughed back.

"Maybe someday they'll appreciate you the way I do," Debbie said.

"Doubtful."

Debbie started to respond but then heard Sugar bark and noticed his snout was covered with something chocolaty.

"Sugar!" Debbie said. "What did you do?" Then she saw the box of Magic Mints torn open on the floor, apparently pulled from her purse.

"Don't worry about it," Cynthia said. "Sugar already has hair on his chest."

Debbie cursed and ran into the kitchen to get a paper towel.

15: The Convenience Store

Mike's red Corvette squealed to a stop in the parking lot of CC Smalls, a grungy convenience store just around the corner from Debbie's apartment. The hazy heat of the summer day matched his blazing mood. He slammed the door behind him as he exited the vehicle and stomped across the sticky asphalt.

He felt grim walking through the smudge-covered glass door, past the overstuffed magazine rack and twenty stacked cases of Pepsi. He was looking for a candy bar, something he didn't normally eat. He headed toward a scuffed-up counter where they kept the chocolate, as well as a gaudy display of lottery tickets.

He shook his head. Man, there were so many suckers out there clinging to false hope. At least his parents had given him a solid foundation regarding success, and so he knew that it was all about hard work—even if it broke his back and crushed his spirit and ruined his life. Hey, was that Debbie's sexy friend, Cynthia, buying a Pick Five?

He felt a surge of excitement. After all, Cynthia would definitely know the story with Deb.

She was the only one in the store at the moment, except for the cashier, who was a guy named Raghu. Cynthia was wearing a pair of lilac stretch pants and a tight pink T-shirt. Her big breasts were bobbing around under the cotton fabric like a couple of rolling coconuts, and she looked freakin' great. Sure, she had a big butt, but it was round and bouncy.

He adjusted the NY Yankees baseball cap on his head and puffed out his chest a bit.

"Hi, Cynthia," he said.

Her eyes got wide. "Mike! Hey, what's up?"

She tossed back her hair and stood up a little straighter, which in a subtle way highlighted her D cups.

He pointed at the lottery ticket in her hand. "So, did you win?"

"I won't know until tonight," she said with a laugh. "But if I do, you can find me down at the pub... Actually, you can find me there, anyway. So, are you going to see Debbie? I thought you weren't coming back for a few days."

"Yeah, I got done a little early, so I thought I'd stop by and surprise her."

"Oh, really? I just left her. I don't think she wants you to take the dog yet—you know, she loves him so much."

"I'm sure she does... I talked to her last night. She sounded a bit out of it. Is she okay?"

Cynthia shrugged and looked away. "Debbie's fine," she said while quickly cramming the ticket into her purse. "You know how stressed out she gets."

"Yeah, I do, but she sounded worse than usual. She sounded like something was wrong."

"No! She's doing great without you. Wait, that's not what I meant. I meant she's doing okay. You know, she's been thinking."

Mike nodded, while noting that Cynthia seemed to be squirming a bit in her sneakers.

"What's she been thinking about?"

"What? Oh, did I say 'thinking'? I meant to say 'drinking.' She's been drinking heavily and everything is great. I'll see you later; I'm late for work."

She gave him a big smile and started to walk around him, but then he said, "Cynthia, is Debbie cheating on me?"

Cynthia stopped walking.

"What? How can you ask me that?"

"So you're denying it?"

"I didn't deny it," she said. Then she blurted, "I mean I didn't deny it *yet*. But I'm denying it now! Why would Debbie cheat on you?"

"You're not a good liar, Cynthia."

"Of course I am! Wait, that's not what I meant, either. I'm not lying."

He spoke in a careful tone, keeping his cool. "You're an honest girl, Cynthia, but you're lying now. I know you want to protect Debbie, and I respect that—but who is he?"

"I don't know. I mean there is no other guy!"

"All right, I guess I'll ask her myself."

She hesitated and then looked into his eyes. "Mike, if Debbie did something wrong, no one will feel worse about it than her. Just keep that in mind."

She turned and walked fast toward the door.

Mike studied her as she walked away. Man, that girl had a nice, bouncy butt. He watched her get into a battered Ford Focus and look down at something in her hands—probably a cell phone. If she was sending Debbie a frantic text message, that was fine. He'd be seeing Debbie soon.

16: Mike Returns

Debbie couldn't move her eyes from the screen. It seemed that Juan Carlos did have a website. He even had an email address listed, and a schedule of shows—and he was playing tonight in New Brunswick, at a place called *Ronnie's Martini Bar.*

That bastard!

Should she contact him? It would be pathetic to go begging after him like a bitch in heat—but god, the sex had been so good. Then again, it wasn't just about the sex; it was about some deeper connection—or maybe it *would* be, eventually—after they'd had a lot more sex.

She heard a sweet chiming tone that indicated a text message from Cynthia. She picked up her phone and read:

Mike is back. Saw him at CCs. On his way over and thinks you've been cheating.

Debbie's head started spinning. It couldn't be! She fumbled for the right button on her phone.

"What do you mean?" Debbie said as Cynthia picked up. "How could he know? What did you say?"

"I didn't say anything," Cynthia protested.

"But how could he know? You must have told him something."

"No! Not on purpose. I mean—no! He just kind of guessed it, and he caught me off guard so I didn't really deny it at first. *I don't know!*"

Debbie sucked in big breaths, trying to keep from hyperventilating.

Obviously, Cynthia had folded while she'd been busy flirting. Damn! She restrained an urge to yank at her hair as the doorbell rang. Damn again!

"I have to go, Cynthia," Debbie said. "The train wreck known as *my love life* is crashing through the door."

"Debbie... I really didn't say anything—and if I did, I'm sorry."

"Don't worry about it. I'll talk to you later."

Debbie hung up the phone and ran to the door. Then she stopped. Was her hair a mess? Should she change her clothes? She was wearing another casual black dress. The doorbell rang again—arrg! What was the use? This was an appropriately grim outfit for the death of a relationship.

She grabbed the doorknob and paused to take a few more deep breaths. *Be cool. Stay calm.* She yanked open the door.

"I'm so sorry!" she wailed. "I must have been out of my mind!"

Mike just stood there silently in his T-shirt, jeans, and baseball cap, looking like a guy in search of a barbell.

For a few long seconds, he just stared. Then he narrowed his eyes and said, "Who is he?"

Debbie wiped away a tear and spoke in a shaky voice. "Some guy in a car I crashed into."

She studied his face, but it remained blank as a block of marble. No, wait, it wasn't completely blank. His eyes were focused in a serious way, and was that a wisp of smoke coming out of his ears? Of course not—she had to get a grip.

He stomped past her and entered the living room. He whirled around to face her and put his hands on his hips.

"Why'd you do it, Debbie? I wasn't good enough?"

"No! You were great," she said, resisting an urge to bite a fingernail. "I was confused. When you said that you loved me it freaked me out. Maybe I don't know if I can handle love."

"But you can handle sex with a stranger?"

"It was an accident."

"Right. Somehow, his naked body accidentally ended up between your legs... So, was it good?"

"What do you mean?"

"Was the sex good?"

What a strange question. Did it really matter? Come to think of it, it probably did.

"Oh," she said. "It was, um—I don't remember. I was pretty drunk. I think it was bad. In fact, it was terrible. It was much worse than our sex."

"What? Our sex is terrible?"

"No! I mean that it was bad sex...unlike our good sex."

He was silent. Finally, he nodded his head. "Okay. I think I see what's going on here."

"Oh...good. What's going on?"

"You got drunk and had bad sex! But that's what happens when you fool around—because crime doesn't pay."

"Right! I know that now."

He gave a sarcastic laugh. "Do you? I'm not sure how I feel about it." He waved his hands in the air. "I'm out there every day working, and sometimes I have a lot on my mind. Sometimes I'm just feeling distracted, and things aren't as good as they could be, okay? Sometimes I'm just too busy thinking, and I don't finish things the best way, and then the freakin' bongos tap out the wrong song. Do you know what I'm talking about?"

Debbie blinked. What was he talking about? But she nodded her head.

"I'm getting out of here," he said.

She felt a tightness in her chest, like it was a sponge being squeezed.

"No, don't go!" she said, and a fresh tear streamed down her face. "I want you to stay... I'm really sorry."

He studied her face. He sighed and said, "Maybe I'll call you later."

He walked out the door without looking back. Debbie watched the door slam. Then she heard the dog bark, and the door opened again.

"I forgot my dog," he said.

Sugar came running in from the other room with his feet click-clacking on the hardwood floor. He snarled a bit as he pranced past Debbie, looking smug.

"Thanks for watching him," Mike said. Then he was gone once more.

Debbie stood still for a long time with a hollow feeling in her stomach. She felt ravaged by guilt, like a birthday cake is ravaged by a pack of three-year-olds. But on the bright side, at least the dog was gone.

Her eyes wandered across the room to the laptop screen. It was still showing Juan's website.

She threw back her head and mouthed a silent scream. That bastard, Juan Carlos! He'd come blasting into her life like a steamy erotic hurricane and now he was gone, leaving her heart in a state of drowned destruction. She replayed the image of Mike walking out the door and felt her insides getting queasy. He'd been the one guy she'd met in the last two years who'd actually cared about her—and now he was gone. *Damn, damn, damn!*

She stared at the living room window and considered jumping, but then changed her mind. She was only on the second floor, and it's quite possible she'd merely break her legs. If she were going to die, she needed to do it right—but could a girl die from eating too many animal crackers? Probably not.

Her eyes wandered back to the website, and her mind rekindled some of the scorching hot scenes from last night. She walked over to the screen and stared at it. Juan was playing at *Ronnie's* tonight. So he would be there—tonight.

There was no way she was going. No way. But if she happened to be in the area, why not stop in and get a drink?

She shook her head and swore to herself. What was she thinking?

She sighed. She knew what she was thinking. Decisions, decisions—but in the end, she had to follow her heart, or maybe just something other than her brain.

She picked up her phone and pressed the number for the diner. She wasn't going in to work tonight, and she wasn't going to write anything, either. Well, maybe a little bit—but then she was heading into New Brunswick.

"Good move," someone said.

Debbie gave a short laugh. "If you approve, Suzy, it can't be that good."

"It'll be better than good. It'll be fun."

17: Trouble At Ronnie's

Once again, Debbie found herself with a white-knuckle grip on the steering wheel of her Honda Civic, taking deep breaths and trying to stay calm. She stopped the car at an intersection filled with cars and flashing lights, near the towering Marriott hotel that marked the entrance to New Brunswick, and tried to ignore Cynthia's advice from the passenger seat. As usual, Cynthia sounded calm and casual, even when dispensing urgent warnings.

"Debbie, let me just say I don't think this is such a great idea, and by that I mean it's a mistake on a nuclear scale. I'm saying you might just come home from this and be radioactive."

Debbie twitched her nose and squinted through her glasses at the glowing taillights in front of her. "Cynthia, let me just say I appreciate you coming with me, and I'm happy for all the advice I'm probably going to ignore."

Cynthia smiled and rummaged through some of the crumb-filled bags of snack food scattered across the dashboard.

"Yeah, and why is that, Debbie? Are you skeptical about my ability to be your coach just because my own love life is limited to a Fender bass? Or is it because you're a girl who's only listening to her vagina?"

Debbie considered the question while looking into the visor mirror to fluff her hair. "Look, I know my hormones are talking to my heart, but what can I do? They won't shut up."

Cynthia laughed. "Maybe they just need to cool off. You know, take a few days and forget about your epic encounter. Maybe sit in a tub full of ice water or something."

Debbie shuddered at the image. It actually made sense to her, but she wanted to see the guy who'd gotten her so frantic. Maybe it was purely chemical, or maybe it involved a deeper connection—or maybe the two were unexplainably linked and she had to do this.

"Besides, what are you going to say?" Cynthia said. "Remember me? The girl you banged the other night before sneaking out the window and sliding down the drainpipe? And can we do it again, please?"

"I'm not going to say anything to him," Debbie said. "I'm going to just pretend I happen to be there."

Cynthia rolled her eyes. "Do you really think he's going to fall for that? You're going to look like a stalker."

"That's ridiculous. One visit does not constitute a 'stalk.' "

"No, but stalking starts with one visit, and it's the one you're about to make."

"I'm not a stalker. I'm just curious about a guy I like."

"Curious about what? His intentions? I think he made those clear when he snuck out of your house like a sex ninja. And what about Mike? You told him you were sorry for cheating, and now you're going to see the guy you cheated with and hope he comes home with you again?"

Debbie stuck her fingers into her ears. "All this logic is starting to stress me out!"

"Logic is funny that way. Hey, put your hands back on the steering wheel."

Debbie grabbed the wheel again, took a deep breath, and then drove the car into the multi-level parking garage on Church Street. The sprawling structure loomed large and grey like a concrete prison, but it was conveniently free of charge on Saturday nights. It was also right near *Ronnie's*.

Debbie hesitated outside the glass door of *Ronnie's Martini Bar*. Glancing inside, she could see the place was filled with hipsters who would probably think her dorkiness was an attempt at fashion. Then again, did she care what anyone thought? She wore a loose black dress because she liked it, and she wore white sneakers because they were comfortable, and she'd had the glasses since she was eight years old.

Cynthia said, "Is that a guitar I hear, or some kind of mating call?"

"You're not funny," Debbie said.

"Oh, I'm funny, Debbie, and that's why you love me. So, did you take a birth control pill before you left? And are we going in?"

Debbie grabbed the door handle. "I take one every day, Cynthia—and yeah, we're going in. Let's do it." She paused to try and slow her heartbeat and then stormed inside.

The room was dark and crowded, but it was also comfortable in a shiny kind of way. The general vibe was "swanky cool paint-by-numbers non-conformist," where everyone was wearing Ray-Bans, Michael Kors, Kenneth Cole—and everyone looked the same. Debbie shrugged. This was just a pricey version of a biker bar, an indie club, or a hippie hangout. It was "clan culture," and further proof that humans weren't as far removed from caves as they liked to believe.

And honestly, this cave could be worse. Sure, it was filled with ostentatious displays of coolness, but it probably had a decent restroom. One of the things Debbie hated about going to dirt-bag bars was the crappy facilities, and she preferred pretentious cleanliness to "keepin' it real" genital crabs any day. She weaved a bit through the crowd, toward the sound of the guitar. Then her heart skipped a beat—there was Juan.

He was perched on a stool at the far end of the room, playing some jazzy stuff that sounded smoother than Spanish olive oil. He didn't remind her of a toreador tonight; he looked more like a dashing troubadour in a sharp white shirt, stylish black jeans, and a virile pair of cowboy boots. Debbie felt her head swim a bit, and she took a few deliberate breaths. *Damn it, I've got to calm down!*

"Debbie? Debbie? *Debbie?*"

What was that sound? Was someone talking to her? Oh, right—Cynthia!

"What?"

"This guy is pretty hot. I'm starting to understand."

"Don't go getting any ideas!" Debbie snapped.

Cynthia laughed. "Gimme a break; he's not my type. I mean he's playing *jazz*... Do you wanna get some drinks?"

"No—wait, yes!"

It would help calm her down, and she needed to get calm, because she felt like someone who was being pushed out of an airplane.

"Great, I'll get you a martini," Cynthia said. "It's on me."

"Thanks."

She watched Cynthia jiggle her way through the crowd, and then the music stopped. A few people clapped while Juan adjusted his tuning. Debbie pretended to be looking at everything in the room except Juan. She began to wonder how this was actually going to work. She began to have some doubts, and she began to feel that tightness in her chest again, and she began to ponder running like a wispy antelope for the door. But then she glanced at the bar—and there was Suzy Spitfire.

Crap, what was she doing here? But of course, Suzy was always wherever Debbie went.

Her hair was dark crimson, and wild like a bonfire, and she had a Series 7 Plasma Pistol slung low across the right side of her black leather skirt. She was staring at a shot glass in her hand, kind of like a monk staring at a holy object. In one quick move she gulped it down and then turned to Debbie.

"I'm busy, Suzy," Debbie said.

"No, you're not," Suzy said with a grin. "But you will be, if you've got any sense. Life is too short to not do whatever makes it better. And that's why I'm taking Shelba's offer for the big payoff; I'm going to deliver a bunch of Baby Bliss dolls to Choccoban. See you later."

Suzy vanished. Debbie hesitated for a few seconds and then found herself walking toward Juan.

She'd never been an aggressive girl. She was more the kind of girl who would stand in the corner with a pathetic friend—unless, of course, she was the pathetic friend. Most of the time she stayed home and read a book. She considered how it still wasn't too late to do that. Juan hadn't seen her yet, and she could turn and run.

She could get the hell out of here and never see him again. She could avoid dealing with all of this humiliation and just suffer a bit of heartbreak—or maybe just "vagina break"—but wait! Juan was looking right at her.

She stopped breathing, but she didn't look away.

In fact, she looked right back. After all, she was just a girl here at *Ronnie's* casually sipping a martini. Of course, she didn't have a martini, because Cynthia was taking forever to get one, but that didn't mean she couldn't look like she belonged. She was just another girl casually waiting for her drink and then maybe a marriage proposal.

Oh, crap! Why was she thinking like this? She hardly knew the guy. In fact, the only thing she knew about him was that he played guitar, had a junky old car, and was a sexual god. But apparently that was enough.

Juan spoke above the noise. "Debbie, how are you?"

She moved closer to him. "Hi, Juan," she said, trying to keep her voice from shaking. "You forgot to say good-bye."

He smiled. "I was going to call."

"You don't have my number."

"Ah. Well then it's a good thing you're here."

"Is it?"

"Of course! So how did you find me? Maybe you should be a detective."

"I used something called the 'internet.' You better not become a criminal, Juan. It took two seconds."

Juan smiled again and then spoke into the microphone in front of him.

"I'd like to dedicate this next song to Debbie, who is smart and funny and very beautiful."

Debbie felt herself blushing. Her face was hot like a geyser.

He started playing some chords, and then he started singing:

"A star so high
Could never shine
Just like the girl
I wish was mine"

He had a smooth, inviting voice—manly, yet still sweet. Debbie wasn't sure what to do. On the one hand, she could stand here and look enthralled, but that wouldn't accurately represent her feeling of rage. On the other hand, she didn't actually feel rage right now; she felt confusion. She was angry Juan had snuck out the door, but she felt euphoric about seeing him again.

She decided to make her face blank like a refrigerator door. Yeah, maybe the best course of action would be to listen to the song with a neutral expression and then head to the restroom before it became awkward. After all, she was no crawling puppy dog looking for love. She'd come here to talk, not beg. But somehow, she didn't feel in control. She felt like a baby chicken that was being eyed by a hungry fox. She felt silly. Suddenly, Cynthia was at her side, offering her a martini.

Cynthia whispered, "Wow, did he write this song for you? I really hate it. I'm also wondering what that witch is doing here."

"What?"

"Velva 'Smokenstein' or whatever the hell her name is. She just walked in the door, and she's coming this way."

Debbie looked through the crowd and felt her stomach tighten into a knot. Yes, Velva was here! She was definitely headed this way.

She was wearing a metallic-blue dress that looked like body armor from a bad sci-fi flick. Her hair was a frazzled pile of white split ends, and her lips were fleshy splotches of bloody red goop. Around her froggy neck was a string of gold-colored beads—obviously, plastic covered with shinier plastic.

Debbie felt lightheaded as she whipped her head around, looking for a place to hide. She whispered to Cynthia in a fierce tone, "We have to get out of here!"

Cynthia didn't budge. "Why? You don't know what she wants—and besides, it might be good to meet her in a public place. This is way better than her stinky kitchen."

"But I don't want to meet her at all! I don't want Juan to know that I know her. I don't want to deal with her tonight."

"So you're going to run? Maybe you and Juan have more in common than I thought."

"Cynthia, this is not a good time for pointing out my cowardly nature—crap."

Velva was smiling at Debbie and pointing. Debbie slumped her shoulders and resigned herself. The only question left was the method of her suicide. She looked around for any loose silverware on the nearby tables. No such luck. And then she saw Velva wave at Juan—and Juan stopped playing.

Debbie and Cynthia looked at each other as Juan spoke into the microphone again. "I'll take a quick break," he said.

He put down the guitar but didn't move from his stool. Debbie studied his face and saw a shaky smile hanging there. Obviously, she wasn't the only one who was nervous. Only now she was more nervous—what the hell was going on?

Velva was standing next to Debbie now. "Hello, people," she said. "This is a sweet little place. Maybe I'll check it out after I get my youth back, which brings up my next point. You owe me a dog, Debbie—and Juan, you owe me ten years. It's time to pay up."

Debbie and Juan looked at each other, while Cynthia sipped her drink.

Debbie squirmed a bit. "What are you talking about? Do I know you?"

Juan said, "What do you mean, old woman? We settled for a plant."

"Right!" Debbie blurted. "An African violet!"

Velva cackled. "I told you both that a plant would be okay *provided you really cared about the plants*. This morning both of you had dead plants—and it's because neither of you cared one bit. So you both lied, and you both need to give me something better right now."

Debbie felt woozy. "What? That's ridiculous!" Then she turned to Juan and motioned toward Velva. "Do you know her?"

"Yes," Juan said. "But she has done nothing for me."

Velva smirked. "Nothing? And what do you call this?" she said, pointing at Debbie.

Juan frowned in Debbie's direction. "I call this a lie. You told me 'no strings,' and yet here she is looking to put a noose around my neck, just like all the others. You haven't kept the agreement."

Velva laughed. "I didn't say 'no strings'—those were your words. I said 'limited after engagement,' which is open to interpretation. You should've read the fine print."

"So now you're an attorney?" Juan scoffed. "Did they give you a free law degree when you bought your broomstick? You know what I meant, old woman—and I hardly consider a real, live girl tracking me down to be 'limited.' You've failed and I refuse to pay."

He crossed his arms and looked smug.

Debbie just stared, bewildered—but the wheels kept turning, and she felt a cold rage building.

She turned to Juan. "What are you talking about? Are you telling me I was supposed to be part of a 'no strings' spell you bought from this shyster? Is that what this is about?"

Juan gave a sheepish smile. "Debbie, you're a very nice girl, but I did make an agreement with this witch, and it was not personal against you. I was just tired of every girl I slept with wanting to turn me into a boyfriend."

Debbie felt like she was drunk. "I can't believe this. And I'm not trying to turn you into anything."

Cynthia grabbed her arm. "Hey, wait! What's the deal with the dog? Why do you owe her anything?"

"Hey, yeah," Debbie said, switching her attention back to the witch. "Why do I owe you anything? You were supposed to improve my sex life."

"I did," Velva said. "You met Juan, and you had great sex."

"You were supposed to improve it with Mike."

"You didn't say that. You said you wanted me to improve your sex life—and Juan improved it, right? That's why you're here."

"Are you kidding me? I'm not here for sex! I'm here because I wanted to see Juan!"

Several people at the nearby bar glanced at Debbie. She knew they had no idea what was happening, but sex was obviously involved and so of course it was interesting.

Juan pointed at Velva. "You see, witch? Is this what you call 'limited'? "

Debbie glared at Juan. "You're such an asshole."

Cynthia shook her head. "None of this will hold up in court, Velva. It doesn't seem to me you've fulfilled your agreements."

"Are you going to take me to court?" Velva said. "You either have to pay up or suffer the consequences."

Juan and Debbie looked at each other once again.

"What consequences?" Debbie said.

Velva laughed. "Are you bringing me the dog?"

Debbie snorted and crossed her arms. "No way."

Velva turned to Juan. "Are you going to surrender your ten years to me?"

Juan gave a haughtier snort than Debbie. "Of course not. You are a fraud twice over—and I wouldn't have paid you even if your spell had worked. So there!"

Velva nodded her head. "Perfect. Since you've both broken a witch's contract, I finally have the power to cast a curse." She raised her arms high and cackled a bit. Then she chanted:

"Power of light
Power of dark
Power of wind
Power of bark
Take this pair
Into a place
Forever locked
In each other's embrace"

Velva smiled through her goopy red lips. "There, it's done."

"What?" Debbie said. "What do you mean? Just like that?"

"Yep, just like that. Were you expecting something more dramatic? A steaming cauldron and all that bullshit? It doesn't work that way in the real world. So long."

Velva turned fast and walked back through the crowd, almost like she wanted to leave before Debbie changed her mind about the Chihuahua. Debbie started to go after her, but Cynthia grabbed her arm.

"Let her go," Cynthia said. "She's full of shit. There's no spell."

Juan also scoffed in Velva's general direction. "Yes, she's a fraud. Her spell did nothing. You hit my car because you weren't paying attention, and that's all. What happened afterward was a spontaneous moment."

Debbie looked at him with her fiercest kind of stare, while Cynthia said, "I'll be going to check out the restroom, unless you want me to stay. Right—I'll be back later."

Debbie watched her go and then felt her chest heaving. Her combination of rage and euphoria was gone. She now felt only rage.

Juan motioned toward a small table for two against the brick wall. "Debbie, I know you're angry. Please, can we talk?"

She said nothing. Then she turned toward the door.

"Please, Debbie, don't go."

She whirled back around, wanting to scream and scratch and lash out with her fists—but she didn't do it, because then she would have to leave him, and she didn't want to leave him. Not yet.

She wanted to stay, and now she was sitting down. What the hell, she would listen to his words and then tell him to drop dead. Of course, she did notice the stubby candle on the table, and she did consider throwing it at him—but then he flashed that seductive smile and sat down across from her. She decided to delay the tableware assault. But it was coming.

"I thought you liked me!" she blurted.

"But I hardly know you."

"You knew me well enough to have sex."

"That doesn't require much knowledge."

"You're such a pig."

He sighed and looked at her with eyes so brown like sweet iced tea.

"Am I? I'm just being honest, Debbie. I like women, and I like you, but I'm not looking for a girlfriend. Why must every physical encounter turn into something more complicated? Can't it just be a moment? I know there are girls who think this way—but not enough of them, and most change their minds soon after."

Debbie gave a sarcastic laugh. "Why don't you try a prostitute?"

Juan shrugged. "I don't care for those girls. I like 'nice girls,' but I'm not looking for a relationship."

"Then you should've told me that."

He leaned forward and whispered, "It didn't come up in our conversation. We were too busy fucking each other's brains out."

She started to respond—and stopped. Whoah, she suddenly felt turned on.

She put her nose an inch from his and whispered back, "Yeah, and it was good, and I liked it—and I'd do it again."

He smiled. Then he reached under the table and began to massage her thigh.

"Let's do it right here," he said. "I wish we could do it right on this table."

He bent his head forward and they kissed.

"Mmm, that would be nice," she murmured.

He laughed and kissed her again, and this time the kiss went on and on, and Debbie found herself sucking on his tongue. She was devouring it like it was a bag of cheese doodles.

Finally, they broke apart. And then everything changed.

18: Sex Hell

Debbie was in a theater.

She whipped her head around so fast she almost lost her glasses. She was standing on a stage, facing rows of empty seats. The lights were low. There was an Italian-style stone bench nearby, and a similarly Romanesque flower pot filled with a leafy green plant. There was also a balcony about two meters above the floor, jutting from the wall at "stage left."

Oh, crap!

She was sure she'd just been in *Ronnie's Martini Bar*, getting happily groped by a smoking hot Hispanic guy who'd jilted her the night before. Then she recalled Velva saying something about a curse—and now she recognized the setting. Had she been sentenced to spend the rest of her life inside Shakespeare's *Romeo and Juliet?* Her eyes went wide and her heart started to pound.

Stay calm! Stay calm!

She took a deep breath and told herself that so far nothing looked too dangerous. Certainly, Shakespeare had more violent plays; her life wouldn't be worth 12 pence if this were the set of *Macbeth*. She wondered about Juan and scanned for him with fast eyes. Then she heard him call out, "Debbie! Debbie! Where are you, Debbie?"

Her heart leaped. It was Juan, and he was up on the balcony!

"Juan! Juan! What are you doing up there?"

Before she could answer, she spotted a set of stairs behind a curtain. She raced toward them and quickly reached the balcony—and there he was, still looking sexy and sleek in his fancy dress shirt, black jeans, and cowboy boots.

She crashed into his arms.

"Juan! Where the hell are we?"

He held her tight and narrowed his eyes. "I don't know, but it seems that the witch is capable of more than we expected."

"Yeah, I see. I definitely didn't think she was capable of conjuring up Shakespeare."

"Shakespeare? Where is he?"

"What? He's not here. But this looks like the set of *Romeo and Juliet.*"

"Ah," he said, glancing around. "So it is. But what is the game? Will we be forced to perform?" He paused for a moment, and then with a gleam in his eye he began to recite:

"But soft what light through yonder window breaks?
It is the beast, and Juliet is the one!"

Debbie tried not to laugh. But then she laughed and shook her head.

"It is the *east,* Juan—and Juliet is the *sun.*"

"What?"

"The *east* and the *sun.* He's comparing Juliet to a sunrise, and the beginning of a new day—and a new love."

"Oh. Are you certain?"

"Am I certain that during one of the most romantic scenes in literature the hero is not calling the love of his life a 'beast'? Yes, I'm certain."

"Hm, you're probably right. I suppose I would make a poor Romeo."

"I suppose, too. Look, we need to get out of here."

Juan's eyes jumped around the large room. "Yes, Debbie, we will. But I don't think we'll simply find a door." He squeezed her a bit and moved his hands down to her rump. "And maybe we shouldn't look just yet."

She pulled back a bit. Was he kidding? They had to escape! They had to run. They had to…

Something was happening. It was like her brain was being consumed by an illogical urge. Of course, Debbie knew this was normal when she wanted to have sex with an attractive guy who she suspected was also the wrong guy—but this was something else. It was almost a druggy feeling.

"Juan, I suddenly feel like I don't want to leave."

"Yes, I know. I'm irresistible."

"No. This isn't about your irresistible, pompous self. This is something else."

"Whatever it is, I think we can find out about it later."

"But that's my whole point; we shouldn't feel this way. I should be in my usual state of perpetual panic. We're under some kind of spell."

"I like the way I'm feeling, and I like the woman I'm feeling in my arms."

Debbie started to object again, but then nodded like she was hypnotized. Something was definitely wrong, but it was making everything feel perfectly right. She lunged forward, and their lips met like a pair of piping hot pizzas, and the voice of reason was sucked away by his kiss.

"I like what I'm feeling, too," she said, and she'd never been more certain of a thing in her life. "But how do we get back to my apartment?"

He flashed a devilish grin. "We don't need to go there." Then he hugged her like an octopus and they crashed against the edge of the balcony. In a flash, Debbie's panties were down on the floor, and Juan's pants were gone, and his fat fandango stick was sliding into her fast and hard.

Debbie gasped. "Wow, that was quick."

"You get me very excited."

"I'm not talking about you; I'm talking about me. I don't usually get slippery so fast—this is like being in a movie. The girls are always ready so quick."

"Mmm," he said. "It's a good movie, and you're the most slippery girl I've ever met."

In the back of her mind, Debbie wondered if that was a compliment. She also wondered who was *really* more slippery, but whatever.

Juan's pace was hypnotic, and his rhythm was top-notch; he had a drum corps built into his brain. He started to pick up speed, and she draped both her arms across the lip of the balcony and pushed her hips upward into his sexy assault. Pretty soon she was moaning and wailing and staring cross-eyed over his shoulder. She was grunting and gripping the edge of the balcony until her fingers ached.

In a quick move, she swung her legs forward and wrapped them around Juan's waist. Wow! She was swinging like a hammock between two trees in the woods, with Juan's hands holding her jiggling bottom. She vaguely recalled the day her mother had forced her to join the Brownies, and she'd gone camping in the woods, and the other girls had laughed at her because the wilderness made her nervous and too many marshmallows made her vomit—but where were those girls now? And did any of them have a merit badge for 'balcony sex'?

Funny, she'd always wanted to do it on a balcony, but she'd never quite gotten around to it. Mike had implied she wasn't adventurous, but Mike's idea of adventure wasn't nearly as radical as her secret thoughts. Of course, in her mind, the balcony experience involved being watched, and not just by a couple of voyeuristic gawkers far below the action. No, her brain was a little more extravagant. At this point, she wondered if anyone else was in the building—and then there was a sound like a blast of thunder, and every seat in the theater was filled.

Debbie's eyes nearly popped from her face.

She saw a rollicking audience of men and women. They were staring at her, and they were cheering. They were whooping and hollering and shouting words of encouragement, and she felt her heart pounding like a pachyderm. She was in a live sex show! How disgusting! How revolting! And what a thrill!

Juan looked at the crowd, and she felt the power of his pulsations increase.

Juan leaned close to her ear and whispered, "Do something sexy, Debbie. You look so sweet."

She smiled and unwrapped her legs from his hips. Her left hand was still on the railing, but her right hand was free. Her breathing was heavy and her fingers were fast. He leaned forward and kissed her long and hard just as her orgasm nearly blew them both off the balcony. At the very least, it shook and shuddered.

But soft what light through yonder window breaks?
It is the east, and Juliet is fucking like a maniac!

In her head, Debbie apologized to Shakespeare. She also heard the roar of the crowd in a more surreal way. They were somewhere in the back of her brain as she yanked Juan closer. He screamed with an orgasm of his own and then slammed into her hard.

Then everything was quiet. She took a few seconds and listened to her ragged breathing. Her heart was still thumping fast.

"Debbie, are you all right?" Juan said.

She felt him kissing her neck, and then he hugged her.

"I'm fine," she said. "That was amazing."

They stood face to face now. She coughed and straightened her dress. She looked out at the room and saw it was now empty—and she felt a wave of relief. She'd been very excited, but now that it was over she had no desire to start signing autographs.

She straightened her glasses and tried to look calm. "Okay, maybe we should figure out what's going on," she said. But she really wanted him to grab and hold her again.

Juan smiled as she pulled on her panties. He looked like he was about to mention the zebra striped design, and he looked like he was about to seize her in a fierce embrace, and Debbie knew she wanted to be back in his arms—but it didn't happen, because a voice was booming from somewhere just above their heads.

The voice said, "Ha-ha! Ho-ho! Welcome to Sex Hell!"

Debbie snapped her head toward the sound.

There was someone else here—or at least someone's head, floating about three meters above the floor and just as far from the edge of the balcony. The head was shaved bald—with two sharp horns on top. It was also bright red with thick black eyebrows and a matching dagger-like goatee. It was a handsome head, in a devilish kind of way, like a pirate, a thief, or a burly bouncer with a Harley out back. His voice was loud and deep and sounded wavy, like it was underwater.

The head said, "My name is Carl, and this is my place. I'm a demon, and you'll be seeing a lot of me. Congratulations."

Debbie glanced sideways at Juan, who glanced back at her. They both said nothing, but Debbie felt her dripping desire changing into dread.

"What's wrong?" Carl said. "Don't try and tell me you're shy. I just watched you do it like a couple of jackhammers in front of a roaring congregation. The nerdy-looking girls are always the best."

"Oh, is that so?" Debbie said, as her fear quickly morphed into anger. "Do the nerdy-looking girls ever point out that you have no arms?"

Carl grinned. "I have them. I just save them for special occasions—like making French toast."

Debbie started to respond, but then Juan put his arm around her shoulder and said, "What do you want, demon? We're not interested in your games."

Debbie jumped a bit when Juan touched her, but then she relaxed. His arm felt good there, and she needed to stay calm and assess the gravity of the situation. She also needed this demon to go away so she could have Juan to herself again.

Carl smiled like a set of steak knives. "Here's what's happening," he said. "Whenever you two start getting it on, you'll end up in Sex Hell with each other—*even if you start doing it with someone else.* And no, it won't always be in a theater, but it will always be an interesting experience. Any questions?"

Debbie narrowed her eyes. "Yeah, I have a lot of questions."

"Good. No more questions!" Carl bellowed.

"God, you're such an asshole," Debbie muttered.

Juan pointed a finger in the demon's face. "Why does Velva want us here, demon? What good does it do her?"

Carl grinned again. "I really shouldn't answer that but since I don't give a crap, I will. When you have sex here it creates a special kind of magic called *sensualla*, and the old hag can use that magic to make herself younger. In fact, you probably just knocked a few years off her crinkled face—but hey, that's like knocking a swig of saltwater out of the ocean, so you better get back to business pretty quick."

"I knew it!" Debbie said. "The things she promised us were scams."

"Right," Carl said. "That would be her style. For this kind of curse to work, she needed you to *break an agreement*. The particular agreement never mattered—as long as she knew you would break it. So she set you up, knowing you probably wouldn't give her your youth or a dog, or really care about a stupid plant. Go figure."

"But that's not right," Debbie protested. "She never defined what it meant to 'care' about a plant! She never defined a lot of things. That agreement was flimsy, and what she did to us is fraud. Can't we take her to court or something?"

Carl shrugged, which was hard for a head to do. "You can probably file a grievance with the Business Bureau of Better Magic, and you'll probably win, but it will take years for your case to get processed. Anyway, that's all I have to say. See you later."

"Wait!" Debbie said. "Is there any way we can break the spell?"

Carl roared with laughter. "The only way to break the spell is to find a Goddess Of Love; she would be able to give you the instructions. But I have no intention of telling you where to find one of those, although there is a nice one living in New Orleans."

"Okay," Debbie said. "Thanks."

"Don't mention it. You'll never get out of here, anyway."

"Thanks again for all the good news. By the way, what do you get out of this arrangement?"

The demon's eyes flashed. "Let's just say I like to watch." And then he was gone.

Debbie turned toward Juan, but before she could speak they were both back in the martini bar.

19: Mike's Conclusion

Mike sat in his living room with a blank expression, staring at nothing.

I can't believe she cheated on me, he thought.

It was night, the lights were low, and his dog was sleeping nearby on the hardwood floor. The television was off and the world of sports was closed, and his empty, hollow eyes wandered toward a bookcase against the wall.

He liked the bookcase because it wasn't a piece of prefabricated junk. It was a genuine article of furniture given to him by his grandfather and made from the wood of a dead tree, and it didn't even hold any books. The main shelves were filled with DVDs and pieces of sporting gear, while the top shelf held a photograph of Debbie.

She had a "Debbie expression" on her face, too—the kind of look that said, "Please don't take my picture," but he had taken the picture, and he loved the picture. He'd put the picture in a frame with a glass front, and he'd planted it on top of his rock solid bookcase, and now the bookcase felt shaky and inappropriate and he wondered how badly it would break if he threw it across the room.

But he wasn't going to do that because he needed a place to keep his catcher's mitt, and so he banged his fist down on the arm of the couch instead. She'd cheated on him, and it was unbelievable. Of all the things she might've done, this was the thing he'd never expected. Sure, she'd made some weird fashion choices, and she'd been inappropriate with snack food at times, but those things were usually not a sign of unfaithfulness.

Maybe he'd never really known her. Maybe all the lovable sarcasm was just a sign of her insecurities. He could forgive her, but could it ever be the same? Maybe it had never been that good. Hell, his family wouldn't have liked her, anyway, and maybe that's why he'd never introduced her. Then again, they would have liked her just fine. Maybe he hadn't introduced her because they *would* have liked her, and he wanted a girl they would not like.

Of course, she still had lots of potential there. One look at her in that black dress and white sneakers or whatever, and they would figure she was weird. Their heads would explode, and their BMWs would vomit caviar.

Somewhere to his left, Sugar stirred and stood up. He wandered over to Mike and barked a few times.

Mike glanced at the dog. Then he studied a certain spot between the animal's front legs, where the dog had a new tuft of hair, and he blinked.

The tuft was red. It could be paint or dye, but he knew it wasn't. He leaped from his chair and took the dog in his hands, bending down to examine the fur close up. The hairs were new and scraggily as well as the wrong color—and they were exactly like the hairs produced by Magic Mints, a cut-rate candy witches sometimes gave away after office visits. The witches got them from a catalog company that sold trashy supernatural surplus, and they were cheaper than magic lollipops.

Mike's jaw dropped. Debbie had made a joke about a witch, and he hadn't given it much thought because she was always joking around. Also, he tended to miss the biggest clues, and it was one of the reasons he was such a shitty witch hunter—but the possibilities were there, and they were looming large. After all, he'd been working with witches and wizards for a while now, and he knew they were a sleazy part of society's underbelly. Could it be that Debbie had cheated on him because of a spell?

He grabbed his NY Yankees baseball cap and jammed it down on his head. Then he started pacing around the room, talking to Sugar as he went.

"So, Debbie's been targeted by a witch or a wizard," he said. He grabbed a baseball bat that was leaning against his grandfather's bookcase and it felt good in his hands.

He smiled and puffed out his chest. "I thought the problem was me, but it isn't. The problem is just an evil spell and that's great! I mean, not really—but at least it makes sense. After all, our sex life was awesome. We rattled the walls and shook the freakin' earth!"

He paused, and then he frowned. "I suppose the shaking would've happened eventually. Sure, we would've moved some dirt after a while."

Then he had another thought, and it froze him like a snow cone.

"Holy crap, Sugar—what if someone is trying to get to me by hurting her?"

He felt lightheaded for a second and sat down. His heart was pounding in his ears. This was awful. This was even worse than the possibility that her infidelity had been inspired by bad sex. Some wizard was out for revenge, and he was trying to hurt Mike by hurting someone he cared about.

His lips curled into a sneer, and he rose to his feet.

"I'm going to find out who's behind this, Sugar, and I'm going to make them pay. And I'm going to rescue Debbie!"

He glanced around the room with raging eyes and snatched a small notebook from a bookcase, determined to create a plan. He sat back down and began scribbling ideas, along with a list of supplies.

Sugar yipped a few times and went to sleep.

20: Return

Debbie looked across the tiny table at Juan. She was back in the martini bar, and his hand was still on her thigh. In fact, it was like they'd never left. She shook her head like a person awakening from a trance and then shoved Juan's hand away from her leg.

"Wow," she said. "Did that actually happen?"

Juan raised his eyebrows. "Are you asking me if I visited another dimension and had a passionate experience with a beautiful woman? Yes, I did."

Debbie couldn't keep from blushing. "This is crazy," she said in a rush. "We need to figure out how to deal with this." Then she considered hyperventilating; it was a start.

Juan nodded. "If I understand the demon correctly, we're forever bound to each other, and if we attempt to stray we'll end up together again, and that is bad."

"Right," she said.

She sat back in her chair, banging her spine hard against the wood. All the sexual euphoria was draining away fast. Her head was pounding, she needed an aspirin, and somebody had a problem with not being allowed to *stray*. Obviously, the demon wasn't Juan's only problem, and she should have known better.

Now he had a tiny smile on his face. "Debbie," he said, "I don't think either of us is ready for an exclusive relationship that involves a demon watching us every time we're together. So we must make a plan. First, we must discover whether or not the demon is telling the truth. After all, he might be lying. It's quite possible we can still... become involved with other people...and nothing will happen."

"Yeah, but that's the problem, Juan. Usually, nothing happens."

Juan laughed. "You're a funny girl, Debbie."

"You won't think I'm so hilarious when I die from a panic attack."

"That would make me sad."

"Would it? It might also free you from Sex Hell. You'll probably be allowed to *stray* from a dead person."

Now why had she said that? She regretted saying it, and she regretted saying it with so much feeling.

He reached out and took her hand. "I don't want to be freed that way. Let's think about things and talk again tomorrow."

She didn't regret it. She didn't regret a thing. She'd tried to improve her life, and she'd learned something about how dumb she could be, but then again she'd already known that, so all she'd really done was reinforce something she'd already known—whatever. She just wanted to go home.

She looked into his eyes. They were warm and inviting like hot chocolate, or hot soup, or a hot, spurting volcano that would scald her into a shriveled pile of ashes.

"Right," she said, and then began scanning the busy room. "I need to find Cynthia. I think it's time to go."

21: Velva Throws A Hairbrush

Velva stared at her reflection in the smudged bathroom mirror. Maybe this would be a good time to clean the glass. After all, she might see a few less wrinkles. Come to think of it, she did look a little smoother. Of course, she still looked like a piece of dried fruit, but it was a less craggy piece. It was more like a dried apricot than a raisin. Maybe soon she'd look like a papaya.

She leaned a little closer to the grungy mirror and then heard the voice of that damned little red monkey down on the floor.

"Checking for a few signs of hope?" Carl said. "I suppose draining an ocean starts with one drop."

She frowned and kept right on staring at herself, tugging a bit with her index finger at the skin under her left eye.

"I do see an improvement," she said. "Stop trying to bring me down. Also, go fuck yourself."

Carl laughed. "I think you'll see a lot of improvement soon. Those two are really hot for each other and they're not gonna stop."

"Perfect, and that's your job, isn't it? To keep them humping until they're dead."

"I don't have a job, honey. I have a *calling*. That means I don't do it for money; I do it for love."

"Oh, really? I'm glad you love seeing people miserable. Someone should make you a saint."

"No one is miserable when they're having sex. The misery happens later, when they try to turn it into a relationship. But you wouldn't know about that, since nobody can stand you for more than a few minutes."

Velva looked around for something to throw, but decided the hairbrush wasn't heavy enough to do any real damage.

"I don't have time for emotional love," she snapped. "I'm too busy with my film career."

Carl rolled his little monkey eyes. "Career? Doesn't that word mean that someone actually wants to hire you?"

"Plenty of people were hiring me before I had my problem. I was in some films."

"Pornography doesn't count."

"I didn't do porn! I sat at the bar in an episode of *Whiskey Wars*, and I rode a bicycle in an orange juice commercial."

Carl snorted. "The bike thing was promising. Hey, wasn't there a woman riding a bicycle in *The Wizard Of Oz*?"

Velva stopped looking at herself and stared at the monkey with true hatred.

"I've been thinking about what you said, Carl, about how I don't care for anyone but me, and it's not true. I'm not trying to hurt anyone. I just want to be young again—is that so terrible? At least I have a reason for doing this. Your only reason is that it gets you off. So you're even worse than me."

Carl chattered his teeth together and considered the statement.

"Okay," he said. "I'm worse than you."

"Good. So now we know."

"Yeah. And you better hope my conscience doesn't start bothering me."

"What are you talking about?"

"I'm just saying I might start feeling guilty, or maybe I might get bored. And then you'll stay older than the mold in King Tut's coffee cup."

Velva laughed and once again returned to her facial examination.

"You'll never feel guilty," she said. "It's not your style."

"That's true. But then again I don't need any of this stuff to get me through my day. So I think I'm going to hold back a bit more of the *sensualla* for myself. Consider it a tax."

Velva's eyes opened like two popping strobe lights.

"What? You can't do that you son of a bitch! *We had an agreement!*"

"You mean like the agreement you had with Juan and Debbie? Who's worse now, you old hag?"

"But I need that magic!" she wailed.

"You'll get it, but you'll just have to work harder for it. Or I guess they will."

Velva clenched her jaw. "I hate you, Carl," she said in a low voice.

"I'll get over it," he said while banging his tail on the floor. "Hey, you know what? I'm over it already."

The monkey vanished. Velva just stared for a few seconds at the spot on the floor where he'd been sitting and then hurled the hairbrush. It bounced on the tile but didn't break. She sat down on the toilet, put her head in her hands, and then let out a choking sob.

It was all so depressing. She wiped a few tears away from her eyes. She hadn't asked to be born a witch—it had happened to her, and all she'd wanted was a damned part in a commercial. Or maybe a small film. Was she really doing any harm? In fact, she was doing Debbie a favor. She'd introduced Debbie to a sexy guy who could bang the hell out of her—hell, Velva was jealous. All she had to look forward to was another evening with her cat.

She sighed. When she looked up, her cat was in the doorway.

"Hey, Bart," she said. "At least you love me, right?"

The cat gave a meow. After all, he was hungry.

22: The Wrong Bomb

Debbie awoke with the sun in her eyes. Apparently, she'd forgotten to pull down the window shades in her bedroom last night. Her eyelids fluttered a few times while her hand instinctively tried to block the bitch-slapping rays—but reality would not be denied, and she suddenly jerked herself into a sitting position.

Where the hell was she? The events of the previous evening flooded her brain like a spotlight. She'd been in Sex Hell. She'd been exhausted after dropping Cynthia off and had collapsed in her room like a corpse, planning to lie down for a minute and then get ready for bed—but the minute had turned into eight hours, and now here she was still dressed in her clothes from last night, and she had to work this afternoon, and then she had to worry about Juan, and Carl, and Velva, and Mike. Damn.

Normally, this would be a good time to start breathing into a paper bag, but then she stared at the picture of Wile E. Coyote on her wall, and as usual, she had a moment of inspiration.

It was time to stop complaining and pick up the pieces. It was time to shrug off the falling anvils, the bone-crunching freight trains, and the rocket-powered roller skates that didn't live up to their warranties. Most of all, it was time to admit she didn't get her inspiration from renowned philosophers or poets or statesman—no, for her, great wisdom came from cartoon characters. A girl needed to grab her inspiration where she could find it.

She leaped to her feet and headed into the bathroom, determined to think positive thoughts. It was the only way.

Ten minutes later, she was stepping out of the shower and drying herself with a fresh-smelling towel. She told herself it was all a dream. She was going to wake up any minute and it would all be over. In fact, she was awake right now! Whew, what a relief. There were no witches or magic spells. There was only another day down at the diner, and another night writing her irreverent masterpiece of a novel, *Suzy Spitfire Kills Everybody*.

"Suzy, why the hell did I listen to you?" Debbie said.

She heard Suzy laugh. "Isn't listening to me kind of like listening to yourself?"

"Yeah, right. But it's only a part of myself."

"It's the good part."

"No! It's the part I shouldn't be listening to!"

"Debbie, I've got some trouble. Tolio and I agreed to deliver the Baby Bliss dolls for Shelba, but she was just using us. They weren't dolls, Deb; the crates were filled with super-secret Fear Focus pistols. And now the Space Patrol is after us—but I'm thinking positive thoughts. It's the only way. Later."

Debbie grimaced and furiously brushed her hair just as the phone rang. She fumbled for her glasses and glanced at the incoming call and felt her heart jump through her rib cage. Mike was on the line, and reality was back, and it was the worst thing ever. She ground her teeth and glanced at that fucker Wile E. Coyote and tried to think. Hey, maybe this would be okay. Maybe, maybe, maybe she could turn this into a good thing. Maybe she would end up drinking champagne and eating a roadrunner for dinner.

She took a second to collect herself and said, "Hi, Mike." She tried to sound strong and sure, but she felt small like a mouse. She didn't feel in control, which of course was nothing new.

"Hi, Debbie," he said, sounding pretty even-tempered. "It's a great morning to go running."

"That's interesting. I was just thinking about how it was a great morning to sit in a chair."

"I was also thinking I could come over."

"What? You mean right now? I just got up."

"That's all right. I'm in the neighborhood, and maybe we can talk. Did you eat breakfast yet?"

"No. I don't know. I mean I didn't eat breakfast but I don't know about you coming over. It might not be the best plan."

"That's not good, since I'm already here. In fact, I'm right outside your door."

Debbie felt like her head would explode.

"Oh, really?" she said, trying to keep her voice level. She threw on her black terrycloth bathrobe and walked into the living room. She yanked open the door, and there was Mike.

Oh crap, she thought. Here we go again.

He was dressed in a pair of Adidas running shorts, a NY Jets T-shirt, and a NY Yankees baseball cap. In one hand, he held a pair of drumsticks—now that was different. He was also holding a gym bag, but it didn't look like he'd been perspiring much. All in all, he looked pretty sexy.

How strange, she thought. Despite everything that had just happened with Juan, she still noticed the sexiness of a different guy in her doorway. But then again, it wasn't so strange. He was attractive, and people always notice each other, unless maybe the house is burning down, in which case there are other things to think about—like maybe being rescued by a really hot firefighter.

"Mike, you're here."

"Yeah, that's true."

"Wow. I wasn't expecting you."

"I know."

"So I'm not sure what to do."

"You might want to hang up the phone."

"Oh, right, the phone." Debbie disconnected the call.

"Can I come in?"

"Sure. I just got out of the shower."

"Yeah, I see. You look good. Did you have an exciting night?"

She once again felt her heart jump.

"No. I went to the theater," she said. Then she quickly added, "With Cynthia."

"Oh. And that wasn't exciting?"

"No! Romeo and Juliet... Just a lot of boring sex and violence and romance. Stupid."

"Debbie, are you okay?"

"Sure, I'm fine. Why do you ask?"

He studied her for a moment and then tossed the gym bag onto the sofa.

"Debbie, I know we've had some problems, but I'm here because I care about you."

Debbie put her hands on her temples and tried to stop the throbbing. She plopped down on the sofa. She wasn't sure what to say, but decided to start talking anyway. Maybe it was time to plunge in.

She took a deep breath. "Mike, I'm not sure why you still want to be involved with me. I cheated on you, and I don't think it's because I'm such a terrible person, at least I hope not. I think it's because maybe we don't have a lot in common. I think maybe we should stop seeing each other."

There, she'd said something. It wasn't even something she'd planned to say until she'd opened her mouth—but she'd thrown it out there like a grenade, and wow, it had felt right, and hopefully it would make something good happen without doing too much damage.

Mike smiled. "Deb, I know about the magic spell. The one created by an evil wizard that caused you to cheat."

Okay, not what she'd expected. Apparently, her grenade had failed to detonate.

"What?" she said. "Mike, I don't think that's true."

"Of course you don't, because you're under an evil spell. That's what makes it evil."

He sat down hard next to her on the sofa. He tilted his head and looked at her like a guy speaking to a little girl who'd just dropped her lollipop.

"Debbie, I know it must be hard for you, but you've got to try and fight it. And keep in mind you won't be fighting alone, because I'm here for you."

"You are?"

"Of course! No phony shyster can compare to someone who *really cares*. Think about what I'm saying! You were conned, honey, by a supernatural con artist, and it's not your fault. But ask yourself, does that guy really give a damn about you? Will he be there when you need him? Where is he now?"

Debbie looked at Mike and crinkled her forehead. She was thinking, but it had nothing to do with his wacked-out information about a non-existent wizard. She was thinking about Juan, and his "no strings relationship," and the way he'd wanted to use her, and the way she'd let him do it.

God dammit! Juan was such a bastard!

She would've tossed a few more mental curses his way—but then Mike kissed her hard. And she kissed him back.

He wrapped his tree-stump arms around her and sucked her face with gusto. She plowed into his lips like they were a bowl of ice cream. Her bathrobe was loose and open, exposing her naked skin. He was moving a hand down her thigh, and she wanted it there. She wanted him to get on top of her right now and pound that silky smooth jazz guitarist right out of her aching vagina.

"Maybe you're right," she said. "Maybe I can fight this thing."

"Of course you can," he whispered. "You just need a little discipline."

"I hate discipline," she murmured. "It doesn't do anything for me."

He just smiled and started ripping off his pants.

And then everything changed.

23: Space Encounter

Debbie whipped her head around fast. What the hell?

She was no longer in her apartment.

She had a sinking feeling in her stomach, like she was on a roller coaster ride and the car had just dropped into oblivion. She recalled the words of the demon, Carl, about how an encounter with anybody would bring her back into Sex Hell with Juan.

She rolled her eyes and let out a moan of exasperation. But this feeling was quickly followed by a tingle of anticipation. Was Juan here?

She cursed herself for the sweet nervous feeling. After all, Mike was probably still groping her on a sofa. But then again, she'd tried to tell him it was over, right before deciding he was a decent guy who might just help her forget about the rotten bastard she was still dying to see. Complications. Ugh!

She took a deep breath and studied her surroundings.

She was in some kind of classroom, but based on the panoramic view through the windows, this wasn't an ordinary classroom. It was a classroom surrounded by gaping gray craters and black, starry-filled skies. Apparently, she was in a classroom on the moon—and she was dressed in some sort of spacey uniform. Holy crap!

She took another deep breath. *Stay calm! Stay calm!*

Wait a second. She wasn't on the moon. She didn't see planet Earth through the windows, and Ursa Minor and Polaris were in the wrong place—and who ever said studying astronomy wasn't cool? Had the captain of the football team ever known what star he was standing under? The popular kids had confused Venus and Sirius all the time.

Enough reminiscing. She examined her clothing, and she gasped. She was wearing a red dress with a black neckline that pushed her breasts up high, almost into her eyeballs. It was also ridiculously short, with the bottom section looking like a pleated skirt that stopped an inch or two below her labia. On her feet were a pair of black space boots with five-inch heels. She also wasn't wearing panties.

Her heart started to pound. She'd occasionally gone commando, especially when she'd mismanaged her laundry—and maybe one or two times when she'd been experimenting. But this dress was too short to be experimenting with anything other than outer space sluttiness. Then again, it was only mildly less revealing than the ludicrous outfits issued to most women in comic books or sci-fi stories. She shivered and realized it was also exciting.

Sure, she was angry at Juan, but now she wanted to see him again. Was it the promise of an unlikely romance? Or was it the promise of awesome sex?

It was both, and her pulse was racing. But then she frowned.

This was crazy. She wasn't going to be entertainment for a demon carrying out the scheme of a witch. No way.

She bit a fingernail and studied her surroundings a bit more. The room held rows of tables. Each table had two chairs behind it, and there were six rows of three tables each. In the front of the room was a teacher's desk, but there was no one behind it. In fact, there seemed to be no one in this interplanetary school but her. This wasn't too alarming; she'd always felt lonely in class. Yes, she'd done a few crazy things with crayons when she was in third grade. Why couldn't everyone just forget about it?

She'd been a good student, and although she'd eventually been an English major in college, she'd spent her early public school days with a strong fascination of science that had nicely complimented her love of science fiction. She noticed a blackboard in the front of the room covered with chemistry equations. She gave a nervous shiver. Chemistry was the stuff that held the universe together, and it was also the stuff that caused people to fall in love. It was all the same thing, and it was one of the things she wrote about in her sci-fi stories.

In fact, her short story, *Test Tube Romancer*, was about a girl who worked in a lab. The girl was supposed to be concocting an artificial food additive for soup, but instead she created a love potion. The potion had a shaky subatomic structure similar to uranium, and it caused people to be magically drawn to their romantic match, and it was quite tasty when mixed with chicken, carrots, and celery.

Debbie examined her reflection in one of the starry windows. Her hair was a mop of limp-looking strands, and her lips were too small, and her eyes were too big, and her chest needed padding—but her ass was definitely tight. It was also mostly hanging out. Wow! It made her feel subservient, which she hated to be in real life—but this wasn't real life, was it? No, of course not. It was something better. She turned around and felt a jolt.

Juan was standing behind the teacher's desk.

He looked sharp as a scissor in a dark suit and tie. His ponytail was like a silky rope, and his goatee was trimmed to a point, and his eyes were shining like pools of hot coffee. He seemed shocked, but Debbie could see him gradually putting the lascivious pieces together. He scanned the room and looked at her with narrow eyes.

"It didn't take long for us to end up together again."

"I guess not," she said, squirming a bit. But then she stopped squirming.

She had no reason to feel guilty. In fact, Juan had told her he wasn't ready for a relationship. Her soft demeanor got hard.

"Are you annoyed, Juan? You did say we should test the demon's words."

"Yes, that's true. But I was thinking I would be the one to do the testing."

"There's no moss growing in my bed, buddy."

He laughed, sarcastic. "So I see. You could have waited until your flesh cooled off."

"My flesh is plenty cool!" she snapped. But then she added, "It was with my boyfriend, okay? We didn't even do anything." For some reason, she wanted him to know that. And then she smiled.

Juan was jealous! He was trying to hide it, but it was as plain as that epileptic twitch on his face. She felt good.

Now he was smiling, too, but it seemed forced. "You look marvelous, Debbie. You should wear scraps—I mean skirts—more often."

Debbie fidgeted a bit in her high-heel boots and wondered how quickly she'd topple over if she took a step. Juan moved in her direction.

"Stop right there," she said, but she didn't mean it. She wanted to mean it, at least for a few more seconds, but just like on the balcony something was making her feel super sexed up. It must be in the air, she thought—some kind of all-powerful aphrodisiac.

Juan was grinning. "So, is this one of your fantasies?" he said, motioning toward their surroundings while briefly studying the blackboard.

He stuck his face close to hers. His lips were like two tempting neutrinos.

Debbie shrugged and tried once again to control her breathing.

"Why not?" she said. "I've always liked learning."

"Maybe you need to learn a lesson about the importance of chemistry."

"I already know it's important. I just can't seem to find the right equation."

His eyes lit up. "I see. Let me show you one of them."

Quick as a flash, he grabbed her shoulders and whirled her around. Her spectacles fell from her face as she was bent over the desk—and then her skirt was flipped up, and he was slapping her bare ass with a heavy wooden ruler.

"Ow!"

"Do you see the equation, Debbie?"

"Oh! Of course not," she said, gasping. "I can't see a thing without my glasses."

"You should have considered that before you started behaving so badly."

She gave a soft moan. "Yeah, I know... I guess you better hit me again."

He was more than happy to oblige.

Slap! Slap! Slap! Slap!

"You need to do what I tell you!" he said, glancing again at the blackboard. "And you need to tell me about...covalent bonds."

She felt her ass tingle as the warmth of her reddening skin spread to better places.

"It involves...the sharing of electrons," she said.

"And what good is that?"

Slap! Slap! Slap!

"It leads to more stable atomic configurations!"

"Yes, and what else?"

Slap! Slap! Slap!

She yelped. "I don't know what else! I ended up studying English."

Was this really one of her fantasies, to be abused by a science teacher in a sci-fi setting? Actually, it was. He hit her several more times while she hoped he had his telescope handy. She hoped he'd brought the big one.

He started hitting her hard and fast—raining blows down upon her bare skin. "Bad girl!" he said. "You're a bad girl who needs to keep her bonds where they belong!"

"Ow! Ow! Oh!" she said. "Oooooooow!"

The spanking went on and on and on. Soon enough, she was squirming and shouting and kicking her legs—but he was relentless. And he was excited.

Finally, the blows stopped, and Debbie took a deep breath.

"Are you all right, Debbie? Are you learning anything? You may stand now."

She stood up and wiped away a few tears. He smiled and gave her a warm hug, followed by a soft kiss. They stared into each other's eyes for a moment—and then lunged into another kiss, and this time it was sloppy and wet and frantic, with their lips locking tight, and their teeth banging together, and their tongues thrashing around. He pushed her down onto the desk, flat on her back, with her head tilted over the edge, her legs in the air, and her mini-dress up around her waist. He leered a bit and started doing the things he did so well. Holy crap, he sure had a tool that made her cross-eyed—and she sure was ready to feel it. He pushed it into her so deep she could almost feel it in her throat. And then he was banging away. *Oh, yeah! Oh yeah!* But when he tried to flip her over and bend her across the desk, she resisted—and he smiled, and kept her on her back, and kept her moaning like she was being murdered. Then she happened to notice a few more things scribbled on the blackboard.

She caught her breath. He saw where she was looking, and he grinned.

"Read it to me!" he said. "Read it now…or I'll give you no more!"

She squealed, and in a desperate frenzy groped for her glasses. Where the hell were her glasses? *Where the fuck were those sex-stopping motherfuckers?*

They were right there on the desktop. She shoved them onto her face and studied the board while Juan moved in and out, in and out, and with her fingers flying and her whole body vibrating, she read the words in a shaky voice.

"Covalency is greatest between atoms of similar electronegativity. Thus, covalent bonding does not necessarily require the two atoms be of the same elements, *only that they be of comparable electro negativity! Ahhhhh!*"

Her orgasm went off like a hydrogen bomb. It rattled every electron in her epidermis and curled her toes into atomic corkscrews—and after her final convulsion she looked into Juan's fiery face and then dropped to her knees, where she crammed that submarine-sized salami into her open mouth.

"Mmmf! Ah! Plah!"

He let out a load moan. She gagged a few times, but held herself steady. When his spasms finally subsided, she leaned back and sighed. She'd always been a decent student, though she'd never learned quite as much about herself as she'd learned today. Apparently, all she'd ever wanted was to suck off the teacher.

Her mouth hung open as she stared at him with wide eyes.

"God, that was disgusting," she said.

"Yes, I suppose. But have you learned your lesson?"

"Oh, yeah. I'll try to do better from now on. Wait—was I trying to do better? I forget what this was all about."

"So do I," he said with a grin. "But I'll try to do better, too."

"If you do any better, I'm going to have a stroke."

He laughed and bent his head down to kiss her on the lips.

It felt good. She kissed him back and wanted to keep doing it—but then she heard the laughter from a place near the ceiling.

Carl the demon was back.

"Ho-ho!" he said in his deep, wavy voice. "That was incredible! Maybe next time I'll have you try a tastier subject, like baking. I'd like to see you do it while you're reading a recipe for chocolate chip cookies."

Juan scoffed. "Don't be ridiculous, demon. We have no interest in your cookie dough."

"Ha, speak for yourself," Debbie murmured. "I do love a good chocolate chip."

Carl roared with more laughter. "Of course you do! I'll put it on the 'sex list.' But there's no rush. It looks like I'll be seeing you both for a while. I just wanted to congratulate you on a great show. See you later."

"Just a second," Debbie blurted, glancing at Juan. "I was wondering if you can tell us…a little more about the Goddess of Love."

Juan rolled his eyes. "Very clever, Debbie," he whispered from the side of his mouth. "Just come right out and ask him, yes?"

"That's what I did last time," she whispered back in a fierce tone.

"I can hear every word you're saying," Carl said.

"Oh," Debbie said. "I guess…we'll try to be quieter next time."

"You don't need to be so quiet," Carl said. "The Goddess of Love is named after a fruit. So there's a clue."

"Thanks," Debbie said. "So why are you telling us this?"

"I have my reasons. Besides, you'll never get free anyway, and I hate that stupid witch even more than I love watching you get banged through a blackboard. I'll see you soon."

And with one final laugh, Carl was gone.

Debbie turned to Juan. "I guess we got some information there."

"Yes, we did," he said. Then he looked away. "I guess you can go back to your man."

"Why? I'll only end up back with you."

"Only if you start taking off your clothes."

"Oh, and is there some reason I shouldn't?"

"No, go right ahead," he said with a smile. "Either way, you'll end up with me."

There was a long silence as Debbie considered what Juan had said. She guessed he was considering it, too. Then everything changed again.

24: Home Again

There was no flash of light or cosmic gong. She was just back on the sofa with Mike, staring up at his chiseled face and NY Yankees baseball cap. She still had two erect nipples, but now she was in her black terrycloth robe, and he was looking into her eyes with concern.

"Debbie, what's the matter?"

"Mike, you're here."

She vaguely wondered if he'd been planning to keep the baseball cap on during sex. She also recalled riding home from *Ronnie's* with Cynthia, and how Cynthia had explained that she hadn't seen Debbie and Juan go anywhere. They'd just started groping each other at the table a bit before suddenly stopping and talking and then going their separate ways.

"Yeah, I'm here," Mike said. "But you seem out of it."

"Oh. Did I go somewhere?"

"What?"

"Did I go anywhere during the last forty minutes or so?"

"Of course not. I kissed you just now, and you started looking distracted."

"Did I black out or...disappear? Did I talk about subatomic particles?"

Mike grabbed her chin with two strong fingers and focused a searching gaze on her face.

"This is what I'm talking about, Deb—the evil spell."

"Mike, no, that's not it."

"Don't argue with me!" he said, jumping to his feet. "I know there's a wizard out there, and I know he just caused you to reject me. What you don't realize, Debbie, is that I work for the Confidential Ultra Force."

"You...what?"

"You heard me, Debbie," he said in a heavy tone, like concrete. "I've kept it a secret until now, but as a member of the C.U.F., I deal with this stuff every day—and now I'm guessing that someone is trying to get their revenge."

There was a time when Debbie would've been surprised to learn that the muscleman jock she'd met in a gym while she had not been exercising was actually a secret agent working in a supernatural world, but on this particular morning, after giving a mind-exploding blow job in an interstellar classroom due to a failed contract with a treacherous witch, she was not overly shocked. In fact, it all seemed painfully normal.

"Mike, I think we need to talk," she said, rubbing her now pounding head. "I don't know what you do all day, but I'm pretty sure none of this is about anyone's revenge."

He wasn't listening. No, he was opening his gym bag and pulling out a fish-shaped bottle opener and waving it around like a lightsaber.

"This is all my fault, Debbie, and I feel terrible about it—but I'm going to save you and set things right. And I'm going to start by pulling that demon's ass out of his freakin' hiding place." He clenched his free hand into a fist. "And then I'm going to break every bone in his body!"

He grinned, looking pleased with his Stone Age solution; Debbie stood up and went to find some aspirins.

"Mike, I don't think that's going to work. For one thing, the demon is just a head."

But he still wasn't listening. Instead, he was now holding up his bottle opener, and he was chanting:

"Spirits of the universe
Lend your ears and here my verse
Feelum, phylum, give your focus
Bring forth he who is a hocus"

Debbie said nothing, choosing instead to walk into the kitchen, grab the aspirin bottle, and then gulp down two pills. When she came back into the living room, she heard a sound like a soft breeze blowing, followed by a couple of sweet, chiming chords on a jazzy guitar—and then Juan was standing there.

What? Yes, there he was, dressed in a pair of purple boxer shorts and a cotton T-shirt. He also looked rather surprised, as did Debbie. Her jaw dropped. Holy crap, Mike really was some kind of wizard! And Juan looked pretty cute in purple.

"Ha!" Mike said, pointing at Juan. "So you're the bastard who put a spell on my girl."

His eyes raged and he lunged forward, obviously planning to turn Juan's face into fleshy pudding. Debbie started screaming.

"Mike! Stop! He's not the one!"

Juan bolted for the door, but Mike was fast and blocked the way. Juan swore and raced into the bedroom with Mike and Debbie close behind. Mike reached out and snagged the back of Juan's T-shirt. The cotton fabric ripped as Juan spun around and jabbed his thumbs into Mike's eyes.

"Ow!" Mike said.

Juan grinned, but then Mike's arm shot out and grabbed Juan by the throat and smashed him hard against the bedroom wall. Mike shoved his fuming face a few skin cells away from Juan's nose.

"You're a sneaky little wizard," Mike said through clenched teeth.

"I...am not...a wizard," Juan said through a few gagging sounds.

"And you're also the guy who's screwing my girlfriend."

"Ah, gag, gag, you might be right...about that."

Debbie felt lightheaded—but she leaped forward and hammered on Mike's back with her fists.

"Leave him alone, Mike! He didn't do anything! Not anything I didn't want! And what I do with Juan is none of your business!"

"I'm sorry, Deb!" Mike barked. "But this is bigger than you and me. I've got a job to protect this planet from wizards and witches, and I'm going to force this wizard to unlock his spell!"

He snarled and dropped Juan onto the floor. Juan was gagging and coughing. Mike aimed his bottle opener at Juan and chanted once again:

"Feelum, phylum, finocus
Breath of summer, scent of crocus
Unlock all, unlatch, unchain
Blow, let go, like summer rain!"

Debbie was kneeling beside Juan now. She noted Mike's silly words—but was Juan okay? Suddenly there was a crash like thunder and rain starting pouring down inside the room. *What the hell?* A deluge of water was cascading from a point just below the ceiling.

Juan stopped coughing and looked at Debbie. Debbie whipped her head around to stare at Mike.

Mike had a perplexed look uncurling across his face. Obviously, he'd been expecting a different result. He frowned as drops of water gushed and fell from the rim of his baseball cap.

"Hm," he said. "I guess that was the rain spell."

Debbie rolled her eyes. "Yeah, I guess. I mean it did end with the word 'rain,' right? Hey, is it raining in the other room? Oh, my god! Is all my stuff getting wet?"

She leaped up and raced into the living room where she discovered another downpour. She grabbed her laptop computer and shoved it into the drawer of her desk. After all, her unpublished novel was stored on that machine, and she needed it to write more unpublished novels.

Through the doorway, she saw Mike shake his head and look down at his bartending tool. "Let's try that one again," he said. He pointed the bottle opener up at the ceiling and shouted:

"Shalom, chrome dome
Sorry schlep
Undo the shoe
Reverse the step!"

There was another crash of thunder, and a flash of lightening, and the rain stopped. Also, Mike fell to the ground like a stricken tree.

Debbie shrieked and ran back into the bedroom, where she stared at Mike's unmoving body. She shrieked again—and then the room was silent, except for the sound of water dribbling from a lampshade, splattering down onto the night stand.

Juan seemed to be okay. He ran a few fingers through his hair to comb it a bit and then leaned down close to Mike's face.

"He's alive," Juan said. "I believe the flash of lightening has knocked him senseless, or should I say more senseless."

Once again, Debbie felt lightheaded; the room was really spinning now. This was terrible! Mike was injured, and it was all her fault. If she hadn't been such a ho-bag whore none of this would've happened. She covered her eyes with her hands.

Juan put his hand on her shoulder. "It's not your fault, Debbie, and I'm sure he'll be fine when he wakes up. Though I'm sure he'll be no smarter."

"He's not dumb, Juan. He was just concerned about me."

She felt a tug at her heart, because that was the thing about Mike. He really did seem to care. But what the hell was the "Confidential Ultra Force," not to mention all the witch doctor hocus-pocus? Obviously, there was more to this guy than she'd ever realized.

"Should I call a doctor?" Juan said. "Or should I call the police?"

She studied him for a second. He looked slick and slippery. Then she looked at Mike, who was starting to move his muscles like a groping ape, the poor guy.

She made a decision. "Juan, we need to go to New Orleans. We need to find the Goddess of Love."

For a long moment, Juan was silent. "Ah, yes," he finally said. "That's a wonderful idea, but we don't know her name, or where she is... We might need more clues from Carl."

"Yeah, I know."

"That's good. I'm ready for whatever he throws our way."

"Yeah, I'm sure you are. We can go as soon as Mike wakes up."

"What?"

"We can't just leave him like this. In fact, we should take him to the emergency room."

"But he tried to kill me! Besides, he's strong and will be fine. He has muscles like a gorilla. I suppose some girls like that kind of thing."

Debbie didn't miss the snide tone in Juan's voice, but she ignored it.

"I know, Juan, but I'm not leaving him here like this. Help me get him up."

Before Juan could reply, Mike's voice boomed through the air. "I don't need your help!" he said. Then he sneered from his prone position and rose to his feet.

"Mike, you're okay," Debbie said, and a wave of relief washed over her.

"I'm fine. And I'm ready for round two."

"Round two?"

"You heard me."

Juan immediately slid closer to the door, just as Mike grinned and started to rush toward him—but he couldn't, because his feet were stuck.

He couldn't lift them at all. He looked shocked—and then his face turned into a mask of fury. He howled and tugged at his feet, but they seemed to be cemented to the slippery wooden floor. His whole head was a shade of chili pepper red as he jabbed an index finger at Juan.

"What kind of spell have you put on me, wizard?"

Juan blinked, obviously surprised. "I did nothing, you fool." Then he smirked and crossed his arms. "But if you're lucky, you'll get free before some pigeons start roosting on your arms."

Mike continued yanking at his feet. No movement. He bent down fast and started untying his Nikes.

"Don't worry, Debbie!" he said. "I'll save you soon!"

Juan said, "Debbie, let's go."

Debbie restrained an urge to pull her hair out.

"Mike, stop!" she said. "I don't need any saving! There's more going on than you know."

He wasn't listening, and he was done untying the laces, and he was leaping out of the athletic shoes—except that he wasn't, because his feet were still stuck to the insides of the sneakers, which were still bonded to the floor.

With a roar he fell on his face.

"Oof!" he said.

Debbie tried to think. This conversation was going nowhere, and Mike would get free eventually. Besides, she could send someone over to look in on him.

"Mike, I'm sorry," she said.

She looked around quick and snatched the fish-shaped bottle opener from the floor. Then she turned to Juan and said, "Let's go."

25: Vinyl Will Set You Free

Cynthia raised her eyebrows as she checked her text messages.

Something was wrong. It was very unusual for Debbie to not immediately return text messages. Debbie was always nervous about who was texting her, and she would stop almost any non-orgasmic activity to see who was on the other end of the line.

Cynthia took a sip of Diet Coke as she parked her Ford Focus in front of the crusty brick apartment building where Debbie lived. She shook the can to make sure it was empty and then tossed it onto the floor of the passenger side, where there was still some good space down there—cool. No need to clean the car just yet. In fact, a messy car was something she and Debbie had in common. They had bonded many times over car clutter.

She turned off the screaming stereo—man, she loved that band, Girl Gorilla. Then she got out of the car and moved fast toward the building.

She considered Debbie's love life and shook her head. Juan was dashing, in a slick-as-an-eel kind of way, but was an eel really dashing? She could never go for such a slippery dude. Sure, he played the guitar—jazz, ugh—but he seemed like a character out of a corny romance novel. He seemed like the kind of guy Debbie might create in a sci-fi story who would ultimately be crushed by an avenging asteroid.

When she got to Debbie's door she paused. Debbie had told her to come by and they'd both go to work together, but then she hadn't answered her text messages. What if Juan had killed her? What if the mustachioed muchacho had only been after her bank account and had freaked out when he'd discovered it couldn't cover the cost of a single burnt burrito?

She rang the bell and got no response, so she rang it a few more times. When no one answered, she twisted the doorknob—and it opened.

She peeked inside. Okay, there was no blood and nothing that sounded like murder. Also, there was nothing that sounded like sex—but what the hell? The hardwood floors were slick and sloshy, and there was a rippling lake over by the kitchen, and every piece of battered old furniture looked soggy and soaked. Obviously, something kinky was going on, and it involved running amuck with a fire hose. She tiptoed into the apartment and quietly closed the door.

"Deb? Are you here? Deb?"

She heard a guy grunt and her heart jumped.

It was not a happy kind of grunt. No, it sounded like someone trapped under a toppled tractor. Then she heard someone say, "I'm gonna get you, wizard! I'm gonna chase you all the way to hell! Just wait until I get my feet out of these socks!"

She charged into the bedroom, and there was Mike.

His was huffing and puffing like a red-faced bulldog. He was trying to lift his feet, which seemed to be glued in place. He was grunting and cursing and bending over to claw at the immobile shapes that were stuck inside his socks that were stuck inside his sneakers that were stuck to the unyielding floor.

Damn, he had huge arms. Wow.

"Hi, Mike," she said, keeping her voice steady. "Is there something I can help you with? Are you angry at your running shoes?"

Mike stopped trying to pry his foot out of his sneakers and looked up.

"Cynthia! Hey, it's good to see you. An evil wizard ran off with Debbie."

"Oh. And did he also glue you to the floor?"

"No. I did that myself."

"Ah."

He stood up straight, crossed his arms and puffed out his chest, seemingly determined to appear in control of the situation.

"Debbie's under the spell of a wizard, Cynthia. He's a scrawny little bastard, and he's got her thinking she's in love with him. I didn't know it at first, but then I used some magic and discovered the truth."

"I see. And was this the same magic you used to get the floor all wet?"

"No. I just messed up with the magic bottle opener. But Debbie and the wizard took that with them."

"Uh-huh," she said, running her fingers through her hair, trying to primp it a bit. "Debbie went to see a witch, Mike. She wanted to… improve her relationship with you, but then she met Juan on the way home, and that's the story. So there's no wizard."

Mike's face went blank as he absorbed the information—and then his eyes lit up.

"Of course!" he said. "No wonder my magic was all screwed up. I've been thinking it was a wizard, but really it was a witch. And I'll bet that matters! Where is Debbie right now?"

"I was going to ask you that."

"Ha! I told you, she ran off with that guy and left me here. As long as she's under the witch's spell she's in serious danger." Then he took off his baseball cap and shook it a bit, sending drops of water flying before jamming it back down on his head like it was the last game of the World Series, and the bases were loaded, and he was heading up to the plate.

"I can use magic to track her down," he said.

"Hm, yeah. Or maybe I could just call her."

"I suppose that might work, too."

Cynthia rummaged in her purse for her phone while Mike kept pulling at his legs and yanking at his feet. She had to admit, he looked pretty damn sexy when he was wet, with his T-shirt clinging to his rippling chest, and his running shorts clinging to his solid-looking butt. She gave him another quick glance and shook her head. He was all set to ride into hell on a flaming horse or whatever to rescue Debbie—really, the girl had no clue what she was missing.

As Cynthia pressed the call button, she wondered about all Mike's talk concerning magic. She'd always thought he was some kind of investigator, but apparently he was a mystical rainmaker. Either way, it seemed interesting—and either way, he was in love with Debbie. Sigh.

"Deb?"

"Hey," Debbie said. "Where are you?"

She sounded nervous.

"I'm standing in your bedroom with Mike."

"Oh, good. Is he still stuck?"

"Apparently. He's also a little wet, but other than that he seems fine."

Mike snatched the phone from her hand.

"Debbie, I know about the witch!"

"Do you? I'm sorry about the way things went. It's all my fault! Please don't hate me."

"You're under a spell, Debbie, and I can set you free."

"I appreciate your concern, but I don't think so. We'll talk when I get back."

"I'm coming after you, Debbie!"

"No, you're not."

"I'll be there soon!"

"Please, don't do that."

"No witch can stop me!"

Cynthia snatched the phone back from him.

"Debbie, where are you going?" she said. "Does this mean you won't be at work later?"

"No, I guess not. Just tell everyone...I had a liver transplant, and I'll be back in a few days."

"I'm not telling anyone that. Debbie—"

"I have to go, Cynthia."

"Wait a second. Where are you going?"

"It's a bit of a ride. I'll talk to you when it's over."

"Debbie? Hello?"

Cynthia shook her head. "She hung up on me. She never does that."

"She's under a spell," Mike said. "The witch is forcing her to love that sleazy shyster and I have to rescue her."

"Mike, I don't think that's such a great idea."

"I'm going after them."

"I think that's a bad plan."

"And you're coming with me."

"What?"

Now here was an interesting concept. Cynthia suddenly felt a little warm. She needed to resist her first inclination here. She needed to keep her heart from fluttering. She needed to keep her nipples from getting stiff.

"Sure, I'll come," she said.

Damn, had she just said that?

"Cool!" Mike said with a grin. "We'll have to swing by my place and pick up a few things. Of course, we'll go to your place first."

Cynthia found herself squirming a little. "How are you going to find them?"

"I told you, I can track them with magic. It's something I've been working on."

"Okay, but what about your feet? I'm just saying it might be hard to follow them, you know, unless they're coming here."

He started to speak and then stopped. A look crept into his eyes, like someone who'd just been slapped a few times across the face with a wet fish.

"Cynthia, can you please go into the other room and find my drum sticks?"

Sure, she could do that. Why not? She figured he needed something to do to pass the time, although hauling a drum kit up here would take a little effort. She returned in a few seconds and handed him the heavy pair of sticks.

"Thanks," he said with a determined smirk. Then he raised the drum sticks high and shouted:

"Rock and blues and lots of booze! Hippie hair and thunder beat—motherfucker move my feet!"

There was a flash of light and a sound like someone banging on a huge bass drum.

Mike lifted his feet off the floor.

Cynthia smiled. "Wow! Nice. That was easy enough," she said.

She decided to ignore the pile of vinyl Led Zeppelin albums that had appeared in the corner.

26: On The Road

Debbie watched the street with jumpy eyes as she navigated her grimy Honda through the honking mess of cars around the train station in New Brunswick. Right beside her sat Juan, grinning as usual. He was wearing one of Debbie's bathrobes over his boxer shorts. It was a sunny summer day, so he also had on a pair of dirt-dark sunglasses he'd found in the glove compartment. He more or less looked like a pervert waiting to expose himself. But at least he was a handsome pervert.

"I'd be happy to pay for your plane ticket to New Orleans," he said. "But unfortunately, I'm low on funds."

"That's okay, Juan. There's no way I'm flying. It makes me too nervous."

She had only flown once, when she'd been nine years old and her parents had taken the whole family to Disney World. Her memory of the trip mostly involved puking on an airplane and then again on Mickey's pontoon-sized galoshes. What could she say? Big plastic characters freaked her out.

"Really?" he said. "So we'll have to drive, and that's wonderful! I've never driven across the country."

Debbie stared straight ahead while chewing on a fingernail.

"Are you hungry?" he said. "We can stop and get some food."

She slapped both hands back down on the wheel and felt her face getting red.

"Sometimes I bite my nails."

"Don't worry, Debbie. This will be a great adventure."

She laughed, but knew it sounded forced. "I'll probably be down to my knuckles by the time we get back." Then she quickly added, "When we're done at your place, we need to go back and get a few things at my place. There's some stuff I forgot."

"That's a bad plan. There is a man stuck to the floor there."

Crap, that was true. She'd left her apartment wearing the first thing she'd thrown on, which of course had been a casual black dress and her white sneakers. She'd also grabbed her laptop and charger out of instinct because she couldn't leave her novel at home, as well as her birth control pills and a safety razor—because pregnancy and hairy legs were two things she wanted to avoid.

Then again, she had most of what she needed. Being a naturally nervous girl, the cargo in her purse was heavily influenced by panic. She carried just about everything except a firearm, and that was mainly because pepper spray was lighter and guns made her very nervous.

Juan directed her to his apartment on Suydam Street, across from a small red-and-white Mexican restaurant that looked like a tin shack with a couple of windows punched into the walls. She parked in front of the multi-family house while noting the clothesline in the backyard, hanging heavy with children's shirts, pants, and underwear. One of the downstairs windows was filled with a Mexican flag.

Juan turned to her with his typical smile. "I'll only be a minute, but please come in."

She tried to hide her curiosity. The fact that the outside looked less than extravagant didn't bother her. She knew Juan was a musician, and was therefore drawn to a higher calling than money. Money had never been important to her, either, except that she needed it to buy popcorn and electricity.

She followed him up a set of creaky wooden steps and onto a gray front porch pockmarked with peeling paint. Juan opened a trashy screen door and they started climbing a stairway up to the third floor.

"I plan to move soon," he said.

"It's not that bad."

"It's not so great, either. But I had my reasons for coming here."

Debbie felt a warm blip of satisfaction. Juan seemed to be apologizing for his home, like he was trying to tell her he had "potential." So maybe he did care what she thought of him.

They stepped into a tiny kitchen. Debbie glanced around, and while the place was cramped, it wasn't that terrible. Everything was old—the porcelain sink, the white painted cabinets, the iron-looking faucets, and the yellow linoleum floor. But it wasn't dirty, and that was good. Debbie could live with old stuff and messy stuff, but not with blatant filth.

She followed Juan into a homey little living room that held a well-worn sofa covered with a colorful quilt, and an ancient television topped with a pair of rabbit ears. There was aluminum foil wrapped around one "ear" of the antenna, waving like the flag of a Third World country. Meanwhile, there was also an actual flag hanging on the wall, the flag of Argentina, right next to a poster of a soccer team. In the corner of the room, by a window overlooking the street, sat a battered old desk made from real wood. It looked like a cozy place to sit and write.

Resting on the sofa, in what looked like the top spot in the room, was Juan's Epiphone Casino electric guitar. It was plugged into a Fender amp sitting nearby.

"I must take my guitar," Juan said. "My guitar is my soul, and I can't travel without it."

"Your soul looks pretty contented. I don't think it wants to move."

"Ah, my soul is not as contented as it might appear," Juan said. "Besides, I'm not bringing that guitar." He walked into the adjacent bedroom and returned holding a guitar case. "I'm bringing this one."

"So you have more than one soul. Why does that not surprise me?"

"I only have one, and it occupies whatever instrument I'm playing." He put the guitar case down near the front door and headed back into the bedroom.

Debbie laughed and followed him.

The space wasn't too tight, despite the king-size bed. The sheets were rumpled and unmade, but that was okay. At least there wasn't a girl under them. Of course, Juan probably preferred not to bring girls to his apartment, since it would be harder to slither away from the scene afterwards.

On the walls were a few abstract paintings. Debbie wasn't an art critic, but these grabbed her attention. They were filled with spicy reds and yellows and cool-as-an-ice-cube shades of blue. They all seemed to have been created by the same artist.

"Did you make these?"

"No. They were made by my mother."

"Wow. They're really nice."

"Yes, she was a talented lady," he said while putting on a pair of black Levis and a summery shirt. He grabbed a few more shirts from a nearby closet and shoved them into a ratty canvas bag. "She died three years ago."

"Oh, I'm sorry to hear that." And she really was sorry. "She must have been young."

Juan kept smiling, but now there was sadness underneath the smile, like something sour under the bright skin of a mango.

"She was much too young to die. She was a good woman who deserved better."

"That's terrible. Was she sick?"

Juan paused, and then stuffed a few pairs of socks into the bag with the shirts. "It was a suicide," he finally said. "Not officially—not according to the coroner. No, he claimed it was from 'natural causes.' But I know she died from sadness and worry. I don't often talk about it."

"Oh, okay," Debbie said quickly. "I was just curious."

"It's all right. I don't mind telling you. And where is your mother?"

"She's at work, I guess."

"Call her and tell her you love her."

"Sure, maybe I'll do that. I mean if I start feeling that way."

He flashed her a warm grin. "You should love your mother, even if she's unworthy."

"I like her sometimes."

"I suppose that's better than nothing. We need to get on the road. Let's go."

She decided not to ask why Juan's mother had been so miserable. Maybe he'd tell her another time, but she felt her heart going out to him. After all, her own mother had a lot of problems, and she seemed to be trying to cure them with alcohol, therapy, medication, and cosmetic surgery. Sadly enough, the alcohol seemed to be the thing that helped her the most.

They switched to Juan's car because he claimed it had more legroom, and Debbie said fine. He turned the radio to a Spanish pop station as the faded black Toyota headed down Route 18 in East Brunswick. As they pulled onto the New Jersey Turnpike, Debbie looked at the traffic and fidgeted in her seat.

Juan glanced at her and laughed. "Are you nervous? Don't be. It's a beautiful day for a ride. It's better than being at work, right?"

Debbie's jaw dropped. Holy crap! She was supposed to be at work in an hour, slinging burgers and fries in the general direction of difficult people, and she hadn't even called to say she wasn't coming.

She began fumbling in her purse, looking for her phone.

"Is something wrong?" Juan said.

"Yeah, I'm supposed to be at work. I better call in and get fired."

In a few seconds she was talking to George, who was the owner.

"George, this is Debbie. I can't come in today. I have an emergency."

There was a pause, during which Debbie envisioned George either rolling his eyes or reaching for a donut.

"Debbie, you called out the other night, and Cynthia already called out today. Do you think I'm stupid?"

"What? Why did Cynthia call out?"

"Why don't you tell me?"

"George, I don't know why Cynthia called out."

"Right. So what's the big emergency?"

Damn. She'd been so busy panicking she hadn't bothered to come up with a reasonable excuse. Oh, the hell with it.

"I need to go to New Orleans and find a Goddess of Love who can rescue me from Sex Hell."

There was a second of silence.

"Well, why didn't you say so?" he said with a mouth full of something, probably glazed cruller. "I thought you were going to make up some kinda dumb story. So I guess you won't be in tomorrow, right?"

"I won't be in for at least a few days."

"And what am I supposed to do?"

Debbie sighed. George wasn't a bad guy, but her whole life didn't revolve around his pickles and pastry.

"I'm sorry, George, but I can't do it."

"Is that so? Listen, Debbie, I like you—but if you don't get your ass in here tomorrow, you're fired. You can tell Cynthia the same thing."

Debbie shook her head and hung up the phone. Why were bosses always so unsympathetic? If she hadn't been working in George's stupid diner, she never would've met the witch who cast the spell in the first place. So it was really all his fault, ha.

So the job was gone. She didn't care—after all, she was a writer, not a waitress. Maybe she could get some quality writing time out of this. Maybe she could even use this experience as the basis for a ludicrous novel.

"Ah, so you're fired?" Juan said. "Too bad. Maybe we can form a group. Can you sing?"

"Like a cat being strangled."

Juan laughed. Then he turned off the radio and fiddled with the CD player, and it started playing an upbeat Latin tune featuring congas and horns. It wasn't the kind of thing Debbie usually listened to, but it had a cool vibe. It was sexy, too—go figure.

They rode along in silence for a few miles, until he glanced over at her again.

"Debbie, what are you thinking about?"

"Nothing. Maybe a story I might write."

"Yes, you are a writer, and we're in the middle of an interesting story. When you write it all down, please don't change my name."

She looked away from him, out the window. "I won't change a thing, unless we have a tragic ending. I don't like tragic endings."

"We have that in common. Will it be a love story?"

"All my stories are love stories, Juan." She squirmed a bit in her seat. "Underneath the ridiculous humor and sci-fi and fantasy, there's always a love story. I guess I'm just that way."

"And what is happening in the romantic novel you're writing?"

Debbie scrunched up her face, like she was trying hard to think.

"Right now, Suzy Spitfire and this guy she just met, Tolio, are flying in her spaceship, the Red Bird. They're in trouble, because they were double-crossed by a mystical guru named Shelba, and the space patrol is constantly attacking them with red hot energy bolts. But through all the stress and adventure, they're together. So the question is, will Suzy and Tolio fall in love along the way?"

He gave a short laugh. "You're a romantic person, Debbie."

She shrugged. "I believe in love." She was about to add, "even if I never seem to find it"—but she bit her tongue. No need to play the pity card.

Juan steered his Toyota into the fast lane and stomped on the gas.

"It's nice to be romantic," he said.

"Oh, really? You mean in a 'no strings' kind of way?"

"Ah… I never said 'no strings' was a wonderful thing. I've just discovered it's who I was born to be, and a leopard can't change his spots. But he can regret them."

Debbie thought about her parents again. Had they ever regretted anything? Probably. But had they kept on doing those things? Of course.

"I think it's good to try and change behavior you might regret," Debbie said.

"Yes, it's good, but not so easy, and it might lead to tragic consequences."

"I'm not writing a tragedy, Juan. Just so you know."

He laughed again. "Very good, Debbie. There will be no tragic ending."

"Is that a promise?"

He took his gaze off the road and stared into her eyes.

"Debbie, that's a promise."

She took a deep breath and bit one of her fingernails.

27: Velva's Instant Assassins

Velva stalked into her kitchen and swept a pair of shoes from the kitchen table. They thudded onto the floor, right near a stack of dusty magazines and a rusty old umbrella stand. Funny, she didn't remember that stand being there yesterday, but then again it didn't matter. All that mattered was the flow of sex energy that was making her young and beautiful.

She pulled a makeup mirror from the pocket of her raggedy robe and stared at her reflection in the morning light. It was the fifth time today she'd studied her face, and damned if it didn't look better. There were definitely less wrinkles creeping across her skin, and her crackly white hair was now showing a few lightening streaks of blond. So things were looking up—except for one problem.

She shoved the mirror back into her pocket and grabbed a glass dish from the wreckage scattered across the counter. She sat at the table and rubbed the dish with the sleeve of her robe, trying to remove some smudges and maybe a few specks of encrusted food. Finally, she held the dish at arm's length and frowned.

She swore a few times and spoke to her cat in a gravelly voice.

"See, Bart, this is what happens when you don't have a crystal ball. I hope I ate something good off of this plate. Hm, maybe a little macaroni and cheese."

The cat barely looked at her. After all, dinner wasn't coming for quite a few hours.

Velva coughed a couple of times, blew some more smoke, and then pulled out her talisman. She clenched the seashell in her left fist while she waved her right hand over the dish.

"Come on, come on," she muttered. "Goddamn it, show me what's going on with my little nymphomaniacs."

There was a low humming noise, and the dish glowed like it was being splashed with moonlight, and then it showed the image of a well-worn Toyota Corolla speeding along the NJ Turnpike. Velva's eyebrows shot up as she saw Debbie and Juan sitting inside the car. She'd sensed her two victims were travelling, and she guessed the reason was not good. She waved her hand, trying to turn up the volume and hear their conversation, but the sound wasn't coming through. It was a weak spell, but her power was low since being kicked out of the Union—and besides, she didn't want to spend too much of her new sex magic on anything other than making herself young and gorgeous.

"Shit," she said and crushed out her cigarette in the lid of an old mayonnaise jar. She kept waving her hands and cursing a bit, but she mostly heard garbled noise, like a radio that wouldn't tune to a station. Finally, she started picking up bits of conversation, but none of it was too revealing. Something about Debbie losing her job, and maybe Juan missing a gig, and a few words about a girl named Suzy Spitfire.

Velva sighed and lit up another cigarette. She was about to stop wasting precious magic on her spy spell when Debbie's voice jumped out of oblivion and filled the room loud and clear.

"I hope we find this goddess quick," Debbie said. "I can't afford to hang around New Orleans too long. Not unless I get a job there."

Then there was a loud pop and the sound disappeared—but Velva had heard enough.

"Son of a bitch," she said. *"Son of a bitch, I don't believe it!"*

She sat for a second with her mouth hanging open. Then she raised the dish high and resisted an urge to shatter it before changing her mind and smashing it down on the tabletop. What the hell, the kitchen was already a mess and it felt good to destroy something.

The cat in the corner leaped up and bolted from the room.

Velva watched the frightened feline run and gave a sarcastic laugh. "Sorry to wake you up, Bart, but my life has once again taken a dive into the shit pile."

She stood up and started pacing around the room.

"*Where are you, Carl?*" she said. "Don't try and hide from me! I know you're in here. Don't make me leave piles of bananas and porno magazines around the house."

She heard a rustling noise and then saw a miniature red monkey sitting on the kitchen counter, right next to an old drink mixer and a couple of broken power tools.

The monkey grinned and spoke in a deep, wavy voice.

"Did you call me, Velva? Do you have some sweet words of praise for my monkey-like magnificence?"

Velva curled her lip into a dramatic sneer. "Did you tell those two idiots how to get out of Sex Hell?"

The monkey laughed. "I might have let a little information slip. Sorry."

"*Sorry?* You are such a moron! This might be a game to you, but I need that *sensualla*—and we had a deal, remember? I get the magic and you get to have fun watching. But now you're trying to help them break my spell."

The monkey grinned again. "Velva, you worry too much. So I tossed them a bone—big deal. I also got them together in a car travelling across the country. Sex in a car is classic! By the time that car gets to New Orleans you'll look like a supermodel. You should be down on your knees, thanking me. But don't worry, I'll accept your apology."

Velva blew some smoke and narrowed her eyes. She crinkled her forehead and considered the creature's smug words.

"Sneaky," she finally said. "Okay, I like some of the idea. Getting them together in the car is definitely nice—but you're still a fucking imbecile! I mean why did you have to give them the right destination?

Couldn't you have given them the wrong city or something?"

"I told you, it was a mistake. Kind of like when you decided to stop brushing your teeth."

"You are such an asshole! Why couldn't you keep your big mouth shut?"

"What's the problem? It's a great plan. Besides, if something goes wrong, you can always find another pair of suckers."

"Yeah, but you know I can only keep one pair at a time under the spell, and I don't want to waste time looking for anyone else. Besides, these two are *really good*. I wonder if you're trying to mess this up on purpose."

"Why would I want to mess up anything? After all, it's not just about watching; I'm getting some of the sex magic, too. I'm having fun, and they'll never get out. Maybe I'll keep giving them information and then toss them a few curves at the last second. Maybe it's all part of my plan."

Velva eyed the monkey and took another drag on her Virginia Slim. "Is that your plan, Carl? Or are you lying to me like you always do?"

The monkey shrugged. "What's the difference? Either way it's what I'm going to do, so you should be happy. You should get down on the ground and kiss my filthy paws, you dried up bitch-turd."

Velva felt every cell in her body burning with hatred. "We both know that isn't going to happen."

"Maybe not today. But one of these days, heh-heh."

And then the monkey was gone.

Velva swore and exhaled a cloud of smoke clear into the living room. Then she opened a cabinet and pulled out a cheap pint of blackberry brandy. She unscrewed the top and took a big swig.

She needed to keep cool. She was probably worrying about nothing. Carl couldn't really free them from Sex Hell, and even if they learned the mechanics of it, they'd still have to overcome some serious hurdles to escape. Still, she didn't like the fact that Carl was fucking around.

She took a few more swigs from the bottle and wiped her mouth on the back of her hand.

Carl couldn't be trusted. Sure, it was in his best interest to keep

Juan and Debbie enslaved—but his interest in the affair was thin, and he was a loose cannon, like a nuclear bomb bouncing around in a kiddie arcade. Plus, he might be up to something, but what?

She sucked down some more brandy, draining almost the entire pint. As she felt the sweet liquid burning her throat, she realized she'd have to take a few steps to keep things going her way, at least until she regained her full power. Then she wouldn't need Carl, or any of those other witches, either.

She scowled. Her magic was limited, and the only way she could get more was for Juan and Debbie to keep going at it—and she hated to waste any of that magic on anything other than the rejuvenation of her gorgeous face. After all, she still had a long, wrinkled road ahead of her.

She walked into her cramped bedroom, where the hodgepodge of debris matched the disaster in the kitchen. She jerked open the bottom drawer of an old wooden dresser and started rifling through the contents, tossing things onto the floor.

She tossed out a couple of pointy hats, and a tube of magic lipstick that forced anyone she kissed to pick up the tab for dinner, and a special bra that increased cup size but unfortunately lowered the intelligence of the wearer—an annoying side effect, but sometimes a little attention was worth a few brain cells. Finally, she said, "Ha!" and pulled out a small glass jar. The jar was filled with jellybean-sized gray blobs, and it was labeled in black magic marker with the words, "Seeds Of Strom."

She hesitated. This was a bad thing she was about to do, even for her, but it had been coming for some time. Sacrifices had to be made, preferably by someone else. She smiled and shook three of the blobs onto the lint-infested carpet.

"A woman's got to do what a woman's got to do, even if it's evil and her mom would not approve. This should be enough, heh-heh."

She shook her head. She really hated to waste her last bit of *sensualla* on this operation, but it was necessary to ensure more *sensualla*. Try to act like a Wall Street investor, she thought. Try to go a few steps beyond devious—because that's where the big payoff was usually waiting.

She ran into the kitchen and returned with a bottle of Beck's beer. She knocked the cap off by banging it on the edge of the gouged-up dresser and proceeded to pour a bit on top of each seed.

She cackled as she reached into her robe to grasp her talisman. It glowed warm in her hand—much hotter than it had been a week ago. Oh, this was good. When was the last time Juan and Debbie had been in Sex Hell? This resurgence of power was a beautiful thing. She grinned through her fence of yellow teeth and chanted a few magic words:

> *"Men so strong just like a tree*
> *Sons of Deutschland come to me"*

Within seconds, the seeds started to grow. Fuzzy gray shapes rose up among the blankets and sheets and shoddy furniture until they gradually came into focus and stood like three tall men. The men all looked identical—clean cut, blond, wearing matching three-piece navy suits and stylish dark glasses.

"Hello, Strom," Velva said.

"Hello," they all answered in unison. Then they looked at each other.

"Yeah, I made three of you," Velva said. "I just thought it might be cool to get myself a little army of Germans—what the hell, you guys almost took over the world a couple of times."

"Ya," said Strom Number One in a thick German accent. Then he whipped off his dark glasses and showed a pair of baby blue eyes. *"But ve need more than drei. And ve need tanks and planes—Panzers und Messerschmitts vould be vonderful."*

The other two Stroms grinned and nodded their heads, while Velva rolled her eyes. "I don't want you to take over the world," she said. "I only want you to assassinate a Goddess of Love living in New Orleans before a couple of people find her."

"Oh," said Strom Number Two. *"Vill be simple, ya? Do you have machine gun?"*

"No," Velva said. "I'll give you better weapons than that. Much sexier."

"Das ist good. Ve fly on plane?"

"No, the potential change in pressure might cause you to disintegrate. Besides, you don't have any identification and all that shit, so you'll have to drive."

Strom Number Three looked at the bottle of Beck's that was sitting on top of the dresser. He picked it up and smiled.

"Wo ist das Bier?" he said.

"In the kitchen, but I've got more in the basement," Velva replied. "I'll give you guys a case and then tell you about your target in New Orleans. And then you need to get going."

The three Stroms looked at each other and smiled. A case of beer sounded good.

28: An Alley

Debbie had to admit the highway looked relaxing, with its leafy wall of green stuff stretching into the distance. Certainly, Juan looked relaxed, tapping along on the steering wheel to the beat of some "strum and drum" guitar tune on the car stereo. But of course, she was not relaxed. She kept fidgeting in her seat, and biting her nails, and playing with her hair. She tried to remember a time when she'd been relaxed, and recalled a moment when she was three years old, before she'd been forced to play with kids who gave her anxiety, and then go to school where more kids gave her anxiety, and then eventually take notice of boys who gave her anxiety, and then go out into the working world where she was constantly filled with anxiety.

Her cell phone rang and she nearly jumped through the roof. She stared at the number and stopped breathing.

"It's Mike! I guess he got his feet unstuck."

"Maybe," Juan said. "Or maybe he groped his way to a phone."

"I never should've left him there."

"Ah, but Debbie, it prevented him from murdering me. Really, it was a fine idea."

Debbie fumbled with the touch screen. "Mike, how are you doing?"

"Hi, Deb. I'm doing great—thanks for asking. Where are you?"

"I'm not home, but I'll be back. I have to do something first."

"You're with the wizard, aren't you?"

"He's not a wizard. He's a musician."

"But you're with him, right?"

"Yeah, I'm with him. I told you, I need to take care of something."

"Where are you going?"

"Please don't keep calling me."

"We're tracking you with a pair of magic bongo drums."

"Okay, that's great. I'm glad you got your feet back."

There was a pause. "Debbie, if you're trying to say my screw-up with the 'foot spell' will cause these bongos to go down the drain, you're wrong. I've got the bongo thing down. Cynthia is holding them right now."

"What?" Debbie felt her cheek twitch. "Cynthia is with you?"

"Hi, Deb," she heard Cynthia say.

"What is she doing there?" Debbie said.

"I asked her to come—because she's your friend, Debbie, and she's concerned about you."

"Let me talk to her."

"Sure."

"Hi, Debbie," Cynthia said.

"What are you doing? And why are you helping him follow me?"

"He asked me to come. I'm barely helping."

"He just said you're tracking me with a pair of bongo drums."

"Yeah, that's true. Can you see how I'm barely helping?"

"I thought you were my friend."

"What are you talking about? *How can you even say that?* I am your friend—and even though I know Juan's not a wizard, I think you might be heading for trouble and I want to help, okay?"

"You want to help? Yeah, I'm sure you do."

"What's that supposed to mean?"

"You know what it means, Cynthia. I think you should turn around and stop 'helping' Mike, okay? I need to take care of something and everything will be fine."

No response. Debbie caught the annoyance in Cynthia's tone, but that was too bad—because she was annoyed, too.

"Cynthia, are you there?"

"Yeah, I'm here. We're on the speaker phone."

"You need to turn around."

"I'm not driving the car, Debbie."

"Fine. I'd appreciate it if you'd tell Mike to turn around, and then I guess what you do is your business."

"Right. And what do you think I'm going to do? Exactly what are you trying to say?"

"You know what I'm trying to say," Debbie whispered fiercely. "But I'm not going to say any more."

"If you've got something to say," Cynthia whispered back, "you should just say it and stop whispering."

"I'm not saying you're chasing after Mike!" Debbie shouted. *"Even though I know that you are!"*

There was a long pause. Debbie realized Mike had probably heard that in the speaker—crap. But she was fuming, and part of her didn't care who knew it.

"That's great, Deb," Cynthia said. "But it's not true. Anyway, why the hell would you care? *You're racing across America with some skuzzy sleaze ball!*"

"Yeah, I know! *But I'm trying to get free from that skuzzy sleaze ball!*"

Juan gave her a sour look. Damn. This just wasn't her day for diplomacy.

"Oh, are you getting free?" Cynthia said. "Or are you just having sex with him over and over again? *I hope you get free before you drop dead from exhaustion!*"

Debbie suspected there were two guys frowning in two different cars.

"Don't call me anymore, Cynthia, okay? And go home!"

In a panic, Debbie hung up the phone before Cynthia could respond with more damage. She never should've picked up that call! She looked over at Juan and saw he still wasn't smiling, which was unusual, since he was the kind of guy who could smile during a car accident. In fact, she'd seen him do it.

"Juan, I didn't mean to call you a sleaze ball," she said in a shaky voice. "I was just repeating what Cynthia said."

He shrugged. "That's all right, Debbie. If you think I'm sleazy, then you've enjoyed being with someone sleazy."

Now he looked smug and Debbie's blood boiled.

"Don't look so pleased with yourself, okay? I didn't enjoy it as much as you think."

"Oh, no? Please forgive my stupidity. I didn't realize your screams of ecstasy were a sign of torture."

"Maybe I was screaming with disgust."

"Yes, maybe. And maybe you are lying, and maybe you enjoyed it—and maybe you want to enjoy it again." He looked right into her eyes as he placed a hand on her thigh. "You're a nice girl, Debbie—a nice girl who likes being a little sleazy."

"You're such a jerk. I don't! There was a drug in the air."

"There was no drug in the air when I met you. There is no drug in the air now."

He moved his hand under her black dress and massaged her upper thigh.

She slapped his hand away. "You disgust me!"

He just laughed and flashed his Coca Cola eyes. Then she saw a rest stop up ahead—unbelievable. He was swinging the car off the road and into the parking area, near some trees but away from the other cars.

"You excite me," he said.

They screeched to a stop fifteen meters from a log cabin-style building with rest rooms and a few scattered metal trash barrels. There were also cars scattered around the parking lot with license plates from surrounding states.

He leaned over and kissed her hard, and she started to push him away—but then she didn't. Instead, she found herself kissing him back, and sucking his tongue, and feeling his fingers everywhere she wanted them.

"There are people around," she whispered.

"Debbie, they won't see a thing."

He was right. In a flash, everything changed.

**

They were in an alley.

Debbie caught her breath. Stay calm, she thought, but her heart was racing.

It was a dark alley, made of cracked concrete that was wet with the sheen of recent rain or maybe a broken sewer pipe. Debbie was standing against a grungy brick wall splattered with colorful graffiti. There was only one way out of the alley, and it was at least thirty meters away—but through that cave-like opening she could see the fuzzy golden glow of streetlights and a stream of rushing traffic.

Juan was holding her in his arms, and he was dressed in a tuxedo. Not Debbie's favorite style for a guy, but she had to admit he looked sharp. He also felt good, pressed against her body with his arms around her back, caressing the skin above her sliver of a skirt.

Holy crap! She was dressed like a street hooker, in a leopard print skirt that hardly reached the bottom of her butt, along with a pair of five-inch pumps and a tube top that squeezed against her perky breasts and nail-hard nipples.

Wow, did she feel turned on. What kind of drug was floating around? She had to find an antidote. But not right now.

She took a deep breath. "It looks like we're in a slum."

"Yes," Juan said. "And it looks like you are its queen."

She tried to control her breathing as his fingers moved down her bottom.

"I don't know," she said. "This queen looks like she desperately needs an illegal narcotic."

"Debbie, you look wonderful."

"I look like a dripping wet slut," she murmured.

"I see, and it's fabulous."

He kissed her hard and she kissed him back.

"Juan, we're surrounded by garbage cans."

"Yes, and there's some space behind that one."

"Which one? The one filled with empty booze bottles and chicken bones?"

"No, the one next to the decaying mattress."

With a crashing sound, they collided with the chosen can and tumbled to the ground.

Luckily, Juan maneuvered her onto the folded mattress. Debbie splayed her legs wide and tried to ignore the disgusting smell of the curdled mattress cloth. This was so gross. This was positively putrid.

"Do you want to be fucked here in the trash?" he said.

"Oh, yeah," she said. "I need a good garbage fuck."

"You slut!"

"You pig!"

That was the end of the foreplay. Juan yanked at her hot pink thong and then tore it off completely. And then his pants were down, and he was sliding into her, and it felt so good.

She groaned and moaned. She reached down and stroked herself, faster and faster—she'd never had an orgasm so quickly. The second and third one didn't take long, either.

He grunted a bit, but he kept going.

He pushed her legs up so her ankles were near her ears, and then he lowered them again and spread them like a pair of wings, and then he tried to flip her over—but she resisted by pushing him down and rolling on top, and yeah it was more work for her, but what the hell, her thighs could use a good workout and this was so much better than that fucking gym membership she'd never used, and they looked into each other's eyes, and he was grinning and she was moaning, and then she leaned forward and gave her thighs a break because, damn, she wasn't an Olympic athlete, but she kept her butt and her body moving, and he kept giving her plenty of motivation.

She knew she'd be sore and tired later, and she knew it would be one of the highlights of her life. Then as she was rising and falling and moaning and wailing she saw a pair of rats.

They were in the corner of her eye, sniffing at a couple of dirty Chicken Mc Nuggets or maybe a few spent shotgun shells. Either way, the rodents were greasy and fat and Debbie just glanced at them and almost puked but then had another orgasm instead.

Finally, Juan gave a loud exclamation and he was done. He stared into Debbie's eyes as she fell forward onto his chest, with her hair hanging down in his face and her body heaving.

They stayed that way for a bit, quiet and still, and let the sound of their breathing mix with the sound of the rats rummaging through the garbage cans and the honks from the nearby traffic.

"I feel disgusting," Debbie said.

Juan smiled. "So you were saying. I think you've said it before."

She sighed and touched the side of his head.

"I feel good, too," she said. She didn't care if he knew it.

She watched his eyes light up, but it wasn't the smirk he'd shown in the car. No, it was a look of pride—and a look of happiness, because he'd made her happy. Now she really did feel good, and it wasn't just between her thighs. No, it was a warm feeling, like she'd just had a shot of good wine poured down her throat and splashed around her heart.

He started to kiss her, and she closed her eyes—and then a voice boomed out:

"Very nice! You two have earned yourselves a bath."

They both jerked their eyes upward, and there was the fiery red head of Carl floating above them.

Debbie and Juan both snorted with contempt.

"Did you enjoy yourself, demon?" Juan said.

Carl grinned. "You know, I kind of did, and I'm also thinking you two might not want to get free of Sex Hell—unless you really prefer a bed to that glorious mattress. Would you like to know what the last guy who slept on that mattress did to it?"

"No, not really," Debbie said through clenched teeth. "And I'd also appreciate a little privacy!"

The stupid demon had ruined a potentially great moment, and she was furious.

The demon just laughed.

Juan scowled up at him. Debbie dismounted and Juan stood up, extending his hand to help her. She tottered a bit and realized that during all the excitement she must have kicked off one shoe. She adjusted her glasses and looked around. It seemed that the shoe had landed in the garbage can with the rats. In fact, they were sniffing it. Fine, it was probably the cleanest thing in there. She decided to remove her other shoe and hope they got the hell out of here before the dirty ground soaked into her feet.

"We'll get free of this place," Juan said. "If we do this again, we'll do it on our own terms."

Carl laughed again. "Of course you will, but you'll probably dump Debbie and do it with someone who's got bigger tits."

"Not true!" Juan said. "I love all kinds of women, even the tiny ones."

Debbie frowned and turned toward him.

"Thanks. I'm glad you'll consider a 'tiny' woman like me."

"That's not what I meant," he said in a rush. "I meant that you are wonderful, even though your breasts are...not huge."

"*Even though?* So I have a defect?"

"No! That's also not what I meant. I meant they're not huge, but very perky, and...maybe I should stop talking."

"Yeah, you should," she said, looking away. Her face was getting very red, and her mind was flashing with past disasters. It was amazing how little it took to turn a wonderful blooming moment into something dead and destroyed.

"Debbie, I think you're beautiful."

"Sure, when you're naked and on top of me."

"That's not true! Do you see how the demon wants us to fight?"

"I thought he wants us to have sex."

"That's true. Demon, you're a fool at your own game."

Carl just grinned. "Am I? Do you really know my game? You'll be back."

And then he was gone.

In a blink, Debbie and Juan returned to the Pennsylvania rest stop.

29: Uncle Clem's Campfire Grill

Cynthia swore quietly to herself. Was there anything on this road besides trees? This is why she preferred to stay in Central Jersey, where she was never more than 100 yards from a place that sold beer and pretzels.

Of course, that wasn't the reason for her bad mood.

Mike turned down the old-school punk tunes blaring on the stereo and looked at her. No doubt he'd noticed how quiet she'd been ever since her fight with Debbie, which had been at least 30 miles ago.

"Are you still upset?" he said. "Don't be. Debbie's under the influence of witchcraft, and we're gonna help her. That wizard doesn't know the game is just starting—or let's say the gig is just starting—and we haven't even played two songs. No one at the bar is drunk yet! So stop worrying."

Cynthia squirmed a bit in her seat. The conversation with Debbie was on her mind, but it wasn't the witchcraft part that was getting replayed over and over in her seething brain. It was the part where it had been stated—in two loud, shouting voices—that there was an issue involving jealousy over Mike.

Mike hadn't said a word about it, but what was he going to say? It was an awkward situation, and Cynthia wasn't used to feeling awkward. Usually, she felt fine—and unlike a lot of people, she did it without prescription drugs.

"I'm okay," Cynthia said, trying to sound casual. "I just feel stupid about what Debbie was saying."

There, she'd said it, and now she felt better. Maybe it was a mistake, but it just wasn't her style to keep things hidden. That was Debbie's specialty, not hers.

Mike laughed. "Don't worry about it. Debbie knows you're her friend—and you know it, too. Like I keep saying, Debbie is under the influence of some bad magic."

"Right," Cynthia said. *Bad magic—from the wizard who isn't a wizard.*

She tried to recall times when she'd flirted with Mike. Was Debbie exaggerating? Of course she was; she couldn't help it if her breasts were huge and her butt jiggled a little. She hadn't done it on purpose.

"Debbie's just being paranoid," Mike said. "Of course I know you've never flirted with me."

Cynthia's jaw dropped as she tried to keep her head from exploding. *You dumb motherfucker, are you really saying you never noticed?*

"Right," she said again, forcing her face to smile.

"Debbie doesn't realize she's the perfect girl for me."

"That's true," Cynthia muttered. "You're both blind."

"What?"

"I said, 'You're two of a kind.' "

"Exactly—well, not exactly. But our differences complement each other."

"Yeah, I guess. Plus, you obviously love skinny women."

She instantly regretted the remark. It made her sound like a jealous fool who was fishing for compliments.

Mike shifted a bit in his seat. "I like a variety of women."

"Oh, really?" she said, hesitating. "What kind of variety?"

Now he pretended to be preoccupied with the gas gauge. Obviously, he sensed himself about to head down another uncomfortable road.

"I'm fine with girls who are curvy."

"Okay," Cynthia said, feeling better. "Curvy is cool." She sat up a little straighter, making her breasts a bit more prominent.

"But it's not just a physical thing," he continued. "It's a whole bunch of hard to define stuff."

"Yeah. I guess that's what attraction is."

And can you see the size of my curves, buddy?

Mike changed his expression to something more businesslike. "Cynthia, we need to get some gas, and how about some food? We can stop up ahead."

"That's a good idea," she said, relieved to be changing the subject—at least for now.

He swung the car off I-95 near Rossville, where there was a dusty stretch of highway filled with cheap motels, fast food places, and gas stations. There were lots of cars from different states in the parking lots, and lots of people waddling around, getting some exercise as they walked from their oversized cars to their supersized lunches. Mike pulled into a BP station and left the car. Cynthia watched him grab the handle of the pump with one of his bulging arms and then cursed to herself.

She had to get a grip and focus on why she was here. But come to think of it, she couldn't deny Mike was part of the reason she was here. So she needed to get a better grip.

She sighed and walked across the sun-splashed asphalt to the gas station rest room, where she discovered a bunch of long-legged insects and some rarely cleaned toilets. When she returned to the car, Mike was just getting back inside.

"Want to check out that place?" he said, pointing down the road to an overgrown log cabin. There was a billboard-style sign out front advertising "Uncle Clem's Campfire Grill: The Best Western Food East Of The Mississippi."

"Sure," Cynthia said. She'd eaten garbage before. It was usually good.

As they got back into the car, the magic bongos started playing. Cynthia raised her eyebrows. This was a wild, frantic kind of banging—not a beat, more like a beating.

"Mike, the drums are going into death metal overdrive. Do you think this is anything serious? Maybe we should toss the bongos and use a map."

Mike glanced at the drums and narrowed his eyes. The playing sounded like a downpour of rain on an old roof made from canvas. He parked the car in Uncle Clem's parking lot while the racket continued.

"That's strange," he said. "It's definitely trying to tell us something. I'm sure it's nothing to worry about."

"Okay. And how sure are you? Is Uncle Clem a serial killer or something?"

Mike shook his head. "No, this kind of playing wouldn't involve food. It would involve a different kind of danger, like a landslide or maybe an assassin."

"And you're not worried?"

"We aren't in an area where any big rocks are going to fall."

"Right. And the assassin thing?"

"Oh, that's true. I guess there could be an assassin around, but keep in mind I've only had beginners magic. It might not be an assassin. It might just be a warning about a stray animal, or maybe a burglar."

"I see. Well, I'm hungry. Let's burgle up some food."

She tossed the bongos aside and they headed into the restaurant. She noticed Mike hesitated and then grabbed the heavy pair of drumsticks that were stashed in the car, next to the seat on the driver's side. This guy sure did like his percussion.

Uncle Clem's Campfire Grill was about what Cynthia had expected. There was a log-wall interior, and waitresses in ten-dollar cowboy hats, and a salad bar piled high with imitation cheese and fake bacon bits—but the price was low and it smelled okay, and upon that concept whole empires were built. They each took a tray and waited on line until they reached "Cousin Bubba's Barbecue Pit" where Cynthia picked out some red hot chili and Mike grabbed a double bacon cheeseburger with French fries. Then they sat in a booth by the window, and Cynthia watched a blue Volkswagen come screaming into the parking lot and slam on its brakes right next to Mike's car.

She had a premonition that something bad was about to happen, and she really hoped it could wait until she finished her lunch. But no such luck.

Three guys in matching three-piece suits jumped out of the car and started looking inside the Corvette.

"Hey, Mike."

"I see them."

"They all look alike."

"Yeah. Maybe somebody around here is selling those suits real cheap."

"No, I mean their faces. They all look exactly alike."

Mike squinted a bit through the glass window. From this distance Cynthia knew it was hard to be sure, but the three guys did look like clones. They also seemed to have matching black staffs, each about two meters long, and they were pointing them at his Corvette.

"Holy shit!" he said. "We're under attack."

A few nearby people turned their heads, but everyone else went right on eating. Apparently, an attack wouldn't be noticed until the food was gone.

Outside, the three guys started shouting as Mike's car was engulfed in a tangerine ball of fire. Then they jumped up and down in celebration and came running toward the restaurant.

Mike's eyebrows shot up. "We've got to move, Cynthia."

"Yeah. I think you're right."

Mike leaped to his feet as the three attackers came crashing through the door.

They stood at the front of the room for a second, scanning the crowd. They seemed a bit confused, and kept glancing at something in the hands of the guy in the middle—until Mike shouted, "Are you looking for me? I'm over here, guys."

He raised the drumsticks high, and a white bolt of energy leaped from the tip of each before fusing into a single bolt that whizzed through the air.

Unfortunately, the bolt was way off target and hit a waitress carrying a tray full of soft drinks. She lit up like a firecracker and smashed backwards into a life-sized cardboard cutout of a cowboy. Glasses of Coca Cola and Sprite flew through the air and crashed to the ground, along with the waitress and her shoddy Stetson.

Shouts erupted from all around. The girl sat up fast and shook her head, and then a nearby kid handed her back her hat. With a dazed look, she put it on. Cynthia guessed that Uncle Clem was very strict about employees wearing proper attire.

"Holy shit!" Mike said with wide eyes. "That shot should've vaporized her."

"What?" Cynthia said. "You want to vaporize the employees?"

"No, of course not. I want to vaporize the demons, but I'm noticing that my bolts are a little weak."

Cynthia was about to point out the advantages of this problem, but then the three guys in black raised their staffs high and fired three bolts at Mike. The blue slashes of energy sizzled through the air.

Cynthia screamed, but Mike was quick. He ducked at just the right time, and the bolts exploded around him—shattering a window, burning a patch of log wall, and completely obliterating Cynthia's unfinished chili.

"Fuck!" she said. She hated when some crazy asshole blew up the chili.

Meanwhile, people were screaming and running for the exits while the three assassins were laughing and firing more magic bolts.

Mike ducked and dodged and then fired a few quick shots of his own. They all sailed wide of their intended targets, striking an old woman with a walker, an elderly man with a cane, and a girl with a seeing eye dog. They all lit up like bright bulbs for one quick second and then went down hard.

Cynthia frowned. Damn, couldn't he hit at least one person who looked deserving?

"Mike, you better stop using that thing."

"Why?"

"Because you're hitting all the wrong people!"

Five more energy bolts exploded around him, causing him to trip and hit the ground as his drum sticks clattered to the floor.

Cynthia's eyes flashed with fury as her brain switched off and her instincts took over. She grabbed the sticks, let out a battle cry, and charged the three attackers.

"Hiyaaaaa!"

The three guys were still laughing and gearing up for another strike—until they saw Cynthia coming. Her face was red, her mouth was open and foaming, and she was waving the sticks like a raging Samurai with a pair of *nunchuks*. Their eyes got wide.

"Vas ist das? Vas ist das?"

"Die Frau ist verruckt!"

Cynthia snarled. "Does that mean I'm sexy? Or just really pissed off?"

She whacked the first guy hard in the face with one stick—*poom!* Then she used a backhand to clobber the guy next to him—*wham!*, and an overhead chop from the other stick to deck guy number three.

What the hell, this was a good time for her first drum solo—punk rock style. She let loose with a flurry of strikes. The bad guys were yelping as she kept swinging. They weren't so tough! They were just a bunch of Deutsch-spouting douche bags. They were scrambling for the exit, slipping and falling and trying to avoid the blows, and then they were running for their car and piling inside and stomping on the gas and driving away fast.

Cynthia put down her weapons and took a few deep breaths. Wow, all this ass-kicking took a lot of effort. Maybe she should start going to the gym. But she wasn't going anywhere until she finished eating her lunch. Actually, she wasn't going anywhere for a while, since Mike's red car looked black and crispy.

She went back into the restaurant where she found Mike already on the phone making calls.

30: Sheath On Fire

Debbie banged her head back against the headrest in the front seat of Juan's Toyota. For the third time in the last minute, she looked over at him and frowned. He was asleep, and he was snoring.

Now this could be a real problem. Something would have to change because she didn't intend to sleep next to a roaring chainsaw every night.

She shook her head and swore quietly. Why was she thinking like this? She wasn't going to marry this guy. They'd never share an adorable dollhouse on a rolling green hillside, or a chic apartment above a silvery city, or some gingerbread castle in a sweet little suburban town. It wasn't going to happen. She was just going to have sex with him a few more times and probably enjoy it and then take her small yet perky breasts someplace else.

Then she glanced at him again—and now, for some reason, he did look better. Maybe because there'd been another nice moment between them, a moment when he'd seemed to really care. How much did breast implants cost, anyway? Mom would know.

Damn, damn, damn! She was doing it again and it had to stop. She wasn't some desperate girl searching for sacks of saline to impress this guy or any other guy, and why the hell was his snoring so loud? It was like being in a hazardous work zone.

Inside her head, she heard the voice of Suzy Spitfire.

"Debbie, just shoot the bastard."

"I'm not going to do that, Suzy."

"Too messy?"

"That's partly the reason. Also, I don't have a gun."

Suzy gave a snort. "I have lots of guns. I have a thousand crates of illegal Fear Focus pistols. Shelba wants to use them to make herself into some kind of all-powerful badass. Unfortunately, Captain Tadrock and his Space Patrol were tipped off about our cargo and now they've got us pinned down in this hell hole of a place... Also, I had a fight with Tolio, who was busy ogling some big-breasted bimbo—and now I'm not sure if I want him around."

"I know," Debbie muttered. "I know all about your troubles. I'll see you later, Suzy."

Debbie sat quietly for a second. Finally, she elbowed Juan hard in the ribs.

"Oof!" he said as his eyes jerked open. "What? What is it? Is something happening? Where am I?"

"You're in a rest stop in Maryland," she said while wiping off her glasses. "You just had sex with me in an alley, and I'm glad the situation isn't keeping you awake or anything."

Juan rubbed his bleary eyes. "Oh, yes, I must have dozed off. But it was wonderful, Debbie."

"Yeah, I'll remember those giant rats forever. Do you realize we didn't get one piece of information from Carl?"

"True, but we're still going to New Orleans. We'll do better with the demon next time."

"Next time? But I don't want to keep going into Sex Hell. I have a headache, and an upset stomach, and probably high blood pressure. I want to find the goddess and get this over with, and I just hope she lives near a hospital."

Juan laughed. "It's not my fault we didn't get information. You started arguing with me."

"What?" she said, raising her eyebrows. "I think you started it."

"I don't recall who started it, but it was you."

"You said my breasts were tiny, and then you made it sound like it was a sacrifice to be in my presence."

He crinkled his forehead, remembering. "Ah, yes," he said. "It was all my fault." Then he put his hand on top of hers and stared into her eyes. "I apologize. You're beautiful, Debbie. I love the way you look, and I swear to you—please, believe me—I think you're very attractive just the way you are."

He leaned toward her as he spoke, and she scanned his face for any trace of insincerity. But she saw none.

Say something smart, she thought. *Accept his apology!*

"Maybe we should get back on the road," she said. Because really, he was good at faking insincerity.

He smiled and put his hands on the steering wheel. "Yes, let's go. Would you like to hear some music?"

"Okay."

He started the engine and in a few seconds they were back on the road, riding fast on I-95 to the rippling sounds of a Spanish guitarist. Debbie stared at the frayed ends of her fingernails, suppressing an urge to bite them. The miles went by, and Debbie found herself fidgeting. Should she say something? What should she talk about? She knew she wouldn't decide until the words were coming out of her mouth.

"So, how long have you been playing the guitar, Juan?"

"Since I was very small," he said with a grin. "I couldn't even fit my fingers around the neck. My father played, and he left a guitar in the house after he was gone."

"Oh. Where did he go?"

"He went here and there, until my mother told him not to return."

"Women tend to dislike guys who keep disappearing."

"He would only leave for a few days at a time, but it was usually to see one of his girlfriends."

"Women tend to dislike that, too."

Juan chuckled a bit. "Yes, he did get himself into trouble." He was silent as a few stunning arpeggios cascaded from the stereo speakers, and then he said, "Don't get the wrong idea, Debbie. I find his life amusing, but I also find his life unfortunate. He caused so much pain for others."

Debbie looked down at her fingernails once again and wondered if Juan wanted to be different than his dad. Many parents consider it an insult when their kid wants to be different from them, Debbie thought. But really, it's okay. It doesn't always mean the kid hates Mommy or Daddy. Sometimes the kid just sees how to do things better.

Juan turned down the volume on the stereo. "Tell me about the first story you ever wrote."

She felt a spark of happiness; he was interested in her stories. Instantly, she had a flashback to a classroom filled with crayons and chaos. "It was called *The Biggest Blackberry*," she said. "I was in grammar school, and it was about all these blackberries on a bush who were talking, and there was one that kept bragging about how he was the biggest and the best. So then a few kids came by, and they noticed how huge and juicy he looked, and they ate him. So he was gone, but the small, quiet berries were still there."

Juan nodded. "You're a champion of the underdog."

"I suppose," she said with a shrug. "But no real writer champions the *overdogs*. It's the way we're built."

Juan turned his eyes back toward the road, but he also reached out his hand once again and placed it on top of hers. This time he squeezed her fingers a bit while she glanced at him sideways. Okay, her heart was fluttering. He started to say something—but then a voice came blasting through the stereo speakers, obliterating the soothing mélange of guitars and ripping a hole through the moment like a knife destroying a balloon.

It was the voice of Carl.

"Hey, hey!" he said. "What's happening here? And why is my voice stuck inside such a boring song?"

Juan and Debbie looked at each other with disgust.

"What do you want, demon?" Juan said. "If you don't like the song, you can go infect someone else's stereo."

Carl laughed. "I think I'll just stick it out for a while. I wanted you two to know that you're doing great so far. Maybe you should pull over and do it again."

"We just did it again," Debbie said. "Why don't you stop bothering us?"

"Oh, is that true? Sorry, time has no meaning to me. The clock is just a thing that ticks. But really, do it some more."

Debbie took a deep breath, trying to control her anxiety. Then she had a thought and flashed Juan a glance, a look that said *maybe we can use this moment to our advantage.* Juan acknowledged the look with a subtle nod of his head.

"Enjoy it while it lasts, Carl," Debbie said.

"I always enjoy it," the demon replied. "And I'll keep on enjoying it because it will last a while."

"Not too long. We know how to get free."

"You don't know how to get free. You don't know anything."

"But you told us, remember? You told us to go find the Goddess of Love. I forget, what was her name?"

"She's got blond hair," Carl said. "That's all I'm going to tell you. Also, she likes ice cream, but that's all you're going to get from me. Yeah, she likes to eat ice cream while she's sitting in her fancy apartment near the flower shop she owns in the French Quarter."

Debbie gave Juan a little smile.

"Anyway," Carl said, "you really need to start thinking about sex again. So I thought I'd stop by and start talking about it, and you'd both get really turned on."

Juan laughed while Debbie rolled her eyes. "I doubt that," she said.

"Oh, really?" Carl replied. "Don't you want to see Juan's big wiener? Don't you want to hump, hump, hump, till your daddy takes your T-bird away?"

Juan and Debbie just shook their heads.

"Why don't you leave us alone?" Debbie said. "Go polish your skull."

Carl made a low growling sound. "I haven't pulled out the big guns yet. I have a romance novel right here in front of me—a top seller, right here—and I'm going to read some of it, and then we'll see who gets hot and bothered."

Once again, Debbie rolled her big brown eyes. Few things turned her on less than romance novels. Really, Carl would be better off making popcorn—but with a sound like a tractor, he cleared his throat and started to read:

"Her hungry mouth consumed his chest, little white teeth nipping, plump lips sucking away, pointy tongue slathering with torture."

"It sounds like she's a cannibal," Juan said.

"Yeah," Debbie replied. "I'm picturing her chin-deep in a bloody chest cavity."

"And down in her loins," Carl boomed, *"it felt like her sheath was on fire!"*

Debbie threw back her head and roared. "Her *sheath*? What is that? Is she carrying a sword?"

"I believe the author is talking about something more sexual," Juan said.

"But what would she have in a sheath? Maybe a bottle of lubricant."

"I think that would be carried more easily in her purse."

"Yeah, that's true. But I usually keep it by the bed and hope I don't use too much, or too little—or spill it all over the place."

"You must pour it into your sheath, like fine wine."

"But I don't have a sheath. Maybe I can get one on the internet."

"You morons!" Carl shouted. *"He's talking about her vagina! Her fucking vagina!"*

"Oooooh," Debbie said, and she looked at Juan, who raised his eyebrows in a mock "who knew?" expression.

"Now that's different," she said. "When my vagina is on fire, it usually means I have a yeast infection."

Juan snickered a bit, but Carl was not so amused.

The demon growled. "I suppose this wasn't the best thing I could've done. But I will be back, and next time—"

Debbie reached out and turned off the stereo. Carl's voice instantly vanished.

Juan grinned. "We should have done that a few minutes ago. So we've learned a few more things."

"Right. The Goddess of Love has blond hair, and she owns a flower shop."

"Yes, that's interesting. I pictured her as a brunette."

"Really? Is that because you associate dark hair with purity?"

"No," he said with a laugh. "It's because I don't."

She considered his words, but said nothing. She bit a fingernail and looked out the window.

31: Velva In A Rage

Velva walked into her kitchen and gave a low whistle of appreciation. The room was less cluttered than it had been a few hours ago. The dilapidated table and piles of reeking junk on the counter had been replaced by a modern Formica kitchen set and a collection of synthesized stone canisters. The stained linoleum floor was now a gleaming layer of white tile—the low budget stuff, but it was clean and bright and on par with things purchased by the average mass consumer.

And her face! She stared into the pocket mirror for the tenth time in the last hour. Her wrinkles were fading. Her hair was less gray. Her ass was getting tight and her breasts were hanging high. Obviously, the magic from Sex Hell was working, and she should be in a fabulous mood. But she was furious.

She grabbed a dish and waved her hand over it. *Poof!* She immediately saw the faces of the three Stroms.

They were smiling. *"Hello, Commandant,"* Strom One said. *"Ve have engaged enemy but they escape. Ve vill soon have them, ya. Now ve drink beer."* He laughed and held up a bottle of Beck's.

Velva thought her eyes would pop out of her face.

"You imbeciles!" she shouted. "You fucking sauerkraut-stuffed pieces of shit! You're attacking the wrong people."

Strom One's smile faded a bit. *"Oh?"* he said. The other two Stroms behind him looked a little confused, but more or less happy.

"I saw the whole thing," Velva said. "You ran like a bunch of little girls—and it's a good thing, too, because *that was the wrong girl!*"

Now the Stroms looked sheepish. This time Strom Two spoke up. *"Commandant, the Magic Tracker light up ven ve find these two. Ve looked for zem in restaurant, and they look not like photo you give—but they attack, and wizard and witch can change, ya?"*

"No ya!" Velva screamed. "Why are you using a Magic Tracker when I gave you a map? You're supposed to kill someone in *New Orleans!* You have her fucking address! You're not supposed to kill anyone else you find along the way! And the way she looks in the photograph is *exactly the way she looks in real life,* okay?"

The Stroms looked thoughtful, or at least gave it a try. Then they went back to swigging their beer.

"Okay," said Strom One. *"Velva, no harm done, ya? So ve find other girl."*

"Yeah, why don't you do that?" Velva said. "And don't fuck it up again. And stop drinking so much!"

The Stroms grinned, and then their images faded from the plate.

Velva cursed and put the dish down. She reached into the pocket of her silk robe and pulled out the little pocket mirror again.

32: After The Attack

Cynthia gunned the motor of Mike's fearsome Corvette Coupe along Interstate 95. The car was now the color of a burnt cinder, but it looked cool in black and the 460 horses under the hood were still kicking hard. She was driving fast, keeping a lookout for three crazy Germans or maybe a police car.

She was trying to stay calm, which was usually not a problem for her, but of course she didn't usually get into battles with people involving white-hot bolts of lightning. Even as a waitress, most fights were limited to a couple of condiments and maybe some French fries.

She looked over at Mike, who was sitting in the passenger seat. Apparently, an enemy energy bolt had exploded near his foot. He'd shaken it off and now seemed okay, though his sneakers were a bit scorched. He was a tough guy but she'd saved him. Come to think of it, she felt a little light and airy about that.

Mike was grinning and checking his phone for messages. "We're lucky the car only had superficial damage," he said. "It would've really sucked to be standing around looking stupid when the cops showed up."

Cynthia shrugged. "Yeah, but they still might be looking for us, because you did kind of blast a bunch of people with your lightning bolts. It's lucky no one was hurt, but I'm sure someone wants to sue."

Mike frowned at the mention of his erratic shooting. "I need to work on my bolts a bit. The one that decked the nun was definitely bad." He sat back and gave Cynthia another grin. "By the way, thanks for saving me. You're a tough girl."

Cynthia felt herself blush. "I'm not that tough. I mean I'm not a wimp or anything, except when I watch corny movies—but no problem. I'd do it again."

"You watch corny movies? I can't picture it."

"I always cry when the guy and the girl get together. Well, not always—not if it's in a horror movie or something—but most romantic comedies affect me. So maybe I'm not so tough."

He hesitated, and then said, "I cry at movies, sometimes."

"No kidding?"

"Yeah, do you think that's lame?"

"No, I think it's...sweet. What movies?"

"Anything heroic, but that can include love. Anything where somebody is brave and fights the odds and wins."

"That includes most romantic stories. The odds against real love are pretty long."

"You don't believe in it?"

She tossed back her hair and smiled. "I do believe in it. But I think it's a tough thing to find, and maybe that's what makes it so special. Do I sound corny now?"

"No. You sound...sweet."

"Oh, crap! I better go back to fighting with the Germans."

Mike grinned once again. "You did a great job. Where did you learn to swing a pair of sticks like that?"

"I'm a musician, remember? Hang around a drum set long enough and you pick up a few things."

"You obviously did. I wouldn't want to mess with you."

"Oh, that's okay, mess away," she said with a laugh. Then she quickly added, "You know what I mean. What am I talking about? I'm not hostile toward people I like."

She felt discombobulated, like her mind was broken—but she also felt a little breathless, and he was definitely looking at her, and it was kind of cool.

He gave her another affectionate glance and then checked his phone.

"Great!" he said with a grin. "The C.U.F .is getting the cops to back off. They're also giving us *zero-point-zero clearance.*"

"The C.U.F.?"

"The Confidential Ultra Force."

"Wow. Does that mean we can destroy anything we want?"

"No, not anything. But most things."

Cynthia opened her eyes wide, impressed. "So you're a real secret agent, huh? Your girlfriend can actually say, 'My boyfriend's a secret agent.' That's even better than 'My boyfriend is a cowboy,' or 'My boyfriend owns a chocolate factory.' "

Mike shrugged. "I suppose she can say that—when we get her free from the spell."

"Yeah," Cynthia said. "Right." Then she had a thought. "I should probably warn Debbie about those German guys. What if they're after her, too? And come to think of it, why were they after us?"

Mike pulled on the brim of his baseball cap, jamming it down on his head. "I'm guessing they're working for the same witch who has power over Debbie—this whole thing is bigger than I thought. Obviously, they're trying to stop us, and they probably won't bother her. But I like the idea of telling her about it. She should know what kind of company she's keeping, even if she can't help herself. Maybe we'll shake something loose."

"I could call her, but I'm driving," Cynthia said. "Why don't you send her a text message?"

"Are you afraid she'll be mad at you?"

"She's already mad at me, remember?"

"That's true."

He cocked his head and studied her outline.

"What?" Cynthia said.

"Nothing. I just never saw you drive a car before."

"Oh. Is it exciting? I mean in a NASCAR kind of way? Vroom, Vroom!"

I do believe he's checking me out. I do believe it's getting warm in here.

"Did I thank you for saving me?" he said.

"Yeah, we did that."

"Let me thank you again."

"Okay, knock yourself out."

He smiled again and started typing on his phone.

33: A Text

Debbie was hungry. It was 6 p.m. and they'd just gotten clear of Washington, D.C. The traffic there had moved slower than a prison wall, and they'd done a couple hours of hard time. Now as they escaped into the hazy sunset above northern Virginia, she almost felt relaxed. She watched the sun's orange fingers shooting into the pinkish-purple evening and then glanced over at her companion.

He looked like a dashing pirate behind the wheel of his Toyota, with a jaunty smile on his face and that carefree ponytail swishing around. She sighed. Playing with pirates was bound to end badly, but she just couldn't stop cavorting with this guy's cutlass.

Juan noticed her open eyes. "So, you're awake. You fell asleep for a bit."

"Did I? I guess I was tired. Do you want me to drive?"

"No. I recall that you crashed into my car."

"Well, this time I promise to crash into someone else's car."

He laughed. "When we stop, we can switch. I think maybe we should get something to eat. What would you like? I'll buy you anything as long as it costs very little."

"Thanks, Juan. At least I know where I stand—right outside of Burger King. But I have a little money." She rummaged through her purse, picked up her phone, and then noticed she had a text message.

Her heart started pounding.

"Oh, my god! Oh, my god!"

"What? What is it?"

"A bunch of guys attacked Mike! And they might be after us, too!" Juan stepped a little harder on the gas as he puffed out his chest.

"What does it say?"

Debbie took a few deep breaths and read:

"Debbie, we were attacked by three demons at Uncle Clem's Campfire Grill. They're dressed in three-piece suits and have German accents. We kicked their butts but they escaped, so be careful. I'll see you soon. I love you, Mike."

She studied Juan's face.

"I don't believe a word of it," he said with a snort.

"Why not? It could be true. He could love me."

"I'm talking about the demons, Debbie! He's trying to scare you."

"Oh," she said. "Right. Well, I'm scared. And I think we should be careful."

"But his story is ridiculous! He could never defeat three demons. In fact, he's probably not even following us. He's probably still stuck to the floor in your bedroom like a fire hydrant."

"I don't think so. I did talk to Cynthia, and she's obviously with him."

"Yes," Juan said with a smirk. "I recall that she's helping him. In fact, she might just be helping him get over his undying love for you."

Debbie flashed him a nasty look, but didn't respond. Instead, she whipped her head around to the rear view window. After all, she had bigger things to worry about than Cynthia and Mike travelling together, and Cynthia's breasts accidentally bumping into Mike's elbows, and her lips accidentally bumping into his penis.

She squinted at the highway they'd just covered. No sign of demons yet, and no sign of Mike.

"I don't think Mike would lie to me," she said.

"Oh, and why not? Haven't you lied to him?"

"Yeah, I have!" she snapped. "And I regret it, because that's how I ended up here with you."

"Ha! I saw no regret when you were lying on that stinky mattress in the alley."

"I was regretting it."

"Or when you spread your legs on that ridiculous balcony."

"There was regret."

"Or when you were dressed like an outer-space slut on the moon."

"The regret was there! It was just hard to see."

"And why was that?"

"Because I was too busy being turned on! Damn!"

Juan threw back his head and roared. Debbie felt her sharp tone melting away, and then she laughed, too.

She sat back in her seat and stared at the ribbon of highway. "All right, so maybe I'm exaggerating my level of regret." Then she leaned toward him and glared through her thick glasses. "But maybe—just maybe—you're a little jealous."

"Jealous? Of what?"

"Of Mike. You seem awfully annoyed when I talk about him—or the way he feels about me."

Juan grunted. "That's completely untrue. I'm just pointing out that he's not a good man for you to be involved with."

"Why do you care who I'm involved with?"

"I don't want you to make a mistake with him."

"And why do you care about that?"

"Because I'm a nice guy, and that's why you like me."

"I never said I liked you. I said I was turned on when we had sex."

"Ah, so you don't care at all?"

"I don't know, Juan. Maybe I'm just like you and it's only a physical thing."

"Ridiculous! My interest in you is definitely not a 'physical thing.' "

"What? Why? What are you saying?" Debbie felt her face getting red. "Are you saying I'm not good-looking enough? I'm not sexy enough?"

"Debbie, what are you talking about? You're twisting my meaning. It was a compliment!"

"A compliment? You mean I should feel flattered that someone like you would want to be with a girl who doesn't have enough 'physical' stuff going on? Because I don't have enough curves? Enough *boobs*? Enough *tits*?"

Now he rolled his eyes. "That's not what I meant and you know it! I meant that you're a very pretty woman but it's not the *only* reason I like you!" He shook his head and sighed. "I already apologized for that misunderstanding. You're such a crazy girl! And you're very insecure."

He stopped looking at her. He gripped the steering wheel hard and said nothing.

It was the first time she'd really seen him angry. Well, good, let him feel angry for a change—but when she sat back in her seat she felt deflated, like a balloon with the air squashed out.

Crazy and insecure. She'd heard it before. Was there no one who found those traits endearing?

Juan kept staring in silence at the highway, and then drove the car onto an exit ramp. They found themselves on an open stretch of road decorated by a smattering of fast food joints, gas stations, and cheap motels. As they drove past a Kentucky Fried Chicken, she noticed the parking lot was full of license plates from other states: Arkansas, Tennessee, Alabama. Obviously, the locals knew better places to eat.

"Maybe we should have dinner," he said.

Debbie sunk down in her seat. She'd been starving, but now she felt like there was a huge knot in her stomach. It felt like there was a giant squid in there. She had demons behind her and a witch in front of her and big trouble in the seat to her left.

Juan parked the car and yanked the emergency brake.

"I'm sorry I lost my temper," he said. "Let's get something to eat and we'll both feel better."

"I'll eat when we get to New Orleans," she said, crossing her arms.

Juan didn't respond. Instead, he got out of the car, walked around to her side, and opened the door.

"Debbie, please have a piece of pizza. You'll still think I'm an asshole, but I'll be a better asshole."

She was quiet for a second and then shrugged. "All right, but it'll need to be a pretty big piece."

"I'll get you a whole pie, covered with sausages and meatballs. By the time you're done with it I'll be a prince."

"I hope the prince won't mind when I puke in his car."

Ten minutes later they were sitting in a red plastic booth inside Billy Bob's Pizza Palace. A fingerprint-smudged window gave them a lovely view of the parking lot, where moms and dads were herding kids back into mini-vans. This looked easy, since all the kids over the age of five were just standing around staring into digital screens.

Juan took a sip of his ice water. "So, are we going to keep fighting? Or are we going to be friends?"

Debbie kept looking around the room with fast eyes. "We can be friends. Or maybe just non-violent combatants."

"Good. Does this mean we can also get a motel room later?"

"Are you making a move on me?"

It was unbelievable the way this guy's mind worked. All conflict could be postponed for the sake of sex.

He held up his hands and grinned. "Of course not."

"Oh."

"Ah. So now you're disappointed."

"Juan, I don't know what I am—besides 'crazy' and 'insecure.' Maybe I'm just a mess."

He laughed. "I apologize once again. I shouldn't have said that, and really, you're not so bad. And I was planning to make a move on you later."

"Oh, really?" she said with wide eyes. "I'll be ready."

Come to think of it, her mind sometimes had the same problem as his.

"Will you be ready with a weapon, Debbie, or with a smile?"

"I could say 'You'll find out,' but realistically, I don't have any weapons."

"Very good. But I suspect you'll come up with something."

"I have been known to manufacture rocket launchers out of banana peels."

At this point, a guy behind the counter called out Juan's name and he grabbed the reheated slices. As he bit into his pizza he said, "You're very funny, Debbie. But I feel there's a serious girl underneath your jokes."

"It's possible, but I've never seen her."

He leaned forward. "I think you see her all the time, and I think she's a good person."

Debbie contemplated whether she wanted to kiss him or throw her hot pizza into his pretty face and watch the gooey cheese stick to his eyebrows.

"Let's find a motel," she said.

***

The motel they found was less than luxurious, but since Debbie knew her last encounter had been in an alley strewn with garbage and rats and possibly a few dead bodies, she wasn't too concerned.

Still, she felt a certain need to not make things too easy for him. Maybe it was just tradition; after all, she'd never been *that* easy, and while she recognized the double-standard concerning female versus male promiscuity, she was also wired to believe she should appear less eager than the guy. Or maybe she really liked to be difficult—or she had some apprehension about going back into Sex Hell.

Then again, her apprehension was muted by her raging hormones. The truth was brutal: She'd had some great times with Juan in Sex Hell, and this was not an accidental trip she was about to take. She was going back there because she wanted to. Was it love? She liked him, she hated him, she liked him, she endured him—whatever. She'd figure it out later.

She fidgeted with her glasses and her hair. She was always planning to figure things out later, but somehow later kept turning into never and never kept turning into another riddle.

Then Juan kissed her lightly on the lips, and she felt a rush in her body. It was like the first time she'd tasted ice cream, or maybe watched a rerun of Star Trek.

"You're a nice girl," he said.

She kissed him back, and then she whispered, "Yeah, but am I really sexy?"

She hadn't planned to say that—but she did. Either way, he wrapped his arms around her and kissed her hard, and they were back in Sex Hell.

34: A Warning

Velva smiled as the woman on the other end of the line picked up. "Velva, how are you?"

"Great, Michelle. I just wanted you to know I've got everything worked out, so if you've got anything new I'll be ready."

"Oh, that's wonderful news. So I guess you're back in the U. S. of A?"

"Yeah, I'm back. My ass is kind of dragging, but Paris was great. I mean except for the funeral."

"It's too bad you didn't go there under better circumstances, sweetie, but at least your mom got to enjoy her dream of living in France, right? That was so nice."

"Yeah, yeah, her dream. So, do you have anything for me?"

"Not at the minute. Stan really liked you for that commercial... It's too bad about your mother, but I'm glad to hear things are settled now. I might have something coming up; it's an indie film about witches—*boil and bubble, toil and trouble!* Maybe I can get you a reading for the lead witch part."

"A witch? Sure, why not? I love witches."

"This is a modern thing, honey. It's not like you're going to be sitting around making a meatloaf out of bat brains, right? The witches are part of a cult in Greenwich Village. They're all young and hot and fashionable."

"Right. And I'll be hot soon."

"What?"

"I said, 'I'll be hot at noon.' That's when I'm getting my hair done."

"Oh, good. Anyway, I have to go to a meeting. It was wonderful to hear from you, honey. We'll talk in a week or so."

"Thanks, Michelle. I'll be here."

Velva hung up the phone. She lit up a cigarette and stared at the black and white poster of Greta Garbo hanging on the living room wall.

The room had changed a lot since Debbie and Cynthia's visit. The rusty, reeking piles of junk were gone. The filthy, fuzzy carpet was now a spiffy hardwood floor, and the furniture was new—and most of it was real wood.

But the movie posters were the same, and those would never change.

Velva glanced at her cat Bart, curled up on a shiny leather easy chair. She blew some smoke and spoke to her feline friend.

"I might be getting a little ahead of myself, Bart, because I'm not 'young and hot' just yet, but I know it's coming and I need to be ready. I also really need this to work out, because how many times can I tell my agent that my mother in Paris died?"

The cat just yawned and stretched his front legs as Velva heard a sound like a soft hum.

"So, Peach is calling me. Maybe she's got some news."

Velva ran into the kitchen and grabbed the humming cantaloupe. She chopped it in half, and there was the radiant image of Peach Blossom glistening on the surface of the truncated melon. There was a smile on her face and a pink flower in her hair.

"Hello, Peach. Do you have any good news for me?"

Peach tossed back her golden locks and batted her wing-like eyelashes. She peered at Velva closely.

"What good news would I have, Velva?"

"How about telling me that you talked to those bitches in the International Union of Witches, and they realize they made a mistake, and they're going to apologize and let me back in."

"Velva, you keep forgetting that I'm one of those bitches."

Velva laughed and blew some smoke. "I didn't forget, honey—believe me. But you're my sister, so that makes you a better kind of bitch."

"Don't count on it. Velva, I'm calling to warn you, and from what I can see it's a good thing I did. Is it my imagination or do you look an awful lot younger than you did a few days ago?"

Velva laughed again. "Is it that noticeable from your piece of cantaloupe? Yeah, I've been using some ancient remedies. I put fruit slices under by eyes. I ate some shitty yogurt."

"Velva, do you really think no one knows what you're up to?"

"What am I up to?"

"Don't insult me, dear. You're using sex magic and *sensualla* to restore your form and your power, and that is a serious infraction."

"I'm not doing that! No one can prove a thing."

"Really? Are you working with a demon, Velva? Is the demon trustworthy? Has he made a side deal with the Union to betray you? A deal where he gets to keep the *sensualla* he got from your victims—and then they give him some more in return for pulling the plug on your plan right before it's finished... *Are you thinking about what I'm saying?*"

Velva frowned. Yeah, she was thinking. Obviously, Peach knew a few things, and one of those things was that Carl had always been working both sides of the soda fountain. But so what?

Velva snarled. "Carl can't keep me from succeeding, Peach. For all his macho posturing, he has no power to stop the actual spell, and that means I'll get my powers back. And once I get my powers back, none of this will matter. The Union ambushed me. They never could've touched me otherwise, and they know it."

Peach shook her head. "You were a powerful witch, Velva, but there's no guarantee you'll ever be that strong again. And they *were* able to take most of it away from you."

"I wasn't ready for them! This time I will be, and I'll be even stronger. Plus I might be in a movie."

Now Peach really rolled her eyes. "Velva, do you ever learn? Trying to get into movies is how you got yourself into trouble. Why don't you just forget about it?"

"Forget about my dreams?" Velva wailed. "I *love* movies, Peach. I want to be in one—is that so awful?"

"Velva, you're such a fool. But I suppose there are worse things you could want. I just never understood why it was so important to you. But you can't abuse other people on your way to stardom. You have to earn it fairly."

"What is 'fair,' Peach? Haven't you ever heard that expression: 'All's fair in love and war?' "

"Yes, I've heard it, but you're not doing either of those things."

"I just told you that I *love* movies."

Peach laughed. "I think you're pushing the boundaries a bit, and I think that's always been one of your problems. So, let's just say, hypothetically, you're doing something you shouldn't be doing, and let's just say, hypothetically, that the Union knows about it. Now what do you think is going to happen? Do you really think they're going to let you regain your powers? Or do you think they're going to do something to stop you—probably right when you think you're going to succeed. *Are you getting my drift, Velva?*"

Velva narrowed her eyes. The drift was coming through, and it was like an avalanche.

"So you're not going to help me, Peach?"

"I'm helping you right now, you idiot! And I shouldn't be. But know this—if you keep traveling down the road to ruin, there will come a time when I will not help you. I won't go against the Union, Velva. I've been young and beautiful for too long."

Velva bit down on her cigarette and stayed quiet. Finally, she said, "All right, Peach. Thanks for the info."

"Don't mention it. And don't expect any more."

Blip! Peach was gone.

Velva swore and walked back into her living room, where her cat was still lounging like a sloth in his new chair. Once again, she stared at the poster of Greta. God damn, that woman was gorgeous—or had been. But Velva knew that she would be equally gorgeous, if only Juan and Debbie would keep copulating.

Peach's warning had been clear. So what was the big, bad Union planning? For some reason they were allowing Juan and Debbie to keep on keepin' on, but did the Union know everything? Did they realize Velva's powers would be completely restored very soon? And if that happened, the Union could eat shit, because Velva would be tough to handle. After all, she'd been one ass-kicking witch in her day—and her day had only been a few months ago.

She sat down across from Bart and took a long drag on her cigarette. "My wrinkles are just about gone, Bart," she said. "My hair is blond again. The body could be a little tighter, but it's still more solid than the average gooey American shithead made out of donuts. I'm almost across the finish line, you hear me? I'm almost there; I'm a couple of Juan and Debbie fucks away. If I can just keep things together a little longer, everything will be great, but if they reach New Orleans, that will really suck. So while I appreciate her warning, I obviously made the right decision to go to some extremes. Does that make me a bad person?"

She crushed out her cigarette. "I do feel bad, but then again, she doesn't want to help me. She's one of the people keeping me down. And what the fuck—I am a witch."

35: Private Dancer

Debbie stopped breathing and absorbed the scene.

She was standing on an open stage in the center of a cramped, dark room. There were multi-colored spotlights above her, cutting through the misty air like laser beams and painting splashes of gold on a nearby brass pole.

In a flash, she realized she was in a strip club—and she was dressed like a stripper.

Holy crap! Her pulse was racing. It was time to go back on the meds.

She glanced down at her outfit and saw a pair of black fishnet stockings with garter straps, a brief black leather skirt with a silvery belt, and a black tie-top. On her feet were rhinestone encrusted platform sandals.

This was ridiculous; she could not be a stripper. She didn't have the body and she didn't have the moves. In fact, she was the most uncoordinated person who'd ever lived, and how high was this stage she was standing on, anyway? It was going to hurt when she tumbled off—or when she walked off. She had no interest in being a piece of swinging meat for a bunch of drooling losers.

She noticed her reflection in the mirror-covered walls and vaguely wondered how many strippers wore eyeglasses. She assumed a few women had tried the "geeky, hot girl" look. But then, Debbie knew she was really just geeky—although she did have a nice butt. Well, it was a little flat. But she did have sexy legs. Okay, they were a little thin. Her hair looked luminous in this lighting! No, it was a bit limp.

She studied the barren bar surrounding the stage. Where was the bartender? She wasn't going to do any dancing, but she certainly needed a drink.

Then Juan appeared. Suddenly, he was sitting at the bar, right near the stage. He was the only one in the room besides her, and he was grinning. The rest of the room remained empty.

She stared at him, and then at all the empty seats—wait a second. Was this show only for Juan? Now that changed things a bit.

"Debbie, you look beautiful!" he said. "And to answer your question, you are very sexy. More than you know, I think."

"Am I?" she said. She wanted to be. She really wanted to be—especially right now, and yeah, she couldn't deny it, especially for him.

She looked around again, and now she almost laughed. Maybe this could be fun. Sure, it was crazy, but what the hell; she was going to go for it.

She'd barely finished that thought when music started playing. Her heart jumped at the sound of the first note, but then settled down as she felt satisfied with the selection. It wasn't the jet engine boom of heavy rock or the robotic pounding of a club dance track. No, she was hearing something smooth and sensual. It was Marvin Gaye singing "Let's Get It On."

So Marv was getting it on and so was she—maybe. Debbie took a deep breath and started to move.

She rocked her hips from side to side. She shook her ass. Juan seemed to be liking it, so she turned her back to him and did it again. Then she spun around fast and kicked off her left shoe, and it sailed across the room. Nice! The right one didn't go quite as far; it was stopped by Juan's forehead.

Whap!

"Oh, my god!" she blurted. "I'm so sorry!"

He just grinned and rubbed his new concussion.

Think positive, she thought. *At least he didn't lose an eye.*

She gritted her teeth, untied her top, and tossed it aside, exposing a black lace push-up bra with underwire cups. It wasn't that comfortable. Really, it was wonderful there were people out there building things like bridges and bullet trains and waste water treatment facilities, but if engineers wanted to make a few million girls happy, they could create a bra with a perfect fit—although this one was adding almost two cup sizes to her perky little peaches—wow!—so she left it on and turned her attention to the silver belt.

Hm, what to do with this. She took it off and started spinning it around, away from her body, like a windmill. Spinning, spinning spinning... Was this sexy? At the very least, it was hot on the stage, and she was creating a little breeze. But does a guy ever get an erection staring at a windmill? Maybe if he's got a real passion for clean energy. She grimaced and stopped spinning the belt, and then tossed it onto the floor. So much for that fiasco.

She narrowed her eyes and forged on, unzipping her skirt and letting it plop to the ground. She stepped out of it carefully, like she was escaping from a manhole. Underneath, she saw the black garter belt with matching straps.

She'd never worn a garter belt before, but it seemed simple enough. She reached down and unsnapped the clips that held her stockings—no problem. But then both stockings fell down around her ankles. Ah, right, that's what the straps were for... So now she was wearing her stockings around her feet. Black fishnet stockings definitely lose a few points of sensual power when they're clumped around a girl's ankles. She had to get them off!

She wanted to slowly remove them, but she didn't want to sit down to do it. She decided to try taking them off while standing up.

She stood on her left leg and unrolled the stocking on the right leg. Unfortunately, she didn't lift her leg high enough, and she couldn't quite roll it over her heel, and then she was hopping around, trying not to fall—hopping, hopping, hopping—yes! She had it off! She tossed it at Juan, who caught it and smiled.

She plunked down quick onto her butt and ripped off the other stocking—no point in pushing her luck. Then she jumped to her feet and threw that one at Juan, too. She also unclasped the garter belt without a problem and tossed it aside.

Meanwhile, Juan had a huger than usual grin on his face. He started banging his hand on the stage and applauding like a wild man.

"Marvelous!" he said. "Bravo! Magnificent!"

Debbie burst out laughing. And then he was laughing, too.

"Juan, are you going to help me get my panties off, or what? Please get up here before I break a hip or something."

She thought it was a good speech. After all, she'd be harder to fuck in a wheelchair.

Juan hopped onto the stage. He reached out and wrapped his arm around her waist as he grasped one of her hands—and began to lead her in a slow dance.

Marvin Gaye was still singing; apparently, the track was on repeat. Debbie was not a good dancer, but Juan was excellent, and his feet glided across the floor, pulling her along, and she followed.

"That was wonderful, Debbie. I'm very excited."

"That was horrible, Juan. I should be shot."

She felt her body pressing against his, and it felt good, and she looked into his eyes, and they were sweet and warm even while he steered her around the stripper pole. How had she managed to not crash into it before? It must be her lucky day.

They weren't dancing now. They were kissing. It was a long, deep kiss, and then he was caressing her. He was running his hands over her body, and he was lowering her onto the floor of the stage—would they ever do this again on a bed?—and he was taking off his clothes, and her panties were gone, and he tasted sweet as an ice cream sundae topped with strawberries, and he had that big banana ready for her, and he was grabbing her hips and moving faster and harder, and they were moving together, and Debbie realized if there was one time when she felt coordinated it was when she was doing this.

Debbie moaned and rolled her eyes up into her head. Her tragic dance had really sexed her up. Juan seemed to feel the same way.

"Uh! Oh! Oh!"

Pretty soon she was having one writhing orgasm after another. The spotlights shining down were nothing compared to the flashes going off inside her head. They were coming like machine gun bursts, and Marvin Gaye was still singing, and Juan was still pumping, and it went on and on until she thought she would either pass out or die.

She lost count of how many times the big siren sounded, but that was okay. She didn't need a scoreboard to know she was a multi-player, and she didn't need a sophisticated app to keep track of the guys who could make it happen.

At one point, Juan tried to roll her over, suggesting she get on all fours—but she resisted, and he was fine with that, and they went back to doing what they'd been doing so well. But she did move her legs up, and then out, and then all the way back, and then wherever. It was all good.

"Oooooh! Oh! Oh, god!"

Juan was done about twenty seconds after her last spasm. He took a deep breath and collapsed on top of her. All her stress was drained away and she felt calm. She felt euphoria. She felt like nothing mattered but this moment—until Carl's megaphone-like voice came booming through the air.

"Ha-ha!" he laughed. "That was a great one! Lots of passion and lots of power! If you two could bottle that heat you could melt the North Pole. In fact, you could turn it into a tropical resort."

His head was hanging above the stage, wearing a jagged grin.

Juan scowled. He rolled off Debbie and grabbed his pants. "You're not funny, demon. In fact, you're nonsensical." Meanwhile, Debbie banged her head back against the floor in disgust.

"Oh, really?" Carl said. "I think I'm pretty hilarious. And I'm the only one around here who gets a vote."

Now Debbie adjusted her glasses and stared up at the floating head with a vicious look. She rose to her feet. She'd had enough of this bullshit.

"Why don't you just let us go? Is it really right for you to keep us here?"

Carl's eyebrows went up. "What are you talking about, honey? I'm a demon. I'm not concerned with *wrong* or *right*. In fact, you should usually start with the idea that I'm going to do what's wrong. That would be a good move on your part."

"That's not nice! We've given you lots of entertainment, and now I'm sick of it! Why can't you just be nice?"

Carl rolled his eyes. "Are you kidding me? No one ever tells me to 'be nice.' *Not being nice is my specialty.*"

Debbie wiped a few tears from her eyes. It was all so ridiculous, and she was exhausted. She put her panties back on and started to cry.

"All I wanted was to improve things," she said between sobs. "I wanted to make things better. I wanted to make *myself* better. Was that so horrible? I want to go home."

Juan slid close to Debbie and put his arm around her shoulder. He glowered up at Carl.

"Are you happy, demon?" he said. "Does it make you feel powerful to hurt this poor girl who's done nothing to you?"

He seemed genuinely enraged, and while Debbie was still upset, she did feel a bit uplifted by his support.

Carl stuttered a bit. "Look, honey—"

"I have a name!" Debbie said.

"All right, all right, you have a name… Uh, what is it?"

"It's Debbie! You should know that! What kind of evil demon doesn't even bother to learn the names of his victims?"

"Now just a second," Carl said. "Let's get a few things straight. First of all, you're not my victims. You're Velva's victims."

"You made a deal with her, so you're just as guilty as she is."

Carl crinkled his forehead. "Hm, I suppose," he said with a grin. "And that does put me in bad company."

"The worst!" Juan shouted.

"But I just told you, I'm a demon. That's what I do."

"Maybe you should aspire to be something better," Debbie said with a sniffle.

Carl raised an eyebrow. "You know, that never really works for me."

Debbie wiped away a few more tears. "You should give it another try," she said, and then sobbed again.

Carl frowned. "Look, honey—I mean, Debbie—don't cry, okay?

Let me tell you something. Can I tell you something? If you get to New Orleans, you might find more friends there than you think."

Debbie stopped crying. "What?" she said.

"You heard me. I'll tell you something else, too—when there's too much fire, look for some water."

"Uh, okay," Debbie said. The demon seemed to be changing his tone a bit. She sniffled a few more times. "I'll try to remember that the next time I burn a piece of toast."

"Good. Look, I'll tell you something else; I've got something for you, okay? Look at this, right here. This will help you out."

A wooden staff appeared in Debbie's hand.

What the hell? She stared at the piece of dead tree and frowned. It was longer than a baseball bat, but lighter. She suddenly recalled being forced to play softball as a kid and failing miserably to hit anything. Supposedly, physical education class was essential to a child's health—because supreme humiliation builds better people.

"What's this?"

"It's the Staff of Sara," Carl said. "It shoots thunderbolts, and don't you wish you'd had something like this when those motherfuckers tried to make you care about their stupid softball games?"

"I've gotten over that," she said.

"Oh, really? Even the way Ben Bolder and Jeremy Klondike and Stacy Hole made fun of you? How about the way your gym teacher, Mr. Buffinsky, didn't care at all?"

Debbie scowled. "I said I've gotten over it."

Carl sort of shrugged, despite having no shoulders. "Suit yourself. I guess I won't tell you that Stacy got pregnant from some drug addict and Jeremy got run over by a truck full of sheet rock."

"You don't say?" she said, cocking her head. "What about Ben?"

"Oh, he's the president of a huge multinational corporation. He's making millions."

"Huh. I guess two out of three isn't bad."

"Yeah, but he's having an affair with his housekeeper, and his wife's got it all on video, and she's gonna divorce him soon and take him to the cleaners. Whoah, is he gonna get his ass kicked."

"Ah. That's tragic."

"You seem so upset."

"You know I'm not," she said with a sigh. "I guess I'm a bad person."

"It's fun to be bad, isn't it?"

"No! And why did you give me the Staff of Sara? And who the hell is Sara?"

Carl laughed. "Don't worry, it's just a brand name. She won't come looking for it. It's a cool little toy, but let's just say it's better at throwing thunderbolts than it is at helping you avoid someone else's."

"I'm a lover, not a fighter, Carl. Maybe I'll just give it to Juan."

Juan's eyes got wide as he reached for it.

"No!" Carl bellowed, and Juan stopped reaching. "It's not for him. Technically, I'm violating some rule or other by giving it to you, so you take it."

"All right," Debbie said. "But you don't have to violate rules on my account. I don't want you getting into trouble or anything with the evil overlords of the universe."

"Ha! I keep telling you, *I'm a demon*. I don't follow the rules. None of us do. It's what makes us so demonic. Now here's something else for you."

Debbie found her other hand holding a huge margarita glass, filled to the brim with a shimmering drink. The gorgeous green pool of Mexican mojo was complete with a smattering of salt around the rim and a slice of impaled lime.

"Gee, thanks," Debbie said. "I guess Juan can be my designated driver. Is this some kind of magic thing?"

"No. It's just to get you drunk."

"All right. Now that's something I can understand."

Carl laughed once again and disappeared.

Juan started to say something, but then they were back in the Big Highway Motel.

36: Wait A Second

Mike knew he was driving too fast, but what the hell, they were barnstorming through southern Virginia, filled with rolling green grass and open blue skies and not much else to crash into. He took his eyes off the darkening hills and highway to glance down at Cynthia's lap. After all, that's where she was keeping the magic bongos, on the seat between her legs.

She had nice thighs. That was the thing about stretch pants, every girl looked great in them. Okay, maybe not every girl, but certainly Cynthia did. Then he wondered what Debbie would look like in stretch pants. He pictured it in his mind, and she looked fine.

Debbie always looked fine. Debbie was the kind of girl who would never gain a pound. Cynthia, on the other hand, was less predictable. Right now she was curvy, but definitely not thin—and why was he thinking about this? Well, because he was a guy. It was his nature to give every woman he saw a quick evaluation every time he saw her.

He grinned, because didn't women do the same thing to men? It was part of being human, and it spanned all types of people. There was an instantaneous "sexual size-up" that happened, sometimes subconsciously but often quite consciously, and he was glad to do his part.

Cynthia raised her arms and stretched. She pushed out her chest, and her breasts strained against the tight cloth of her T-shirt. Jesus Christ, they were like a pair of wild, marauding cantaloupes. Do cantaloupes maraud? Who the fuck cares? What a pair of tits.

He had to get a grip. He was on a mission to rescue his girlfriend from an evil wizard. That bastard! He'd get what he had coming. Hang on, Debbie, *I'm coming to save you!*

But Cynthia was a nice girl. She was so laid back. That was one bad thing about Debbie; she was tighter than a suspension bridge over a sea of crocodiles. Cynthia, on the other hand, was smooth like a good milk shake. But then again, he was pretty tense at times. He was so obsessed with his goals that he didn't enjoy himself much along the way, and he really hated that about himself.

"I'm no fun," he muttered.

"What?"

"Did I say something?"

"Yeah. You said that you were no fun."

"Oh. I guess I was talking to myself. Just ignore me."

"I think you're fun," she said with a smile. "That time over at Uncle Clem's was the best date I ever had, ha-ha." Then she said, "I mean, it wasn't a date—well, you know what I mean."

Mike laughed. "Yeah, I guess that was a pretty good time. Except for the part where I got my ass kicked."

"But it took three of them to do it."

"Yeah, that's true," he said with a grin. Then the bongos started playing.

"Damn," Cynthia said. "Does this mean more trouble?"

Mike narrowed his eyes and flexed his right biceps. "Maybe it means our German friends are up ahead."

"Huh. Or maybe it means we're about to find Debbie."

"That's true. It could mean either one. I really should figure out how to work those stupid things."

He turned off the CD player to concentrate on the drums. They were banging out a flutter of beats. The beats were settling into a pattern, and it almost sounded like a convoluted shuffle—but how could he be sure? The truth is that he didn't listen to that kind of music. He had a very narrow musical focus, and he should have brought a different Magic Tracker.

He leaned forward a bit and peered at the road. He saw an

18-wheeler and a lot of empty highway. Could it be they'd passed Debbie and Juan? Could it be that the bongos were a total fiasco, and they were driving in the wrong direction? Could it be that it was evening, and they would need to stop soon, and he might just get to share a room with Cynthia?

He imagined her naked and bent over a chair. It was an innocent thought. Or maybe not innocent, but harmless. Now the images where she was kneeling in front of him with slobbering gusto—those were less harmless, although exciting.

He had to focus. Cynthia was a sweet girl with a great sense of humor. Of course, Debbie was sweet and funny, too. But Cynthia was very relaxed, even while exuding a certain animal sexuality, and the passion she'd shown in that battle with the demons—she had totally saved him. She really cared about helping him, and it made him feel warm and fuzzy.

These were crazy thoughts. He loved Debbie. He wanted to find her and protect her. But man, he'd like to bang Cynthia just once. Well, not more than once or twice—damn! That was a bad, bad thought. There was no way he was going to do anything with this girl, even though he suspected she was willing.

Get a grip! Her flirty comments could be a delusion. Debbie was her best friend. If he made a move on Cynthia and she rejected him, he'd look like the biggest asshole in the world. But what kind of thought was that? He wasn't going to make a move. He wasn't going to do a thing. and he didn't want to do a thing. It was just hormones and pheromones and testosterone and the close confines of the car. Also the fact that he'd wanted to fuck this girl senseless since the first time he'd seen her—dammit!

It would be nice to lie in bed with her. She would feel sweet lying against his chest. It would feel good to wrap his arm around her and squeeze her tight. She was a good girl. She had character.

"Hey, the bongos aren't playing anymore," she said.

"What?" he said.

"The bongos. They stopped. Maybe they were just excited about something."

"Hm, maybe," Mike said, squirming a bit in his seat.

"It doesn't look like we're going to catch them today."

He shrugged. "But we have no idea how long they're going to drive. If we stop too soon they'll get too far ahead of us."

"Yeah, maybe, but we can't drive all night."

He saw her expression was neutral. Of course, that should be expected. It's not like staying in a motel together meant anything. He never should've considered it. Obviously, they would either get separate rooms or share a room like two friends. It was a perfectly common thing to do. Besides, how could he look Debbie in the eye after cheating on her?

Wait a second. Debbie had already cheated on him, so why was he being so unshakably faithful? Then he recalled the witch. It was the witch who'd put a spell on her. Otherwise, Debbie was just a girl who'd dumped him, leaving him free to jump on Cynthia. Damn that witch!

Wait another second. Was he mad at the witch for casting a spell, or mad at the witch for not casting a spell? This was getting confusing.

Cynthia said, "Maybe we can just get a drink somewhere and call Debbie in the morning."

"Why do we want to call Debbie?"

She gave him a sideways glance. "Because we're trying to rescue her from Juan and the witch?"

"Oh, yeah, right—I know," he said. "But if we call Debbie, she'll know we're still chasing her, and then Juan will know, and maybe the witch will know. Nah, I think at this point I'd rather leave everyone in the dark until we show up. I want to take them by surprise."

Cynthia sighed. "I understand, but we can't drive all night."

Mike shifted a bit in his seat. There was an exit up ahead.

He didn't say a word, but he smiled at her as he swung the car off the highway and onto a stretch of road containing a few restaurants and some motels. He parked the car and yanked on the parking brake.

"I guess we'll stop here," he said.

"Yeah, this looks good, or at least not too terrible—or at least better than sleeping in the car. Hey, the bongos are playing again. Sounds like some kind of smooth jazz."

Mike picked up the drums and studied them. He looked around and said, "Cynthia, I don't understand these stupid things. Let's go inside and see if they've got any vacancy."

37: The Big Highway Motel

Back in the motel, Juan said he needed to get some rest and Debbie agreed. He was friendly and sweet but didn't say much. Maybe he was just tired, or maybe he wanted to avoid the ongoing conversation about their relationship—fine. Debbie was always up for a good round of non-communication, so she finished the margarita Carl had given her and went to bed.

Now she was lying in the dark, feeling restless and edgy while Juan slept beside her.

She tossed and turned and saw her entire sexual history undress itself before her eyes—the drama, the agony, but mostly the comedy. Was it so ridiculous for everyone? Maybe not, but she doubted she was the only person with a list of naked catastrophes. Hormones tended to create some very fucked up situations. In fact, it was the main thing they were good for. Then she heard Juan's voice.

"Debbie, what are you thinking about?"

She instantly felt warm and happy, glad he was awake.

"I thought you were asleep," she said.

"I was, but now I'm not. It happens."

"Oh… Well, I walked in on my mom and her boyfriend once. That's what I was thinking about."

"Walked in?" he said with caution. "You mean while they were being…intimate?"

She laughed. "*Intimate* makes it sound like it was classy, but it wasn't. I came rushing home from school and opened the back door and there's my mom, half dressed and bent over the kitchen table. The guy was behind her with his pants down. I remember there was a tuna fish sandwich on the table, and a can of Budweiser, and an open bag of marshmallows. I remember thinking it was a weird combination—marshmallows and tuna fish."

He turned his head and stared at her through the dim light. "How old were you?"

"Ten."

"Were your parents divorced?"

"No, not yet. They stayed together for another four years."

"Ah. What did your mother say? Did you keep it secret from your father?"

"My mother looked right at me; it was so crazy. Can you imagine what it's like to see your mom getting it doggie style over the kitchen table? She said, '*Oh! Oh! Debbie! Oh! Close the door!*' and I did. Then she said, '*Oh! No! I mean go back outside—and then close the door! Oh! Oh!*' So then I did that. But they didn't stop, and I stood out in the yard listening to the guy's body slapping against her butt... Then later she came to talk to me. She was drunk, and she told me that 'Harry was a special friend,' and I shouldn't tell Daddy about him. I remember thinking, *Is that the best you can do, Mom?* If I have any talent as a fiction writer, I didn't get it from her."

"Ha. Did you tell your father?"

"No. I was too traumatized. My dad was a mechanic from Montreal; he met my mom when she went to Vermont on vacation. She decided to drive across the border to see the city, and her car broke down—and there he was, ready with his big box of tools. So she came back to Jersey with a new thigamajig under her hood and a cheap ring on her finger. Then he moved down here and opened up a shop, where he spent a lot of time fixing cars and collecting girlfriends. So really, he was too busy working on cars and cheating on my mom to find out that she was cheating on him. It was weird. And right around that time, the stories I was trying to write got pretty sardonic and twisted.

I guess it was a form of venting, or maybe escape. Or maybe I just liked it. My parents didn't like sci-fi or fantasy, and I guess maybe that was part of the appeal."

"Ah. That particular position—is that why you don't like it?"

She hesitated. "No. I don't like it because…" Her voice trailed off. Then she said, "That's only a small part of why I don't like it. I don't like it because it's impersonal, which suits my mom, by the way. She also has an anxiety problem, and she's been in therapy for years, and she takes medication—and I never wanted to do those things. But I *have* done those things." Debbie sighed. "At least I didn't inherit her obsession with tanning and Botox. Of course, I'm not ready for Botox yet, so we'll see, ha. I guess you think I'm defective."

In the darkness, she saw the bright teeth of his smile. "No," he said. "I think you're a very nice girl. I'm not perfect, and we have things in common."

"Oh, yeah? Like what? Crappy parents?"

"Yes. Though my parents were good."

"You said your father was a lecherous philanderer."

"He was good, except for that."

"But that's a *big except*, Juan. If you're hurting someone, then you don't really care about that person. That's the way I see it, anyway."

He was quiet for a bit, staring now at the dark blob of the ceiling. Was he considering her words, or was he just at a loss for words that would defend his beliefs?

Finally, he said, "I suppose in some ways I admired my father even while I hated the result. I don't want to be like him, but I wonder if it's too late."

"It's not too late. You haven't caused anyone to die yet, right?"

"Not yet. But I'm still young. Will I ever cause such heartbreak?"

"I don't know, Juan. Maybe when you meet someone who wants to marry you, you'll find out."

He gave a sardonic laugh. "Only a fool would marry a dog like me."

"That's interesting. I often feel the same way—like no one's going to want me."

"You're no dog, Debbie."

His hand drifted over to hers, and she let him hold it.

She tingled a bit inside. She wanted to feel his touch—but she didn't trust him, and it was unfortunate because she liked him, and he seemed to like her, too. He also seemed to genuinely care about her at times, such as when he'd stood up to the demon after she'd become upset; but he wasn't admitting any real feelings for her, or apologizing for running away after that first night. He was only teasing her with a comforting hand and a few kind words, and it wasn't enough.

Then again, the only reason she didn't hurl herself on top of him and kiss his face until her lips were broken was because they'd end up in Sex Hell again, and she was too emotionally drained for that right now. But would she do it if the threat didn't exist? Would she fantasize about loving this guy, and about him loving her?

Yeah, she would. In fact, she was doing it already—and it was probably a huge mistake, but she just couldn't help it.

She noticed Juan was sleeping again. That was a good thing because he did need to get some rest. She wished she could sleep, too, but knew it was unlikely.

She rubbed her forehead and tried to drive every thought about love and relationships from her mind. *Go away, go away, go away!* But as much as she wanted the swirling storm of thoughts to disappear, they were still there, bombarding her brain like hale. She closed her eyes tight.

"Suzy, we need to talk," Debbie thought.

"I'm here," Suzy said, accompanied by the sound of a magazine locking into a Series 7 Plasma Pistol. "I can relate."

"I don't trust Juan, Suzy. But I like him."

"I hear you. I don't trust Tolio—and I shot him."

"What?"

"Just kidding! I didn't shoot him yet; he's good in a scrap. Helped me stand up to Captain Tadrock and the Space Patrol. But I can't trust him with my heart."

"Right. So what are you going to do?"

"Cut it out of his chest. Or maybe just get some sleep. You do the same."

Debbie knew Suzy was right. She pushed her head back deeper into the pillow, hoping for the best. She wanted to sleep. She needed to sleep. She tried to empty her head and make the world fade away. Unfortunately, the couple having sex in the room next door kept making things difficult. They were really going at it.

38: Oh, Yeah!

Cynthia walked into the motel room, right behind Mike. Man, he had a great walk. Her heart was pounding. It sounded like a drummer with a 26-inch bass drum was in there.

They could have gotten separate rooms, but it seemed dumb to spend the extra money, especially since they were going to end up in the same bed anyway, right?

That was a crazy thought. She was supposed to be out here helping her best friend, not stealing away her man. But then again, her best friend was showing her appreciation by letting some man-whore bang her at every rest stop along the interstate—and she had the nerve to be angry about Cynthia's help. Debbie wanted her cake and she wanted to eat it, too, and then she wanted some more, and then she wanted to make sure no one else got a piece. That skinny bitch.

But Cynthia loved Debbie. They'd known each other since they were little kids. Sure, she'd been into music while Debbie had been more into books, but it was the same stuff. Debbie hated slick best-sellers the same way Cynthia despised putrid pop. Plus, Debbie liked all that punk rock. They'd been to all those concerts together. They'd gotten drunk together. They'd puked their brains out together. Bonding through puke! There is no substitute.

They'd tried smoking pot together. Cynthia had gotten some weed from a guy who sat in front of her in history class, sometime between World War I and the New Deal. Cynthia smiled, recalling how Debbie had predictably freaked out and claimed she was having a heart attack and then a stroke and then preliminary lung cancer. Cynthia had just laughed and told her to shut the hell up and let's get a pizza.

They talked about everything: love, sex, lack of love, lack of sex, food, movies, music, books, and more. Actually, not much more—because what else was there? If Debbie hadn't been so uptight about her sex life with Mike, none of this would've happened. But Debbie was always on the ledge, close to the edge. It was one of her most endearing qualities, even though it often made her impossible.

Mike tossed his little travel bag onto one of the two twin beds. He put his drum sticks down next to it and looked her way.

She smiled. "Two beds but only one bathroom? I want my money back. Then again, you're paying for it—which I keep saying you don't have to do. I can pay my own way."

"Don't even think about it," he said with a grin.

"Okay, in that case I'm going to take a shower."

"That sounds like a plan. Everyone's cleaner without dirt."

She briefly imagined asking him to join her, but of course she didn't.

She really needed to cool down. Yeah, make that water ice cold.

The shower wasn't too bad in this place. It was generic and functional. The water felt slippery, and her hands were a little shaky with the soap. Everyone thought she was so laid back, and she was—but she wasn't proactive when it came to guys. She didn't mind showing off her stuff and jiggling a bit, but that was it. She'd make a few jokes, but nothing too obvious.

She wondered what Mike would do if she walked out of the bathroom naked.

It was just a thought. It was nothing she would ever do.

She still imagined the rest of the scenario, and it was fine. It was exciting, especially as she ran her fingers over her most thrilling places. She really needed to get some clothes on.

She took a few deep breaths, then toweled herself off and got dressed. She brushed her hair, which was a little damp but not really wet because she'd decided not to wash it. She didn't want to look like a drowned rat tonight.

She wanted to play it cool and be herself, but she didn't feel like herself. She felt like a panting animal in heat—how ridiculous. Was this a physical thing, or an emotional thing? It had definitely started out as physical, but she really liked Mike. He was chivalrous, and mysterious, and capable of jealousy in a sexy way—and he was committed. He was committed to his causes, and to his women. Maybe that's what was turning her on. Also, that rock hard body. Sigh.

She ended up sitting on the bed while Mike was in the shower. Too bad she hadn't brought a bass with her, or maybe a guitar. She could serenade him. They could sing a duet, and then tear each other's clothes off.

It was hot in here. Was the air conditioner on? Was there anything to drink around here? There was a place across the highway that sold liquor. Whoah! Now that could be a real game changer.

"Mike, I'm running across the street for a minute. I'll be right back."

She heard a muffled response through the bathroom door, but she was already gone. When he walked out of the bathroom, Cynthia was on the bed, drinking a bottle of Corona.

"I thought I'd start a party," she said.

He smiled. "I have to get up early, but I guess one couldn't hurt."

"It hurts less after five or six—trust me."

"That's true. Do we have five or six?"

"Yeah, but I was thinking about drinking five, which would leave you with one."

"You'll be pretty drunk after five."

"I wish. I really should've gotten a bottle of vodka."

He seemed to hesitate about where to sit, and then plopped down on the bed across from her. She took another sip of beer. She felt better already—perfectly sober, but a little more relaxed, and a little more inclined to puff out her chest. Of course, she didn't want to do anything too obvious, but then again, she wasn't wearing a bra under this T-shirt. In her defense, it was not a see-through shirt, and she never wore a bra when she slept.

Well, well, Mike was sneaking glances at her nipples.

That's not a problem. She was sneaking glances at him, too. The guy had big arms. The guy had a big everything, or so Debbie had said. She needed to calm down. This was so wrong!

But it wasn't wrong. If Debbie were really a friend, she'd understand whatever happened, and nothing might happen—nothing at all. She and Mike might just lie in these pathetic little twin beds, furiously masturbating all night long.

She was really feeling hot. Why didn't he make a move? *If he does, I'm going to go for it!* But he was probably still thinking about Debbie—Debbie, Debbie, Debbie. Just one little sign, Mike, and all this can be yours.

She considered how, if this were a movie, some ridiculous thing would happen and they'd end up in each other's arms. An earthquake might do the trick. Sure, if the ground shook hard enough he'd get bounced into the air and then end up on top of her. But there's never a fucking earthquake around when you need one.

This was getting silly. They weren't even talking much. She was just drinking her beer and looking at him, and he was drinking his beer and looking at her—and his eyes were hitting all her hot spots.

She had some real hot spots, too, and it had been way too long since anyone had visited them. Of course, she'd had her chances, because she went out a lot and the average guy will do it with anyone. But she wasn't interested in guys who were repulsive, or sleazy, or wimpy, or dishonest, and that ruled out a lot of them. Like many girls, she didn't say 'no' because she was pure and chaste—she said 'no' because she was disgusted.

She wasn't disgusted right now. She was warm and steamy and interested.

She got up and walked over to a window that viewed the deserted highway. She took another swig of beer and hoped he was checking her out. She had a feeling he was, but it wasn't a sure bet. After all, Debbie was very thin, with a nice, tight kind of butt, while Cynthia had a bigger, bouncier look. But see, that might be one of Mike's problems. He didn't know what he really liked.

He was standing next to her now. That had been quick. Maybe he did know.

"Nothing going on out there," he said.

"Yeah."

"Maybe we should get some sleep."

She turned toward him. "Sure." They were very close together now. Her nipples were grazing his chest.

"Cynthia, you look nice."

In her mind, an alarm went off. He was making a move. It was a slow move, like a glacier plowing its way up a mountain, but it was a move. Well, she wasn't going to let it go by without giving the ice pile a kick in the right direction.

"Thanks. So do you. But I think these pants make my ass look big."

"No way!" he blurted. "I love your ass! I mean, it's…not too big."

"Huh," she said, feeling pretty good now. "That's nice to know."

"Right."

They stared at each other, like two people standing on a high wire, and for a few long seconds neither one spoke. But Cynthia took another sip of her drink. All right, the hell with it—full speed ahead, baby.

She took a deep breath. "Mike."

"Yes?"

"Do you want to fuck me?"

His eyes got wide.

"Absolutely."

"So what are you waiting for?"

Their lips locked hard. He tasted like beer, but that was fine because she loved beer. She also loved having her shirt ripped off and getting her nipples sucked—and he was pretty decent at both. A little rough, but she liked it that way. As rough as he was, he wanted to please her, and that was a turn on.

She was going to please him, too. Oh, man, was she going to make him happy.

39: Shootout

Debbie watched Juan flirt with the granny waitress who took their order. He was peppering her with compliments, including a line about her hair; it was a beautiful shade of white, like "Christmas snow." The guy couldn't open his mouth without telling a woman how nice she looked. The bastard.

Then again, it was nice that he complimented *all* women, not just the pretty ones. The guy really liked women. It was a problem, but it was also kind of sweet.

Debbie bit one of her fingernails and dumped way too much sugar into her coffee. In the surrounding room, a few other bleary-eyed travelers were getting coffee and eggs, rushing to get back on the treadmill to nowhere. From the window, she watched the sun rising like a pink grapefruit above the matchbox motel where they'd spent the night. The building was right across the parking lot, adjacent to the dusty stretch of road connecting to the nearby interstate, still empty at this hour. She hadn't gotten much sleep and figured she looked like hell.

Juan said, "You look bright like a flower this morning, Debbie."

"Thanks, but I feel more like a piece of ragweed."

"You're an adorable weed. You're a weed that outshines any rose."

She rolled her eyes and smiled. "You're very good at flattery, Juan—or maybe you're just a good liar."

"I only speak the truth. But why did you bring that in here?"

He was nodding his head toward the Staff of Sara. For some reason, Debbie had brought it into the restaurant.

Debbie shrugged. "I don't know. Carl said it could protect us, so I thought I'd keep it with me. I guess there's a primitive feeling of comfort that comes from holding a big club."

Juan grinned, of course. Probably some juvenile joke about his big, hard stick, Debbie thought. She stared at the peppers-and-onions omelet on her plate and realized her stomach was too jittery to eat.

She poked a fried potato with her fork. "I had a hard time sleeping," she said. "Especially with those two people in the next room going at it."

"Really? I didn't notice."

"Are you kidding me? There wasn't a lot of screaming, but the bed was really rocking." She leaned forward and whispered, "And then they were obviously doing other things...in other places."

"Ah, and how can you be sure?"

"I had my ear against the wall."

He laughed. "Why didn't you tell me you were so excited? I would've been happy to help."

"Juan, you were snoring like a tractor. So between the snoring and the stuff next door, I was wide awake."

He took a sip of coffee and grinned again. "I'm sorry about that. Next time you should wake me, and we'll give those two a run for their money."

"Hm, I don't know if I can run that far. Those two sounded like they were trying out for the Olympics, and I think they're going to win."

"Nonsense! They'll never defeat us, Debbie. We're an unbeatable team."

She gave a tight smile and said nothing. Then she stared out the window, across the desolate parking lot, where she saw something that almost made her head explode. Mike and Cynthia were walking out of the Big Highway Motel.

In a flash, her mind connected the undulating dots. Holy crap!

Cynthia was glowing like a glass of champagne; she was smiling and laughing like the whole spurting bottle. Mike seemed more reserved, but he had his arm around her, chuckling at her jokes while she tried to knock the NY Yankees cap from his head. There was something magical going on, and it had nothing to do with a dried up old witch.

Debbie took a few deep breaths and tried to stop a key artery from popping. *Stay calm, stay calm, stay calm!*

Maybe the two people in the adjacent room had not been Mike and Cynthia, even though they'd always been hot for each other, and had been traveling together, and had just exited the same motel in each other's arms surrounded by a smoldering volcanic afterglow. Or maybe this was just Debbie getting what she deserved, after cheating on a decent guy. Damn, that was a real kick in the teeth. She hated the kind of logic that crossed paths with grim reality before demolishing her dental work.

Juan seemed happy enough, droning on in the distance, but Debbie wasn't hearing him. She was too busy noticing that Mike and Cynthia were coming this way—and come to think of it, Mike had attacked Juan the last time they'd seen each other, so there was more involved here than the fact that her best friend was now having roof-raising sex with him.

"Juan, it's Mike!"

Juan put down his coffee and peered out the window, studying the scene. He gave an indignant snort and puffed out his chest. "There's nothing he can do," Juan said. "We have every right to travel together. Besides, it seems he has a new girlfriend."

"What are you talking about?" Debbie snapped. "They're just travelling together, trying to catch us. It doesn't mean they're involved."

"Are your glasses not thick enough, Debbie? They look like a happy couple, and why is that a problem? You left the man stuck to the floor in his socks."

"That's because he was trying to kick your ass."

"He was kicking no one's ass. He couldn't even raise his foot."

"Juan, we have other things to worry about."

"No, we don't. After all, you've accused me of jealousy when you are the one who is most jealous—jealous that your friend is with a man you don't even want."

She felt like clobbering him, but it wasn't her style. She considered screaming, but that wasn't her style, either. Her style was to make a few smart remarks and then go home to wallow in a state of misery and denial—but she wasn't feeling too smart, and she couldn't go home. Luckily, she was saved from needing a response by the door opening and a new catastrophe entering the room.

Mike saw her right away. "Debbie!" he said. Then he stared at Juan. "And you!"

Juan smirked. "Yes, me. Would you like to join us for breakfast? The omelets are quite good, but I suppose a jackass prefers weeds and grass."

Cynthia put her hand on Mike's arm, apparently to keep him from charging forward—and it worked. But he still raised his drumsticks high and started shooting. He still missed by a good five meters.

With a sound like bacon frying, his first bolt crackled though the air and struck an old woman's plate of poached eggs—*kasplish!* Yolk and egg whites splattered in every direction, along with a thousand bits of fried SPAM. Shouts erupted, and Debbie felt her head start to spin.

"*What the hell are you doing?*" she shouted. "Leave him alone!"

She threw up her hands, not really considering how one of them was holding the Staff of Sara—and a bolt of lightning leaped from the stick, sailed through the air, and detonated in a windy explosion that destroyed the cash register and sent nickels, quarters, and small bills flying across the room.

Debbie froze. This thing was powerful—and it also wouldn't quit shooting. Bolts of white light flew from the staff, one after the other, and Debbie couldn't make them stop. To make matters worse, the searing tongues of electric death weren't really aimed at anything. They seemed intent on spreading around as much mayhem and destruction as possible.

Zip! Poom! Zip! Poom! Zip! Poom!

The flying spears of energy destroyed a dessert counter, a soda fountain, a bubble gum machine, and a pile of brown bananas. Debbie was shouting and holding one end with both hands while the other end kept firing. She was trying to let go but her hands were stuck. Then she was magically yanked toward the center of the room, where she began spinning in a circle, around and around, like she was at the hub of a hellish carnival ride.

Customers were screaming and ducking under tables—and then running for the exits, along with two waitresses and a cook. Things in the room were being shattered and destroyed. Mike pushed Cynthia to the ground. Juan ducked down under the table, narrowly avoiding a blazing bolt.

Debbie was shrieking and holding on and blasting away. From the corner of her eye, she saw Cynthia leaping to her feet.

Debbie felt a jolt of alarm—a wave of lightheaded panic at the thought of vaporizing her best friend.

"No! Stay there!" Debbie yelled.

But Cynthia kept coming. She timed it just right, too—tackling Debbie around the thighs while Debbie was turned in a different direction. Debbie crashed to the floor and the staff popped loose from her hands. It also stopped firing, but the fight wasn't over.

Cynthia had fury in her eyes. She jumped to her feet and looked down at Debbie.

"What the hell are you doing, Deb? You could have killed us all!"

Debbie groped around for her glasses. Juan was there, handing them to her and helping her to stand. Debbie turned toward Cynthia and said, "Yeah, I know—and I'm sorry! Do you think I was doing any of that on purpose? It was an accident! But why are you even here? None of this would've happened if you'd just gone home!"

"Why should I go home?" Cynthia shouted. "I'm trying to help Mike!"

"Yeah, I heard you helping him last night. Does anyone really need that much help, Cynthia? I'm surprised he can even walk!"

Cynthia's face turned red. "What I do with Mike is none of your business! You dumped him!"

"I didn't dump him! I was trying to improve things with him, and I got sidetracked."

"Sidetracked? By picking up a guy you met in a car accident? By letting him maul you in a martini bar? You were chasing after Juan way before the witch tossed you into Sex Hell!"

"And you were chasing after Mike the whole time I've known him!"

"That's a lie! I never did any chasing."

"No, of course not—but you sure did a lot of jiggling."

"I can't help it if I jiggle! You're just mad because you can't do it."

"I can jiggle if I want to!"

"With what? It's not jiggling if nobody can see it!"

Juan and Mike looked at each other, like they were pondering the right moment to get involved or maybe just stay out of it. Meanwhile, customers who were still left in the room peered from under tables or moved quickly toward the door.

Juan said, "Ladies, please, there's no need to fight. We can settle this like reasonable people."

Cynthia shoved a finger into Juan's face. "Shut up, sleaze ball! Guys like you are exactly why nice girls end up so unhappy."

"He's not a sleaze ball," Debbie said.

Mike laughed. "Oh, come on, he's pretty sleazy. He's at least eighty percent sleaze."

"Not true!" Juan said, indignant. "Thirty percent at most!"

Debbie rolled her eyes. "The exact amount of sleaze isn't the issue. Mike, you have no right to keep interfering in my life!"

Cynthia smirked. "Fine. But you've got no right to interfere in mine."

Mike looked at Debbie. "You were chasing after Juan before the witch put a spell on you?"

Debbie felt her face getting red. "No! I didn't meet Juan until after I met the witch, and that meeting was part of her spell."

"So you didn't really dump me after all!" Mike said. "The witch set you up with Juan, just like I've been saying."

"No!" Juan said. "Or maybe yes—but the chemistry between us was real."

"Does it really matter now?" Cynthia said to Mike. "Do you still want her instead of me?"

"Well," he sputtered, "I still want to free Debbie from the spell."

"And then?"

"And then..." His voice trailed off.

Debbie studied the situation in front of her. Cynthia was angry. Juan was angry, or at least annoyed. Mike was confused. And those guys pulling up outside in the blue Volkswagon? They looked enthusiastic, but not in a good way.

Cynthia saw them, too. "Holy shit! It's the Germans."

Debbie stared at three guys whooping and hollering and hanging out of the windows of their car. They were dressed in dark, matching three-piece suits, and they were drinking beer, and they were looking drunk and dangerous.

The vehicle slammed to a stop and they leaped out.

They pulled out three wooden staffs and aimed them at Mike's Corvette. There were three flashes of light, and the car burst into flames. There was no doubt; it was straight to the junkyard in a ball of fire. They raised their beer bottles high and screamed a lot in German.

Debbie felt lightheaded once again. Who the hell were these guys? Obviously, the people Mike had warned her about.

Mike was moving fast. He raised his drumsticks and crouched behind a pylon. "Everyone get down!" he said.

Cynthia ran to his side. "Mike, no! Let's get out of here. Besides, you know you can't hit anything with those."

"Yes, I can," he scoffed.

Juan grabbed Debbie's hand. "Let's go," he whispered, motioning toward a back door.

Debbie paused. Her head was spinning and blood was rushing in her ears. She was no fighter—but she was no deserter, either.

"No," she said. "I'm staying."

Juan waved his arms and motioned toward Mike. "For what? To watch that idiot get himself incinerated?"

"That idiot is trying to protect me."

"I'm also trying to protect you—by getting you to a safe place.

If Mike and his girlfriend are smart, they'll do the same."

"*She's not his girlfriend!*" Debbie screeched.

"Debbie, I should leave you here. But I won't!"

He grabbed a few dishes from a nearby table and ducked down behind a garbage can near the front door. Debbie crouched down beside him. "Don't get hurt, okay?"

"That's a wonderful idea. I'll keep it in mind."

The three guys burst into the diner like an intoxicated tornado. One of them tripped and nearly fell, but he managed to recover without dropping his staff, or his beer. One of his partners looked at him and said, "*Get it together, Strom!*" Then he addressed the entire room. "*Ve are all Stroms—Strom, Strom, Strom—and ve are coming to conquer!*" The three of them grinned and raised their beer bottles high—just as Mike fired a bolt and watched it come pretty close to hitting its mark, passing within an inch of Strom's ear.

"*Ya!*" Strom shouted. "*They have ze weapons!*"

Juan snarled and started hurling the plates. He threw two standard dinner plates, a dessert plate, and a coffee cup—and every one of them hit a Strom.

"*Oof! Oof! Oh! Ze bastard is throwing ze dish!*"

They recovered fast and commenced firing energy bolts.

Woosh! Poom! The bolts whizzed at Mike and Cynthia.

Cynthia ducked down, while Mike stood calm and returned fire. One of his bolts exploded between the Germans and sent all three sprawling in different directions.

Meanwhile, Juan leaped toward Debbie's discarded staff. Debbie saw him grab it and felt her stomach leap into her throat. *If he gets hurt I will kill myself!* The Staff of Sara had been a disaster when she'd used it—but of course, he wasn't as nervous as Debbie.

Juan grinned and aimed it at one of the Germans.

A fiery tongue of light leaped out and struck Strom, who was immediately engulfed in a beery fireball. Smoke and flames and maybe a few hops seemed to burst from his body—but he wasn't vaporized. The blast just frazzled his expensive suit and made the rest of him look like a burnt piece of bratwurst.

The other two Stroms stopped to survey the damage, and that's when Mike fired a bolt that nailed another Strom right in the chest—*poof!* Another ball of flame, and another burnt piece of meat. He hit the floor hard.

"Nice shot!" Juan said.

"Thanks!"

The last Strom standing grimaced and ducked down behind a lunch counter. When his head popped up again, he was wearing a pair of goggles over his sunglasses.

"Ze extra protect me as I shoot big ya!"

Then he put the staff on his shoulder, like a rifle, and screamed: *"Yihaaaaaaaaaaaaaa!"*

As he swung the staff in an arc, a wall of white light and fire swept across the room, searing everything in its path.

Debbie screamed. Mike moved toward the blazing wall of destruction with his drumsticks held high. Juan dove toward Debbie and pushed her to the ground.

Debbie took several deep breaths and raised her head, looking around for Cynthia. Where the hell was she? Then the wall of flame collided with one of Mike's outstretched drumsticks—and the wall stopped.

Strom scowled and gritted his teeth. He continued to try and move the staff, but it wouldn't budge.

Mike continued to grimace as beads of sweat popped from his face. Strom sneered. *"You vill die sure! My staff is too big! Too hard! Too thick!"*

Mike smirked. "Mine is bigger and harder and faster! Wait a second, that's not what I meant—I meant it's not that fast. In fact it lasts a really long time."

Debbie groaned as the sophomoric shrapnel flew, and then she felt Juan's arm circling her shoulders. Meanwhile, Cynthia appeared next to Strom. Apparently, she'd been crawling across the floor. In her hand was the staff of Strom's fallen brother. Strom glanced at her and showed a look of alarm—just as she brought it down on his head.

"Augh! Das böse Mädchen ist zurück!"

The staff fell from his hands, and the wall of power disappeared.

"What did he say?" Juan said.

Debbie shook her head and tried to catch her breath. "I think it was something about an overdue library book. But you know, I could be wrong."

Either way, the battle wasn't done because the first two Stroms were back on their feet, and one of them was firing colorful darts of energy. They whizzed through the room like crackling jellybeans and detonated all around Mike.

Zip! Poom! Zip! Poom! Zip! Poom!

The Strom with the staff was laughing as he fired, but then he stopped shooting to take a big swig of beer. Meanwhile, Debbie was huddled with Juan under a table by the window, where he was preparing to fire a few more shots. From across the room, she saw Mike crouched beneath another table, no doubt waiting for his chance. Before either guy could move, Debbie decided to take action.

"Hey, Strom!" she shouted.

Mike and Juan hesitated. Three voices from different parts of the room said, *"Ya?"*

"Why are you shooting at us?"

The Strom who was standing with the staff took another swig of his drink. *"Vat you mean? Ve shooting, yes, it is the shoot ve do."*

"Yeah, but why? We haven't done anything to you. Why are you attacking us?"

Strom gave her a blank look. Obviously, he wasn't used to communicating with people he was trying to slaughter.

"Ve shoot, yes, it is vat ve made do by ze vitch."

"Why does the witch want you to shoot at us? I thought she wanted to keep us alive."

Strom grinned. *"Come to say, the shooting is the idea ve had. The vitch had some idea not so much fun."*

"I see. So in other words, you guys are not really following her instructions."

"No, we do not follow!" Strom said with a laugh. *"Ve follow instructions some and then it is time for beer."*

The three Stroms all raised their bottles high and saluted each other.

Debbie looked at Juan. "I tried, but I think these guys are pretty determined to keep drinking and shooting. Obviously, they're not interested in finding…the Eternal Beer Castle.

"*Vat? Vat do you talk about? Ve get beer for free.*"

"Yeah, but this is better beer," Debbie said. "This is beer made with magic—the drunker you get, the better you shoot. It's what we're searching for. It's a powerful place, but the witch wants it all for herself."

Juan rolled his eyes while the Stroms just snickered.

"*Do ve look so drunk, Frau, that ve believe story so dumb?*"

Debbie frowned. "Well, you guys do seem pretty far gone."

"*Ve are!*" they shouted in unison. Then Strom One said, "*But ve are not gone so much for that!*"

Two of the Stroms started shooting again. The third guy was still behind the lunch counter where he'd lost his staff to Cynthia. He grabbed at it and the two began pulling back and forth. Meanwhile, Juan and Mike started blasting away, returning the fire from the Stroms.

Electric charges were once again whizzing around the room. Big and small explosions commenced, and Debbie was disgusted.

Her attempt at diplomacy and then subterfuge had failed, but she hated this ridiculous violence, and she especially hated when it was directed at her. There had to be a way to stop it, and she meant on both sides. Then she glanced up at the ceiling and noticed a sprinkler system.

She recalled the words of a certain demon: "*When there's fire, look for some water.*"

She knew a sprinkler produced water, and maybe these staffs that fired lightning would be shorted out by a little water—or a lot of water. If not, it would still be harder for everyone to fight in a downpour. Of course, she also realized the sprinkler hadn't gone off, despite presiding over a room filled with smoke and small fires. So it was probably broken, but then she had another idea. She reached into her purse and fumbled around fast, pulling out Mike's fish-shaped bottle opener—the one she'd snatched from her bedroom floor.

Juan looked at her. "What are you doing, Debbie? This is no time for a drink."

"I'm not looking for a drink. I'm going to make it rain in here."

"Oh, is that so? And I suppose you know a magic spell that will make it rain inside a restaurant?"

"Actually, I do."

She raised the bottle opener high, just as she'd seen Mike do in her apartment. She also tried to recall the words he'd spoken—and luckily, her memory for words was legendary. She could recall silly poems she'd been forced to memorize in third grade, and this was just another silly poem. From the back of her mind, the words came to her.

"Feelum, phylum, finocus
Breath of summer, scent of crocus
Unlock all, unlatch unchain
Blow, let go, like summer rain!"

There was a crash like thunder and a deluge of rain began to fall.

The Stroms were busy furiously firing as the rain came pouring down, and their staffs were drenched. This did not stop the weapons from functioning—but it did stop the Stroms.

"Augh! Das Mädchen hat Wasser vom Himmel geschickt!"

Far away in her kitchen, a certain witch was watching the action in her brand new crystal ball. She was cursing the idiotic, non-obedient Stroms and was now rooting for their destruction. Why had she created such imbeciles? But now she grinned.

The Stroms had been made from a combination of magic, a seed, and beer water. They were indestructible—unless they were drenched by water that resulted from a magic spell, at which time they would return to being seeds once again.

Velva marveled at Debbie's dumb luck and then shrugged.

"What did I tell you, Bart?" she said to her cat. "It's better to be lucky than to be good."

40: Back On The Road

Debbie watched through the downpour as the three German boozers began to change. First, she saw a modification in color. Strom's skin turned an empty shade of gray, like a dead piece of chewing gum. Then his nose, eyes, ears, fingers, and other unseen parts melted into the shapeless lump that was now his body. Finally, the lump shrank, leaving only a soggy three-piece suit behind.

Unfortunately, his voice remained for a few more seconds, despite his lack of a mouth.

"Ve vill find you, Frau, and ve vill have revenge! Ugh! Oog! Ahhh!

Debbie didn't like the implication of these words, but she figured she'd keep Mike's bottle opener handy. She also didn't like how only two of the Stroms were immediately destroyed. The third one ran into a restroom and she wasn't sure whether or not it was raining in there. It was always possible the spell excluded restrooms.

Mike ran after the final Strom with his drumsticks held high. No doubt he was following that ancient maxim: *Never rest until the final Strom is destroyed.* Debbie knew Mike loved a good rout, and she guessed he'd feel great kicking the crap out of a Strom who was busy melting in the toilet.

Debbie had mixed feelings. She wanted to make sure the final Strom was washed down the drain, but she also saw an opportunity. Juan saw it, too.

He tugged at her arm. "Let's go," he said.

They bolted for the back door. She glanced behind as they left and saw Cynthia looking at them. Cynthia looked undecided about what to do, but Debbie didn't wait to find out what she did. They were in the parking lot now and racing toward Juan's car.

Debbie wasn't much of a runner. She was more of a sitter, or maybe a 'layer.' Was 'layer' an actual word? Yes, of course, it was part of a cake. Sometimes it was hard to stop thinking like a writer, or maybe just a dessert lover.

Juan grabbed her hand. "Hurry, Debbie! I'm sure they will follow."

Debbie yanked her hand away. "I'm not running anymore. Leave me to die." She was breathing hard and wiping her glasses on her sleeve.

"I won't do that," Juan said.

He slowed his pace and walked by her side. She glanced at him, and she felt warm and fuzzy. He'd run from her bedroom, but he wasn't running now. He even leaped forward and opened the car door for her before bolting around to the driver's side. As they drove past the diner, she saw water pouring from the doors of the building and into the parking lot, like the place was bleeding. She saw Mike and Cynthia at the doorway, watching them go. He was shouting about something. Cynthia just smiled and waved her hand.

Debbie waved back. She wasn't sure what the wave meant, but she guessed it was a friendly gesture. Then again, she'd had fights with Cynthia before over the years, but never over a guy, and never over Cynthia's tendency to jiggle.

Debbie shook her head. It had been a stupid argument. Cynthia couldn't help her jiggling; it was the way she was built. As for the remark about Debbie's own lack of jiggling parts, it was nothing Debbie hadn't joked about herself a thousand times. None of that was the real issue. The real issue was Mike, and the fact that Cynthia might have been dead right about everything she'd said.

She took a deep breath and looked at Juan. He'd been downright chivalrous in there, risking himself and trying to protect her. Maybe there were good reasons why she was in the car with him, and maybe they didn't all involve sex.

"We're both soaked," Juan said. "Maybe we should get out of these clothes."

"You're always trying to get me naked, Juan."

"That's not what I meant," he said with a laugh. "Even if it's true."

He looked at her and grinned. "You're quite a fighter, Debbie. You were magnificent."

She shrugged. "You were doing more fighting than me. I'm no brawler, Juan. I can't even kill a spider."

"You were amazing. It was more subtle, but you took charge."

"I don't usually do that, either."

"You'll learn to do it someday. All women want to take charge of a man's life. It's in the female blood."

She rolled her eyes. "You were doing great for almost two minutes, Juan, but now you're blowing it. Comments like that make my blood boil. That's what's in my blood now—a lot of steam."

"That sounds very sexy."

She was about to respond, but then he pulled up her soaking wet dress and laid a hand on her bare thigh.

"Very pretty," he said. "You are the sexiest woman in the world."

She put her hand on top of his, and he moved it higher, and he moved it correctly, and she couldn't believe how much heat she had going on so fast.

"Pull over," she said. "Do it now."

He almost swerved the car into a tree, but then he saw a little strip mall, and a parking lot, and an area away from the stores near a dumpster. Their lips locked as he yanked the parking brake. She grabbed his head and pulled him into her fiery kiss.

She vaguely considered the fact that they were in a public place, but she knew it wouldn't matter. No one would see them in Sex Hell.

41: Queen Of Sex Hell

Debbie was sitting on a throne.

It was a cushy chair shaped like a heart, sitting in a spacious room with stone walls, and decorated with zebra striped rugs, pictures of Wile E. Coyote, and a heavy wooden table in a corner that held a laptop computer and a pile of chocolate bars.

Her eyes jumped around while she caught her breath. Okay, so far this didn't seem too bad. Her flowing green gown looked elegant, in a non-black kind of way. All she needed now was a decent book, and maybe a shot of tequila to calm her down. Also, where was Juan? That philandering troubadour better be around somewhere.

She pressed a candy-colored button on the arm of the chair, and two doors at the end of the room swung open. Her eyes got wide as a pair of strong-looking women strolled in. They were tall, and had hair like platinum linguini, and wore blazing red dresses with metal accessories and slick black boots with death-defying high heels. One was holding a jewel-encrusted scepter, and the other was clutching a bowl of popcorn.

"Does Her Majesty require a snack?" said one of the women. "Or would she prefer to just sit around and act like a queen?"

Debbie considered the question. It seemed like there should be a separate button for each of those options, and she pondered calling an electrician. "I'm really not hungry," she said. "I guess you can leave that stuff over there... Hey, wait! Can I please have the scepter?"

It was heavy and bursting with baubles, and it felt powerful in her hand. But she realized it was also more or less useless, except maybe as a nutcracker. Debbie liked walnuts, but she didn't see any nearby.

She pressed another button on the chair and the doors swung open again, and two more towering ladies appeared—only this time Juan was walking between them. Now she totally stopped breathing. He was dressed like a bullfighter, in tight black clothing with sequined gold trim, and his arms were bound behind his back.

He flashed a smile filled with smugness. "So, it looks like you're in charge after all, Debbie. But I didn't know that killing a bull turned you on."

She bristled at his arrogant tone. She bristled at his cute little smirk, and his lean, muscular body, and his suave Hispanic charm, and his—where was she going with this? She was bristling, god dammit.

"Be quiet," Debbie said. "I don't want to hurt the bulls. In fact, I love the bulls, and now that I'm queen the bull fights will be replaced with something else—something where no one gets hurt, but the outfits are still tight and sexy."

Juan laughed and then shook his ass back and forth a few times. "I do feel kind of sexy, but I can't play the guitar with my hands like this. I also can't make a sandwich. Why don't you be a good little queen and show me to the royal bedroom?"

He gave her another shining smirk and shook his ass again.

Debbie narrowed her eyes and considered whether to laugh or scream.

She held the scepter high. "Guards! Throw him into the royal dungeon!"

As soon as the order left her lips, she felt wonderful. In fact, she felt great! This queen gig was so uplifting. She was bursting with confidence and totally in charge. She vaguely wondered how long it would last.

Juan raised his eyebrows. He looked surprised, but obviously not scared. In fact, he looked eager to get to the dungeon. Then one of the women said, "I'm sorry, Your Majesty, but the dungeon is closed. The walls are being painted."

"What?" Debbie said, lowering the scepter. "Are you kidding me? Who paints the walls in a dungeon?"

"You ordered it, Your Majesty. You said it looked too depressing and stressful, and you asked for a calmer shade of blue."

"Oh. I guess that does sound like something I would say."

She sighed and took a few deep breaths. Now this queen gig was making her nervous. Then she looked over at Juan, who still had a lascivious leer plastered all over his pretty face.

Her nostrils flared. "Untie him and put him on the floor. On his back!"

Juan grinned again. Obviously, nothing would ever wipe the smug expression from his smirking lips—but she was going to decide what happened today. She was going to show this cocky trouba-dour-turned-toreador who was calling the shots.

He was on his back now, staring at the ceiling. She took a step forward, feeling like a queen but also failing to notice the throne was on a raised platform. She missed the step and tumbled down on top of him.

"Oof!"

That was fine. She'd been planning to be on top, anyway, and that's where she was—with her head between his knees and her feet around his face.

She sat up and slid toward his head, letting her knees rest on either side of his torso. Her flaring gown completely covered Juan's head and upper body, but she knew he was under there, right between her thighs. She also knew she wasn't wearing any panties.

"Juan, do you see the situation?"

"Yes, my queen," he said in a muffled voice. "Mmmmf, at this distance, I require no telescope. Let me say that the view is quite magnificent."

She smiled again. It was going to get a lot better. "Stop talking and get busy."

In general, being on top wasn't Debbie's favorite position. It was tiring, and why should a girl get all worn out trying to enjoy herself? But in this particular case, she wasn't doing much, except for occasionally letting Juan know what she wanted. And she wanted it for a long time while he was getting nothing.

At least not right away. But at some point he tried wriggling out of his tight pants, and at some point she helped him do it. But she still gave him nothing. She just watched the effect her queenly position had on him, and she enjoyed it. Obviously, he was a devoted subject, very attentive—standing at full attention, in fact. She gave him a couple of strokes here and there, and it seemed to inspire his devotion even further, but she wasn't in the mood for that. Not yet.

Quick as a flash, she jumped up and turned around, so she was no longer facing his feet or his stupid bobbing boner. Then she sat back down on his face, with her knees on either side of his shoulders, giving him a different angle into the royal treasure chest. Yeah, much better. She hiked up the front of her gown with both hands and held it back, close to her hips, so she could look down and watch things unfold, all the while rocking forward and back, forward and back.

Whoah! He was really in there! His tongue and his mouth and his whole shiny face! *Oh god is that hot! That is so hot!* She felt herself breathing hard. She felt like she was about to have the happiest heart attack of her life.

Her first orgasm was like a blast from a hundred silver trumpets—and so was the next one, and the next one. And through it all, Juan kept right on going. He is so incredible, she thought. Give that man a medal! Get that man an aqualung! Then the gown came off and the positions started changing.

Debbie was on her side, and on her back, and on her knees. She was back on top, back on the bottom, and back to wishing she wasn't on yet another hard floor. Still the raging action continued, and her body was racked by spasms, and she acquired a few bruises that were absolutely worth the pain. Her mind started to melt like a lump of burnt butter. Maybe she didn't need true love, or maybe she didn't need it as much as she needed this—or maybe she was falling in love because of this, or maybe she'd been in love for a while, or maybe she didn't care right now. The same non-conclusion kept rearing its fleshy head and then fucking the hell out of her.

She wasn't sure when it ended, but at some point she blinked and found herself lying beside Juan in a large bed with puffy white sheets, in a cozy little room with a window that overlooked a sprawling hillside bathed in the light of a thousand stars. There was a nightstand near Debbie's side, complete with a bowl of crispy hot popcorn.

Juan was smiling and eating a handful of the corn.

He put his arm around her, and she kept it there. She had nothing to say. She felt wonderful, and there was no point in ruining it all with a bunch of questions about anything deeper than this moment.

Of course, Carl had other plans, and his voice boomed through the air.

"That was amazing!" he said. "There was some very hot magic going on there. I'm going to need a blizzard to cool that room down."

Debbie and Juan looked up, and there was Carl's head floating in a corner of the room, right above what appeared to be a dusty exercise bike.

Debbie banged her fists down against the mattress. She hated to see his shiny red face again—but interestingly enough, she didn't feel as stressed about it as usual. Maybe she was getting used to him, or maybe she just didn't care anymore.

"Thanks, Carl," she said. "I'm glad you had a great, pervy time watching us... And thanks for the magic staff. Was it supposed to cause me to almost kill everyone in the room?"

Carl laughed. "What do you mean? Juan used it with no trouble."

"Yeah, I noticed. Was it designed so it wouldn't work for a woman?"

"No, it was designed so it wouldn't work for someone spastic."

"Then why did you give it to me?"

"You seem pretty coordinated when you're naked."

"Did you think I was going to be naked in a diner?"

"Look, I like the way you made it rain. That was very impressive."

"Great. Maybe when I get out of here I'll get a job working for a farmer."

Carl grinned. "You're a real smart-ass, you know that, Debbie? Are you sure you want to leave? You're having a better time here than most of my visitors. Some of them start off with real gusto but then end up with pretty routine, run-of-the-mill sex, despite my best efforts. Some of them just end up making excuses and asking for a television."

Debbie shrugged. "Where are they now? Would you let us out if we were boring?"

"Ha. That's the best question you've ever asked, but it's irrelevant. There's only one way out for you, Debbie—and you do have a shot."

She cocked her head and studied her tormentor. Under the blanket, she was still clenching her fists.

"Oh, really?" she said. "Then why don't you just tell us the name of the Goddess of Love? I'd really like to know that."

The demon laughed. "I can't make it too easy for you, honey." Then he grinned again. "Her name is Peach Blossom."

There was a noise like a gong, and Carl was gone.

42: Velva Buys A Ticket

Velva strolled through the noise and clatter of Newark Liberty International Airport with the springy step of a tigress. Eyes popped open, heads swiveled, and several guys gave themselves whiplash.

She smiled. Her legs were long, her skirt was short, and her hair splashed down like wanton waves of gold. She had curves that could cause a car crash, but most people in here were walking.

She stood online at the ticket counter and basked in the furtive glances of her admirers. There were plenty of attractive young women in the world, but she was something more. She was a magical sex goddess right out of a classic Hollywood movie—only she was in full, bursting color, and her spirit was enhanced by the pulsating power of the *sensualla*.

She tossed back her hair and congratulated herself. She'd really picked a hot pair when she'd chosen Juan and Debbie. Of course, Velva had trained for a while under a succubus, and that experience had helped her to spot their powerful libidos—but even she hadn't been expecting something on such a fearsome scale. Debbie's sex drive was almost supernatural, despite her plain appearance. But then appearances and sex drive were often unrelated. The sexiest person on the planet could be deader than a doorknob, while the less conventionally attractive would often burn the bed sheets into cinders.

She grinned. She only needed one more dose, and the odds of

Juan and Debbie getting free before they had another skin-shat-tering encounter were pretty low. In fact, they'd probably be going at it before Velva boarded the airplane. Too bad they didn't realize the sexual magic would eventually turn on them like an addictive narcotic, and they would die in the midst of a climactic moment—but sacrifices had to be made, and luckily, they would not be Velva's.

She had another thought, and she frowned. Everything could still be lost. The magic had done its work well, but unless she got her power to a certain level, it would not be permanent and it could be easily taken away. Plus, her traitorous sister, Peach, would probably help Juan and Debbie if they arrived at her doorstep, and that treach-erous demon, Carl, would probably help them get there—and that back-stabbing Union was behind it all.

That's why she was here at the airport. Those drunken, strudel-sat-urated fuck-faces had totally blown it, so now she would take care of business herself.

She approached the young girl behind the ticket counter.

"Hi, honey," Velva said in a sexy voice. "Give me a round trip ticket to New Orleans."

43: Hey, We're In Mississippi

Cynthia stared in silence at the leafy green trees along I-59, and at the light rain coming down. They'd just crossed into Mississippi, heading toward Meridian, and that meant Mike was going to announce their progress—big deal. She and Mike had hardly spoken as they'd driven the rented Jeep Grand Cherokee through Tennessee and Alabama, and the thought of a third state without any real conversation was a grim prospect.

She glanced over at his blank face and wondered if he was feeling the tension. The air was heavy with unspoken words. Sure, there was some idle chitchat sprinkled around as token gestures of good faith, but they were like crumbs of stale cake during a famine. They were temporary fixes stalling the inevitable Hindenburg hanging in the air.

"Hey, we're in Mississippi," he said, right on cue.

"That's good," she said.

"I've never been here before."

"Me neither."

"Too bad about the weather."

"It could be worse."

"I hope it stops raining."

"Yeah, me too. And I hope last night actually meant something to you."

She was tired of talking about the fucking weather.

He kept staring at the road. He didn't smile, but finally took a breath and said, "It meant a lot to me, Cynthia. You're a great girl."

"Great at what? At sex? I thought it was about more than that."

He squirmed a bit in his seat. "Cynthia, it was amazing, and I really like you. But you know why we're on this trip."

"Yeah, I know, and you know why I came, right? Because I liked you, and I thought it was a way…to get to know you better."

His eyebrows shot up. "What are you talking about? I thought you wanted to help free Debbie."

"I did, but that wasn't the only reason I came, and I think you knew that—and I think that's partly why you asked me to come, even if you can't admit it now. So I guess I'll just say all this stuff and feel like a fool. You were never really attracted to me, and everything that happened last night was spontaneous, and you never thought about me at all—right? I misunderstood everything, and it's all my fault."

He looked at her and then returned his gaze to the road.

For a long moment, there was no talking. Finally, he said, "Do you still want to help Debbie?"

She rolled her eyes. "Yeah, of course! Debbie's been my best friend forever, and I care about her more than anyone else in the world. We've been through a lot together, and I'm not going to let all this bullshit mess it up. In fact, we'll still be friends long after you're gone, Mike. I'm sure of that."

She sighed. "I shouldn't have said that… I'm sorry. The truth is I appreciate the way you want to rescue her. I hope some day if I need help, someone will come and help me the way you want to help her."

He hesitated, and then put a hand on her knee. "Cynthia, if you need help, I'll be there."

She gave a weak smile. "Thanks." Then she looked away, hiding her red-rimmed eyes. "Hey, we're in Mississippi," she said.

"Yeah."

They drove a bit more, not speaking while she rehashed the conversation in silence. She wondered if he was doing the same. She saw a sign for a rest stop.

"We need to get gas," Mike said.

As he pulled the vehicle up to the pump, he turned to her and said, "I want to rescue Debbie. Once that happens, I don't know."

She looked at him and said nothing, but her heart was beating fast.

"And by the way," he said, getting out of the car, "I *always* thought you were attractive."

She forced herself not to smile—but she felt a joyful spark, like a flower rising from a pile of April snow. *So this wasn't over yet!* She contained her feelings and only shrugged. After all, she was no beggar, and "I don't know" was still an insult, and this whole relationship thing was a two-way street.

"Okay," she said. "We'll get Debbie out of Sex Hell, and then we'll see how we feel. *I'll see how I feel.*"

He smiled and adjusted the brim of his baseball cap. "Fair enough."

She watched him work the gas pump. Damn, he looked good. She pretty much knew how she was going to feel. She sighed. Then she thought about Debbie.

What was her oldest friend in the world doing? Hopefully, she was okay.

She laughed to herself. Knowing Debbie, she was all wrapped up in the adventures of Suzy Spitfire.

44: Debbie Writes

Sparks and smoke swirled around Suzy Spitfire as she wrestled with the jumpy controls in the cockpit of her spaceship, The Red Bird. She'd been trying to outrun disaster for too long—most of her life, really—and now it seemed to be closing in as the beat-up spacecraft screamed through the blue skies above the glittery city of Choccoban. She swore in three different languages as a voice crackled in her headset. It was someone from the spaceport below with the most obvious kind of news.

The voice said, "Red Bird, you're coming in too fast... You're wobbling all over the place... You're fucking up everything!"

Suzy laughed. "Yeah, that's usually how it works before a crash. Have a fire truck standing by, okay? Bring the big one."

She glanced at the seat beside her, where Tolio was staring out the window with his coconut brown eyes. He was gripping the chair hard, but smiling. Despite the air of calamity, not a single hair on his pretty head was out of place. She had to admit, nothing seemed to frazzle the guy. Was that why she liked his world-class, philandering ass? It was one of the reasons.

Another shudder went through the ship. "How badly are we hit?" Tolio said. "That Space Patrol is being very difficult. They just won't let us go."

"It's Captain Tadrock," Suzy said. "He's my own personal demon. He's

been watching me for a while, and he's seen me in a few compromising positions, if you know what I mean. But don't worry, we'll escape. I once landed this baby in a cornfield and didn't squash an ear."

45: New Orleans

Debbie and Juan and his beat-up Toyota came careening into the glittery oasis of New Orleans a few hours before nightfall.

Debbie closed her laptop and stared at the bleary orange sun sinking above the highway. Her head was pounding like there was an inmate inside trying to escape. She chewed on a fingernail. She needed to relax, but a chaotic jumble of thoughts kept getting in the way.

She glanced at Juan and saw he was smiling. Somehow he took things in stride, and she admired that.

"We're here," he said. "I've always wanted to see this city."

"Yeah, me too, but I was hoping to do it under better circumstances."

"Debbie, we're in the middle of a great adventure. What could be better than this?"

"I really don't care for adventure," she said while massaging her temples. "My favorite adventure involves a book and a new kind of chocolate bar."

"Ah, I'm sure they have some fantastic chocolate here. How can you not like adventure? You're a science fiction writer."

He gave a nod toward her computer.

"I like *imagining* adventure," she said. "I don't like actually doing it."

"Adventure is an attitude, Debbie. It's not about climbing a mountain or drinking tequila. It's about living the life you want to live. That's something few people do, and that is true adventure."

"Juan, I'm a waitress in a diner."

"No, you're not. You were fired."

She laughed. "I guess that's true. So maybe poverty will be a great adventure."

"You'll be richer than any banker on Wall Street."

"You're an idealist, Juan. But that won't keep you alive."

"It's worked so far. Debbie, why are you a waitress? Because you're a writer. You're doing what you must to pay the bills, but that's just a physical thing. In your head, you're not there. You're in a place few will know, and you're more free than many."

She started to respond, but stopped. Everything he was saying was exactly what she believed. Of course, there were days when egg and orange juice stains made it hard to *really* believe, especially when they covered her battle flag of liberation—but she still believed it, and it would always be one of her "pry it from my cold, dead fingers" philosophies, and she loved the way he believed it, too.

"Yeah," she said. "I think you're right, but sometimes I wonder if I'll ever give up. Sometimes I wonder if I'll just fall into step with the blank army of normalcy."

He shook his head. "A real musician is always a musician. If you're a true musician, playing music is a way of life—and if you stop playing, your true self will die. If you're really a writer, you will write. You are a writer, Debbie. You are real."

She fidgeted with her hair and stared out the passenger side window. "How do you know I'm so real, Juan? You've never read a thing I've written."

"I can tell. You have the soul of a writer. You must let me read something."

"Maybe I will. But you'll probably read one story and think my soul is filled with dangling participles and questionable story arcs—or just empty schlock."

"I won't think those things," he said. "Besides, I like science fiction and satire. I like it more than you like the music I love." He motioned toward the stereo, which was playing a jazzy guitar tune.

"No, I like this music!" she said. "It has…personality. I also like the stuff with lyrics, like the song you played in the restaurant."

"Ah, yes. I wrote that for you."

She rolled her eyes. "I tend to think you've said that to at least ten other girls."

"Ten? Only ten?"

"Very funny. Sorry to imply that you were less of a bastard than I thought."

He gave a short laugh and then grinned. "Debbie, it's possible I wrote the song for other women—but when I sang it that night, it was only about you. That's the truth."

Debbie gave him a skeptical glance, followed by a brief fantasy where she was kissing him on a beautiful bridge above a shimmering river, and then lying in bed with him, just talking, and then he was playing the guitar, and she was writing a novel, and they were eating dinner and drinking wine at a rustic restaurant overlooking the rolling hills of Spain, and life was going by and it was better than it had ever been before.

"Do you know where you're going?" Debbie said.

"No. But I think we're there."

"Maybe we should try looking up the name Peach Blossom somewhere."

"Yes, but maybe first we should find a place to stay and get something to eat. Maybe we should take a little time to enjoy ourselves—and no, it doesn't have to be about *that.*"

"What are you talking about?"

"You know what I'm talking about."

"Okay, maybe I do. You're talking about sex—again."

"I was saying we don't have to do it."

She cocked her head. Here was an interesting idea.

"Oh, really?" she said. "You'd want to be with me for an entire evening and not have sex?"

"Only if you wanted it that way. But you won't."

She laughed, indignant, and tossed back her hair. "Do you really think I couldn't do that?"

"Do you really want to? Besides, you haven't refused yet, Debbie."

She started to speak—but stopped.

Holy crap—come to think of it, he was right. Apparently, Juan thought he was irresistible, and why shouldn't he? After all, she'd done very little resisting. It's true she hadn't wanted to resist, but he had a lot of nerve thinking she couldn't do it. She stared down at her thighs, and felt a quick sexual fantasy lapping at her brain—and then she stopped it.

Maybe it was time for a test. Maybe it was time to stop bouncing around on the sticky road of pink and wet gratification and start thinking about what else she wanted. Maybe it was time to stop lying to herself about her confusion and admit exactly what it was she wanted, and that she was afraid to confess to—and then make it happen or not happen.

She wanted to be with Juan, and not just in a sexual way. She'd had a great time, but it was over now, and she was not going to have sex with him again unless she could have what she really wanted.

She imagined another scene of undulating flesh. No, it was not going to happen. Then another one, and this one was intense. She was being spanked and then pounded hard on top of a desk in an outer space classroom, and it was mind-blowing, and come to think of it that one had actually happened. But it wouldn't be happening again, no matter how hot and excited she got.

She squirmed a bit—wow, pretty hot and excited, but it would not happen. She pictured a steel padlock between her legs and almost laughed out loud. Could she keep it closed if he started acting like he sincerely cared about her? Yeah, because he might be lying just to get her naked, but what if he wasn't lying? She had to stay strong, find Peach Blossom, get out of Sex Hell, and then see what happened.

Juan put his hand on her thigh. "Are you all right? You seem lost in thought."

Debbie caught her breath. Red alert! She wanted that hand to keep moving, but there was no way. She put her hand on top of his—and then peeled away his grip.

"I thought we were getting something to eat," she said.

Juan smiled and put his fingers back on the steering wheel. "Yes, what would you like? I only want you to be happy."

"We don't have much money left, Juan. Do they sell potato chips in this town?"

"We'll do better than that. I have some room left on my credit card."

"I thought you had no credit."

"I exaggerated. I was saving it for a dramatic moment."

"Was that the dramatic moment when I ran out of money?"

"Precisely. But really, I was planning to spend it on a celebration. Maybe we'll begin to celebrate early."

"Yeah, I like that plan. That way, if we fail, we still had a party."

"You see? You *are* adventurous. See if you can find a good place."

Debbie reached into her purse and grabbed her phone—and then she saw a message from Cynthia, and her heart started pounding. What did she want? Did she really think their lifetime of friendship could be restored by a little communication? The message said: *Deb, where are you going? Mike's magic bongos have crapped out. You're my best friend. Love, Cynthia.*

That was a short message, and she had no intention of telling Cynthia and Mike where she was going. Those two would only bring a brawling disaster.

Meanwhile, Juan was navigating the streets of New Orleans.

Debbie took her eyes off the digital screen for a second to notice the flavorful scenery of Bourbon Street, with its brick and mortar saloons, and wrought iron railings, and flamboyant balconies, and gas lampposts, and a street that bubbled with a raucous river of people. Signs in bright windows advertised blues, jazz, beer, and general good times.

It was very romantic, in a commercial kind of way. She wondered what the place had looked like before it realized what it was supposed to look like. Probably the same, only dirtier—and better.

Juan touched Debbie's knee. "Life is short. Who knows if we'll ever be here again? We need to think about what's important."

She looked at him, and then made a decision. She sent a text message.

We're in New Orleans. You're my best friend, too. Love, Debbie.

46: From The Dumpster

Strom's head rose from the garbage like a periscope rotating in a pool of filth.

Strom was inside a dumpster, and it was a hot dumpster. The summer sun was cooking the metal container into a stinky stew of discarded hamburger bits, French fries, and coleslaw, as well as some less edible stuff, like burnt chairs, bits of a dessert bar, soggy ceiling tiles, and a pile of exploded bananas.

So vat? This does not change mission much, no.

Strom was mainly looking for the other Stroms, and they were easily found. But they looked different now. They used to be a pair of sharp-looking assassins in three-piece suits—but now they looked like two wide-shouldered women dressed as police officers. He was also starting to realize he was probably a "she" as well. When he spoke, he heard the sound of a female voice.

"*Oooh, ve change, ya?*"

"*Ya. Wir sprechen noch Deutsch?*"

"*Ein, zwei, drei—ya, some Deutsch and the English, too.*"

"*Vy you dress like police?*"

"*Sie sind wie ein Stormtrooper verkleidet.*"

"*Do I vere high heels?*"

She wasn't wearing high heels. In fact, they were all dressed like professional cops, complete with guns, badges, and glistening black combat boots. Unlike the previous Stroms, they were not identical. But they were pretty close—all Aryan blondes with blue eyes, red lips, and a lust for violence.

"*Do veapons ve have?*"

"*Ya! Oh ya!*"

Strom reached into the dumpster and pulled out a couple of rifles, a pistol, and a few hand grenades.

"*Das rifles and pistolen.*"

"*So kill Peach Blossom still?*"

"*Ya, and Velva.*"

"*And the others?*"

"*Kil wir sie alle! And ve do without court order!*"

"*We must follow.*"

"*Schauen sie dort!*"

Strom looked out at the Big Highway Diner and spotted a camera crew, as well as a pickup truck that said, "Fix It Fast General Contracting"— and a police car.

"*Lass uns gehen!*"

They were on their way.

47: Here At Last

"I made it to Choccoban, Debbie."

"I know. And I made it to New Orleans, Suzy."

"That's great. I'll bet you can get into a lot of trouble there."

"Yeah, well, I'm trying to get out of trouble. But I'm not exactly sure how to do it."

"Usually when I get into trouble, Debbie, it's because I did something stupid. And usually when I can't get out of trouble, it's because I keep doing the same dumb thing. Like that time I lost a hundred thousand *loot cards* playing number 97 at the Crystal Casino. I mean, motherfucker, you would think after 600 spins my number would come up, right? But it never did, and I had to blast my way through every toll booth on the way home."

"So you're saying I should stop gambling?"

"No! I'm saying go ahead and gamble—just don't keep playing the same losing game."

"What if they're all losers?"

"Start drinking heavily."

"I'm not sure if that's the best advice, Suzy."

"There are no certainties, Deb. Take a shot and hope for the best."

48: Bar Fight

Juan stuffed another crusty shrimp into his mouth and asked the bartender for more beer.

"This is wonderful," he said. "It reminds me of the food in Spain."

"You've been to Spain?" Debbie said.

"No, but I've seen it on television. They had shrimp there."

She laughed and looked around. The room was smoky and dark, and filled with gruff old blues, sweet wafting smells of seafood, and stumbling tourists with glazed eyes. Debbie tried to feel comfortable, sitting in a corner at the bar, but her stomach was in knots. She took another sip of wine. One ticket to *comfortland* coming up.

"I've never really been anywhere," she said. "No one in my family ever went anywhere except the liquor store." She held the glass high. "I guess the drunk doesn't fall too far from the other drunks."

"You're not a drunk," Juan said. "And all things are fine in moderation. That's what my father used to say."

"Is that the guy who was never home?"

"He was home a moderate amount of the time."

"You haven't been home for days. He would be proud of you."

"Yes, he would be proud—that's true."

He took another gulp of his beer and said nothing.

"You don't want your father to be proud of you?" Debbie said.

He hesitated. "Sometimes yes, sometimes no." He smiled and then looked away.

Debbie wondered what he was thinking. She felt his arm around her waist, pulling her closer, and then she knew.

"You look very beautiful tonight," he said.

She laughed again. *Not so fast.*

"I look like hell," she said. "I've been in the same clothes for two days, and that's pretty much how I feel—like a stinky old dress hanging in a consignment shop."

"It doesn't matter. You're the most beautiful girl in the room."

Debbie glanced around again and shook her head. "Thanks, but really, I'm no better than sixth or seventh."

"You put yourself down, Debbie, but you shouldn't. You're smart and talented and funny, and these things make you beautiful. Plus, you *are* a sexy woman."

"Juan, we don't even have a room yet."

His hand dropped down and squeezed her thigh.

"We don't need one."

This was true. The instant trip to the other dimension known as Sex Hell made finding a place very convenient, and though Debbie was determined to stay out of there she felt herself getting excited. It didn't matter whether the flattery was sincere or not—it totally worked. Her heart was speeding up, and her blood was rushing around, and in a second they would be there.

She jumped off her stool. "I'm not playing that game tonight, Juan. Forget it."

His eyebrows shot up, but his smile remained. The smug bastard, she thought.

"It was just an idea," he said. "I was making a suggestion. Maybe we should go for a walk."

"Yeah, good idea. I'll go first."

She ran toward the door. He was right behind and would have easily caught her—but a beefy bouncer grabbed his arm.

"Hold it there, bub," the big guy said. "You gonna pay for the food and drinks?"

He was wide as a pickup truck, with a shaved head, a full beard, and a canvas of tattoos covering his gorilla-sized arms.

"Yes, yes, of course," Juan sputtered. "But my girlfriend has my money."

Debbie stopped running. She opened the door to the street, smiled at the bouncer and said, "I'm not his girlfriend." Then she walked out into the night.

49: Debbie And The Demon

Debbie felt warm pinpricks of rain on her face. The fuzzy tangerine sun had been replaced by a cloudy night sky, and a stabbing drizzle, and a breath of hot, steamy air. She wiped off her glasses and absorbed the sticky evening.

The streets of the city were filled with the clatter of cars and conversations. The sidewalks were pulsing with ramblers and tourists and it was fine. While she'd never felt comfortable in a crowd, the thought of living away from the bustle didn't thrill her. For some reason it was good to taste the soup of humanity, even though it often brought bubbling anxiety and shrieking hot stress.

She felt like a rope ready to snap. Stay calm, she thought, and stop thinking about Juan. But she still kept thinking about him. She took a deep breath. It would be nice to have a friend around, but lately friends were in short supply. Of course, most people had few real friends, whether they knew it or not. The average person with a hundred friends was someone who didn't know how to count very well.

She looked around with anxious eyes as she approached another pub full of festive music, blackened catfish, and beer. Another drink would be great, but she was already tipsy and low on cash. She'd hardly eaten, but her stomach didn't want food. Cynthia, where are you? she thought, and felt empty inside.

She paused at the door of the pub. The sign in the window said, "The Big Dog." She was going to keep walking, but there was something that drew her in. Maybe it was the way the room was bathed in golden light, or the way everyone inside seemed to be so alive. She wondered about the day of the week, but right now it didn't really matter. Maybe it never did.

She wasn't dressed for this place. Her casual, wrinkled black dress and white sneakers didn't fit in with the scruffy, smiling locals, and the drunk, unruffled tourists. But then, her outfit didn't fit with any place back home, either—except her living room.

She noticed a few people staring at her, and she fought an urge to flee. What the hell, she was too tired to do any fleeing. She saw one dull-looking dude smiling in her direction. His hair was short, and his head was narrow, and his eyes were small and dark like the eyes of a pig, and now he was walking toward her. Her heart started racing. Why did guys always approach her in these places? After all, she wore loose clothing, and industrial strength eyeglasses, and she lacked the bobbing breast-magnets of the C and D cup women—yet guys always talked to her. Maybe they thought there was less competition for a girl like her, ha.

She tried to look away, hoping this empty-eyed predator would take a hint. No such luck.

"Hey, what's up?" he said. "Are you looking for someone?"

"Yeah. I'm looking for a woman named Peach Blossom. Do you know her?"

"Never heard of her. Do you want something to drink?"

Smooth, Debbie thought. No idle chit-chat—just get her drunk as soon as possible.

"No, thanks," she said. "I don't drink."

"Oh." His face deflated like a bad tire. Apparently, there was only one tool in the toolbox.

"My friend wants to meet you," he said.

She snorted, hoping the "friend" wasn't in his pants.

"What friend is that?"

"That guy over there." He pointed to a round table in the corner.

Debbie followed his finger with her eyes—and her eyes almost popped from her face.

Sitting at the table was Carl, the floating demon-head of Sex Hell. Only this time he'd brought his whole body with him. He looked huge, and she wondered why she hadn't noticed him before, especially since he was bright red like a Christmas ornament. He also wore no shirt.

"That guy?" Debbie said. "The big red demon?"

"No, no, the guy standing behind him in the black leather pants."

"What?"

"Just kidding! I meant the big red demon. Anyway, I've got to go... By the way, my name is Jay."

"It was nice meeting you, Jay."

"Maybe I'll see you later."

"I doubt it."

Jay shook his head and walked toward the door while Debbie threaded her way through the crowd. Carl was grinning, and his massive, muscled body glistened in the golden light.

"Hello, Debbie," he said.

"Hello, Carl." She crossed her arms, determined not to appear nervous despite her pounding heart. "Are you here for a particular drink special? And by the way, is this a dream?"

"Why would you ask me that? Do you dream about me?"

"No, but I'm wondering why no one else is looking at you. You do seem a little conspicuous, you know, being huge and red and half naked."

He laughed. "No one else is seeing me like this. You see the real me, but they're seeing just another random dork."

"Oh, you mean like the guy who was talking to me before?"

"Yeah, like him. What's the matter, you didn't like Jay? I told him he would strike out."

"I'm not really in the market for a relationship right now. I guess I should ask why you're here."

He grinned again. "I wanted to tell you not to have sex with Juan until you find Peach."

"Oh, really?" she said, eyeing him with suspicion. "I thought you wanted me to keep having sex."

"Yeah, I did, but now I don't. So keep your panties on."

"Well, that's funny. I guess you caught me on a good day, because I wasn't planning to do it with him right now. I'm holding out."

Carl smirked and slapped his hand down on the table. "Right! And you've never said *that* before."

"Hey, I liked him, okay? Besides, I turned him down before I came here."

"Yeah, I know, and it's a good thing. I didn't realize how close the witch was to getting enough *sensualla*. You picked a good time to leave him there jerking off—but it was close, so I thought I should talk to you. I'm going to help you get out of Sex Hell."

She narrowed her eyes. This was not making sense.

"Why the big change of heart, Carl? Are we boring you now?"

"Ha! That's a good one. Debbie, I could watch you all day, but it was never really about that. Let's just say the situation has changed, and we're now on the same side."

"You know, I can't really see myself on your side."

"Then get a thicker pair of glasses because that's where you are. And stop fucking."

"Okay, fine," Debbie said. "And how about you stop putting that aphrodisiac into the air that turns me into a sex maniac."

"What aphrodisiac?"

"The drug or spell or whatever it is you've got floating around in Sex Hell."

"Oh—right. Look, there's something in the air, but it's just a tranquilizer. It calms you down without any side effects. It doesn't do anything for your sex drive."

"What?" Debbie felt like she'd been slapped. "Are you kidding me?"

"No. Not a bit. You're a little high-strung, so I added something to help you relax and enjoy yourself. But that's all."

Debbie shook her head, still stunned. "Wow. So I must be really attracted to Juan. And my sex maniac tendencies must be natural."

"Oh, yeah," Carl said with a leer. "Your attraction to each other is epic, and your personal sex drive could level a city. Maybe you should try writing erotica."

"I don't want to write erotica!" Debbie snapped. "Why can't you just let us out?"

"It doesn't work that way. You are bound by a magical contract I made with a witch."

"Can't you just break it? She broke the one she made with us."

"Yeah, but you are part of the Third Dimension, which you laughingly call the 'real world.' And in your world, contract disputes get settled by lawyers or maybe some simple violence and murder. But in places beyond the Third Dimension it doesn't work that way. So you and Juan need to cool it until you find Peach. She'll tell you what to do."

"Why don't you just tell me where Peach is?"

He grinned and handed her a card with an address printed on it. Debbie studied it for a second and then shoved it into her purse.

"You can even tell her I sent you," he said.

"Thanks, but why should I trust you?"

"I'll admit, it's normally a bad idea—but I've taken a liking to you, Debbie, so shut up and enjoy it."

"Thanks, I think. Is there anything else I need to know?"

"Yeah, quite a bit, but I can only tell you so much."

"And why is that?"

"Because only you can free yourself from Sex Hell. Peach will get you started, and I can watch it happen, but you need to do it yourselves. You'll see what I mean—or you won't see."

"Great," she said and looked away. "Well, thanks again, Carl."

"Oh, come on, I'm not so bad."

"Yeah, when we want the same thing. Otherwise, you're not so good."

"I'm good enough," he said, standing up.

Debbie's eyes went wide. He was not half naked as she had thought. No, he was totally naked and had a monstrous erection. It was at least twelve fat inches and pointed at her like an engorged cannon.

Carl smirked. "Are you shocked? Threatened? Disgusted? Fascinated? Or just turned on? I know the truth."

Then he vanished.

Debbie stared for a bit at the spot where he'd been standing, and then turned and headed for the exit. But Carl wasn't quite done with her, and his voice sounded in her head.

"One more thing," he said. "Check out the Wheel Of Gold down the street. Also, watch out for more assassins."

"That's two things, but thanks again."

"Don't mention it. See you later."

Debbie shuddered and stepped outside.

Her head was pounding. Her vision was blurry. Her mind was swirling with crazy thoughts.

Was any of this actually happening? She'd always said that truth was stranger than fiction. She'd always felt that fiction was just as real as what passed for reality.

It all happened on a higher plane, in a place where fantasy mixed with reality. It was the place where Suzy Spitfire lived. But Debbie didn't bother talking to Suzy. She knew Suzy was busy.

50: Debbie Writes Again

Suzy Spitfire peered from a crooked doorway in a crowded neighborhood near downtown Choccoban. She was standing in an alley, but on the nearby street she could hear a screaming party going on. It was Carnival Season, and people were playing jubilant music non-stop while they sucked down drinks and stumbled around. The alley had already been used for a few acts of debauchery and two acts of vomiting, and it wasn't even noon.

She smiled to herself. The whole city was rowdy and disgusting, just the way she liked it.

Suddenly, she was staring into the cool eyes of the tall, shiny guy standing next to her—a guy in the cherry red uniform of the Space Patrol.

"It's been a while, Suzy."

"Yeah, it has."

"I see you've still got that leather skirt. And the gun."

"Yeah, and I'm still killing people with both of 'em."

"Do you miss me?"

"I miss parts of you, Tadrock. I'll let you guess which ones."

"I always knew you loved my blue eyes. So, here we are."

She tossed back her mop of dark crimson hair. "Right. Look, you've been dogging us for days, and I just can't seem to shake you. But I'm telling you, I got into this whole thing by accident. I thought I had a deal with Shelba, the Mystical Guru, but she was just using me. Can't you just give us a break?"

The guy grinned and then shrugged. "I'm just doing my job, Suzy. And you're just a girl making a lot of mistakes."

"I've made a few."

"Was I one of them?"

"Hell, yes. Any more dumb questions?"

Tadrock laughed. "Fair enough. How did you get mixed up with this guru? And this guy?"

Suzy shrugged. "Shelba made me some sweet promises she didn't keep, and then introduced me to Tolio—a guy I don't trust. So maybe I should just say 'fuck it' and rob that casino downtown."

"What casino? The Silver Shot of Happiness? It's impregnable! Even on a typical day, it's very tough to win there. The odds are long."

"I like 'em long, Tadroc—otherwise, they're just too short. So, do you want to buy some Fear Focus pistols? They blast an opponent with his own insecurities and cause instant heart failure."

Tadrock shrugged. "No thanks, but be careful. Someone might use one of those on you."

"Ha. I'll take my chances."

51: Cynthia Refuses

Cynthia gazed through the windshield at the colorful streets of the French Quarter. It looked like a rollicking mishmash of gritty music, fiery food, and touristy good times. It looked like a place that would be better without all the tourists. In any event, Mike didn't seem too interested in finding a party.

His eyes were busy scanning the scene, jumping around like drunken searchlights. Obviously, he was looking for Debbie. Cynthia wondered what would've happened if she hadn't told him to come here. Maybe he would've created another idiotic pair of magic bongos or whatever. Either way, it was good they were here. She wanted to find Debbie as much as he did. In fact, she wanted to see Debbie more than she wanted to get naked again with Mike.

She recalled a time in high school, when Tommy Standish had spent a week flirting with Debbie, but then rejected her because his jock friends ostracized him for it. Mike reminded her of Tommy in a physical way—a big athletic guy. But unlike Tommy, Mike was upfront about his feelings for Debbie. Tommy had been tough on the outside but he'd had the backbone of a jelly donut. A guy with a real backbone doesn't reject love over social status. Mike also threw thunderbolts, while Tommy had never thrown anything but a football. Really, the hell with Tommy and high school and the whole fucking football team. Come to think of it, they'd lost every game that year.

Mike reached down and touched her knee.

"What are you thinking about?" he said.

"Tommy Standish."

"Oh, is he a musician?"

"No. He was more of a fraud."

"An ex-boyfriend?"

"No. He wasn't my type."

Mike smiled. "And what's your type?"

"I like a guy who knows what he wants."

He turned his gaze back to the street. "I guess that's good to know... Maybe we should get a place to stay. Maybe you can ask Debbie where she is again."

"I sent her another text, but she didn't answer."

"Maybe you can call her."

Cynthia shrugged and pretended to touch the screen of her phone before jamming it against her ear. She was calling nobody. She didn't want to talk to Debbie with Mike around.

"No answer," she said. "I'm not leaving a message."

Mike didn't say anything as he swung the car into a Hampton Inn parking lot.

They were soon walking into a hotel room. It was bland like a greeting card, yet comfortable, with a panoramic view of the glittering streets below. There was also one queen-sized bed.

"Didn't they have a room with two beds?" she said.

"Oh, I didn't ask. I figured whatever they had would be fine."

"Is that what you figured?" she said with a short laugh. "You just make sure you stay on your side."

He took a step toward her, wrapping his arms around her waist.

"Cynthia, there's no reason we can't be friendly."

"I am being friendly, but friendly doesn't include everything."

He raised his eyebrows. "What are you talking about? Did I say anything like that? I know we have to sort out a couple of things."

"I'm glad you know that. Let me know when you're done sorting, and I'll tell you if I'm still interested."

He took off his baseball cap and tossed it onto the bed. Then he stared at her, and he grinned. "Cynthia, you look great." He took a step forward and wrapped his hands around her waist again.

His hands felt good there, and her nipples reacted. He hesitated, and then lunged forward and gave her a kiss. She kissed him back, but then pulled away. "Thanks," she said, "but I don't think we should do anything like that right now."

"It was just a kiss."

"Yeah, but an evening of awesome sex starts with a kiss, and I'm not interested in anything awesome right now."

"I didn't say we had to do anything."

"That's good," she said in a breathy whisper. "In fact, that's just perfect, because I don't feel like unsnapping my bra, and sliding off my panties, and dropping to my knees, and sucking you and fucking you and letting you bang me through the wall—I don't feel like doing any of those things right now. Do you see what I mean?"

His eyes were wide. "Yeah, I see."

"Oh, good."

He took a deep breath. "Do you think you might feel like doing any of that stuff later?"

"No," she said and smiled.

"Oh."

"I want to take a walk."

"Great!" He snatched his hat from the bed. "Let's do it!"

"I want to go by myself."

"What? Alone in the city?"

"I've been alone in the city before."

"Oh, I know... I just thought we could walk around together."

"We've spent a lot of time in the car, and I just want to be alone to think."

"Okay, sure," he sputtered. "I suppose. What are you thinking about?"

"Whatever pops into my head, I guess. I'll see you later."

She opened the door and started to leave.

"Wait!" he said. "Do you have your phone? Call me if you need anything."

"Yeah, I've got it. Thanks."

She once again grabbed the doorknob.

"Wait!" he said. She turned back around—and he was just staring at her, not saying anything.

Finally, he said, "Cynthia, do you have to go?"

"Yeah, I do. I'll see you soon."

She closed the door hard and headed fast toward the street.

It hurt to leave him. She was aching to stay. It would be so easy to run back into the room, and throw her arms around him, and kiss him a hundred times, and have raging sex until she collapsed, and then walk around this glowing city with him by her side—but no. The hell with that and the hell with him. At least for now.

She walked quickly, putting some immediate distance between herself and the hotel. She practically sprinted a few blocks before finally slowing down. Then she stopped and caught her breath. Hey, this was an awesome city, and it was time to relax and soak up the local color. And the city was filled with color. It was a three-dimensional canvas bursting with the shades of humanity.

She passed a few pubs that seemed inviting, but finally found herself standing in front of a place called The Wheel of Gold. Then she walked inside, and there was Debbie.

52: Reunited

Debbie didn't go to bars alone. She usually went with a friend, and that was usually because the friend wanted to go, and the friend was usually Cynthia. Tonight, she was alone in a bar recommended by a demon—and was that Cynthia standing in the doorway?

Debbie's heart jumped. Then Cynthia looked at her, and Debbie's face bloomed with a huge smile. Cynthia raised her arms in a pre-hug position, and then Debbie did the same, and they ran toward each other and collided in a whirlwind embrace like two long lost lovers. It was every bit as good as sex with Juan. It was even better.

"Debbie! What are you doing here alone?"

"I was thirsty, and I didn't want to have sex with Juan. What are *you* doing here alone?"

"I wanted a drink, and I didn't want to have sex with Mike."

"Wow. United in alcohol and celibacy."

"Again!"

They both laughed and plopped down at the bar.

The bartender glided over to them. She was a tall, dark woman with smoky eyes. "Hello, I'm Aruna," she said. "What would you like?"

"Something strong," Cynthia said. "And more than one."

Aruna poured a pair of shiny green margaritas, and Debbie instantly relaxed. They'd found a bartender who could read minds. The two friends sipped their drinks and looked at each other.

It was a good room for a talk. The lighting was soft, the crowd was thin, and the music was subtle like a good guitar lick. In the background, a guy was playing solo on a Gibson hollow body—light, feathery riffs with a whispering digital echo. It was cool and calm.

Debbie fidgeted with her drink and sighed. "Cynthia, I apologize. Everything you said was true. I cheated on Mike and then ran off with someone else, and it's all because Mike wasn't the right guy, so I shouldn't be mad at you for jumping in like a big slut."

Cynthia laughed. "I'm not big. I'm curvy."

"Okay, you jumped in like a curvy slut."

"Right," Cynthia said, taking a gulp of her drink. "And I'm sorry I flirted with Mike and then had sex with him after you dumped him and started acting like a crazy whore who's obsessed with some sleaze ball."

"Hey, I'm not a crazy whore. I had great sex with a guy I liked, and at the very worst I'm just crazy."

"Are we making up here?"

"We're making progress."

"It seems minimal."

Debbie put down her drink. "I missed you."

"I missed you, too."

"I'll forgive you if you'll forgive me."

"I'll forgive you if you'll buy me another drink."

"I'm a little light on cash."

"Okay, I'll buy the drink."

"Deal."

Aruna poured them another round while Debbie filled Cynthia in on her adventures. Cynthia listened with wide eyes, and then brought Debbie up to speed on the situation with Mike. Also, the possible non-situation.

Debbie took a big swallow from her glass. "I'm glad you got things to work with Mike, at least one time. He wasn't too happy with me. I guess we just weren't compatible in that area."

"Debbie, you weren't compatible in any area. You had nothing in common."

"What do *you* have in common with him?"

Cynthia shrugged. "I don't know, but whatever it is, it seems to work. I think he likes curvy girls, and he plays the drums, and he's someone I can be around... *I don't know!* What the hell do you like about Juan? Is it the sleaze factor? "

"No! Well, maybe. But really, the things I've done with Juan weren't sleazy; they were just interesting. Either that, or I do like sleazy sex more than I realized, ha... Anyway, that isn't what I like about him. Juan's a nice guy. He is! And he has a way of relaxing me."

"You mean with his penis?"

"Yes! And other stuff. It just works. He's very idealistic, and he has this whole thing about his dad, and I relate to his love of music. Plus, he's so damn sexy. *I don't know!*"

"I suppose it could work out."

"It's possible. But then again, I don't trust him, and I can't love a guy I don't trust. Or maybe I can, but I'll always be miserable."

"Maybe he'll show you that he really cares."

"Maybe. But I just want to get free of the whole Sex Hell thing and then worry about it."

"Debbie, I'm a little drunk."

"Yeah, me too, and it's good. It means I'll stumble back to the hotel and just pass out. I told Carl I wouldn't do anything with Juan until we find Peach, and that's fine with me."

"And where is this Peach? "

"Carl told me, but I can't tell you."

"What do you mean? You told me you were coming to New Orleans, didn't you? What if you get in trouble? I need to know where you'll be."

Debbie hesitated, and then fumbled around in her purse. She knew the many clichés concerning a girl with too much junk in her pocketbook, and she embraced them all. But eventually she found the card Carl had given her, and she showed it to Cynthia, who wiped off a few stains from a couple of stray chocolate bars and studied the writing.

Debbie slapped her hand down on the bar. "You can't bring Mike over there! He would just screw things up with his whole Wyatt Earp routine. And I'm not even gonna talk about his crooked thunderbolts."

"He was getting good with the thunderbolts, and we might be able to help."

"I don't want you to help! I just want you to know where I ended up in case I don't make it back."

"Debbie, you're coming back! And we're going to help you."

"No! Cynthia, you have to promise me you won't come over there tomorrow—please."

"Debbie, I can't even promise you I won't go back to the hotel and bang Mike's brains out."

"*I don't care if you bang Mike's brains out! Just don't come over there!*"

Cynthia sighed and shook her head. "Okay, we won't go over there."

"Do you promise?"

"Sure, until I change my mind."

"Do you think we should get another drink?"

"No. Let's get out of here."

53: Peach Blossom

Peach Blossom loved her home in the heart of the French Quarter. It was a burgundy brick house surrounded by a mossy stone wall. The place had a swimming pool, and a balcony, and a courtyard that bloomed with flowers and trees. In the first light of day, as the hazy sun was rising over the sleepy city, she sipped a cup of tea and smiled from her balcony at the garden below.

She'd made decent money as a florist, but it was nothing compared to the cash she'd made as an investor. Of course, a florist had to provide beautiful flowers, while an investor only had to predict the future. This was easier for a girl with a long future, and Peach had been working for five hundred years. She looked good for her age.

The doorbell rang, and she put down her tea. Who would be here at such an early hour? She knew her downstairs tenants were away in Europe, and she was expecting no visitors herself. She felt a chill in her spine, despite the tropical air, and her nose tingled with the touch of a cold memory. It couldn't be! She smoothed a wrinkle in her sizzling yellow sundress and walked to the intercom.

"Who is it?" she said.

"Hi, Peach. It's me, Velva."

Peach felt every nerve in her body go on a state of alert.

"Velva! What a surprise... I'm upstairs. Come on up."

"I'll be right there."

Peach took a deep breath and reached for the talisman hanging around her neck. It was a miniature glass hand, outstretched in a gesture of welcome, and she rubbed it a few times to power it up. She was guessing Velva hadn't come all the way to New Orleans just to say 'hello.'

When Velva came striding into the living room, Peach knew she'd been right. Peach's jaw dropped. Velva 'the hag' was gone, and here was Velva the movie star. Velva struck a dramatic pose, like a splash of blond blasphemy preening on a red carpet.

"Nice place, Peach. Do you still sell flowers, or did you discover something more interesting to do with yourself?"

Peach's ears perked up at the change in Velva's voice. The sound of gravel grating against a chalkboard was now smooth and sultry, like a late night mating call in a subterranean nightclub.

"I still sell flowers, Velva, but I don't think you're here to buy a white hydrangea. I see you've been busy."

Velva shoved a manicured hand into her purse and pulled out a cigarette. She lit it up and let it linger in her mouth before taking a long drag.

"Yeah, I've been violating the terms of my sentence from the Union."

Peach narrowed her eyes. So they were getting right to the point. "Yes, I see. Obviously, your violation has been going quite well."

"Thanks. But I keep wondering, Peach, if I'm going to get to keep it. I keep wondering if maybe those witches know what I've been doing, and if just maybe they're planning to pull the rug out from under me at the last second, right before I reach the top. It's the kind of thing they'd do, you know? Let me coast along, riding an orgasmic wave created by two perfect sex maniacs—and then, with the help of that traitorous bastard, Carl, yank it all away at the last second because that would hurt even more."

Peach shrugged. "Yeah, that is something they'd do, but not just to cause you more pain. They'd also be able to bring you up on charges for violating your original penalty—which would lead to an even worse penalty."

Velva blew a stream of smoke. "Why do they hate me so much?"

"The rules are the rules, Velva, and you tend to break them."

"We're witches. We don't have to follow rules."

"We do! You just think you're special. You've always been that way, even when we were young."

"That's because I *was* special! Didn't I make pancakes when I was three? And didn't I turn Grandma into a rattlesnake?"

Peach laughed. "The pancakes tasted like gooey flour, and Grandma turned *herself* into a rattlesnake—so she could kill Grandpa. You had nothing to do with it."

"Is that so?" Velva said with a smirk. "You were always jealous of me, Peach... You know those two are headed here, right? They're looking for a Goddess of Love. Now why would they be doing that?"

Peach's eyes got hard like frozen blueberries. "I don't know anything about the whereabouts of your victims, Velva—and I've never been jealous of you, and I told you, I'm not going to go against the Union. Why should I? You violated the witches' pact of non-magic for trivial affairs."

"They weren't trivial! I wanted to be a movie star."

"And then you violated the terms of your penalty by working with a demon to create illegal *sensualla*. So you really have no one to blame but yourself."

"We're sisters! You should want to help me."

"I tried to help you, Velva—and plenty of evil bitches happen to be somebody's sister."

"Are you saying I'm evil?"

"Why did you come here?"

Velva crushed out her cigarette on the top of a table. Peach frowned and watched the ashes smolder.

"I decided to give you a chance to help me out," Velva said. "I also wanted to see if you're afraid of the Union—or if you're part of it."

"Fine," Peach replied. "Now that you see *I'm part of it*, what's your plan?"

Peach didn't wait for an answer. Her eyes flashed like fireworks as she raised her palm, and an icy blue bolt of energy lashed out and slammed into Velva's chest. Velva flew across the room and crashed into the rail above the balcony.

"Oof!" she said, and then flipped over backwards and tumbled into the swimming pool below—*sploosh!*

Peach ran to the rail and looked down, searching the rippling waves. Velva seemed to be drifting somewhere near the bottom. Peach grasped her talisman and prepared to fire another strike—but she wasn't quick enough, and as the pool burst with orange light she was yanked from the balcony and swept down into the water—*kasploosh!*

"God damn you, Velva!" Peach shouted. She was in no mood to get wet, and she was in no mood for her sister's murderous attitude. She shot to the top as the water churned. It was heaving and swirling, and she had to struggle to swim—and then she saw the tentacle.

It came whipping out of the water like a groping snake and wrapped itself around her. Two more tentacles followed fast. Peach frantically splashed and cursed, trying to get free, but the giant arms were too strong and they pulled her down.

The pool was only eight feet deep—or at least it had been a few minutes ago, but it was much deeper now, and the water was murky and green, and Peach felt herself being pulled farther down and then she saw the monster, with its beak full of jagged teeth, snapping from a thicket of twisting tentacles, drawing her in toward a bloody, shredded death.

But not just yet! Peach stopped trying to yank herself from the goliath's arms, and instead wrapped her fingers around her talisman—and with a blaze of burning light she became a tiny fish, and the tentacles were gripping nothing, and the fish shot free before they could close around her again.

The monster let out a bubbly roar as Peach broke to the surface and instantly transformed into a bird, dripping wet, flying high and flapping its wings and coming to rest on the balcony above, where she was suddenly Peach once again.

This time she was very quick. She gripped the talisman and with another fiery flash the pool burst into a boil. In an instant, steaming hot water churned and swirled like a gargling cauldron. A deep moan came from somewhere below, and then the tortured squid shot to the surface, flailing away in the middle of the tumultuous, chlorine-infested sea.

Peach threw back her head and laughed. "We certainly know how to cook seafood in New Orleans, Velva. Stay right there while I go get a few vegetables."

The squid vanished beneath the waves. Peach grinned—but her happiness was brief, as a steaming meteorite shot from the pool. Peach ducked as it hissed above her head like a searing cannonball and shattered the glass door behind her before crash-landing in the living room.

Peach whirled and ran into the room just as the hot rock was turning back into Velva. She was dripping wet, and her face was a bit red from being boiled, and her eyes were filled with hot rage.

Peach gave her a droll smile. "Velva, your makeup is running, and your hair is a mess. I hope there aren't any paparazzi hanging around outside."

Velva snarled. "You've grown stronger than I remember, Peach. I guess kissing ass all day has its rewards."

"I don't kiss ass, Velva. I kick it." Then Peach pointed a finger at Velva's sneering face and fired a blast of blue light—but Velva was fast. She blocked the bolt with her palm, and it ricocheted back and struck Peach in the chest.

Peach screamed as she was hurled across the living room and into the kitchen, where she crashed into a cabinet and fell to the floor, along with a few dishes and a teapot. Then a jar of honey tumbled from a high shelf and broke on top of her head, and she was covered with sticky goop, and a cabinet popped open and a furious swarm of bees came roaring out and attacked her.

Peach screamed again. Velva shook with spasms of laughter, while somewhere in the background the doorbell rang.

Peach was on her feet and covered with bees. She stumbled around the room, draped in a writhing blanket of buzzing insects. Then the shape inside the swarm collapsed. The bee cloud briefly hit the floor before rising up and dispersing like noisy smoke. The tiny spider Peach had become was barely noticeable as it crawled into a crack under the kitchen cabinets.

Velva frowned and searched the room with fast eyes. "How much fucking magic do you have, Peach? I'm thinking you've just about used up whatever you had stored. Come on out so I can stomp on you once and for all! I'll send the gooey mess to Mom—*Your favorite daughter is done bugging me. Love, Velva.*'"

While Velva was busy talking, the spider was busy moving—and then growing. From the center of the kitchen floor, it started getting bigger. Velva spotted it and grimaced. It was the size of a hand, and then a cat, and then a large houseplant. And then it stopped growing.

Velva grinned. "Is that all you've got? One spider the size of an oversized petunia? I knew you were running dry, Peach."

Then Velva watched as the spider split into two spiders of equal size, and the two became four, and the four became eight.

"Motherfucker," Velva said. Everyone hates to fight the big bunch of spiders.

The oversized arachnids charged toward her. Velva shouted and yanked open the door to the stainless steel refrigerator. Normally, it would be full of shelves, but her touch caused the shelves to vanish, and she jumped inside and slammed the door shut.

The spiders swarmed onto the appliance, while the doorbell rang again.

The spiders ran around the refrigerator, thumping fast with their fuzzy feet, finally stopping and lining up on the body of the fridge, along the seam where the body met the door. They worked together, and started to push the door open—and then the refrigerator lit up, crackling as a surge of electricity exploded across its steel surface. It was like the refrigerator had been struck by lightning, with white electric light flying in all directions but ultimately piercing through the renegade arachnids.

The spiders squealed in high-pitched agony as the voltage fried their hairy legs and bodies. They fell from the refrigerator as smoking mounds of burnt hair and flesh, and their hard exoskeletons thudded against the kitchen tiles.

A smoke alarm started to shriek, and the door that led to the stairs from the vestibule below swung open.

Debbie poked her head inside and sniffed the air. Obviously, someone had burned the toast, although it didn't really smell like toast. It smelled more like crabmeat. Juan was right behind her as she walked into the room.

"Hello," she said, adjusting her glasses. "Is anyone here? We're looking for Peach Blossom."

Debbie noticed the kitchen was a mess. Either there was a party going on, or a couple of witches were trying to kill each other. At any rate, she was glad to finally be here. Then the door to the refrigerator popped open and a glamorous, somewhat beat-up looking blonde came stumbling out.

The woman frowned and shoved her feet into a pair of 5-inch pumps on the floor. "Hi, can I help you with something?" she said.

Debbie stared in silence. "Hello," she finally said. "Are you Peach Blossom?"

The woman paused and seemed to consider the question. "Yeah," she said in a slow drawl. "How did you guess?"

Debbie and Juan looked at each other.

"Someone told us you would be living inside a refrigerator," Debbie said. "And it's very nice. I love stainless steel."

The woman glanced at them sideways as she lit up a cigarette. "Everybody does. So, what do you want?"

Debbie hesitated—something didn't seem right. Somehow, she'd expected a Goddess of Love to show more hospitality. She wasn't looking for a hug and a French kiss, but a little personal warmth would've gone a long way, and maybe some coffee from that silvery cappuccino maker in the corner.

Also, there was that heap of giant, dead spiders on the floor. Normally, this would have been a five-alarm stressor, but Debbie put her panic attack on hold by temporarily denying their existence.

"We heard you can get us out of Sex Hell," Debbie said.

The woman started to answer, but then stopped. A smile slithered across her face.

"Sure. I can get you out right now. I'll cast a reverse spell, and you'll just need to have sex a few more times, and it'll all be over. So why don't you two go into the bedroom or out on the balcony and get busy."

Debbie cocked her head and frowned.

"Are you really Peach Blossom?"

"Of course!" the woman replied. "Don't I look just like her?"

"What's with the giant dead spiders on the floor?"

"What giant dead spiders?"

"The ones right there. They're all over the floor."

"Oh, those giant dead spiders. Those were…my pets. I went on vacation to New Jersey, and I forgot to have somebody feed them, so they starved to death."

"That seems pretty unlikely."

"Okay, I went on vacation to Las Vegas."

"You're not a very good liar."

"What are you talking about? I'm a great liar! But of course, I'm not lying now."

Juan crossed his arms. "Ha! You're even dumber than Velva."

The woman's face twisted up like an angry corkscrew. "Velva's dumb? She put you into Sex Hell, didn't she?"

"Yeah, she did," Debbie said. "But that's because she lied to us. Velva's a very dishonest person."

"She's not dishonest! She just wants to be a movie star."

"What?"

Debbie kept watching the woman, but she also noticed the dead-looking spiders were moving, gathering into a pile, and changing into a woman. The woman was willowy in a yellow sundress, with long blond hair, calm blue eyes, and a small glass hand hanging around her neck.

"Hello, Debbie," she said.

Debbie took a breath; she suddenly felt relieved. "Are you Peach Blossom?"

"Yes. And this is my glamorous sister, Velva. I believe you knew her when she was ugly on the outside as well as on the inside."

The glamorous woman smirked. "I'm not Velva. I'm Peach, and you two need to start having sex right now or you'll never get free!"

"Don't do it," the willowy woman said. "If you do it one more time, Velva might reach the Key Power Threshold, and that will be bad."

"I'm not Velva! I'm Peach! And I need to kill this imposter! In fact that's what I was doing before you two came barging in here and interrupted me."

The glamourous woman turned and waved her hand. A nearby pantry opened, and with a thunderous roar and a burst of flames a dragon leaped out.

It wasn't big as dragons go, but it was bulky for the average kitchen space. It was black and red with purple wings, lemon-yellow eyes, and talons as sharp as silvery steak knives. It let out another threatening roar as smoke poured from its quivering nostrils.

Juan cursed and put an arm around Debbie, while Debbie took a step backward. The willowy witch grimaced and wrapped her fist around the glass hand on her neck. The dragon roared again and flashed its jagged teeth. It looked ready to pounce on her—but then the oven popped open, and a huge pot roast came floating out.

A mouth-watering smell instantly wafted across the room as the drifting dinner settled on a nearby kitchen counter. The dragon glanced at it, raising its eyebrows.

The glamourous witch pointed at the beast and said, "Don't touch it, you moron!" But with one quick motion, the dragon snapped the meat into its jaws and gulped it down. The witch rolled her eyes as the monster turned back to face the other witch, who stood her ground as the dragon stopped moving.

The dragon seemed to be considering something, but then it let out an ear-shattering moan, and its ping-pong ball eyes rolled up into its head—and it collapsed with a thud onto the floor, kicking its legs and thrashing its long neck. It shrieked and it cried as it writhed on the ground, swinging its tail, battering the cabinets, knocking over the chairs, and destroying a toaster oven. Juan squeezed his arm around Debbie's shoulders as she watched without breathing. Finally, the beast let out one last howl and vanished.

The glamourous witch swore. "The old poisoned pot roast trick, huh, Peach?"

The willowy witch laughed. "The old dragon-in-the-pantry trick, huh, Velva?"

"Ah-ha!" Juan said to the glamorous witch. "You just called her Peach! So you really are Velva."

Velva frowned. "Did I call you Peach? That was a mistake; I meant to call you Velva. I am Peach."

Debbie rolled her eyes. "I think you better give it up, Velva. It's obvious who you are now. Wow, you do look a lot better."

Velva smiled. "Hey, I couldn't have done it without you."

"Gee, you're welcome. So why don't you let us go?"

"I couldn't do that even if I wanted to. But I don't want to, at least not until you do it one more time."

"Don't do it!" Peach said. "Velva is almost at Tier Six, the Key Power Threshold. A witch who reaches Tier Six can suck magic from just about anywhere, and as such becomes extremely powerful. Besides, she won't let you go. She'll keep on using you until you die."

"What?" Debbie said. "We're going to die?"

"Oh, did she forget to mention that part?" Peach said with a sarcastic smile. "Yes, you can only last so long in Sex Hell before your body burns out. In fact, you probably don't have too much time left."

"That's not true!" Velva said. "You've got at least one good fuck left—wait, that's not what I meant. I meant that you can...last in there forever, if you...eat right and exercise."

Juan's eyes blazed. "You're a liar! I'll never have sex again, you evil witch. Not with any woman—not even Debbie!"

"Not even?" Debbie said, raising her eyebrows. "Are you saying you'd rather do it with me than any other girl?"

Juan took her hand. "You are a good girl, Debbie. You are the best."

Peach smiled, but Velva was furious. She stabbed a finger at Peach and said, *"You bitch! You're trying to ruin everything, and I won't let it happen! If they get out of Sex Hell I will crush you, and I will crush them, and I will find two others, and I'll be the most powerful witch in the world!"*

Then she raised her hands high, and the kitchen disappeared.

***

Debbie caught her breath. She was now standing in a forest. She blinked, and then she cringed.

If there's one thing she hated, it was the "great outdoors," a place filled with bugs and slime and dirt and primitive restroom facilities.

Juan was by her side. "I guess we're not out of the woods yet. Are we in Sex Hell?"

Debbie shook her head. "I don't think so, but then again I'm not sure." She sighed. "You *were* kind of turning me on."

"I never touched you."

"Yeah, I know, but you said nice things."

"Ah, I'm sorry."

"That's okay. I liked hearing them… We are done helping that witch."

He nodded, and then the ground started shaking.

Debbie and Juan looked up—and there was Velva. They had to crane their heads to see her face because she was now at least fifty meters tall.

Debbie felt her heart begin to pound, but she took a few deep breaths.

Stay calm! Stay calm!

"So, the biggest asshole in the world just got bigger," she said.

Velva looked down from above the trees. "The biggest asshole has a big foot, little girl. But I'm not going to stomp on you yet, because I'm still pretty sure you'll end up naked with this guy again."

Juan smirked. "That might be true, witch, but it will be when we are free."

"Are you sure about that?" Velva said. "I don't think it's going to take that long." Then she waved her hand—and it started to snow.

Debbie raised her eyebrows. There was nothing about snow that excited her. She didn't hate it, but she wasn't one of those winter sports freaks who slept with a pair of skis, either. She mainly liked snow because it sometimes gave her a good excuse to not go to work. But as the flakes began to hit her, she felt something stirring inside—her heart was beating fast, her breath was getting short, and that spot between her thighs was getting very warm.

The snow was filled with some kind of sex drug! It wasn't just a tranquilizer, like the stuff in Sex Hell—this was the real deal, and she was incredibly aroused.

She turned toward Juan. "Red alert! This snow is some kind of super aphrodisiac. I'm feeling really excited."

Juan's eyes were glazed over with lust. "Yes, I know what you mean, but we must not do anything."

"Maybe we should get an igloo together, make out a bit, and then stop once we get to Sex Hell."

She shook her head. Had she just said that?

"The effect might last once we're there," he said. "Besides, I don't know how to build an igloo, so let's just find a place on the ground."

"Bad idea," Peach said. She was standing next to Debbie. She waved her hand in Debbie's face, and *poof!*—the snow turned into a shower of confetti.

"Whoah!" Debbie said. "Thanks! Where did you come from? Are we celebrating something?"

"I came from over there, near the dishwasher. We're still in the kitchen, but don't worry about it. And yes, we're celebrating the impending destruction of the big, bad, witch."

From up above, Velva cursed. "So there you are, Peach! Congratulations at finding your way into my forest spell. It was pretty quick thinking on your part, but it will take more than a little colored paper to ruin my party."

Then Velva shrieked and lunged forward with her massive foot, stomping down on Peach. Debbie screamed, while Velva grinned and ground her shoe down on the soft ground, over and over—but when she lifted her foot to view the mangled destruction, there was nothing there but dirt.

"Damn," Velva said. "I should've guessed she'd do that."

A deer burst through the trees. The sleek-looking doe gazed up at Velva and laughed, and then said, "Yes, it seems that all the magic in the world won't make you any smarter."

Velva snarled. "I'll crush you, Peach. Once and for all!" Then Velva started stomping after the pretty creature of the forest.

She stomped and thumped with her huge feet and then stomped some more as the deer ran in circles through the dense bushes. Debbie watched with her heart in her mouth, while Juan put his arm around her shoulders.

Velva kept shouting, and knocking over trees, and crushing bushes and shrubs, while totally failing to hit the deer with either foot. Finally, the deer found a clearing in the brush. The doe turned to Velva and said, "You might look young, Velva, but you're clumsy as a corpse—and twice as slow. Catch me if you can!"

Velva grinned, while Debbie felt her head spin. The open space seemed perfect for Velva, since there was nowhere to hide. The deer took off with the giant in hot pursuit.

Debbie ran to the edge of the woods and watched. Velva was gaining. She was almost on top of Peach! But then Debbie noticed a problem—Velva was wearing high heels. She was moving fast, but tottering as she ran, like a drunk on the verge of toppling over. And then one of her huge heels hit a rut in the grassy field.

"*Motherfucker!*" Velva screeched as she crashed to the ground, landing face first in a greenish, algae-covered pond—*sploosh!*

Debbie burst out laughing. "I guess that's why Davy Crockett never wore heels. They're just no good for deer hunting."

The deer galloped back to Debbie and Juan and once again became Peach.

"Let me congratulate you two," Peach said. "Velva has been expending an enormous amount of magic to do these stunts, and that means you both produced an amazing amount of *sensualla*. You're obviously a fantastic couple."

Debbie felt herself blushing. She saw Juan look away quick—but was he also smiling?

"Anyway, this is no time to celebrate," Peach said. "I can't believe Velva has this much magic left—at least I hope not because I'm almost done myself. On the bright side, we're forcing her to use a lot of it. Oh no! Look!"

Velva was getting up. She was laughing, staring at Debbie and Peach—and then she raised her hand, and everything changed again.

Poof! Just like that, they were on a beach.

It was a beautiful beach, a sweeping stretch of sand splashed by a jewel-blue sea, ringed by a thin line of palm trees that stood just before a wall of steep, rocky cliffs. The sun was high in the balmy sky, looking like a blurry orange, and a salty breeze was blowing in above the foamy surf.

Debbie shook her head and shielded her eyes from the sunny glare. "Where are we now?" she said.

"We're still in the kitchen," Peach replied.

"Oh. But it looks so much bigger."

"It is bigger."

"But how is that possible? Aren't there some basic laws of physics that need to be followed?"

Peach laughed. "Magic doesn't conform to physics. That's what makes it so magical."

Debbie took a deep breath and tried to control the tight feeling in her chest. "I didn't bring any sunscreen," she said.

"You don't like the beach, Debbie? But you didn't like the forest, either. What kind of setting would you have preferred?"

"Maybe a bookstore. Where's Velva? Is she resting?"

Peach scanned the scenery. "That's a good question. Rest will not give her more magic. She either needs to get it from somewhere or create it herself. But she's using quite a bit to create these landscapes, and she's got to be running low by now—or maybe not. Look!"

Peach pointed out at the surf, and Debbie felt her heart start to pound. An army of giant jellyfish was coming out of the sea. They were fat, grayish blobs, each one about the size of a bean bag chair, and they were wriggling across the sand—and there were a lot of them, at least 50 or 60 with still more on the way.

"Wow," Peach said. "How much sex did you two have?"

"Not that much," Debbie blurted. "But it was intense."

Juan grinned. "It was fantastic. I'm surprised these creatures aren't larger."

"Congratulations once again on your earth-rocking orgasms," Peach said. "But they're large enough, and I've seen these things before—not too fast, but relentless. And I'm almost out of magic."

The advancing monsters were heading toward Peach, who started backing away. But the cliffs were only a short skip from the surf, looming like a prison wall of stone.

Debbie bit her fingernails. She could see Peach wasn't that confident, not with her power supply fading fast. Well, if Peach dies, there was no way Debbie was going to have sex with Juan. In fact, she'd never have sex again—the hell with it! But what if the witch threw down another pile of sex snow? Ugh! Debbie took a few more deep breaths. Then Juan held her hand.

"Don't worry," he said. "The witch will lose."

"How do you know?"

He smiled. "Something will happen."

Debbie bit another fingernail, and was about to object—and then something happened.

A pile of rock in the face of the cliff crumbled away, and a police car came bursting through the rubble. It barreled across the dunes with its siren screaming and its red and blue lights ablaze.

Debbie pointed. "Look! Somebody called the cops! Great, maybe they can lock up Velva."

"I don't think those are the police," Juan said, grabbing her elbow and motioning toward the nearby line of palm trees. "Let's get out of here."

Debbie eyed the police car with suspicion, and then said, "Right."

Meanwhile, the marauding vehicle immediately plowed into a couple of jellyfish, which burst like plastic garbage bags filled with sticky goo—*sploosh!* Grayish pink goop splattered across the vehicle's windshield and then scattered across the sand. Then a whiny roar rose from the rest of the jellyfish army.

The car slammed to a stop, and three tall blond women in police uniforms leaped out with their guns drawn. They were grinning and shouting in German.

"Töten die Monster! Alle töten!"

Debbie's jaw dropped. More Germans! She tried to recall her basic German from High School. Apparently, the female Gestapo wanted to kill the monsters, and then kill everyone. They were very consistent.

Zap! Zap! Zap!

Fiery bullets of energy shot from their guns, and every one hit a fat jellyfish, and every fat jellyfish burst into a mishmash of flying slime. *Sploosh! Sploosh! Sploosh!*

The German girls were jumping up and down with huge grins on their Teutonic faces. Obviously, they'd been hoping for an exhilarating shootout, and there was nothing more exhilarating than a good massacre.

But maybe not so exhilarating. The jellyfish sent up another collective moan—and then they vanished. For a second the sea was calm, lapping at the sandy beach like a baby's bathwater. Everyone stood still, scanning the surf with nervous eyes. Then Debbie gasped and pointed as Velva came walking out of the waves.

She was no longer young and beautiful. Her hair was white once again, except for a few green highlights that were probably seaweed, and her face was wrinkled and leathery. For some reason, her sludge-colored gown didn't appear to be wet—but her eyes glistened with white-hot hatred.

"You idiots!" she screamed. Then she pointed at Peach. "You're supposed to kill her!"

"*Yah!*" a German girl said. "*Ve vill—ven ve done killing you!*"

They started blasting at Velva. Velva raised her hands, which caused the bolts of energy to bend around her, and then she returned fire with a few bolts from the tips of her nicotine-stained fingers. Her onslaught struck one German in the chest and she tumbled to the ground. Quick as a flash, she was back on her feet. She was a bit cooked, but not much worse than medium-well. She grinned and fired another shot.

Peach crouched down with Debbie and Juan behind a cluster of palm trees. "Did you see that?" Peach said. "Velva's bolt barely did any damage to that girl, and that means she's weak—what a relief."

"Great!" Debbie said. "So maybe you can blast her."

Peach shook her head. "She's still dangerous; she's going to be like a wounded animal at this point. Besides, I'm also almost out of magic, and now I need to deal with these German-speaking demons."

"Water destroyed them before."

Peach's eyes lit up. "Really? Velva used water-soluble assassins? Ha, no wonder they're shooting at her—those things never work right. She always did like to shop in the bargain bin. Give me a second."

"Look!" Juan said. "Someone else is coming."

The vehicle came thundering around the far end of the rocky cliff. It was a red Jeep Grand Cherokee, and behind the wheel was Mike. Sitting beside him was Cynthia.

Debbie shook her head. Damn! Getting drunk was a bad way to keep a secret. She craned her neck to follow the action, while trying to slow her speeding heart.

She saw that Mike had a grimace on his face. He was apparently sizing up the situation, and he was doing it fast. He obviously didn't know what the hell was going on, or where he was—but he saw the three cops on the beach firing the bolts of lightning, and he headed right toward them.

One of the Germans pointed her finger and shouted, and the other two whirled to face the charging SUV. They started shooting at the vehicle, striking it in a wide range of places. The windshield shattered, the headlights exploded, the front tire blew out—and then it veered off course, hitting a dune and flying into the air before crashing down onto the sand and toppling over onto its side.

The German girls whooped and gave each other high fives. Then they turned their attention back to Velva, who was now running for the palm trees. They started blasting at her.

Debbie felt her head spinning.

"Are Mike and Cynthia okay?" she said.

"Stay here," Juan said. "I'll go see."

She grabbed his arm. "No! It's too dangerous."

He grinned. "It's not my destiny to die on this phony beach."

"I don't believe in destiny."

"Maybe it's my destiny to change your mind about destiny."

She gripped his arm tighter. "Juan, don't go. Please."

"She's right," Peach said. "Not until I get done with one last spell."

She grasped the talisman around her neck, and a wind began to blow, and the sky began to fill with storm clouds. The Germans stopped shooting at Velva and looked up as the first crash of thunder sounded, and then the sky seemed to split open and the rain gushed down like a fire hose had been opened somewhere in the heavens.

In an instant, the Germans dropped their guns and yanked out umbrellas.

They were wide, industrial strength umbrellas, and they clutched them tight against the wind. As it became apparent the water would not be reaching them, they starting whooping and laughing and congratulating each other.

"*Ready ve ver, Frau!*" a German shouted above the deluge. "*Ready for trickery, ya!*"

Debbie winced while Juan shook his head. Peach just grimaced and grasped her talisman one last time—and a huge wave rose up out of the sea, and crashed onto the beach, and washed over the three wide-eyed policewomen before they could even scream.

When the wave receded, they were gone.

"Woo-hoo!" Debbie said. She turned around and gave Juan a hug. Then she pulled away quick—after all, she didn't want to end up in Sex Hell.

But still, it felt good. And then they saw Peach down on the ground.

"Peach!" they both shouted as they knelt by her side.

Peach was trying to get up, but she fell back down.

"I'm out of magic, kids," Peach said. "Plus, I'm damn tired. Quick, help me up. We can't let Velva know."

But Velva did know. Farther down the beach, she was grinning. She was soaking wet and looking like an old mop, but her cracked face was filled with a face-splitting grin.

"That was your last spell, Peach," Velva said. "You're all done and I've still got some left. Bad luck for all of you!" Her face turned a raging shade of red. "You've turned me old again, and you'll pay for that. And when you're done paying, Debbie and Juan won't have anyone to help them escape from Sex Hell—and I'll end up young and beautiful again! Ha-Ha! Now prepare to die!"

While she was busy laughing at her murderous plans, Mike emerged from behind the Grand Cherokee. Apparently, he'd scrambled out during the storm with Cynthia by his side. He puffed out his chest, gritted his teeth, and raised his drum sticks high.

Velva spotted him. She sneered and fired a quick shot at his head. She missed, and the bolt ricocheted with a pinkish spark off the vehicle's rear bumper. Then Mike took aim, and he fired—and his shot missed, sailing into the water. He let out a shout and sent another bolt into the beautiful blue sea. He let out a battle cry and *splooshed* yet another shot into the waves.

Peach grabbed Debbie's arm. "Who is that idiot? Those sticks are charged with a lot of proprietary magic. It's too bad the only thing he can hit is the ocean… But if I could get that magic, I might be able to do some damage."

Debbie paused. "How does that work? You can just suck it out?"

"Not exactly. Physically, we're still in the kitchen, but at the same time, we're also in a realm of imagination—a higher plane. It's hard for me to explain; it's a place where magic and imagination come together."

Debbie's eyes opened wide. "I *knew* it," she said. "I've always thought that imagination might exist in an actual place, a place other than my brain!" She was about to say something more, but then Mike let out a scream and fired another fearsome thunderbolt—and it struck Debbie right in the forehead. In a flash of blinding light, she screamed and fell to the sand.

Oooh. Everything was hazy. What had just happened? She heard people shouting around her. No one shouted louder than Velva.

"You dumb shithead!" Velva screamed. "I need that girl!"

Debbie felt like she was in a dream. She watched Velva start blasting at Mike as Cynthia yanked him behind the destroyed Jeep. She felt Juan holding her in his arms as her eyes fluttered open.

"Debbie, are you all right?" Juan said.

Debbie blinked a few times. What was going on?

Everything was blurry. Everything felt light and distant, like she was in some kind of electric fog.

"Where am I? I feel strange. I feel like I'm dreaming."

She heard Juan swear and felt him shake her a bit. Velva also swore as the zinging crackle of more shots filled the air. And then there was a shriek of sound and everyone stared up at the sky.

Something was moving fast. It was a smoking hot spacecraft shaped like a bird, and it was screaming above the water. It was weaving and wobbling and flaming—and then it was crashing down onto the surf, spinning and sliding and skidding across the sand before slamming to a stop in a fat dune.

Velva's witchy face flashed with a what-the-fuck-now kind of stare. Everyone else stared, too. Through a wall of smoke and flame, they watched as a door on the side of the ship flew open, and a woman stepped out.

She was dressed in a black leather skirt and a pair of matching thigh high boots. Her dark red hair was blowing in the ocean breeze—and her hands were pointing a Series 7 Plasma Pistol across the sand.

Velva shook her head. "How many assholes are coming to this party?"

Suzy Spitfire smiled. "I only see one. And she's about to leave—the hard way."

Then she aimed her pistol, but not at Velva. She aimed at a point high above Velva's head, at the top of the nearby cliff—and she hit it. With a salvo of perfect shots, the flaming Plasma Bullets struck the rocky overhang, and with a roar like exploding dynamite a pile of boulders came tumbling down.

Velva's eyebrows shot up as her mouth dropped open.

"Motherfucker!" she said, and then she was buried beneath the avalanche of stone.

A shout went up from the beach as Juan, Peach, Mike, and Cynthia all said "Woo-hoo!"

Debbie just stared with a blank expression. Was all this happening?

Juan squeezed her hard. "Debbie, are you all right?" he said. He gave her a hug—and then they were back in Peach's kitchen, standing next to Peach, who was standing next to a burnt-looking refrigerator and a shattered cappuccino maker.

Mike and Cynthia were farther away, in the living room.

Meanwhile, Velva was lying face down on the balcony. She moaned, and they all tiptoed toward her.

Her hair was long and dry and white, and her face was shriveled like an apple head doll, and her tattered gown was the color of bread mold. In every possible way she looked more ancient than the dirt below a dinosaur. Her eyes were closed.

Peach stared down at her. "Hm, she'll live, but I don't think she'll be doing any tricks for a while."

Cynthia gave Debbie a hug. "I decided we should come. So we walked into the house and then we were on a beach, and then this Jeep was sitting there, around the bend, over by a tiki bar, so we took it for a ride and ended up in a shootout—and then I'm not sure what happened."

Debbie smiled. "I'm glad you're here. And I have no clue what happened."

Peach said, "I think the magic in your friend's inaccurate energy bolt somehow combined with your imagination and created that…person."

"Right," Debbie said. "That makes sense. But I created Suzy long ago. I think the magic just helped her show up."

Cynthia and Mike looked at each other like they were having an aha moment. Then Cynthia said, "So that's Suzy Spitfire; I like her style. Hey, can she play guitar? She'd be perfect in my band."

Mike said, "She's got a lot of personality. She seems pretty confident."

Debbie laughed. "Yeah, she's pretty sure of herself. I wish I could be that way."

Almost instantly, Debbie heard a voice in her head. "I wish you could be that way, too, Debbie, because Shelba had one trick left, and she tried to kill me with a Fear Focus pistol. But it didn't work, and I shot her dead. So believe in yourself, Debbie—it's the only way. Remember my words."

Debbie crinkled her forehead a bit. "Sure, I'll remember," she said out loud.

"What?" Mike said.

"Nothing," Debbie said in a rush. Cynthia just laughed.

Meanwhile, Juan gave Velva a suspicious tap with his toe. "I don't trust this witch."

Velva's eyes popped open. "You're smarter than you look, stud—because I've got one trick left!" Then she stared at Peach as her hand shot out, grabbing Debbie's ankle. Peach's mouth dropped open, as if she could read Velva's mind but couldn't believe what she saw.

"You wouldn't dare!" Peach said.

Debbie tried to twist away, but Velva's shriveled hand held her like a clamp.

"Just watch me!" Velva said.

Peach grabbed at Debbie. "Let go of her!"

"Soon enough, sister! I'll send her back to you when I'm done, ha-ha!"

Debbie shouted and tried to yank herself away. Juan and Mike both dropped down and grabbed at Velva's hand, trying to loosen her grip.

"Let go of her!" Juan said. Mike and Cynthia said the same.

Then Debbie screamed, and everything disappeared.

54: In The Witch Hole

Debbie opened her eyes—and then slammed them shut.

She didn't want to believe what she'd just seen. She stayed in the dark, listening to the sound of her heaving chest and her thumping heart, and then she opened her eyes again.

She felt every hair on her body stand up on end.

She was flat on her back, tied to a table in a black room. She could see some shadowy shapes—a chair, another table, and a few items on top of the table that looked like bottles and hoses—and she could move her head left and right, but her limbs were held tight by some kind of strangulating clamps. Her glasses were off kilter, sitting on her forehead a bit above her eyes, and she tried to jerk her head and make them fall into place but they didn't. She heard someone moving around nearby.

"Who's there?" she said.

She heard a cackle as a candle was lit on another table, and she saw Velva's crooked form, and then Velva's gnarled face was hanging there, with her white hair falling down like dead grass, and her head like a hoary spider. Velva smiled through her crooked yellow teeth and used a finger like a withered branch to nudge Debbie's glasses down over her eyeballs.

"Hello, Debbie. It seems like a long time since we met in that diner, huh?"

Debbie took a deep breath. "You know, I'm starting to wish I'd just gone home and had a frozen pizza."

Velva cackled again. "Always cracking jokes, right? I've got nothing against you, so don't take it personal; I mean what I'm about to do."

Debbie struggled with her breathing—*stay calm!* Then she squirmed a bit in her bonds. "What are you going to do?" she said, trying to keep her voice from quivering. "And where are we?"

"We're in a Witch Hole. It's a cubbyhole in another dimension. There are thousands of them, but most of them aren't charted and can't be easily found. No one can find you here, honey—and you won't be getting a charge of magic to help any imaginary friends appear, either. It's just you and me. I used my last bit of magic—my secret, emergency stash—to get you here, so I better get to work creating some more."

Debbie bit her lip. "Okay... And what does this have to do with me?"

Velva turned away and melted into the shadows, but Debbie could hear her moving bottles and pouring liquid on another nearby table.

Velva coughed a few times and said, "I need a new source of power, Debbie, and that source is going to come from you—from your sexuality. There's a lot of energy there, and when I'm done sucking it out of you, I'll be young and powerful again."

"But isn't that what you were doing before?" Debbie said.

"No. I was feeding off the *sensualla* you and Juan produced. I wasn't just plugging right into you and taking all you had, and all you ever will have."

"Wouldn't that have been easier?"

"It depends. The Union has harsh penalties for harvesting *sensualla*—but they have much harsher penalties for this."

Debbie blinked. She felt like she'd just had a spike driven through her skull.

"Are you going to kill me?"

Velva sighed. "Look, I don't want to, okay? You're a good kid, at least in a smart-ass kind of way. But you're also a super-orgasmic girl, and I need that power. I want to be a movie star."

"A movie star?" Debbie said. "You think that's more important than my life?"

Velva shrugged. "Everyone's got a dream."

Debbie banged her head back against the table and struggled in her bonds. But she was helpless.

She took a few more deep breaths. *Don't panic! Don't panic!*

Velva stuck a hose onto the middle of Debbie's forehead. Debbie didn't feel any kind of puncture wound, but she certainly did start to panic, and then she started to scream.

"Let me out of here! Help! Help!"

Velva smiled and stuck the other end of the tube into her own forehead.

"I'm not sure why the hose goes into your head," Velva said. "That's what the instructions say. Seems to me it should get plugged in somewhere else, right?"

Debbie stopped struggling. *Stay calm! This is not happening! Stay calm!*

Velva lifted her hands and muttered a few words, and the tube started to glow with pink light.

"Oh, yeah," Velva said. "I feel it already."

Through the flickering light and shadows, Debbie could see an immediate effect. Velva's wrinkles started to vanish. Her body was changing, too—it was getting more shapely and firm. Her breasts were increasing in size and it was happening fast. Meanwhile, Debbie felt a tiredness in her bones, like all her energy was draining away.

She tried to scream again—but no sound came out of her mouth. She felt too exhausted. She felt too sleepy. Maybe she could just drift off for a minute and then wake up and everything would be fine.

Velva grinned. "This is incredible! I should have just done this from the start... I'm gonna need a way bigger bra. Your sex power was being wasted on those perky little things. But it's gonna love being part of a great-looking woman, ha-ha."

At the sound of Velva's voice, Debbie's eyes popped open. She had to fight through this! She squinted a bit and tried to concentrate—maybe there was some way to stop it. She also whispered, "I wasn't that bad looking."

Velva smirked. "You were okay. Most guys will have sex with anything, honey."

Debbie felt her head start to spin. If she was going to be murdered, fine—but she didn't feel like being humiliated.

"Juan liked the way I looked!" she snapped. "And so did Mike. I was fine the way I was."

"Yeah, that's great. You were fine."

"I wasn't that bad!"

Velva frowned—and Debbie noticed something.

She squinted at the tube and stared hard. Had the flow of pink light just slowed a bit?

"Don't go getting any ideas!" Velva said. "You were nothing special, Debbie. You're too skinny, with no boobs, no butt, big glasses—forget it!"

In the back of her brain, Debbie felt a spark of hope. Something was up. She wasn't sure what it was, but she had to keep it going.

"I have a great butt!" Debbie said. "I looked good to lots of people, including some very attractive guys. My whole life, people have found me attractive—and sexy."

The pink light stopped moving. Debbie still didn't understand what was happening, but now she was excited.

"What the fuck are you talking about?" Velva said. "You're an ugly bitch and you know it! Quit acting confident just to ruin my spell! God damn you!"

Debbie's mouth dropped open. Was it possible Velva couldn't steal someone's sexuality if her victim had some self-confidence? Debbie knew she had never really been completely confident in that area—until now.

"Juan was very attracted to me! And so was Mike! And so was Ben, and Eduardo, and Tyrone, and Richard!"

It was all true. They were all guys who had approached her, looked at her, come on to her, dated her, and had sex with her—not necessarily in that order.

Velva was screaming now. Her hair was fading back to gray, and her butt was dropping like a sack of stones. And all the pink stuff had drained back into Debbie.

"You fucking ugly bitch!" Velva screamed. "Do you want a mirror to see what you look like?"

Debbie smiled. "Maybe you should use that mirror, Velva. I'm the only one here who's looking good. I'm beautiful."

Velva swore and tried to rip the tube from her head—but it wouldn't budge.

"What the fuck?" she said. "God damn it, this thing is stuck! *I'm going to wither away!*"

Velva kept losing ground. Debbie wondered if Velva's sexuality was now draining into her, and she grimaced. That wasn't something she wanted, but what the hell, maybe it would give her a few magic tricks to use, ha.

Velva's eyes were wide with desperation now, as she tried to yank the tube out of her head. But it still wouldn't move. Finally, she grabbed a knife and tried to cut the tube in half, but it was useless. Velva pulled out a small mirror and stared into it.

She was aging at a fantastic pace. Her head was like a shriveled coconut, and her body was sagging like a tree made out of pizza dough. She yanked and pulled at the tube but it was no use.

"Motherfucker!" she said.

Then she stared at the knife in her hand, and she stared at Debbie. Debbie opened her eyes very wide.

"Sorry, honey," Velva said with a leer. "But I've got to end this now."

"No!" Debbie said, and she thrashed in her bonds, but she was still held tight, and she screamed as Velva lunged with the blade, aiming for her neck, and she braced herself, waiting to feel the sharp steel piercing her throat—but it didn't happen.

Velva froze in mid-lunge. Her face contorted like she'd been shot, and then with an agonizing moan she fell forward. Debbie screamed again as the knife stabbed down into the table, so close to her throat, and then she watched as Velva slid to the floor.

From somewhere below, Debbie heard Velva wail.

"You bitch! You killed me! And I'm never gonna be a movie staaaaaar!"

She was cursing and thrashing around. It sounded like she was suffering through a series of convulsions—and then the sounds stopped. There was one last scream, and the tube fell from Debbie's forehead.

Debbie let out a long sigh of relief and rested her head back against the table. She closed her eyes and listened to the sound of her own breathing. Finally she tried to move again and discovered that her bonds were gone. She took another deep breath and sat up.

She saw Velva's hideous dress on the floor, but there was no sign of the witch. She leaped off the table and kicked the dress with her toe, but there was nothing there besides some ashes and scattered cloth. And then she was back in Peach's kitchen.

55: Sex Hell Challenge

Debbie saw Peach, Mike, Juan, and Cynthia staring at her with eyes wide like hubcaps. No one spoke for an instant—and then she was surrounded by hugs, shouts, and kisses. Debbie returned all the frantic embraces and then sat down in the living room to tell everyone what had happened. When she finished, they all just stared at her again with looks of amazement.

Debbie wiped off her glasses and looked at Peach. "Is Velva dead?" she said in a shaky voice.

Peach hesitated. "Probably. That would be the logical explanation for why you were returned. Of course, she might still exist in a very weakened form. At the very least, she'll never get out of wherever she is."

Mike banged a fist into his open palm. "That's not the answer we're looking for, Peach. That witch needs to be stamped out permanently."

"Yes, I agree," Juan said, and his voice was quivering with rage. "We must find her and make sure she's finished."

"Right," Cynthia said. "Hey, we know where she lives."

Everyone was ready to go to war, and Debbie found her eyes tearing up. She didn't have a lot of friends on social media sites, but she had them where it counted—right here in front of her. She wiped a few drops from her eyes. "I'm pretty sure Velva is done," she said. "If I see her again, maybe I'll just take away her cigarettes. That probably would've been the easiest way to stop her." Then she looked at Peach and said, "What about Sex Hell. Does killing Velva free us?"

A blanket of silence smothered the room.

"No," Peach said, shaking her head. "Once you're in Sex Hell, the only way to escape is to complete *The Sex Hell Challenge*."

Debbie and Juan both rolled their eyes. It sounded like Peach was talking about a game show, or maybe a mixed drink.

Mike motioned toward Juan. "I suppose you'll be doing it with him."

"Is that a problem?" Cynthia said, cocking her head.

Mike hesitated and then put his arm around her.

"No. I'd just like to do what I can to help. Debbie, Cynthia and I are together now. I hope you don't mind."

Cynthia looked at Debbie and smiled. "We worked things out."

Debbie felt her head spinning a bit, but she smiled back. Good for them.

"That's great," Debbie said, and she meant it. She wanted to look at Juan, but instead avoided his gaze.

"So how do we do this?" Debbie said. "Is it something we can study for?"

Peach laughed. "No, you really need to go through a particular event, and there's no way to fake your way out of it. And I have to warn you—it's not that easy, and you might end up unhappy."

Debbie tried her best to look calm. "Let's do it," she said.

Juan wrapped his arms around her. "You will be happy, Debbie. It's your destiny."

She gave a short laugh. "I told you, I don't believe in destiny."

"There's more to life than what you believe. You need to consider the unbelievable things that will happen anyway."

Debbie considered a few of them. "Okay, Peach, send us in."

"What? Don't you want to rest first? After what you've been through?"

"No," Debbie said, shaking her head. "I seem to have a lot of energy. Maybe it's the stuff I inherited from Velva, or maybe I'm just hyped up on stress and anxiety—but I'm ready now."

Juan nodded his head. "Let's do it."

Peach started to object, but then just smiled. "All right," she said. "Good luck." And she grasped her talisman.

"Wait!" Mike said. He stepped forward and gave Debbie a hug. "Good luck, Debbie." Then he turned to Juan and stuck out his hand. "Good luck to you, Juan. Make sure she comes back okay." Juan nodded and smiled. "Thank you. We'll be fine."

Cynthia gave Debbie a hug that almost crushed her. "You better come back okay," Cynthia said, and her eyes were full of tears. "I mean who am I going to get drunk with?"

Debbie laughed and wiped away a few tears of her own. She was about to make a joke but changed her mind. "I'll be back," she said. "Have a margarita waiting."

Then Debbie heard Suzy's voice inside her head. "I don't think I can help you with this," Suzy said. "My own relationships have all been a case of 'flaming hot match meets smoldering jug of gasoline.' But I'll tell you, Tolio is turning out to be okay. We make a good team—and teamwork is important, right? And we're going to rob that casino, The Silver Shot of Happiness. Good luck, Deb."

"Thanks," Debbie said. "Good luck to you, too."

"Are you sure you're ready?" Peach said.

Debbie and Juan looked at each, and they nodded. Peach once again grasped her talisman. Then she shouted, *"Here stand two lovers, Juan and Debbie—or are they lovers? They will soon know the answer... As a Goddess of Love, I invoke the Sex Hell Challenge!"*

Debbie never felt a thing, but she immediately found herself back in Sex Hell.

***

She was surrounded by green things, and it was hot.

This looks like a jungle, she thought. For some reason, she wasn't surprised. She saw chaotic foliage, and tangled vines hanging down, and trees disappearing into the misty air. The soaring trees formed a dark canopy overhead, but spears of yellow light still shined through. The humidity was smothering, like a steam bath. In the distance, she heard the scream of a wild bird and the sound of gurgling water. Below her feet, she felt soft earth mixed with small bushy things, along with stems and stones.

She shook her head. A forest was bad enough, but a jungle was like a forest on steroids. The insects were bigger, the snakes were longer, and there were drooling animals mucking around, looking to devour ignorant tourists.

Juan was by her side. "It's very warm in here. I don't suppose there's a thermostat in this place."

"I always said sex and love belonged in a jungle," Debbie muttered.

"And so they do!" a voice boomed out. Debbie and Juan looked up, and there was Carl's floating head.

Carl grinned. "Welcome to *The Sex Hell Challenge!* Do you have what it takes to get out of here? I guess we'll see."

Debbie looked into his eyes. "You sound like a sports announcer," she said. "Are you selling tickets or something? Is this being broadcast across the universe?"

"No, but it should be," Carl said. "You two are very entertaining. I'll bet you could beat the crap out of all that bullshit on cable TV."

"Thanks," Debbie said. "But that doesn't say much. So, what do we do?"

Carl grinned again. "Don't be fooled by my bouncy demeanor. This is serious."

Debbie raised her eyebrows. "Bouncy? I wouldn't use that word to describe you. *Bouncy* is kind of like *rambunctious* or *raucous*—which fits your personality, but it's not really the opposite of *serious*."

"All right, then *upbeat*, how about that? But I guess that's not really the opposite of *serious*, either."

"No, but I'd say it works, because you're using *serious* in a way that implies something that's *grave*, *grim*, or *sober*—all synonyms of *serious* that are opposite the general idea of *upbeat*. So I'd say that's fine."

"Oh, good," Carl said. "Because I ain't got no intention of fucking up my sweet grammar."

Juan shook his head. "Are we going to get on with this, demon?"

"She's the one who yanked open the thesaurus, sleaze ball."

"I'm not a sleaze ball!"

"Hey, I'm sorry. I'll look for a synonym. How about *salacious piece of shit*?"

Debbie frowned. "That's a little harsh. Although he is salacious."

"I am what?" Juan said. "Please remember English is not my first language."

"*Salacious* isn't necessarily bad, Juan," Debbie said. "I have salacious thoughts; most healthy people do."

Juan smiled. "That's good to know."

Carl laughed. "Either way, I'll remember that scene in the alley forever, especially since I recorded it. So are you ready for the rundown?"

"I guess so," Debbie said. "But it's hot in here. I don't like to have sex when it's too hot."

Carl smiled at her, and the trees parted, and now there was a lagoon by a hillside with a waterfall tumbling down between slippery, moss-covered rocks. There was also a cool breeze in the air.

"How's that?" he said.

"Better, thanks."

"Don't mention it. It's probably a little too cool for some of these plants to survive—but hey, do I look like a horticulturist? None of this conforms to your idea of reality, anyway. I can put a fucking igloo in here if I want to."

"Please don't," Juan said, "I don't like the cold."

"It's not all about *you*," Carl said. "This challenge is generally slanted in favor of the guy, so I'm trying to help Debbie out."

Debbie felt her heart stop. "What do you mean? We're competing against each other?"

Carl grinned yet again. "Here's how it works: You two will have sex. The first one who has an orgasm is freed from Sex Hell. The other person is also freed—but that unfortunate person will never be able to have another orgasm. That's it."

Juan and Debbie looked at each other.

"What?" Debbie said. "Are you kidding me? Why?"

"I didn't create the place," Carl said. "But that's how it is."

"That's not fair! Why does one of us have to suffer?"

"It's the penalty you pay for playing. There are stakes and pitfalls. You should have known better."

Juan frowned at Carl, then grabbed Debbie's shoulders and stared into her eyes. "Let's not do it," he said.

Debbie hesitated, and then shook her head. "We can't get free of each other without getting out of here. And besides, this is no way to have a relationship."

"That's true," Carl said. "Plus, you can't keep coming here, anyway. You'll eventually die. Sex Hell is a toxic place, and you two have almost reached your limit. It's time to move on—or not. So what's it gonna be?"

"I'm not in the mood," Debbie said. "I'm also way too nervous to have an orgasm." She threw up her hands. "Let's do it. I don't care!"

She was tired. She was tired of the drama, the effort, the emotional torture—she was done.

"What do you mean?" Juan said.

"I mean I've had a pretty good run. I've had more orgasms than most people ever have, and I'm tired of this. I just want out."

Juan moved close to her, and put his hands on her waist.

"No, that's ridiculous. I want you to escape."

"That's very sweet of you, Juan—but really, I'll be okay. I don't want you to suffer without sex for the rest of your life."

"I won't suffer. I'll play the guitar and drink wine until I puke. I want you to be happy."

He wrapped his arms around her.

"Juan, I don't care. I don't want to get out of here at your expense—and it will never happen anyway. I can't do it under pressure."

"You can."

"I can't, and I won't."

He kissed her hard. His lips melted into her own.

"I want to free you from this," he said. "I want you to escape."

Debbie realized she actually felt a little turned on—what a sneaky bastard, she thought. But it was fine. She also felt overwhelmed, buried, drowned; she'd had enough. Love and sex and sex and love and does he love me and do I care? Let him do it and get me out of here. *Lots of girls live without orgasms and I'll just be one more. And lots of girls live without love. Put me down for that one, too.*

She pushed him away, and then ripped off her panties. He looked at her with wide, lust-filled eyes. And then she was on the ground, on a soft bed of mossy earth, and he was naked and on top of her. She wasn't feeling much, but she could moan and pretend. Just a few more minutes, she thought, and this will be done.

But Juan kept kissing her. He was also moving slowly, like a man in no hurry. There was no kind of pounding—and really, Debbie liked a good pounding. But this wasn't bad at all. She stared up at the blue sky, and the swaying jungle trees, and then looked at the water lapping at the edge of the lagoon, and felt Juan's huge erection inside of her, and she thought that if this were the last time she ever had sex, it would be okay. She was going out in style.

It went on and on. Was he going to finish this, or what? Then he reached down with his hand, and started to stroke her a bit with his finger, which never worked when someone else did it—but he didn't know that, so why was he doing it?

"Juan," she whispered. "What the hell are you doing? Just finish."

He kissed her neck. "No. I want you to do it first."

She felt a jolt. For the first time, she realized he was telling the truth.

"Juan, are you serious? I told you, I don't want that."

"I won't have it any other way. You're the best girl I've ever known. You deserve a wonderful life...with someone better than me."

Debbie's eyes were wide with disbelief. "Juan, that's the nicest thing anyone has ever said to me."

He kissed her again. "I meant every word."

She felt herself moan—and this time it was real.

"Juan, I don't want to hurt you. I want you to do it first."

He pumped into her harder now. "Debbie, I cannot."

She moaned again. "You have to. I'm getting excited."

"I like you excited. I want you to be excited for the rest of your life. You're the best girl in the world, and I care for you more than anything."

She felt things starting to build.

"Juan, you're the best guy for me... I want to be with you!"

"I want to be with you, Debbie."

"Oh… Oh…"

"Mmmm!"

She was getting close now. But she didn't want to do it.

"Debbie, I love you."

Damn, that was going to put her over the top.

"Juan, I love you, too." She could barely speak now, but somewhere in the back of her mind, she had a thought.

"What if we do it together?" she said.

His eyes lit up. "Yes! We can do it!"

"Yeah—right now! Now!"

The orgasm blasted through Debbie's brain. But it wasn't like a bomb or an earthquake or a tidal wave of wet destruction. No, it was just warm—very warm. It was warm like a wave of happiness pouring from her heart, and she knew that Juan was feeling the same warmth, and that made her feel even more warm and wonderful.

And then it was over.

He was still naked on top of her, and he was kissing her, and she was kissing him, and nothing had ever felt so good, not the biggest bowl of popcorn, not the coziest book on a cold winter night, not the sweetest, jug-sized margarita—nothing.

Then he rolled off her and stared at the sky. She rolled sideways and put her arm across his chest.

"I wonder what happens now?" she finally said.

Juan smiled. "I don't know. But I know I'm in love."

She smiled back and gave him a kiss. "Me, too."

They turned their heads fast as the familiar voice of Carl boomed through the balmy air. "Isn't that cute," he said.

Juan scowled. "So, what is the score, demon?"

Carl grinned. "Congratulations! You figured it out. I had a feeling you would. You're both free, and you can both come and come and come again! Good luck."

He winked at Debbie, and he was gone. And then they were once again in Peach Blossom's kitchen.

56: The Final Chapter

Debbie sat in front of her laptop and typed the last few lines of her novel. She crinkled her forehead, and then reread what she'd just written. It was done—finally.

"It came out great," Suzy said. "I mean despite all the changes."

"Yeah, I decided to change a few things."

"Debbie, you changed everything. You made it into a completely different book."

Suzy Spitfire was sitting on the couch with a beer bottle in her hand and a pistol by her side.

"That's not true," Debbie said. "I kept Tolio in there."

"Were you trying to do me a favor? I'm not sure if you did."

Debbie laughed. "All my stories are love stories, Suzy. And you and Tolio make a good pair."

"Sure, for now. We'll see."

"I'd like to talk, but I've got something going on."

"I know. I'll see you later, Debbie. Break the bed, okay?"

Debbie laughed again. Suzy did the same and then vanished.

Debbie looked at the clock. Crap! Juan was coming over, and she had to get ready. They were going to a Greek restaurant with Mike and Cynthia, and it promised to be a good time. There was a lot of wine and *mousakas* waiting for them.

The doorbell rang. More crap! She wasn't dressed, and she hadn't taken a shower, and she had no shoes—where the hell was that other shoe? She hadn't seen it in days. She yanked open the door and there was Juan.

He gave her a big smile.

"Debbie, it's so good to see you. You look beautiful."

"You're a little early, Juan, and I look like garbage."

"You're a slender flower, Debbie, rising out of a shining city of light. I thought I'd come early." He grabbed her in his arms. "I thought I'd spend some time with you before we went out."

She rolled her eyes. "Juan, I just told you, I'm not ready. I didn't even take a shower yet."

He grinned. "Then let's go into the shower."

"Really? That's pretty kinky—the *shower*. What kind of girl do you think I am?"

"I think you're a crazy girl in the middle of a romantic adventure."

They kissed, and she felt her insides tingling.

Debbie smiled. "I write the stories around here, Juan—and this isn't the middle. It's just the beginning."

THE END

About The Author

Joe Canzano is a writer and musician who lives in New Jersey, U.S.A. For the latest news about Joe's books, subscribe to his newsletter. You can find it at www.happyjoe.net, where you'll also find more information about Joe than you'll ever need.

He invites you to email him at mail@happyjoe.net.

Author's Notes

Debbie's story *The Biggest Blackberry* was actually written by my father, Fred Canzano. He told it to his kids when they were small. He always wanted to see it published and now in a way it has been.

You might notice that Debbie's surname, "de La Fontaine," starts with a lowercase letter. This is not a typo. Some people are destined to go through life with such a name and must constantly endure the inevitable misspellings and corrections.

Thanks to everyone who's been supportive, especially my wife, Jill. Thanks to all the great authors who've written so many inspiring novels. Thanks to everyone who's ever tried to do anything creative— good or bad—because as Teddy Roosevelt once said, "It is not the critic who counts."

Most of all, thanks to you for reading this book. I appreciate it.

Novels by Joe Canzano

MAGNO GIRL
SEX HELL
SUZY SPITFIRE KILLS EVERYBODY
SUZY SPITFIRE AND THE SNAKE EYES OF VENUS

For more information check happyjoe.net.

CPSIA information can be obtained
at www.ICGtesting.com
Printed in the USA
BVHW030224310720
585128BV00001B/21